# ABOUT THE AUTHOR

A. J. Cronin, doctor and novelist, was born in Cardross, Dunbartonshire, in 1896. On his return from World War I he graduated with honours from the Faculty of Medicine at Glasgow University. Later he took up practice in London until, due to declining health, he started writing.

His many novels include THE CITADEL, THE STARS LOOK DOWN, THE KEYS OF THE KINGDOM and THE SPANISH GARDENER, all of which have been successfully filmed. The collection of short stories, ADVENTURES OF A BLACK BAG, became the basis for the long-running TV series, *Dr Finlay's Casebook*. A. J. Cronin has also written his autobiography, ADVENTURES IN TWO WORLDS.

For some years until his death in 1981, A. J. Cronin lived in Switzerland.

*Book by A. J. Cronin*
*published by New English Library:*

# GRAND CANARY

## A. J. Cronin

NEW ENGLISH LIBRARY

First published in Great Britain by Victor Gollancz Ltd, 1933

All rights reserved. No part of this publication may be
reproduced or transmitted, in any form or by any means,
without permission of the publishers.

First NEL Paperback Edition January 1975
Reprinted April 1977
Reprinted March 1983
Reprinted June 1985

**Conditions of sale:** This book is sold subject
to the condition that it shall not, by way of
trade or otherwise, be lent, re-sold, hired out,
or otherwise circulated without the publisher's
prior consent in any form of binding or cover
other than that in which it is published and
without a similar condition including this
condition being imposed on the subsequent purchaser.

NEL Books are published by
New English Library,
Mill Road, Dunton Green,
Sevenoaks, Kent.
Editorial office: 47 Bedford Square, London WC1B 3DP

Printed and bound by
Hunt Barnard Printing Ltd., Aylesbury, Bucks.

0 450 02047 9

# CHAPTER I

HE was still a little drunk as he came out of the sleeping-car with Ismay and walked along the platform towards the baggage office. And he was still bitter - charged with that searing bitterness which, like an acid, had consumed him, drunk or sober, for the past three weeks. The platform swayed gently beneath his feet; the cold haze of morning that filled the high arches of the station pressed round him like a thick sea mist. He saw nothing. He walked rigidly like a man in a dream. He drew up.

'A cabin trunk,' he heard Ismay explain, 'checked in from the London sleeper. The name is Leith.' The clerk, pulling a pencil from his ear, ran down the list.

'Consigned to the *Aureola*,' he said. 'Right. Slade's agent is here.' And without turning his head, he shouted:

'Slade!'

A man with a mottled face hurried forward, an invoice book clutched to his reefer coat, a finger pointed to the peak of his gilt-badged cap.

'Dr Leith, sir. Yes, sir. You'll leave everything to me, sir. I'll meet you with your luggage at the Princes Jetty. Ten o'clock sharp, sir. This here is your voucher.'

He scribbled on a blue sheet, tore it raggedly, and, looking indeterminately from one to the other, finally offered it to Ismay.

'Sign here, sir. No - on my slip, if you please.' His nicotined fingernail made a crease on the crinkling paper. 'Nothing more to come, I suppose?'

Ismay shook his head, half turned to offer the book to Leith. But he thought better of it. As he wrote neatly *H. Leith* he said to the porter:

'Many people travelling?'

'Eight passengers this trip, sir. A full cabin list. Nice business for Slade Brothers - oh, very nice, sir.' From his subservient satisfaction he might have been principal shareholder in the company; and with an air even more proprietary he added -

5

producing the title triumphantly: 'Lady Fielding and party are travelling, sir.'

Leith, listening with a set face, moved his hands restlessly in his raincoat pockets and shivered: after the steam heat of the train it was cold upon the draughty platform. He had not slept; his head was numb; the sudden shriek of a departing engine set a nerve twitching in his left cheek.

'For Christ's sake, Ismay,' he broke in jerkily, 'how long are we going to stand here?'

At once Ismay swung round.

'All right, Harvey, all right,' he exclaimed in his mild persuasive voice.

Harvey sneered.

'If you must have your little society gossip, let's get out of this blasted wind.'

'We're just moving,' Ismay said quickly. 'This instant.' He dismissed the porter with a shilling, and as they started off together he pulled out his watch. 'Nine o'clock. We'll breakfast at the Adelphi.'

'What do I want with breakfast?'

Ismay slid his eyes towards his companion, gave him the shadow of a smile.

'Then we'll kill an hour in the lounge.'

'What do I want with the lounge?'

Again Ismay smiled, a wry, acquiescent smile. They had emerged from the station into Lime Street, and, on the pavement, swept by a fine drizzle of rain, fronted by smoke-smeared buildings and sluggish clanging trams, environed by all the bleary life of a half-awakened provincial city, Ismay paused.

'Well,' he remarked in a tone kept carefully reasonable, 'I don't know the full resources of Liverpool at this hour. Not wholly exciting, I should imagine. In addition, it appears to be raining. You won't eat and you won't sit down. The ship doesn't sail until ten-thirty. So perhaps you'll say what you do want.'

For a moment Leith seemed to contemplate this distantly, with a sort of brooding derision.

'Want,' he echoed dully, as though scarcely conscious of what he said. 'I want to know why the devil I'm here at all.' He paused, then his eye fell upon the other's blunt, unconquerably good-natured face.

'Sorry, Ismay,' he said slowly, moistening his lips, 'I'm not quite - you see - ' Then his nerves got the better of him and he cried out: 'For God's sake don't stare at me like that. Let's get to the blasted jetty if we're going. Anywhere, so long as we keep moving.'

So they set out to keep moving, steering a course through the wet streets, encompassed by a hurrying stream of elbowing clerks and typists, trudging past opening shops and cafés and offices and squat bounding taxis which invited them in vain. Beside Ismay's short, well-groomed form, clothed with the dapper opulence of the successful man, Leith's striding figure struck an arresting, almost painful contrast. He was tall, badly dressed, and spare, with an angular leanness which gave his movements a queer abruptness. His face was very pale, unshaven, the features set to a fine edge as though chiselled. In the fixed harshness of his expression openly displayed there was something burning. It was like a burning contempt of life - bitter, scornful, austere. And yet his wide, dark eyes betrayed him. They were wounded eyes with far-down glinting depths in which a sensitive comprehension lurked and quivered. His brow, too, was fine and high; feeling was there as well as mind. Yes, feeling, the dreadful feeling of despair! For now that mind, cleared by the keen wet air, lay focused to a dreary concentration. Why, he thought over and over again, why am I here? Only doing it because of Ismay; yes, because he stood by me. I don't want to go. Don't want to go. Don't want -

To be left in peace, to be by myself, to forget - that's what I want. And above everything to be alone - alone! But he was not alone; nor could he forget: the most irrelevant and trivial distractions drew him back inevitably - painfully. Immediately in front of him two little typists travelling to work with brisk calves were exchanging confidences - loud and coquettish - of their conquests of the previous night; and giggling: tehee, tehee! Snatches of their chatter came drifting back like wafts of a bad air, nauseating him.

'Mine was a nice one, mine was. In drapery, if you please. Least, he said he was. And the band played "Believe it if you like".'

'Mine had pimples, rather. But you should have seen his style. Oh, my! Swish wasn't the name.'

To him, sunk now in morbid introspection, their simpering, cheaply painted faces, their vapid minds, their weakly, rabbit bodies, endowed grotesquely with the means of propagation, became a sort of nightmare - a clownish symbol of humanity. These, and those like them, he would have benefited. Saved - that

7

was the word; a beautiful, oh, a luscious word. But they wouldn't be benefited, they wouldn't be saved, not now. How funny, how damned funny! He wanted to laugh, to stand stock still in the middle of the wet pavement, to throw back his head and laugh and laugh.

Suddenly Ismay spoke.

'Nearly there now'; and he indicated cheerfully a snatch of the Mersey river seen distantly between two house-roofs which lay below the cobbled street down which they tramped.

Leith, his head bent, his shoulders hunched, made no answer.

They went down the hill, past dirty plate-glass windows masking ropes and binnacles and ships' gear; through a muddle of mean dockside alleys. In five minutes they had reached the Princes Jetty. There, the ubiquitous luggage man awaited and approached them as confidently as if he had known them from birth.

'Tender's here,' he declared at once, and, ceasing to rub his hands together, he indicated almost with ownership a small steam tug which gently rose and fell, nosing its fenders against the quay. 'And your baggage is aboard. All correct, sir. Absolutely all correct.'

'Well,' said Ismay, moving forward with a tentative air.

They went aboard, leaving the mottled-faced man obscurely grateful by the gang plank, and, passing forward beyond a massed disorder of trunks and leather bags, suitcases and wrapped-up travelling-rugs, beyond a small group of people staring with the nervous hostility of strangers, they stood silently in the bows.

The river, gliding without effort, was a cloudy yellow, windless and smooth, yet scored by thin curves where eddies ran; in midstream, anchored at ease, lay steel ships of burden; away to leeward some barges loitered, and always this river flowed towards the sea. Away and outwards towards the sea.

It was quiet, save for the slapping of the current, the far-off chink of hammers, the soothing rattle of a distant winch, till all at once a ferry, noisy and troubled, shot like a flustered duck towards the farther bank. Then, as in sympathy, the tug whistled and cast off its ropes. They began to sidle from the pier.

Again Leith shivered, struck by a sense of quitting the land. A rawness rising from the water enwrapped him, mingled with a presentiment so strangely agitating he felt shaken. His eyes, reaching ahead, drew magnetically to the lines of a ship of some

8

three thousand tons, blue-flagged for departure, her dark brown funnel lightly smoking, her shut ports palely glittering in the cold grey light. Dimly he traced the name upon her stern - *Aureola*. She was small and built for cargo; but a lovely ship, her bow keen, her stern fine, her hull graceful, tense.

'There's your hooker, then,' murmured Ismay, breaking his tactful silence at last. '*Aureola* - a lovely name. *Aureola!*' He let the syllables slip over his tongue. 'Sounds fine. Good omen, too, I'll be bound.'

Because he felt the name was lovely and somehow rhythmic, Harvey forced himself to sneer. He gave a hard satiric laugh.

'More uplift, Ismay? A mystical light by the bow and haloes wreathed around the mast. You expect me to come back wearing one. Purified and ready to begin all over again.' He broke off, sorry already that he had spoken. He was on edge, his nerves overstrung; he needed a drink; yes, that was it, he must have a drink to steady himself. With the cold insight of a scientific mind he admitted his agitation, and placed it to its just cause. But what did it all matter anyway? Finished - everything!

And yet it was strange, very strange, this sudden queer excitement piercing the dreary oppression of his mind. As the tug drew alongside the *Aureola* he felt it strike at him again. He stood apart, heedless of the other passengers, of whom vaguely there were four, now disembarking from the tender - a small, stout woman; an oldish, clumsy-looking man; another man, tall, very assiduous and talkative; and a young woman in the background - but he took no notice of them. Climbing the ladder to the deck, he looked round - like a man expectant of something he knows not what. Yet he saw nothing; no one but a steward whom Ismay at once appropriated. Thus the mood broke sharply and fell away from him. He followed Ismay and the steward along the alley-way to the brief row of cabins which constituted the passenger accommodation of the ship, bowed his head, entered his cabin dully. He sat down upon the settee, morosely contemplating the shining white-enamelled cell which must enclose him for the next four weeks.

Vaguely he heard Ismay talking to the steward; vaguely he saw them go out together. He didn't care whether they went or stayed. No, no, that was wholly untrue; and above everything - yes, even now - there must be truth. Ismay's kindness: coming from London like this, arranging the whole dismal business; it was a sign of something far beyond the mere friendship which had linked them at the hospital. Ismay was a good fellow, a little officious perhaps, but that surely was permissible, the prerogative of a successful surgeon.

Success! He winced from the word and stared at the bunk which he must occupy, a bunk white as a shroud and narrow as a coffin. There had been three coffins, long and black, the coffins of three men borne with all the ghastly panoply of death to the grave. He had never seen these coffins, yet, as he sat, a sound like that of chanting swelled over him in waves, hollow and sepulchral. Wearily he raised his hand to his brow. He had heard no chanting. Never. Was he mad or drunk? His jaw set rigidly. At a sudden sound abruptly he lifted his head. It was Ismay: returning alone, closing the cabin door, looking at him with sudden resolution.

'I'm going now, Harvey. The tender's just pushing off.'

'You've been away a long time,' said Harvey slowly. 'Where have you been?'

There was a short silence.

'Speaking to someone - the steward,' said Ismay at length. 'Explaining about your - your breakdown.'

Harvey stared at him fixedly.

'You will try, Harvey,' went on Ismay quickly. 'You promise me you'll try.'

'Try what? I told you I'd stopped trying. Let someone else have a stab at the trying. I'm done with it.'

'But listen; nobody believes - oh, I'm tired of telling you - every decent man knows - '

'What do they know?' Harvey cried bitterly. 'Nothing. The whole blasted brigade.' The nerve in his cheek began to work again painfully, excitedly; he went on with savage mimicry: 'Take the coloured water three times a day. Come and see me next Tuesday. Yes, dear lady, two guineas, if *you* please. Swine - the lot of them ignorant, greedy, self-sufficient swine.'

'But look - '

'Stamping along their measly little ruts. Snouts in the muck of ignorance. Rooting the same patch. Year in, year out. Blind to truth. On and on. Blind.'

A supplicating note ran into Ismay's voice:

'But hang it all, man, be reasonable. There's yourself - your future. You must think of it. You must.'

'Future?'

'A brilliant future.'

'Who said so?'

'I said so. And you know it. For God's sake don't smash up that, Harvey.'

'It is smashed. Smashed to bits. And the bits belong to me. I'll do what I damned well like with them.'

'Can't you think of humanity then?' cried Ismay. 'Sneer if you like. I will put it like that. I know you'll do great work. I feel it. You've got it in you just - oh, just as Pasteur had. I'm positive. Don't let yourself go to pieces like this. It's too horrible.'

Carried away by his feeling, he bent forward and said again entreatingly: 'Can't you think of humanity?'

'Humanity!' Harvey burst into a loud, derisive laugh. 'I hate every son of a bitch who ever had the belly-ache.'

There was a pause filled by a quiet sound of feet on the deck above; then all at once Ismay awkwardly discovered his own emotion. He let his attitude relax, forced the anxiety from his face.

'I'll say no more, then,' he declared in his ordinary voice. 'I'm going now. But I know you too well to have any fear. All that you need is this breathing-space. Four weeks - it isn't much. But it's enough. I've got faith, you see. Perhaps I know you better than you know yourself.'

'You know, do you?' sneered Harvey. 'My God!'

There was another pause: Ismay held out his hand.

'Good-bye.'

'Good-bye,' said Harvey shortly; he hesitated, then added slowly, with averted head and a sort of laconic compunction, 'And thanks.'

'It'll be good to have you back,' said Ismay. 'Back and ready to begin again.' He smiled his dry, reassuring smile; then the door closed behind him and he was gone.

Back - ready to begin again? Sitting there alone as Ismay had left him, he had the rushing conviction that he would never begin again. But what did it matter, anyway? That was all past, finished, done with; and in the meantime he wanted a drink, wanted it so badly he felt the moisture run into his mouth in reflex to the thought. Strange how alcohol had helped him. It was a drug, and as such he recognised it - a useful drug which he had applied deliberately to his own condition, blunting the edge of his suffering, dulling the quivering agony of his mind. Dispassionately he studied the question. He was no drunkard. He was a scientist, bound to no banal moral code, admitting no virtue but truth - that truth which he had always sought - impervious to the stupid, the obvious, and the orthodox, demanding the freedom to arrange his destiny according to his will. It was a lucid thought and not without a certain bitter comfort.

He remained quite still, craving to drink, feeling the fine tremor of his fingers run into his arms in spasms of nervous irritation. But oddly, with a fierce and introverted grimness, he withheld the moment of his deliverance. He would drink when the ship got under way, but not before. And so he sat waiting; waiting for the ship's departure.

## CHAPTER II

THE ship, too, seemed waiting. In the waist, the cargo hatches lay secured, tarpaulined and in sea shape. Beyond, at the donkey engine, two men in blue jerseys stood alert, shrouded by a coil of hissing steam. In the bows the boatswain fingered his whistle, and by the gangway Hamble, the purser, hung about, dusting the lapels of his monkey-jacket, caressing his small moustache, fiddling at his stringy black tie, all with a sort of nervous anticipation.

The tender had long ago stood off. On the bridge deck, gazing intently towards the quay, there was firmly planted a short man in uniform who now, without moving his head, hailed the bridge. At once the siren sounded - a long and mournful note, repeated and again repeated. At the same econd a swift moving shape darted from the dull background of the docks towards the ship. On it came, an open motor-launch, impelled to speed by the siren's troubled moaning, threshing a curving wake with every indication of despatch. In three minutes it bumped alongside.

Beyond the rich baggage which it contained and the waterman - plainly distressed to be involved in the supreme disaster of a ship's delay - the launch held three passengers.

And now they came on board.

Daines-Dibdin, a long, rangy, senile gentleman with a monocle embedded in his eye, came first. He was a reddish, withered gentleman, but he was, in his preserved way, utterly immaculate and well bred. He stood, at a glance, for the correct thing, and there was about him a perennial aspect and a certain doltish inevitability as though one day he might use Bond Street as his highway and the next, with a fresh shave and serene stupidity, the middle of the Sahara.

Breathing heavily, he reached the deck and turned to assist the others - a woman and a girl - now clambering up the gangway. At that moment Harvey, chafing at the delay, flung open his cabin door. His brooding eye, arrested suddenly, fastened on the scene of the arrival: the formal reception, Hamble's deference, the rapid attention to the baggage, the agitated scurrying of the stewardess, the unusual stir created. With cold detachment he noticed these evidences of social consequence, and a moment later, as the two women advanced along the deck, he inspected them stonily.

The elder was tall, with a full and elegant figure, a languid air, and a manner so completely assured it aroused unreasonably a sort of irritation. Perhaps it was Elissa Baynham's manner which had irritated two husbands through the divorce courts. Perhaps not. Certainly, at thirty-two, she was physically quite magnificent. But it was a careless magnificence. Only a tenth part of her mind seemed occupied by external affairs - a tiresome business! - the remainder was concentrated upon herself. If her face showed no animation it was because she had now decided that the situation was unworthy of her attention. Yet her expression was striking - faintly challenging and, now that her features were in repose, arrogant, almost sullen. She was handsome in her vivid way. She had a dashing colour, her eyes were splendid, her mouth wide, her teeth strong and white.

Beside her the girl seemed strangely young; that, indeed, was the quality in Mary Fielding which instantly possessed the eye; though she was twenty-five, she looked, at times, no more than fifteen years. She was of medium height, her figure slender, small-boned, and light. Her hands and feet were small, her face both eager and alive. Her hair, of a deep rich brown, was worn short, falling away from a wide forehead; her teeth were small and perfect; her eyes blue, with irises circled curiously by much darker rings; and very deep they were - brimming with light that seemed upon the edge of darkness. Though there were moments when those eyes could hold a strangely puzzled sadness, now they were dancing - singularly gay. She was dressed quite carelessly in brown tweed clothes that hung about her in some disarray.

They drew near. And, preparatory to their passing, Harvey

pointedly averted his gaze. It was then that Mary Fielding saw him.

She gave a little gasp; her face went quite pale; and into the brightness of her eyes there flashed a look both joyful and afraid. She hesitated, made to stop. And then, lifting his head, his gaze met hers. He did not know her, had never in his life seen her before. He stared at her in stony and complete unrecognition.

At that her eyes fell. Again deep within her she felt frightened, terribly frightened, and yet glad. Her face was still white as she walked forward with Elissa. Out of the corner of his eye Harvey observed them enter their cabins, which, with a cold indifference, he saw to be adjoining his own.

The doors closed; he forgot about it all. Wearily he turned and leant against a stanchion. A bell rang sharply from the bridge, then rang again; a muffled throbbing stirred inside the ship, which pulsed as with the awakening of life. He felt the vessel slowly move and, like a man released by a sudden signal, he swung abruptly round.

## CHAPTER III

HE stepped into his cabin, flung himself upon the settee, and immediately pressed the bell. He waited; then with a sudden impatience he rang the bell again. Violently. In a moment the steward entered, flurried and apologetic, sweating from his haste. He was a little fat man, bald on top of his head, with brown bulbous eyes that popped out of his round face above the whiteness of his short drill jacket.

'What's your name?' asked Leith abruptly.

'Trout, sir.'

'You thought twice about answering the bell, Trout.'

'Very sorry, sir. I've been extra busy with the luggage. You see, sir, Lady Fielding just came aboard now. And I had to look slippy of a sudden. Sir Michael Fielding - her husband - is a big man with Slade Brothers. Large interests in the company he has, sir.'

'Fielding?' said Harvey. 'You mean the specimen with the monocle?'

Trout looked deprecatingly at his cracked boots, rubbed his moist palms along the shiny seams of his blue serge trousers.

'Sir Michael is not travelling, sir. You might mean the Honourable Daines-Dibdin, intending no offence. An oldish gentleman, sir, but very classy, as you would say. He came aboard with her ladyship and Mrs Baynham.'

Harvey looked gloomily at the steward's bald head.

'I've got no title, Trout. And no influence with the company. But I've got a devil of a thirst. So fetch me a bottle of whisky. And look sharp about it.'

There was a pause during which the steward's eyes remained irresolutely upon his boots. Then he said:

'Yes, sir,' in a constrained voice, as though the words came from those very boots; and he turned and went out.

The satire faded from Harvey's face, and, raising himself, he gazed through the square glass port. Why had he bullied the steward? It wasn't like him to do that. A dark melancholy flowed into his eyes as he stared at the blurred river-bank slipping past like a grey veil unwound slowly across the screen of his sight. Life slipped past now in just such a fashion. Remote, empty, meaningless.

He moved uneasily, gritted his teeth. Why did the fellow not come? Was he never coming? He waited with quivering nerves, then on an impulse he jumped up and flung out of the cabin. The deck, swept now by the freshening wind of the estuary, was deserted as he crossed to the companion, descended, and entered the saloon. It was a small place, but very bright and clean, panelled in white wood, the floor covered by a Turkey carpet, the shining mahogany of the long fixed table splashed by a pot of blazing geranium. And seated in the corner with his boots upon the cushions was a very big man of about sixty with a large square-cropped grey head on which his bowler hat reposed at an angle both rakish and profound. He was ugly, his eyebrows mere grey tufts, one ear a flattened wreck, but over all his seamed and battered face there lay a look of jaunty affability. He wore a very shiny blue serge suit, much too small and much too shabby. And yet he carried that shabbiness adventurously. The tight short trousers upon his bulky legs gave him quite a dashing air; his neck-tie bore a large imitation pearl pin; and his linen was clean - at least in parts. There he sat composedly, and in his knobby, enormous hands he gravely held a certain volume with a paper back. As Harvey entered he lowered the book, over which his lips had moved, looked across the steel-rimmed spectacles on his broken nose, and in a seductive Irish voice remarked:

'Good mornin' to you.'

'Morning.' Harvey sank into a chair, rang the bell, and began nervously to drum his fingers upon his knees. In a moment the table steward entered.

'Steward,' said Harvey in a controlled voice, 'I ordered some whisky to be sent to my cabin - No. 7. Send it up, will you? In the meantime bring me a brandy and soda.'

At once the steward's face exhibited an ill-concealed embarrassment.

'Dr Leith, sir,' he hesitated. 'No. 7?'

'Yes.'

'I'm sorry, sir. The bar is closed.'

'Closed?'

The steward bent over and lowered his voice with awkward, too obvious tact.

'Closed to you, sir. The captain's orders through Mr Hamble, the purser.'

Harvey's fingers ceased their drumming; he sat quite still, transfixed by the unexpectedness of the reply. Then his lips drew to a narrow line.

'I see,' he murmured to himself. 'I see.'

Dimly he felt the two men watching him; dimly he saw the steward slip out of the saloon; but he gave no heed. Ismay, of course, had done this - Ismay, priding himself upon his friendship, his influence, his ability to arrange the universe, had interviewed the captain - oh, it was maddening. . . .

Suddenly the man in the corner spoke.

'Do ye know, now,' he said - and unexpectedly his battered face was illumined by a friendly grin - 'they're cranky, some of these skippers, cranky as a cracked payanna. Sure, if I was you, I wouldn't be gettin' up in the air about sich a thing one way or t'other.' He paused, but, though Harvey gave no sign of having heard, with undiminished gusto he went on: 'I saw ye in the tinder comin' off. Me name's Corcoran. Jimmy Corcoran. It's a name well beknown, up and down, off and on.' Again he paused naïvely, his good ear expectantly advanced, as if to hear some confirmation of his repute; then he added:

'Heavy-weight champeen of the North in '88. The only man that went the length with cracky Joe Crotty. Might have been a world beater if I hadn't bruk me leg. Faith, there's many's the one knows Jimmy Corcoran, and all about him. Tinker, tailor, soldier, sailor, never a rich man and never a thief, that's Jimmy C., always in form wherever he be's. And always in trouble, like the Drury Lane lady. Them's me ould mother's words - the finest woman, rest her soul, that ever came out of Tralee in the Kingdom of Kerry.' He sighed gently, pulled a metal snuff-box from his waistcoat pocket, tapped it with reminiscent sentiment, and took a generous pinch. Then, holding out his book, he enquired artlessly, 'Did ye ever read Playto? Well, well, he's the boy that knew which was what. He's took me through some queer spots off and on. A great boy was Playto. You should read him, young fella, if you're not too busy.'

Harvey made no reply. He scarcely realised that he had been addressed. With a fixed expression he stood up, turned, and walked out of the saloon. He ascended the companion, made his way to the bridge deck. Here the chart-house and the captain's quarters faced him, set solidly beneath the bridge, and through an open doorway he saw the captain writing at a baize-covered table. He gathered himself, knocked upon the door which stood hooked back, and entered the cabin.

Captain Renton looked up sharply. He was a little bantam-cock of a man with frosty eyes and a chin: his short, fairish hair, turning grey in patches, had a strangely piebald look; his monkey-jacket, worn too small, gave his figure an air of tautness; his whole attitude was spry, uncompromising, and direct. Before him on the panelled bulkhead was a crayon portrait of Nelson, whom he had once been told that he resembled and for whose memory he had an inordinate regard.

'Well, sir,' he exclaimed immediately; then added: 'I hope you see that I'm engaged?'

'My name is Leith,' said Harvey in a hard voice. 'I've got something to ask you.'

'You must ask another time, Dr Leith. Give me an hour. The pilot's still on the bridge. I'm always busy when I sail.'

A spot of colour worked itself into the greyness of Harvey's cheek, but he made no sign to go.

'You've given orders to the steward -'

'I give what orders I choose in my own ship, Dr Leith.'

There was a pause, during which the two looked at each other; in Harvey's eyes was hidden a singular distress.

'I'd like to indicate,' he said at last in a laboured tone, 'that it's against all reason to cut me off short at a second's notice. I know

17

what I'm talking about.'

'No doubt, Dr Leith,' answered Renton crisply. 'But I'm the person who does the talking here. And I've talked with your friend, Mr Ismay. Desperate cases require desperate remedies. You'll not touch a drop in my ship. You may as well make up your mind to it. I dare say you'll thank me when we get back.'

The colour died out of Harvey's face and his lip twitched with the bitterness of his thoughts.

'I see,' he cried. 'I'm to be saved. To come back with the halo. In spite of myself. Good God! It's too funny for words. Long live humanity. Love one another and be kind. They've kicked me into the bloody pit and now they're going to bloody well kick me out of it.'

The captain turned his eyes away, stared at the drawing upon the bulkhead opposite, then let his gaze wander back to Leith. As he spoke he tapped the table gently with his pen.

'You've had a bad time. I'm aware of it,' he said in a quiet, altered voice. 'Yes, a bad time. If I may say it, you have my sympathy.'

'I don't want your sympathy,' Harvey said savagely; then he stopped. His face quivered and hardened; without a word he swung round; pushed through the open doorway. Already he felt ill; his head throbbed with a heavy pulse; the daylight stabbed his jaded eyeballs; a deadly wave of weakness flowed into him. He swallowed down his sickness and entered his cabin. There, standing rigid and intense, he seemed as in a vision to see the impotence of all life and to feel dumbly the wretchedness of his own. As he flung himself upon his bunk a low sound broke from his lips that was like a sob.

## CHAPTER IV

In the next cabin a man and a woman were praying, standing together in the narrow space, with hands clasped and faces uplifted, linked by the ardour of their spiritual communion.

He was about thirty, of a fine upstanding figure, an imposing presence, well dressed in a grey square-shouldered suit, dark, deep-chinned, and handsome, with a full lip, a humid eye, and a nostril that could curl with eloquence. His hands were white and smooth, moving at times - responsive to his happy fervour. He it was who prayed aloud in a sonorous voice coloured not unpleasantly by an American accent.

'And give to our mission, dear Lord,' he went on earnestly, 'all blessings and all benisons. Let the light be shown in these benighted islands where there is darkness and many are lost - ah - roaming in the wilderness, ignorant of the true word of the Seventh Day Unity. Suffer us, Thy servants Robert and Susan Tranter, to be Thy instruments of grace. Be with us, Saviour. Be with us. Favour Thy servant Robert with a fuller knowledge of the foreign tongue. Vouchsafe to Thy servant Susan continued strength and purity of soul. Be with us, Saviour, oh, be with us, we beseech Thee. Give us fortitood to withstand sickness, temptation, and the scoffing of unbelievers. Let us follow after charity and desire spiritual gifts, and above all let us remember that all things are possible in Him who strengtheneth us.'

When he had concluded she said aloud, 'Amen'; then in the same quiet tone she added, her face holding a warmth which enriched her words: 'And please, O Lord, let my brother Robert's health improve, for Jesus' sake. Amen.'

She was not so tall as her brother, nor was she as handsome. Her figure was too solid, rather disproportioned, her hands large, her ankles generous; her nose was blunt, mildly upturned; her cheeks wore a fresh scrubbed look; yet the face, though plain, held a singular candour. Her eyes perhaps expressed her honesty; they were brown, small, but very bright; bright with a twin devotion - to her God and to her Robbie.

There was a moment's silence, then, suddenly relaxed, they looked across and smiled, as people do who love each other.

'I guess I'll tuck into my unpacking now, Robbie,' she said at length. 'Guess I better not leave that till it blows.'

She was an indifferent sailor; when, two weeks ago, they had crossed a turbulent Atlantic she had shown a lamentable lack of equipoise. Even now he wagged his head jocosely at the memory.

'No basins this trip though, Susie girl. Not a one. Believe me, with the Lord's help we're going to have it calm as Galilee after the storm. And it's not *that* long. I figure it's seven days to Las Palmas - where we lay up one day. One more to Orotava, and say another to Santa Cruz. Gee! It's nothing, Sue, to a hardened vessel like yourself.' He sat down upon the settee and, without crossing his legs, placed his hands upon his knees, watching her with affectionate regard as she drew out and began to unstrap her trunk. 'You know, sis,' he went on reflectively, 'I've got a hunch we'll strike a rich vein of salvation out there in Santa Cruz. The vine is heavy within the vineyard - that's the Rev Hiram McAtee's own words; he wrote me a real letter; he's one good man, he sure is, and I did set value on his brotherly greeting and encouragement. But there's no doubt, sister, the time is ripe now. The revolution has produced enormous change. In Spain - mother country, as you might say, of these islands - the old order is tottering to its fall. As I wrote to the Rev Hiram, this surely is the living moment to advance the genuine word of God in that special field.'

She had not really been attentive, but she knew his periods, and now, as he drew breath, looked up with her responsive smile.

'I'm right glad to work with you anywhere, Robbie. And it's a big thing for me to know that the climate is going to build up your health. Did you remember to take your extract this morning?'

He nodded his head magnanimously.

'Of course there will be prejudice. And there is the language. But we'll put it across, Sue. We've done it before and we'll do it again. I guess Santa Cruz isn't any different from Okeville. Personality counts in business anywhere. Good enough. I'll say it counts double in the biggest business deal in life. And that, Sue, is putting over the word of God.' His eye glistened; his hands moved; for all his hyperbole there lay a passionate conviction behind his words. And the glistening eyes kindled as he saw himself, virile servant of his Saviour, missioner of the Seventh Day Unit of Connecticut, spreading the word of God in Santa Cruz, saving the precious souls of a sin-steeped Spanish population. 'Already we've met kindness, Sue,' he went on after a moment. 'It's auspicious. The captain raised no objection to the harmonium standing in the saloon. I put it to him as simple man to man. "We'll pay the freight, captain," says I outright. "We're no pikers. But I don't want my sister's instrument harmed in the hold. It's collapsible and small. And between us we prize it more nor a genu-wine Stradivarius."'

'Maybe you might take service Sunday, Robbie,' suggested Susan. 'It would come pretty handy in the saloon.'

'Maybe, maybe. Anyway, things have started real favourable.' He glanced round the cabin. 'I'm just sore you didn't manage a cabin to yourself, Sue. It's kind of raw for you rooming it with a stranger.'

'I don't trouble, Robbie. The main thing is you're fixed right.'

'You haven't seen the lady, sister? A Mistress Hemmingway, wasn't it, they told us? English - bound back for Santa Cruz, where she's lived a big number of years. If a Christan, she might have influence.'

No sooner had he spoken than the cabin door swung open and without warning a stout little woman with a red face launched herself in from the breezy deck.

''Streuth,' she gasped, 'what a gyle! It would knock the pins from the twelve apostles.' She arranged her skirt with a certain volatility. 'Sancta Maria, it's too much of the mucho - drove the blood right into my 'ead.' And patting her left breast sympathetically, as though to encourage her heart to draw the blood back again, she stood striving to regain her wind.

She was fat, was Eliza Hemmingway, so fat her breadth seemed almost to exceed her stature; the depth, indeed, of her advancing bosom so reduced the cabin space that Robert found himself retreating defensively against the farther bulkhead. Her face was shrewd, hard-favoured; her eyes bright black beads; her cheeks plump and shiny; her forehead squat, rather like a toad's; her expression, in consequence, a strange mixture of the bold, the cheerful, and the malicious. Her hair was dark and oily, very profuse. Upon her upper lip a few stray roots sprouted unashamedly, emphasising her air of spirited effrontery. She was draped in clothes of a lively plum shade, and around her neck, suspended, was a black handbag which gaped upon her bosom like a pelican's pouch.

Tranter stared at her with extreme distrust.

'Would you care to sit down, ma'am?' he said at length, doubtfully indicating the settee.

She shook her head till the earrings rattled, eased her corsets with a tug, then with an impulsive movement went forward and spread herself largely upon the lower bunk.

'Carajo coño, that's better,' she declared, pointing her native cockney with the Spanish idiom. 'Come up the ladder too 'asty, I did. 'Aving a small pow-wow and a drop of brown with the wardress - meanin' the stewardess.'

A chill seemed to fall upon the cabin for almost a minute, then with a sort of uneasy politeness Robert said:

'I had hoped, ma'am, my sister Susan might have the lower

berth. She's a kind of poor sailor and she'd feel the roll much more up top there.'

Mother Hemmingway wrinkled up her squat brow and grinned like a ferret.

''Oo finds keeps,' she quoted slyly. ''Oo loses - you know the rest, mister. 'Ere I am and 'ere I stye. Why didn't you swipe it before I come in? I respects your 'on'able request. I respects your feelings as a brother. I'm heart-broke for Susan. But it's age before honesty these dyes. So it's up aloft for Susannah, and 'ere below for the elders. Carajo coño, and by Jesu-Maria, I only 'ope and pray she won't sick down on me.'

There was a stricken silence intensified to horror as Mother Hemmingway slipped her fat ringed hand into her open bag, drew out a small brown cigar, struck a match on the side of the bunk, and nonchalantly lit up.

'Carajo,' she went on coolly, pursing her lips to a small round hole from which trickled a thin thread of smoke. 'It brings a smile to my fyce to get back on the briny. Yes, mister. I'm all agog for the islands. Blymed funny, though. There's dyes in Santa I'm that mucho longin' for Wapping, I'd give fifty peseta for a sniff of the pubs on a foggy night. 'Uman weakness - 'ome, sweet 'ome, you see - like you blubs w'en you 'ears Melbar on the phonograph. But, by Cristo, w'en I am 'ome I'd give five 'undred peseta to be hout of it.'

'You live, then, in Santa Cruz?' said Robert stiffly; only for his sister's sake did he feel himself constrained to conversation.

'Thirty year come next Ascer.sion Dye,' answered Mother Hemmingway with a reflective wave of her cigar. 'My 'usband, blast 'is mem'ry, was master of the *Christopher* - little coasting barque - five 'undred tons - guano tryde. I can smell 'er as I lies 'ere on this bunk. Thirty years come next Ascension Dye 'e went on the lush roundin' Teneriffe like 'e 'ad the playful little 'abit. Lost 'is course and lost 'is bleedin' ship. Run 'er on the Anaga rocks, slap-bang like that, and sunk 'er to the bottom of the deep blue sea. 'E'd 'ave sunk me too if 'e'd 'ad 'is dyin' wish. Out of spite, you see. But I done a Crusoe on 'im. The only one syved from the wreck, like Corney Grain used ter sing. That's 'ow I come to 'it Santa Cruz. And, Madre de Dios, come to think on it, that's 'ow I styed.'

'You have certainly acclimatised yourself, ma'am,' said Robert uncomfortably. 'Do you find the Spanish people agreeable?'

'Tyke as you find,' replied the other complacently. 'I can't sye I likes and I can't sye I 'ates. They're 'uman, ain't they? And they ain't all Spaniolas on the islands. You'll see every colour of 'ide from a full buck negro to an 'alf w'ite blonde. But wot's the odds? I think on the proverb: We're all alike under our skins. And I love my coloured brother just the syme. That's gospel, that is, in the Book, strike me blind. 'Ooever comes to my plyce gets fair word and no favour.'

'You are in business, then,' queried Robert stiffly, 'in Santa Cruz?'

'I'm in business, señor. I just keep a little hanky-panky towny place.'

Susan, in her corner, had been silent, studying the other woman's face, but now she asked almost wonderingly:

'What kind of a place, ma'am, do you keep?'

Mother Hemmingway knocked her ash to the floor and spat a shred of leaf sideways from her tongue. Then she turned, compassed Susan with her knowing bead-like eye, and smiled with her lips.

'A kind of an 'otel it would be, dearie. Very simple. Bed and breakfast - odds and hends in that line. Nothing flash. Just a plyne goddam honest business.'

There came a silence, then Susan, inhaling unexpectedly a breath of smoke-filled air, began suddenly to cough. It was a momentary spasm but, accentuated by a vague preliminary undulation of the ship, it recalled Tranter's attention to the odious business of the cigar. When he had given Susan a glass of water from the carafe on the tip-up stand, he cleared his throat uncomfortably and said with some earnestness:

'I trust, ma'am, you are not going to resent my words. We are Christian people, myself and my sister, missioners of the Seventh Day Unity of Connecticut, and we do not hold with the use of tobacco, especially in the case of females. And more. You see, my sister cannot stand the odour of the weed. With this in mind, might I beg you, in the name of Christian charity, to withhold from smoking in the cabin during this present voyage?'

Mother Hemmingway's jaw dropped; she stared at Robert; then all at once she began to laugh. She laughed with a secret convulsive merriment which shook her fat body - as in the contortions of a terrific grief - like a blancmange agitated by an earthquake. She declared at length:

'That's blymed funny. Mucho richo, señor. Thanks for the caracajada. Beats the bleedin' band. Wye, don't yer know, charity

23

begins at 'ome. 'Ere,' she tapped her still quivering bosom. 'Wye, I punishes an 'undred cigars a month - my own brand - Perfecto 'Emmingway - made special at Las Palmas. Might as well ask me to give up my gyme of w'ist. No, mister, I wouldn't stop my seegarillos if you offered me salvation on a plyte.'

Robert flushed richly, but before he could reply Susan interposed.

'It's no good, Robbie,' she said, aside. 'Let her be. I'll manage.'

Mother Hemmingway caught up the words.

'Of course she'll manage. Me and 'er'll be bosom pals when the ship gets into Santa.' She darted an oblique glance at Robert from beneath her bulging forehead. 'You're good-lookin', mister. But you want to see the joke. Sabe. Laugh and grow fat.'

Again Tranter made to speak, but he looked at her and thought the better of it. He turned instead to Susan and, his colour still high, remarked self-consciously:

'I guess I'll get round to my cabin. Reckon I might put through an hour's study before we eat.'

She nodded her head, pressed his hand understandingly as he opened the cabin door and with his head in the air stepped out.

On deck it was cold, and the wind blew with force, striking gratefully on his heated face. The estuary now lay behind, the land likewise a thin elusive blur upon the ship's port quarter. Soon he felt calmer - it was typical of his emotional nature that he would cool as quickly as he flushed - and with a step again springy he swung into the alley-way towards his cabin on the starboard side. As he did so, Mrs Baynham entered the passage from the opposite end, her tall figure trimmed to the breeze, which already had whipped a fine blood to her cheeks. He stood aside, hat in hand, to let her pass, and as she brushed by him in the narrow alley he said suavely:

'Good morning.'

It was, he knew, no more than courtesy: and courtesy had its roots in Christian charity.

But she did not even look at him. Her big sulky eyes seemed fixed upon infinity. Then she turned at the corner and was gone, leaving a queer uneasiness about him and a tenuous fragrance which vanished instantly upon the breeze. He stood still, quite unusually upset by this rebuff following so closely upon the other; then he moved off slowly. It was the wind, he thought, his face downcast; she couldn't have heard. And, only half reassured, still thinking of her look, rather unhappily he entered his cabin.

# CHAPTER V

THE ship was slapping into the Irish Sea, the bugle had blown, and with one exception the passengers met together at lunch and seated themselves at table with the captain. The *Aureola* was at heart a cargo ship - often the phrase banana boat was levelled with derisory intent - but not to Captain Renton. To Peter Renton she was a ship, a sweet taut ship, and he that trim ship's master. For he had a deep instinctive understanding of the sea and a rare sense of that dignity which, he held, should vest those who seek it out. His own kin for years had followed the sea; he knew their histories and the histories of others more eminent than they. He had served his time in sailing-ships, and known the rigours of the South-West Passage. His library held books on famous mariners, on Nelson, whom he revered. And when the spirit took him he would speak with kindling eye of these great men and their connection with the islands where he coasted: of Columbus sailing from Gomera to discover America for Spain, of the assault on Las Palmas by Drake and Hawkins, of Nelson losing an arm at Santa Cruz, and Trowbridge battering his way through the Plaza de la Iglesia when all - beside the Spanish treasure - seemed lost.

That was the man and this his method: with an autocrat's eye and tongue he kept his vessel fit, ran it to a proper order even to the niceties of his table - which he held to mark the standing of a gentleman. At table, in his phrase, he liked things so: the napery spotless, the glass gleaming, the cutlery ashine, a fresh flowering plant to soothe the eye. And, though his officers messed aft, he had his whim, fostered by a social sense, to dine with his passengers. 'A captain is a lonely man,' he would say, 'and this his compensation.' And again: 'To a point my passengers are my guests.'

At this moment, critically eating his omelette, he sent his scrutiny round the table. Lady Fielding was on his right; and next to her, stiffly upright, Daines-Dibdin, whom he classified already as an ass. Then came Mrs Baynham, a d——d fine woman, he thought, but a devil to go; and Tranter, the missionary man, a dull effusive fellow - he had never liked the Yankees: his grandfather had been shot running the blockade on the S.S. *Alabama* - but sincere, at least, he felt. Upon his left sat Susan Tranter, of whom, despite his prejudice, he vaguely approved; she had a queer directness in her face which pleased him. And next to her a vacant chair, which made him frown. Then came Corcoran, whom he had met on shore - a little matter anent the easing of the passage money! - and whom he couldn't help but like. And finally, as far to leeward as he could arrange - she had sailed with him before - the vulgar bulk of Mother Hemmingway.

And now, his inquisition ended, he gave an ear to the conversation. Dibdin, his neck craned forward, his long, bony face filled with mulish curiosity, was speaking.

'Captain, what's that odd box over there? Bless my soul, but it's an odd affair.'

'It is a harmonium, sir,' Renton answered shortly, 'belonging to one of the passengers.'

'A harmonium,' echoed Dibdin blankly, and his eyebrows flew into his scalp. 'But aren't they finished? On my oath, I thought harmoniums had gone out with hair-nets.'

Mother Hemmingway leered down the table.

''Aven't you ever been to a revival meetin'? That's w'ere 'armoniums sprouts like hartichokes. And this 'armonium's on the syme gyme.' She jerked her thumb towards Susan. 'It's 'ers. Goin' with 'er brother to convert the Spaniolas. An invalid 'e is.' And, having discharged her information like a cuttle-fish its venom, she returned cheerfully to her hash.

There was a short silence, then Mrs Baynham looked across at Susan.

'Is your brother really an invalid?' she remarked pleasantly. 'He seems a healthy-looking animal.'

Susan bit her lip and lifted her eyes resentfully to face the other. It cost her a painful effort to control a rising dislike for this indolent creature who now so brazenly mocked her Robbie.

'My brother,' she said steadily, 'is not particularly robust.'

Tranter laughed, that deep pleasant laugh which even in the pulpit he freely used.

'Come now, Sue' - and his tone was unusually mild - 'Mrs Baynham was just asking. And there ain't no harm in asking. The fact is,' he went on seriously, turning to Elissa, 'that I am quite organically sound but rather anaemic. My physician back in Connecticut - well, to cut a long story short, he found my haemoglobin index registered point five off normal. I follow the new liver extract treatment; and we hope of course that the sunshine of the islands will send that odd index right up where it belongs.'

She stared at him incredulously, then gave a short amused laugh.

'Dibs,' she exclaimed, 'you've got a vast experience, indecent and otherwise. You've never met a missionary with an index?' She paused gracefully. 'In the meantime, will someone give me the butter.'

Tranter, at whose plate the butter-dish stood, made an effusive movement of apology.

'I'm deeply sorry, ma'am,' he murmured, passing the dish with a little flourish.

She turned her head, stared through him with her large blue eyes, then deliberately looked away.

For some moments Mary Fielding had been gazing abstractedly at the unoccupied chair, and now, as on an impulse, she turned towards Renton.

'That empty chair, captain.' She smiled and gave a little shiver with her shoulders. 'Isn't it unlucky - so early in the voyage?'

The captain straightened the napkin upon his knee.

'I am not superstitious about chairs, my lady. It is simply a place, that chair, set apart for one of my passengers. And if the passenger in question does not choose to occupy it, I infer simply that he has his own good reasons for not occupying it. And so I go on with my lunch.'

'You are too heartless, captain,' said Mrs Baynham languidly.

'But you intrigue us. Didn't we see this - er - passenger in question as we came on board? That wretched-looking man standing in the alleyway. You did see him, Mary?'

There was a tiny pause.

'Yes, Elissa,' said Mary, 'I did see him.'

'He looked teed up - all gaunt and burning you know. Delightfully intense,' said Elissa. 'Let us hear more about him, captain.'

'Some more of this omelette, Mrs Baynham,' said Renton abruptly. 'We make a speciality of this dish on the *Aureloa*. It is from my own receipt. Made with pimentos. I got it from a Spanish cook in Palma. Or would you care to have some hash?'

Elissa smiled gently.

'We were talking of the missing passenger, weren't we? Who is he, what is he, where is he?'

There was a short pause. The situation, for some reason, took on an edge of sharp discomfort. From beneath his bushy eyebrows Renton surveyed Elissa, then he answered very shortly:

'His name is Leith, ma'am. Dr Harvey Leith.'

Instantly there fell upon the table a dead silence. Everyone stopped eating and looked up.

'Leith! Dr Leith!' Elissa seemed to meditate, and her glance strayed from the captain to the empty chair. 'Just too extraordinary.'

Then Dibs gave his little nickering laugh and exclaimed:

'Why, the papers have been full of a fellow called Leith - Harvey Leith. And I'm hanged if it wasn't a doctor, too. You know, the fellow who . . .'

Renton stared straight in front of him with a face which appeared carved from wood.

Suddenly Mother Hemmingway giggled.

'Blimey if it ain't funny. The syme name as our absent friend! Wot a joke! I can tell from the captain's face it's the syme man. You can paint me pink if it ain't.'

There fell another silence, during which Renton's features remained impenetrable and unrelaxed; yet, stealing a quick look at him, Mary could see that he was vexed.

'Confounded scandal,' declared Dibs excitedly. 'Nothin' short of murder, don't you know.'

Unexpectedly, Jimmy Corcoran laid down his knife and fork which he had been holding upon their ends. His large seamed face was quite impassive as he said gently:

'Ye know what yer talkin' about, don't ye? Ye know a lot. Science. Everything.'

'Eh, what?' said Dibs; he was a little deaf on one side. 'What was it?'

'Nothin',' Jimmy said calmly. 'Just plain nothin' at all. I'm not a talker, ye see, but I've been listenin' to ye since we come in. And I'm just thinkin' how much ye must know. It's marvellous. Sure, it's marvellous. Ye've devoted yer life to study. Playto was a child beside ye.' He blinked at the skylight and took an enormous bite at his roll.

'You read the papers,' said Dibs, bridling like an old woman. 'You know I'm speaking the truth.'

Jimmy went on chewing stolidly, then he said:

'Uh-huh! I read the papers an' I read Playto. There's a difference.'

A faint shred of colour stole into Dibs' toughened skin. His

28

eye-glass glinted agitatedly.

'But you can't get away from this thing,' he exclaimed. 'It's hitting you in the eye. The Press shrieked about it. The fellow's inhuman.' His voice finished on a high note which made Renton frown and abruptly lift his head. In a firm tone he said:

'I think that is enough. I don't like scandal. And I won't have it in my ship. This Dr Leith is the man you speak of. There is an end of it. Gossip has ruined many a man. And it's ruined many a ship. When I'm afloat I won't have it. You understand. That's all.'

A full minute passed, then Robert Tranter made a gesture of generous assent.

'I guess I'm with you, captain,' he gushed. 'That's the true spirit of human brotherhood. There was a question asked, "Who will throw the first stone?" Well, I reckon it'll be none of us. My sister and I saw this man on the tender. And, believe me, he looked so afflicted I felt right there I wanted to offer him my sympathy.'

Susan Tranter, with her feet pressed close together and her eyes upon her plate, felt herself glow at her brother's words. Harvey Leith - Dr Harvey Leith! - to think that it should be he whom she had read about with such distress. Even before she had known she had noticed him upon the tender, observed his air - like a man who has lost his faith - and marked especially his eyes. They suffered, those eyes, like the eyes of the wounded Christ. An impulse of compassion quickened within her. Oh, how he must have suffered! Instinctively she aligned herself upon his side against the hard indifference of the Baynham woman. Her pity flowed; and born of that pity - for surely it was pity - came the happy thought: I may help him. Yes, I feel that I shall help him. Stealthily almost, she raised her eyes.

The meal was ending. No one, apparently, had very much to say.

And Mary Fielding, who had said so little, was now, like Susan, completely silent. Her face wore once more that sad and puzzled look as though again she strove to capture something both elusive and obscure. Her eyes were still troubled as she rose from the table and went with Elissa upon deck. For a moment they stood balanced to the gentle pitching of the ship, their skirts wrapped tight about them by the wind, regarding the cheerless prospect of the following sea. Land had faded, and the waves came swinging down astern - long, grey, crestless billows which seemed to urge the vessel inexorably upon her course. Forward upon her fixed, predestined course. Forward, evoking a curious sense of recollection. Forward – to what? The thought confused her as the bleak discomfort of the scene broke over her.

Her husband, who viewed always with half-humorous distrust her impulse towards simplicity, had not wished her to take this most fantastic trip. She could see his face now as, approaching him, she had resolutely declared:

'I must get away, Michael. By myself. On some little ship. Anywhere - so long as it is quiet and away. I really must. You'll let me go.'

Why should she have wished to get away? Surely it was inexplicable. She was happy at Buckden; she loved, at least, the mellow Tudor place set in its rolling oak-studded parks, loved the odd things that one could do there: to ride alone in the hidden glades, to bathe unseen at early dawn in the pool, to feed the timid nuzzling deer by the silver birches, all by herself.

And she was happy with Michael. Happy? Oh, yes, happy enough. She was fond of Michael. She liked him; she had always liked him. He it was who mildly pointed out a dozen reasons which might deter her; and then, with that graciousness which was his charm, who had consented. A delight to humour her caprice - that was his attitude; he did not really understand. But inevitably he showered consideration upon her, arranging that Elissa should accompany her, that Dibdin should escort them both. Poor Dibs - no money for all his name - had leaped at the job. Dibs was like that; he lived on people, subsisted on invitations, so that his two rooms in Davis Street saw him little. Poor Dibs! All manner, front, nothing inside! He had never read a book in his life, never done anything. No! she was wrong. He had shot, also by invitation, a large number of birds and animals.

She was sorry for Dibs. Yet she would have preferred to come alone; but that, of course, was quite impossible.

Oh, why was her mind running on like this? She was confused, evading something - yes, evading that meeting . . . that strange meeting of the morning. . . .

Suddenly Elissa moved.

'I'm cold,' she said, tapping her feet upon the deck. 'Let's go into my cabin.'

In the cabin she switched on the tiny electric heater, tucked a rug round her knees, remarked sulkily:

'It'll take a lot of sun to make up for this agony you've landed me into, Mary - cramped on this wretched little ship with no maid and those ghastly - oh, those most ghastly people. Why, oh, why did you ever want to come?'

'I don't know,' said Mary hesitatingly. 'I felt all screwed up inside. And somehow I had a fancy to come - a strange sort of fancy.'

It was true. Often she had strange fancies - of a place hauntingly familiar, of a perfume lingering, elusive, of a garden, sweet-scented and profuse, set in the shadow of a snow-capped peak, bathed in clear moonlight, hushed by the whisper of a distant sea. Often this garden came to her in sleep and she would run gladly and wander there, fingering the flowers, lifting her face to the moon, feeling a lovely inner joy which irradiated her like light. Next day she would be sad and quiet and alone; she would feel herself odd, strangely out of key, separated from the ordinary things of life. Once she had told Michael about her garden. He had laughed kindly, after his fashion, with the calm precision of possession.

'Still a child, Mary,' he had said. 'You must learn to grow up.'

It was all so unsatisfactory. She did not understand. It worried her, this strange fantasy which struggled secretly, like a plant reaching from a dark place towards the sunshine. And sometimes she feared it, because in reaction it had brought her so much pain.

She looked up suddenly. Elissa was staring at her.

'You're a funny little sprat, Mary,' she laughed. 'You're like a child looking at a rainbow. Exactly that. Hand me a chocolate. And for heaven's sake put something on the gramophone. For I'm bored - oh, so terribly bored.'


## CHAPTER VI


ONE bell had sounded in the second dog watch, and the echoes still jangled in Harvey's ears as he lay half undressed upon his bunk staring fixedly at the row of bolts which ran across the ceiling. Nineteen white-enamelled bolts, round-headed and symmetrical, all neatly in a row; he had counted and recounted them as a man half crazed by lack of sleep might vainly number sheep. Sometimes, amid the creaking and sighing of the ship, he heard the clink of hammers on these bolts, and sometimes that hammer-beat was in his brain. His hands clenched, his face pale and haggard, he had a look strangely persecuted. Clearly he suffered; but he endured that suffering with a stoic bitterness. At times the thought flashed into his mind: a few steps to the ship's side and then cold darkness - the end of everything. But that was too easy; he always recoiled from the impulse. At other times, with a self-analysis almost grim, he made attempt to trace the morbid pattern of his sensation. He had always had this impulse: a curious instinctive searching, the burning desire to strike into the heart of reason.

It was the motive which had actuated his life.

His upbringing had been austere. His father had been a schoolmaster: no comfortable tutor at an expensive establishment, but an ill-paid, hard-driven teacher of science in a Birmingham Board School. Yet William Leith had a mind; he was ambitious, a man far before his time; and far above the soul-destroying task of thrusting reluctant youths through the crude elements of chemistry and physics. But for him the task was a necessity. Julia, his wife, was one of those women whose whole existence might be epitomised in the word: Demand. Insatiably she demanded clothes, money, and his affection. She taxed his slender income to the uttermost; she complained of that income's insufficiency; she harassed him; she exhausted him in mind and body, then with sublime bathos she ran off with a commercial traveller. Neither her husband nor her son heard of her again.

When she deserted him, William Leith was already suffering from an early phthisis lesion - his cough had been the crowning inadequacy which thrust Julia into the travelling salesman's arms - and now the condition rapidly advanced. He did not seem to care. He let ambition slip, turned his gaunt and brilliant mind upon his son, named in a whim of early arrogance, for the great Harvey. Thus there germinated in the boy a forward passion for scientific research and, incredibly - though he had never loved his mother - a precocious contempt of women.

When Harvey was twelve years old, William Leith died of a pulmonary haemorrhage. It was a staggering blow. Harvey had loved his father and lived with him in close companionship.

He fell now to the care of his aunt - a nagging and impoverished spinster who, accepting him of necessity, regarded him thereafter solely as an incubus. But young Harvey had his ambition. His own brilliance and a dogged pertinacity of purpose sent him through the rest of his schooling, then, with three scholarships, to the provincial medical college. He had seen his father fail for lack of opportunity in a career purely academic; and he felt instinctively that medicine would give him surer chance of success. Besides, biology was his bent. At Birmingham he was regarded as the most distinguished student of his time. But after his graduation, which gave him every prize that could be won, he had refused an appointment to the City Hospital and abruptly taken himself to London. He had no aspirations towards a successful practice. No craving for a consultant's chair, no ambition to acquire a fortune in exchange for bedside condolences. His inspiration lay deeper, his ideal stood higher. He had that unique incentive which few men through the centuries have possessed - the genuine passion for original research.

He had no money, nor did he desire it, except for the bare necessities of life. He took rooms in Westminster and set to work. His struggles in London were severe, his privations many. But he gritted his teeth, tightened his belt, built everything upon his ideal. He discovered the prejudice which bogs the feet of genius, especially when that genius is sponsored by a provincial school of small repute. Yet rebuffs served merely to harden his purpose; he lived like a monk, he fought like a soldier. He obtained a minor hospital appointment in a nearer suburb; then, after three years' grilling work, he was given the post of clinical pathologist at the Victoria Hospital. A small and unimportant hospital, perhaps; old, too, and conservative in its methods; yet actually this marked the most important step in his career. That night he went home to his rooms in Vincent Street and stared at the portrait of Pasteur upon his desk - Pasteur whom alone he admitted to be great; then he smiled his rare, unusual smile. He felt the power surge up within him to conquer.

He had swung inevitably into the field of serum therapeutics. And he had a theory, based upon a long series of agglutination experiments, a vivid advance upon the work of Koch and Wright, which he felt would revolutionise the entire principle of scientific treatment.

It was immense, his idea, magnificent - bearing not merely upon one particular disease, but bigger, much bigger, embracing in its ramifications the whole wide field of preventative and curative inoculation. He burned with this conviction. Singling a specific point of attack, he chose the condition of cerebro-spinal fever;

partly because of the mortality of the disease, partly because of the comparative failure of all previous sera.

So at the Victoria he began. For six months he worked intensely upon his serum, the routine work of his appointment accomplished through the day, this special work at night. His health began to suffer, but he exhibited no gratitude when advised by his friend Ismay to shorten his laboratory hours. Instead, he lengthened them, driven by that burning zeal within him. Nervous, irritable, and overstrung, he still felt himself approaching definitely towards success. Moreover, a seasonal outcropping of sporadic meningitis occurred about this time, and the mere consideration of the existing treatment in all its pre-Adamite ineffectuality - the phrase was his! - goaded him to further effort.

Late one night he completed his last conclusive tests against controls. Over and over again he checked his results. Satisfied? That was no word. He was elated! He flung his pen into the air. He knew that he had won.

The next day three early cases of cerebro-spinal fever were admitted to the hospital. It was for Harvey no mere coincidence but a logical concession from circumstance, the tacit pre-admission of his victory. At once he approached the hospital authorities and offered to exhibit his serum.

His offer was curtly refused.

Harvey was staggered. He did not know he had made enemies, that his careless dress, sardonic tongue, and arrogant disregard for etiquette had made him an object of antipathy and suspicion. Already the biting truth of his pathological reports had soured the temper of the diagnosticians and, like all who disdain the footsteps of their predecessors, he figured in the eyes of many as an upstart, a firebrand, a clever, but a dangerous fellow.

But, though he was staggered, Harvey did not accept defeat. No, no; that was not Harvey.

Instantly he launched a campaign. He approached individually the various members of the staff; produced the evidence of his experiments; he laboured painfully to convince those more favourably disposed to him of the value of his original work. Infuriated by the inertia of conservatism, by the whole muddling process of authority, he pressed his case urgently. The very bitterness of his air breathed conviction. There was humming and hawing; reference to the institution's sane policy; talk of a general staff meeting. Meanwhile the three patients progressed with inexorable rapidity into the advanced stages of the disease.

Then with suddenness and magnanimity the opposition weakened; it was decided with due gravity to permit the application of the new therapy; a sort of ponderous consent was conveyed - in writing - to Harvey. He leaped to the opportunity, rushed immediately to the ward.

It was, of course, too late. He should have known it. The three patients, now six days in hospital and ten in the grip of their morbidity, were comatose, clearly moribund. And the circumstances, alas! were no pre-admission of Harvey's victory, but a trap sprung by destiny in his face. On the one hand, an expectant and antipathetic audience awaiting with a sneer the consummation of the miracle; on the other, three subjects his calmer judgement would have instantly rejected as far beyond the aid of any human remedy.

But he was not calm. Strung to an unimagined tensity, he could not allow to his opponents the gratification of seeing him withdraw.

He had a desperate belief in his serum. And he had the fatal urge of eagerness. Grimly he accepted the responsibility, injecting massive doses directly into the cerebral ventricles of all three subjects. All that night he remained in the ward. Again and once again he repeated the dosage.

Early next morning, within the compass of the same sad hour, the three patients died. They would have died in any case. It was inevitable. Yet it was a bad business for Harvey - though one from which his resilient spirit would inevitably have recovered. But there was worse to follow. A loose tongue wagged spitefully outside the hospital. News of the incident reached the newspapers, flared in a garbled form, and spread like wildfire through the popular Press. There was a terrific outcry levelled at the hospital and at Harvey. He gave no heed, meeting the biased clamour with quivering contempt. Unshaken, he saw now that he had intervened too late. To his cold and scientific mind the deaths of the three individuals represented no more than the termination of an inconclusive experiment. Because he desired no popular success, the flagrant uproar of the herd was to him as nothing.

But to the hospital it was not as nothing. And the authorities, alas! gave heed.

Pressed by the force of outside influence, the board met - a full meeting - *in camera*. The governor, like Pilate, washed his hands; the protests of the discerning few who believed in Harvey proved unavailing; there was a sort of scurried feeling that the incubus must be removed.

Upon the day following the meeting, Harvey went into his laboratory and found an envelope upon his desk. It was the formal demand for his resignation.

Incredulously he faced the shattering injustice of this final blow. It was beyond reason. The very walls rushed in upon him.

Four years' work, his whole soul straining in the cause of science; four years' searching for the heart of truth; and now - he saw it in a flash - outcast, no position, no opportunity, no money. And his name a public obloquy. With luck he might secure himself, perhaps, a paltry assistantship to some unknown practitioner. But for the rest - he was finished.

An agony of self-satire was in his soul. Without a word he rose, burned the records of his research, smashed the flasks which held the product of his work, and walked out of his laboratory.

He went home. He faced the situation with a scathing, pitiless irony. But he wanted to forget - to forget as quickly as he could. And he began, not from weakness, but from a bitter hatred of life, to drink. His attitude was not heroic, but derisive. Alcohol - it was a drug: and as such he would use it. He was alone; the thought of women had never entered his head; and, with no capacity for friendship, only Gerald Ismay, the surgeon, had been there to witness this spectacle of saturation.

But Ismay had been there. Yes. Each day of those three deadly weeks he had been - quite mildly - there; and by insinuation and insidious tact had finally advanced the suggestion of this voyage.

Why not? A man might drink the better and lose himself the quicker upon a lonely ship. He had agreed, unthinking of the trap which Ismay had contrived. And now he was here; aboard this wretched ship; deprived of liquor; feeling so ill the sensation was like death.

All at once he turned his head upon the pillow and with a start came back to himself. Someone had knocked upon the door. And immediately the handle turned and Jimmy Corcoran sidled his bony frame into the cabin. For a moment he stood grinning ingratiatingly, hat still on head, then he flexed both arms as though nonchalantly to elevate dumb-bells of enormous weight.

'How goes it, me boy? In other words, how does it go? D'ye feel muscle comin' back on ye yet?'

Harvey stared at him with an injured eye.

'How do you know that it doesn't go?' he muttered.

Corcoran smiled again - in a friendly, intimate way. He touched his hat a shade farther back.

'No lunch, no tay, and now, by the looks on it, no dinner. Faith, it wouldn't take a detective to see that ye was out. And, knowin' somethin' about the old K.O., I just looked in to see if you was scramblin' to your corner again.'

'The Good Samaritan,' sneered Harvey.

'Sure.'

A short silence came; then, at a sudden thought, Harvey raised himself upon his shoulder.

'They've been talking about me.'

'That's right,' Jimmy agreed; he hitched up his trousers and sat down easily upon the settee. 'They've been talkin' about ye all right. Had the whole of yer history weighed in and tested. A gintleman was sayin' things. What they don't know about ye now could be writ on a threepenny piece. But don't get yer rag out. Stay cool and stick yer chin down, fella.'

'For God's sake,' cried Harvey in an agony of irritation, 'don't call me that. Call me anything under heaven but that.'

'Sure,' said Jimmy agreeably.

A silence fell, during which Harvey pressed his damp hand on his brow; then suddenly, with a concentrated bitterness of tone, he exclaimed:

'Why do you come in here? Can't you see I want to be left alone?'

Jimmy pulled the metal snuff-box from his waistcoat pocket, dipped in a broad forefinger and thumb, inhaled gravely, then dusted himself gently with the palm of his hand.

' "Whin the object of his desire has faded," ' he quoted oracularly, ' "then he departs and is seen no more." That's Playto, that is. But faith, ye wouldn't be askin' me to go yet awhile. Me that took a proper notion on ye the minnit ye come into the saloon. Sure, I knew booze was the trouble as soon as I clapped oi on ye. It's sent many's a good man for the count. I followed the beer meself in the ould days. Cyards and the dthrink - ah! -' He sighed and looked at the other sideways with a sort of sly solemnity. 'But divil the one or t'other am I after touchin' now. Mind ye, despite me faults and failings I've always spoke the thruth. Let a man be tinder to the thruth and I'll rispect him. And me heart draws to a man that's had a rap from distiny.

37

Faith, I've had a troublous life meself, up and down, off and on, since first I seen the light in Clontarf sixty odd year ago. Me folks was poor - proud people, mind ye, from Tralee, but poor. I got me early eddication holdin' horses' heads in Sackville Street, and learned me letters spellin' the Guinness's advertisements. Ye wouldn't believe it, me that reads Playto like a scholard.' He paused, as for encouragement, but Harvey's eyes remained tightly shut. 'Then I went in for the game, the glorious game. A foine set figure of a lad was I. Unsurpassable. There wasn't a man could stand in the ring against me. In Belfast I knocked Smiler Burge over the ropes with one crack of me left. Sure, I'd have been the world's champeen if I hadn't bruk me leg. But bruk me leg I did. And carry the mark to this day. Faith, it robbed the world of a champeen. That's how I came to emigrate in the black nineties.'

Harvey groaned.

'Is that the end? If so, will you kindly get out?'

'The end?' cried Jimmy. 'Faith, 'twas only the beginning. Since then hivin alone knows what I done. I marked billiards in Sydney. Then I marked time in Mexico in wan of them popgun revolutions. The next year I was in the Bull Gulch gold rush, and the next I took a pub in San Francisco. But sure, I couldn't stand the loife. Then I tried a turn at farmin' in the Southern States. And I liked that best of all. If ever the ship comes in, that's where ye'll find Jimmy C. - wid a cow and some hens in his own backyard. But I took a foolish fit and wandered off to Colorado, scratchin' silver. And after that I travelled with Professor Sinnott's circus. Dear old Bob, I hopes to see him soon. I'm joinin' him in Santa Cruz, ye see - there's business all fixed and waitin' - a great affair. Ah, but these was the palmy days with old Bob Sinnott's show. Every evenin' for a twelvemonth I intered the din of the untamable lioness Dominica. She'd attacked and killed three keepers - so 'twas said upon the posthers. But in the end she died on Bob and me. 'Twas somethin' out of the monkey-house got in her grub. And thin the circus busted.' He sighed, thrust his thumb in his armhole. ' 'Twas a sorry day, I tell ye, when I took good-bye of Bob.'

Harvey turned restlessly in his bunk.

'I wish to God you'd take good-bye of me.'

'I'm goin',' cried Jimmy. 'Of course I'm goin'. I can see yer feelin' none too grand. I only wanted to inthrojuice meself and let ye know I'm at yer service. Faith and I am. And don't be

judgin' by appearances, me boy. I may look down on me luck.'
He stopped and straightened his paste tie-pin with an air. 'Sure,
'tis only timporary. 'Tis now I'm on the best thing ever was.
Wid the Professor, ye understand. A foine affair. It's goin' to
make a fortune for yer good friend Jimmy C.'

He paused so impressively that Harvey was compelled to look
up. And he found that disarming grin upon him. He hesitated.
There was about the shabby old adventurer an irresistible
humbugging charm that killed the angry words upon his tongue.
For a moment the two looked at each other. Then Corcoran
stood up.

'Ta-ta for the moment,' he murmured airily. 'And don't forget
what I've been tellin' ye about the man. Just say the word and
he's at your beck and call.'

He lunged forward, tilted his hat, and with a final nod
swaggered through the door. He wore the gratified air of one who
had discharged a duty to himself and to his neighbour. Humming
gently, he advanced along the deck with his eyes skinned for
Mother Hemmingway. Faith, there was just time before dinner
for a little dhrop of porther and a quiet hand of the cyards.

Harvey, in his cabin, pressed his brow against the cold brass
rail of his bunk.

How, he thought, did I endure it - that anthropoid attempt to
kindness? - the traditional Irishman blundering in to bolster
him up with friendliness. Oh, it was lunatic, the situation. Again
he twisted nervously beneath the narrow sheet, wishing desperately for sleep.

For a full half-hour he was alone.

Then Trout came into the cabin with a shining brass can of hot
water in his hand and a frightened expression upon his indeterminate features. Bestowing the can tenderly upon the floor, he
said gently:

'Shall I lay out your things, sir?'

Harvey did not open his eyes; without moving his head he
muttered:

'No.'

'Shall I bring you some dinner, sir?'

'No.'

'Is there anything more I can do, sir?'

In the cabin forward the gramophone began shrilly, for the
tenth time that afternoon, to play: 'Give me all your kisses.' A
shiver as of pain passed over Harvey's face. The strident melody,

rich in sickly and offensive sentiment, turned in his soul with shuddering revulsion and, like a man overborne from the last of his restraint, he started up.

'My head is splitting. Ask them - ask them for pity's sake to stop that gramophone.'

There was a quick pause, shocked as the look upon Trout's face; then, as though a hand had snatched the needle from the disc, abruptly the music stopped. The silence, so sudden it was oppressive, lengthened until Trout said tremulously:

'It's thin, sir, that bulkhead. Your voice goes through if you call like that.'

Then Trout went out; but in five minutes he was back, bearing on stiff extended fingers a napkin-covered tray. A bowl of steaming soup stood on the tray, and beside it a tiny silver-topped tube holding some flat white tabloids.

'Some soup, sir?' pleaded Trout, as though to exculpate himself from a grave transgression. 'It's nourishing, sir. Sydney soup, sir. The captain would have me fetch it up. And Lady Fielding, sir - hearing you had a headache, she asked if you'd care to have some aspirin.'

Harvey's lips stiffened. He wished in the same instant to scream, to curse, to weep.

'Leave it, then,' he said in a low voice. 'Leave it by the bed.'

Then he lay back, closed his eyes, hearing the creaking and sighing of the ship as it bore onwards, cleaving the outer darkness. Cleaving onwards, a strange symbolic force which carried him against his will. Onwards, sighing gently. As though around there were voices, strange voices whispering, whispering to him.


# CHAPTER VII


THEY were three days out, the wind still pouring favourably from the south-west, the *Aureola* riding the placid swell with Cape Finisterre fading upon her port quarter. The morning sun blazed fitfully out of a ragged sky and warm intermittent showers had flattened out the sea.

A pad of feet came from the starboard deck, but in the saloon below Robert Tranter and his sister were seated before the open harmonium.

'It's a great tune that, Robbie,' she said reflectively, lifting her hands from the keyboard and turning the sheets of music on the stand. 'And you certainly sing it fine.'

'Yes, it's got a swell swing has old "Glory".' His ear, held sideways towards the skylight, seemed to attend the returning tramp of footsteps above. 'Don't you think we might close our practice now, Sue? The sun's on the shine.' He smiled, 'I guess the choir might go up top.'

Her fingers ceased to move; slowly she turned her warm brown eyes upon him.

'But we've only just begun, Rob. We *said* an hour, didn't we? And it's the hour I like best in all the day - all quiet and together down here.'

'I know, Sue,' he said with a little laugh. 'I certainly enjoy our practice. I kind of guess it's just because I'm restless - you know the feeling - when you get your foot on the deck.'

She looked at him intently: looked away again; pressed a long soft chord from the bosom of the instrument.

'I don't take much to the folks on this boat,' she exclaimed suddenly and without apparent reason. 'I don't take overmuch to that Mrs Baynham.'

He contemplated his white stiff cuffs, neatly projecting, linked by severe gold links.

'Ah, no, Sue,' he protested in an odd but unselfconscious voice. 'I'll say you're wrong there. Yes, I'll say you're wrong. I feel she has good - great capacity for good in her.'

'She's guying us, Robbie. She mocks at everything, even - even at God.'

He gave a deprecating pressure upon her arm with his large white hand and quoted:

' "Let not your good be evil spoken of." I guess, Susan, it's none too good for us to criticise.'

'You're interested in her,' she said quickly. 'I can feel it.'

He made no evasion.

'I'll admit, Susan, that I'm interested in her,' he answered, gazing back into her eyes calmly. 'But it is because she has a soul to save. I reckon I've had to mix up with plenty women in the past. Well! Did I ever give you the slightest reason to doubt me?'

It was true. He had encountered many women responsive to his spiritual fervour - responsive with a devotion which he had

41

come to feel, complacently, his due. But never for a moment had he entertained towards them any sentiment which merited even a shadow of reproach. His affections were centred exclusively upon himself, on God, and on his sister.

Born in Trenton of pious parents, he was one of those individuals who seem destined for the ministry from their earliest days. His father, Josiah Tranter, was an unsuccessful tradesman, a bearded, ineffectual little baker - rigid adherent of the Sect of the Seventh Day Unity - who leavened his loaves with Leviticus, whose doughnuts even had a stale and spiritual flavour. His mother, Emily by name, a quiet woman with a zealous eye, had come from a sound Concord stock. She was silent, good, sustaining successive business failures of her spouse with commendable patience and fortitude. Her happiness lay in her children, particularly Robbie to whom beneath her tranquil surface she was passionately devoted. And indeed Robert merited that devotion. He was dutiful, intelligent, instinctively fervent, never in mischief, and when visitors would pat his head and demand: 'Well, son, what d'you think you're gonna do?' the boy would answer quite sincerely: 'I'm going to preach the gospel.' And with delight his high intention was fostered and encouraged. A tract even was written about him by a visiting pastor who had dwelt at the baker's house, entitled: 'Saved at the Early Age of Nine.' Thus he knew betimes the ardour of salvation.

Susan, inevitably, though of a tender disposition, took a back seat in the home. She was devoted to her brother; she was a good girl: but she was not a paragon. Thus whilst Robert entered theological college she was allowed without demur to enter as a probationer-nurse at the John Stirling Hospital.

The years rolled on and the day of Robert's ordination gloriously arrived. What a moment of pride for the little baker and his wife! Forgetting the toil and rigours of those years of scrimping sacrifice they dressed in their sober best and entrained joyfully for Connecticut.

But there was sad perversity about that train. Six miles out of Trenton it fouled a point and ran into the embankment. Little damage was done: only two lives were lost. But these were Josiah and Emily Tranter. Robert, of course, was painfully upset. There was a touching scene when the news was broken to him as he came out, ordained, from Unity Temple. Susan said less. She could not be expected to feel the blow so keenly. But she fainted twice in the ensuing month whilst on duty in the wards

They said at the hospital she had a heart lesion and advised her kindly to relinquish the idea of institutional work.

Thus she came to live with her brother at Okeville, his first pastorate. Here she lavished everything upon Robert. She desired no more. But he, though zealous and successful, was less settled. He was restless. He had inherently an ardent and romantic mind. He wanted, though he knew it not, to see the colour and to feel the texture of the world. After one year he resigned his pastorate, entered his name for the foreign mission field.

His sincerity was known, his capabilities recognised, his step approved. It was understood that his health was not robust. Moreover, in the movement the directing mind of the Rev Hiram McAtee was turning - like Alexander's - to fresh fields of conquest. There had been, too, under special circumstances, a persistent demand from the Canaries. Robert was sent out, not to China nor the Congo, but to Santa Cruz. And Susan, of course, accompanied him.

That briefly was his history. And now he faced his sister with a tolerant eye.

'I surely am serious, Sue,' he went on steadily. 'Believe me, I have a hunch that Mrs Baynham might be saved. There's more hope for the conversion of the scoffer than the soul which is just plumb apathetic. And it would be a great happiness indeed to me if I should be the Lord's humble instrument to bring this soul to grace.' His eye kindled: he thrilled to the glory of the thought.

She gazed at him in silence, touched by a troubled colour, and almost wistful. Then with a gust came a swirl of rain upon the skylight, succeeded by a laughing exclamation from above. There was the sound of footsteps upon the companion, and Mary ran through the doorway, her small white sand-shoes spattered, her wind-blown hair clustered with pearling raindrops.

'It rains, it rains,' she chanted. 'All hands are piped below.'

Elissa, Dibdin, and Corcoran followed her into the saloon.

'By George!' said Dibs with a nautical stagger, 'that was a squall. Sudden if you like - what?'

Elissa, having shaken the lapels of her coat, was staring at the Tranters. 'You've been singing,' she announced loudly. 'How terribly diverting. And the harmonium - too, too sweet. You treadmill upon these pedal things, don't you? But you mustn't stop. You must entertain us. Delicious. Too simply delicious.' And ranging herself beside the others on the long plush settee she assumed an air of bland expectancy.

Awkwardness at once was in the air, but though Susan's flush still lingered her voice was firm.

'We have been singing to our Maker,' she said distinctly. 'We don't just regard that as an entertainment.'

Elissa affected a puzzled frown.

'Can't you sing something?' she protested. 'I mean, couldn't you entertain your Maker and us - both at the same time?'

Dibs let out his usual laugh, but Susan's eyes darkened and her lips became quite pale; she seemed struggling for words when Robert spoke.

Looking directly at Elissa he said:

'I'll sing for you, Mrs Baynham, since you ask us. We aren't that unobliging after all. I'll sing something you might like to hear. And I guess God won't mind hearing it either.'

He swung round with a half-conscious, vaguely ceremonial air and in an undertone said a few words to Susan sitting bolt upright, rigid as a rock. For a full ten seconds, it seemed as if she would not stir, then, with a movement, almost of resignation, her body slackened, her hands reached out to the keyboard, she began to play. It was the negro spiritual 'All God's Children,' and as the thin melodious treble of the cheap harmonium rose into the saloon Robert began to sing.

His voice was good, a baritone which, though it boomed a little in its lower and vibrated in its upper reaches, had nevertheless richness and resonance. And with full eye and straining throat he tried hard to sing his best, which made him rather emotional, even theatrical. But nothing of his mannerisms could destroy the touching beauty of the air, echoing in that cabined space and soaring outwards to dissolve thinly upon the vast dimensions of the moving sea.

Corcoran listened with lifted battered ear and faintly nodding head - to him it was a tune; Dibs, his upper lip retracted questioningly to show his yellowish teeth, was thinking of his lunch; Elissa's sulky inanimation betrayed nothing but a bored contempt. But Mary, curled upon the settee, her slender legs bent under her blue serge skirt which, drawn tautly back exposed the beauty of her thigh, listened like someone in a dream. Her eyes were utterly remote, quite heedless of the singer. Her expression, a moment ago so eager and intrepid, was now forlorn; upon her lovely face there lay a queer lost look. Shadows all fretted and perplexing floated across her vision; in her ears a fountain surged and splashed; white moonshine mingled with the fountain's note. Again she felt herself trembling as upon a deep chasm of discovery.

Suddenly the voice rose and for the last time fell to silence. No one spoke. Mary was too moved to speak. Then deliberately Elissa yawned behind her hand.

'Thank you so much,' she said languidly. 'I heard Robeson sing that. He did it quite beautifully.'

Tranter flushed to his ears with mortification; Susan got up with the abruptness of an automaton, began to collect her music.

Then Mary said:

'It was lovely - lovely.' She hesitated, seeking to shape her thought. 'Something behind it - that meaning you can't find on the surface of things.'

'Faith and yer right, lady,' said Corcoran gallantly. 'There's more goes on below the surface than works out by rule of three. Things you'd never dream about - the queerest things ye can't for the life of ye explain.'

There was a short silence. Then Mary rose and without a word went out of the saloon.

On deck the rain had ceased. Leaning across the rail she felt the clean wind come crisping through her parted teeth with a sound like the sighing of a great seashell. For no reason whatever her emotion was intense. That meaning you couldn't find on the surface of things! Oh, she was stupid, too stupid for words. But she couldn't help herself. Blindly she reached out her arms. With palms uppermost and thin fingers uncurled, she surrendered her whole soul to the listening horizon.

Below, the group had not held together: Corcoran and Dibs had vanished separately to their cabins, and Susan, too, stood now in the middle of the floor, her music clasped under her arm, her brown eyes fixed on Robert, who still sat by the harmonium.

'Are you coming, Robbie?' she asked quietly. 'It's about time you had your extract.'

Like one removed from serious thought he lifted his head.

'I'll be along right now, Sue. Will you put out the' - he smiled in a big brotherly fashion - 'the darn stuff.'

'Come now. You'll forget for certain if you don't.'

He still smiled at her; spoke with unusual lightness:

'Pour out the dose, Susie, and if it's not gone in half an hour I'll swallow the bottleful.'

Her fingers tightened against the green cardboard of the music case, but she managed to answer his smile, then she turned, retreated noiselessly from the saloon.

Elissa, removing her gaze from vacancy, let it fall by chance on Robert.

'She's jealous of you,' she said - then added her jibe: 'What on earth for?'

'Susan and I live for each other.'

'And for God?'

'Yes. For God.'

From across the cabin she contemplated him as from across a continent, her gaze charged with lifeless scorn yet holding a sort of antipodean wonder, seeing him the most abject creature, the most insufferable bore, the most contemptible prig who had ever whined a psalmody. His dark eyes absorbed her scrutiny with all that it contained, and he broke out suddenly:

'Why do you despise us, Mrs Baynham - my sister and me? We haven't your breeding, your poise, we're not in your social grade. But for all that, ma'am, we are human. At least I guess so. We're ordinary human beings trying to be honest and good.'

She lit a cigarette without interest. But he rose, strode over to the settee, and impressively seated himself beside her.

'Mrs Baynham,' he said earnestly, his voice full, soft, and ceremonial. 'I've wanted the chance to talk to you. And say' - his eyes blazed suddenly and his voice quickened - 'I am real honest about this. You think my sister and myself are fakirs - what you would call plain humbugs. It isn't true. There's been mud thrown at us evangelists. Books have been written - guying us - our accent, our clothes, everything. It's shameful! And before God it isn't true. There's been cases, I grant you - bad cases - men and women with commercial minds who prostituted the gospel for money. But for every one of these shams there's a hundred others with a positive and burning belief. You'd think, to read those books, there wasn't an ounce of good intention or endeavour in religion. That every minister doubted what he preached. That's a downright lie. I believe with every fibre of my being. Mrs Baynham, ma'am, granted you're not in sympathy with that belief, at least have the goodness to admit that we are sincere.'

She threw him a patronising glance.

'What a long speech. What does it mean? And what does it matter?'

'It matters more than you think, ma'am. And you know what it means. Believe me, it grieves me to see a woman of your talents

46

and capacity and beauty so blind to the meaning of life. You are not happy. You have tried everything and enjoyed nothing.'

Her eyebrows lifted.

'So I've enjoyed nothing?'

'No!' he cried. 'Nothing! And you'll never be happy until you find God. There lies the only joy in life.'

She inhaled a long puff of smoke and studied the cigarette's fat glowing end. He was sincere; she admitted it with a kind of lustreless surprise; and a vague whim rose and sank within her - his profile rather good, she speculated, his figure big, quite solid, but there were tiny hairs sprouting in his nostrils and he was a bore, oh, yes, such a frightful crashing bore. She found herself saying:

'And you've got all the happiness you want?'

'Cannot you see,' he answered glowingly, 'I am happy? Salvation spells happiness, here and hereafter. That's a cinch - a certainty. If only you could see it! Oh, I wish I could convince you, ma'am.'

Wrapped unapproachably in her indolence she said:

'You mean then - you want actually to - to save me?'

She had a vague derisory impulse to employ another predicate - but she refrained.

'My mission is to lead people to salvation,' he cried, and a strange sincerity rang through the florid words. He bent towards her, his eye humid, fervent: 'Won't you try, Mrs Baynham? Won't you try to come to God? You are too fine really to be lost. Come! Come! Oh, let me help you to come!'

She sat motionless, holding in her body a secret, contemptuous hilarity which suddenly swelled unconquerably. She burst into an uncontrollable fit of laughter through which, like the trumpet note of judgement, there came a bugle's clarion call. It was the signal for luncheon.

At last she turned to him.

'I've just thought,' she declared brokenly. 'You haven't - you haven't taken your liver extract.'

## CHAPTER VIII

JUST after seven bells on that same day Harvey Leith came out of his cabin for the first time since the ship had reached blue water. In the alley-way he paused, dazzled by a sunlight which his unaccustomed eyes could not sustain, flooded by a strange pariah sense of isolation. In that merciless light his face betrayed what he had suffered. The ridges of his cheeks were gaunt, but though weakness still assailed him he was better - incomparably better. Trout had shaved him, assisted him to dress in the non-descript grey suit, and now observed him from the cabin door-way with a bland creative pride. The little steward had been assiduous, and Corcoran, too, had come often to the cabin to plague him with companionable philosophy during those last three days.

He was not ungrateful, yet for all their succour he felt a stranger upon the ship. And so desired it. Supporting himself against the rail he slowly ascended the companion-way to the bridge deck. Upon the port side, wrapped in a rug, sat Mother Hemmingway, her fat, ringed hands like blobs of butter upon her lap, her figure spineless as a bag of dough. Since at this moment she neither smoked nor ate she was doing nothing - she merely sat. But when she saw Leith her beady eyes glistened with their bright, malicious stare.

'Well, well,' she cried. 'If it ain't the strynger. Sancta Maria, but you don't 'alf look scuppered. My 'at and parsley, you gives me quite a turn.'

Harvey gazed downwards at her bulging cheeks so blotched they seemed to ooze blood.

'Ought I to apologise?' he asked stiffly.

'Ah!' she exclaimed in a friendly tone. 'I don't think none the worse on you 'cos you was lushed. Carajo, no, sir. And it's 'ell when you're knocked off it pronto. Wot you need is a drop of nigger's blood - stout and port that is. 'Streuth but it's lively.' She winked. 'Say the word and I'll do you a turn.'

'No thanks,' said Harvey flatly. And he turned to go.

' 'Ere, don't go awye,' she cried volubly. 'Sit down and be matey. My tongue's 'angin' out for a parley-vous. With that bleedin' old snob at the tyble ye can't get a word in edgewyes. 'E's too stuck up for Gawd Almighty. "Do you 'unt?" says 'e to me to-dye, meanin' to tyke me down a peg. " 'Unt," says I - "I don't know an 'orse from an 'am-bone but if you try to make gyme of me I'll 'unt the bleedin' 'ide off your back." ' Indignantly she tossed her earrings; but immediately she smiled. 'Now you're different. You've been up against it, cocky, like I 'ave. I likes you for it. Strike me blind if you 'aven't got my bleedin' sympathy.' She closed one eye cunningly. 'You'll ave to come and see me at my plyce in Santa. We'll 'ave a snack and an 'and at German w'ist. 'Undred and Sixteen Calle de la Tuna. Make a note on it.'

'Your kindness is overwhelming. But I hardly think I'll be able to come.'

'You never knows your luck, cocky.' She peered up at him. 'And while we're talkin'. Wot's your friend Corcoran's gyme? 'E's on 'is uppers for all 'is blarney. And I've rooked 'im of his petty cash at rummy. Wye is *e* comin' out to Santa? I don't rumble 'im no'ow.'

Harvey shook his head.

'I haven't the least idea,' he said coldly; then before she could reply he turned and passed quickly out of earshot.

He went round to the starboard side, seeking seclusion. But though some chairs stood about untenanted, two were occupied. He did not care. Suddenly he felt weak and sat down.

The sun was warm, a healing warmth which lay like balm upon his half-closed eyelids and sank into his weary body like a caress. The corners of his mouth, drawn downwards into bitterness, faintly relaxed. The wound in his soul remained raw and bleeding; but for a moment he forgot its pain. The air was light. The water glinted in great soft curves. The ship sailed southwards. Incredibly, about its steepled rigging two swallows circled, cherishing this chance oasis upon their passage, holding to safety till they should sight the land.

All at once Harvey opened his eyes, conscious that someone was gazing at him. Immediately Susan Tranter looked away, an unexpected flush rising, then fading on her cheek.

She was seated in the neighbouring chair, darning a grey woollen sock, a work-bag by her side, a note-book and a pencil upon her knee. So quickly did she turn that the note-book dropped upon the deck and lay open beside her strong, square shoe.

He picked up the book, aware with the instant comprehension

which was his faculty that it was her diary: keeping a conscientious diary, mending her brother's underwear - that, he thought grimly, is her type. But as he held the note-book in his hand a page fluttered and quite by accident his name, a phrase upon the finely written sheet beyond that name, leaped to his astonished eye:

'I do not believe the story to be true. He has a noble face.'

That was all; the book was now closed, back upon her lap; his expression had not changed. But she was still vaguely discomposed, feeling that she must speak, not knowing what to say. At last she ventured:

'I hope - I hope you feel better.'

He turned away. Nauseated by his discovery, by the gawky sentiment implied, he hated her solicitude; yet there was in her attitude a diffidence which compelled him to reply:

'Yes, I'm better.'

'That's great,' she went on quickly. 'When we make Las Palmas on Saturday you'll feel that fine you'll want to go ashore and climb the Peak.'

He stared morbidly in front of him.

'I shall probably go ashore and get drunk. Not heroically drunk you understand. Just undramatically fuddled. Stupid oblivion.'

Something in her eyes winced; she made to protest; but she controlled herself.

'We wanted to help you, my brother and I, when you - when you were sick. He wanted to come to your cabin. But I kind of guessed you'd like to be left quiet.'

'You were right.'

His agreement seemed conclusive, constituting a final silence. Yet in a moment she bridged that silence.

'That remark of mine sounds so officious,' she said diffidently. 'I just must explain I've had nursing experience. Three years in the John Stirling clinic. And fever training also. I've nursed most things - from malaria to teething fits. It'll help Robert's missionary work, you see.' She paused to snip competently a tag of wool, and ended: 'But I guess it's healthy enough in Laguna.'

But he wasn't listening. As she spoke, his eye, roving nervously, had fallen to studying the girl in the chair which faced him four yards away. She was sleeping, her small bosom rising and gently falling, her hands relaxed, her lashes casting blue shadows upon her pale, sun-warmed skin. Each lash was long and curled to a point with a separate, lustrous individuality. Her coat, of smooth brown pelt, lay open at the neck, exposing a row of pearls, each pinkish, translucent, soft, and larger than a pea. She slept warmly like a child, her body acquiescent yet filled with a flowing beauty. Loveliness lay upon her like a bloom. And in her sleep her mouth seemed smiling.

Finding him frankly inattentive, Susan had fallen silent: but from time to time she followed his stare with little darting glances cast off across her flying needle, glances which focused alertly upon a tiny ring of yellow silk that glinted unguarded above the sleeping girl's knee. Finally she seemed compelled to speak.

'She is very young - Lady Fielding,' she said carefully, in a tone charged with determined generosity. 'And real beautiful.'

'Her two virtues, doubtless,' he answered frigidly. And the instant he had spoken he regretted it; he had the strange sense of striking something lovely and defenceless.

Susan did not encourage his irony; nor did she rebuke it.

'Those pearls,' she continued in the same colourless voice. 'Each of them would help keep a starving family for a year. Don't you think it a terrible pity, Dr Leith? Poor folks starving to death in the slums - and these gew-gaws! Honest, they're so useless.'

'I have no interest in starving slum families,' he said with sardonic bitterness. 'Except in so far as they do starve to death. That would improve the race. It needs it. You know of course that I am practising the killing-off principle. Three blameless fellow creatures wiped out before I came on board. A good start!'

Her eyes were troubled. Drawn to him by pity she felt now instinctively the hurt within his mind. And his face - it made her catch her breath, so like that painting she had once seen, the profile of the wounded Saviour. She must speak.

'Her husband, Sir Michael Fielding,' she went on at random. 'He's awfully rich. Plantations on the islands. That's only a side-line, I reckon, to him. But we heard tell of it through our enquiries. Real fine reputation, he's got. And of course his name - historic! Guess he's a bit older than she. A Mainwaring, Lady Fielding was, before her marriage - folks always been connected with the sea. Leastways so I'm told. Kind of queer she came away without her husband. I wonder why?'

'You might ask her,' he said rudely. 'I don't like scandal even when it is text-flavoured.'

She stared at him, her eyes confused, her look altered suddenly to dismay.

'I'm sorry,' she said in a low voice. 'Yes, I shouldn't have said that. Reckon I'm sorry.'

Then eight bells slowly chimed and at once the bugle sounded lightly for tea - Trout had the faculty of varying his note to suit the dignity of the meal. And at that moment Mary Fielding awoke. Susan, her workbag packed and in her hand, had risen to her feet. Her face was now composed and she addressed Leith quietly:

'If you're coming down now I'll be glad to pour you some tea. It's strong, the ship tea. Gets black if you let it stand.'

With head turned sideways against his chair and all his morbid agony returned, he pretended not to hear. He wished no tea, black tea, curdled with that milk of human kindness which welled from her warm eyes. His face was still averted as after a moment's pause she moved silently away.

And now he waited, with curious unrest, the departure of the other; waiting chafingly till she too should go to pour that black and bitter tea.

But she did not go. Instead, Trout appeared upon the deck bearing a tray set pleasantly with the ship's pink rose-sprigged china. New scones were on the tray and thin-sliced lemon and a silver box graved with a deep-cut crest.

Then she spoke, as though addressing the ambient air.

'I always have tea on deck when it's like this. The sun . . . it makes everything taste so good. Now will you or won't you have tea up here? Say no if you like.' Her voice was light and charming - it made him feel surly, ill-looking and coarse. Urgently he desired to rise and walk away, to make a violent gesture of negation with his arm, but, before he could do either, the cursed Trout was back, placing another cup upon the tray almost with reverence, and tiptoeing away as though he had received a sacrament.

'I like Sea-Trout,' she announced mildly a moment later. 'He's married to the stewardess. They have six children, all on shore. Think what fun if they could all come together on a cruise. I must ask Michael to let me do it some day.'

He had a disturbing vision of the *Aureola* sailing strange seas, manned by the steward's six children; then he became aware that whilst she spoke she was holding out to him a cup of tea. He took it mechanically, observing gloomily that in his fingers was still a tremor which made the thin spoon chatter upon the saucer.

She read his thoughts.

'My hand shakes most frightfully too, at times,' she said. 'When I pour out at Buckden. We have the most stately tea-parties sometimes. Michael adores them. I go all sick inside.'

He was silent. She baffled him. He looked at her thin fingers: blue-threaded beneath the smooth white skin; at the loose, gold circlet, somehow grotesque, a wedding ring upon a child's small hand and he saw that slender-wristed hand holding a massive Georgian teapot, trembling faintly from its weight.

'You don't know,' she went on, 'how lovely it is to get away from things. You feel yourself getting more and more crushed up, like your nose was pressed against a window-pane. Then you think, "I must, oh, I must get away - away from everyone." Have you never wanted that?'

Instinctively he fell back upon his satire.

'Yes,' he said. 'But often without success.'

She smiled at him guilelessly with her eyes.

'You're quite right. I say things stupidly. Can't express what I mean. I'm not too competent. But this sun' - she sighed - 'all lovely in my eyes. Have some more tea. It's Twining's. Can you taste orange in it?'

'No,' he said shortly, 'I can't. I'm not used to expensive tea. And I've been drunk for the last three weeks. At the moment my palate is rather blunted.'

She took no notice of his rudeness, but lay back holding her face to the radiance mingling upon the sea and sky.

'Don't you ever feel happy,' she asked dreamily, 'without knowing why? Just without any reason?'

'There is no reason,' he answered morosely. 'Happiness is an unreasonable state. Examine it and it disappears.'

'You don't want to examine it,' she murmured; looking at him directly, she went on with perfect simplicity, 'I'm happy now at this moment. I must tell you. I know; yet I can't actually explain why.' She spoke more slowly and very seriously like one groping beneath the surface for words. 'It's so puzzling. The moment I saw you I had the feeling that I knew you, that I had met you, that you would understand. Like a memory - deep down, a long way off. Don't you know the feeling? You might get it on a calm very quiet and sunny evening - something coming back to you. You want to sit perfectly still, not moving a finger, listening.

But it's all very odd, mixed. I can't explain. But it's there, oh, it's there.'

Her charm and her beauty were extreme, making him instantly antagonistic - suspicious of her sincerity. Deliberately he set himself against her. He gave a short laugh. He could not comprehend the sudden rushing desire which rose in him to hurt her. All his life he had evaded beauty: obsessed by work as an anchorite by prayer, he had thrown but a passing glance upon a sunset, a budding tree, a woman's face: he had set himself apart. And now the sight of her young body, her hair enriched by the level sunlight, her lovely vivid face, animated him with a poignant, unaccountable distress which welled up bitterly within his breast.

'I'm sorry,' he said in a cutting tone. 'I haven't the remotest idea what you're talking about. I am concerned with the facts of life. I am a biologist. I have no time for vague emotions and silly fancies. And I am certain that we have never met.'

A look of strange disappointment flowed into her face.

'Surely,' she said suddenly and paused. Then, as though she mustered all her courage she exclaimed quite breathlessly: 'You don't know - you wouldn't know what I meant by the - the House of the Swans? And the garden with the freesia flowers? And the fountain with the old cracked rim where those funny little lizards lie and sleep? Oh, I'm not asking you for any silly reason. I'm just asking you because - because I must.'

For a moment he could not believe that she was serious; but her gaze - so grave and so intent - held him strangely. He shook his head.

'I don't know what you mean.'

'I thought,' she murmured, 'I thought you might know.' And as though to give him yet another chance she persisted with eyes that now looked far away: 'The gates have swans worked upon them as well. You go up the drive, past the little yellow lodge. And there's an old, stiff tree with smooth, round branches standing in the corner of the courtyard. Surely you know it?' An almost painful eagerness crept into her voice. 'Surely you've been there too.'

'No.'

There was a long silence; her breast rose and fell.

'I thought,' she said again inarticulately, 'I just thought you might know.'

He was startled to see that there were tears standing in her eyes, and, despite himself, he asked:

'Where is this place - the House of the Swans?'

She looked out upon the moving sea.

'It's a place I go to sometimes,' she said very slowly. 'And sometimes I've felt that - that somebody goes with me. But it's quite plain I've been mistaken. I've made a fool of myself for nothing. You don't understand.'

Again he was inexplicably moved; deeply within his soul there was a stirring as from a movement of uncertain wings. He leant a little forward; but before he could speak, a stamp of feet came from beneath. Tea was over, the saloon had disgorged itself and now the others were mounting the companion-way. Tranter's voice boomed out:

'There's room for us here, folks.' And immediately they all came on the upper deck.

At the sight of Harvey there was a general pause. Dibdin fiddled for his monocle. Elissa stared with her careless curiosity. And Tranter's eyes kindled. He rubbed his hands and beamed.

'Well, well,' he gushed. 'Glad to see you up, friend. Most glad indeed. Wanted to drop in on you before but Sue here, she wouldn't stand for it. Say, I surely am happy to see you up and sat there so nice and comfortable.'

' 'E wouldn't sit by me,' said Mother Hemmingway with a malicious titter. 'But 'e's sat by 'er lydyship all right. That's wot it is to 'ave blue blood in yer veins.'

Robert's laugh boomed out again. He advanced and laid a large fraternal arm on Harvey's shoulder.

'You'll count on me from now on, friend. I guess I'm not so anglified and tony as her ladyship here but I'll sit with you any time you please. Yes, sir. I guess I'd like you to know right now - if there's anything I can do, anything at all, you may reckon it as done.' His eyes swivelled for a moment towards Elissa. 'Believe me, if we can't help one another in Christian charity . . .'

Harvey stiffened in his chair. He who had lost everything, to be fronted by this odious windbag. It was intolerable. With nervous violence he rose, conscious suddenly that he was ringed by stares. Only Mary, with her eyes still reaching out upon the sea, seemed not to be looking at him.

'You flatter me,' he said to Tranter in an ominous voice. 'Really I'm not worthy of your interest.'

'Not at all, friend, not at all. Why, I reckon . . .'

'Shut up,' Harvey hissed. 'Don't bray at me.'

Tranter's face, flushed by hot tea and manly sympathy, fell ludicrously.

'Why,' he stammered, 'why - I guess I was only offering my sympathy as a minister of God.'

'God!' said Harvey in a low, embittered tone. 'He must be a queer god to let you rant about him.' And lowering his head, he brushed past and made for the companion.

Exactly at that moment Renton came out of the chart-room. He gave no attention to the situation before him. On his face was an expression preoccupied, almost perplexed. In his hand he held a marconigram.

Elissa it was . . . inevitably . . . who sighted the prospect of news; and in her languid style she exclaimed:

'You don't say, captain, that it's something to relieve the boredom?'

Renton raised his eyes from the flimsy white slip and faced the group.

'It's nothing,' he answered, infusing the words with a certain lightness. 'Sorry to disappoint you. Nothing at all.'

Harvey waited to hear no more. His feet already were upon the ladder. Descending with feelings curiously lost and unsubstantial, he plunged again into the solitude of his cabin.


CHAPTER IX


ON Saturday they made Las Palmas - a windless morning land-fall. Gliding along the sunrise into a sleeping harbour, sliding past silent ships with masthead lamps still palely winking, the *Aureola* laid her brine-encrusted hull against the mole.

Three hours later, to the rattle of the fore-hatch winches, Harvey awoke. For the first time in many nights he had slept well, and with limbs relaxed he lay quite still watching the glowing shaft of sunlight irradiate the whiteness of his cabin wall. A strange lightness was in his body, and in his mind a singular incredulity that he should feel so far refreshed. Strange, too, was the solidity of his high berth which lacked that floating unreality of the last few days. And as a distant chime of land bells fell upon his ear, with sudden comprehension he knew the ship to be in port. Stirred by a queer excitement he got up, slipped on his bath-robe, and went on deck.

There the full freshness of the morning fell on him like dew. The sky was blue; the air actinic, rare; the sun, dazzling downwards from the mountains, spangled the sea with glittering scales. Before him lay the bay, edged by a frill of foam, and beyond, the town, climbing in multi-coloured tiers towards the yellow hills. It held warmth and profusion: reds and greens and glaring white all sprawled about in vivid, tropic beauty. And over all, transcending bay and town, triumphant over the nearer jagged summits, rose a distant peak, elusive somehow, and mysterious as a mirage, thrusting its snow-capped cone above a milky ring of clouds, seeming to swing suspended between earth and heaven.

Filled with a strange wonder, Harvey stood staring at the Peak, quite motionless. Lovely as some celestial strain the vision held him, struck him with a sharp and subtle pang. Was it the meaning of the vision or its beauty which so hurt him? Spellbound, he caught his breath; he could not bear to look nor yet to look away.

With a wrench he tore his eyes away, walked to the ship's side and surveyed the yellow, dusty mole which swarmed now with a sort of languid life. On its sun-baked stones some twenty peons in bare feet and calico trousers were unloading sacks of flour with picturesque indifference. They were in no hurry. They talked, smoked, spat, stood about and laid casual hands upon the sacks as though the last thing desired of them was despatch. One of them with a washed-out ochre shirt kept singing in a high-pitched voice a swaying little tune which rose with irritating sweetness. He listened in spite of himself.

*El amor es dulce*
*Y el que lo desprecia un loco.*

Though he knew little Spanish the meaning of the words was clear: Love is sweet and he who scorns it is a fool.

Impatiently, as though he sought an antidote to sweetness, he let his gaze slip down the quay to where some ill-conditioned mules with raw, galled rumps and sad, skeleton ribs hung forward on their shafts, attached to high-wheeled wagons. One coughed suddenly like a human, agitating its coronet of circling flies, collapsing almost from sheer debility. But the driver, crouched upon the box paid no attention: with hands flapped across the reins, a flower stuck behind his ear, he snored contentedly.

Abruptly Harvey turned away - he could not endure to look at these wretched brutes. One instant - the beauty of the island shore, the sublimity of that mysterious Peak; the next - this sluggish spectacle of morbid life. Restless, queerly agitated, he began to pace up and down with quick nervous steps. He looked at his wrist-watch - quite late, already nine o'clock - demanding of himself impatiently what he should do. He was in port, free of all fatuous restraint, free, too, of that enforced society which had so infuriated him; and with sudden surging recognition came the knowledge that he could land from this hated ship and lose himself again in that oblivion he could invoke at will. He could forget now those torturing visions of the past, those shapes, mingling the living and the dead, which like some feverish nightmare had beset him. His lips drew together; his jaw set. Of course he would go, he had determined it from the first; life held nothing that could alter his decision; yes, he would go deliberately, nothing would prevent him.

And yet he did not go. He went on walking up and down, feeling the sun warm upon his shoulders, feeling almost furtively the presence of that sublime Peak behind him. He had to stop again and turn to look at it. As he stood thus he heard Renton at his elbow:

'A noble sight, Dr Leith. It is the Pico de Teyde, on Tenerife. And if you will believe me it is a full seventy-three miles to the westward. It dominates these islands. You will see it more plainly at Santa Cruz.' Side by side they gazed at the mountain; then Harvey said slowly:

'Yes, it is a noble sight.' Then, quickly satirising his own feeling: 'A vision of paradise!'

'A paradise that has its drawbacks occasionally,' Renton said crisply. He paused, looked up at the other.

'There's a nasty little business on the hills back of Santa Cruz. I had the news by wireless yesterday. They have yellow fever there!'

There was a sudden silence.

'Yellow fever,' repeated Harvey.

'Yes! The outbreak is in Hermosa - a village just outside Laguna. Fortunately it is confined.'

Again there was silence.

'You'll keep that information to yourself,' said Renton at length. 'You are a doctor. That's why I mention it. But I see no reason to set the others worrying unnecessarily.'

'You haven't told them?'

'No, sir. I have not. I believe in holding my tongue until there is some cause to speak. I have told you the outbreak is confined.'

'Yellow fever is difficult to confine,' said Harvey slowly. 'It is mosquito borne. And it is a dreadful scourge.'

The captain bristled; above everything he hated contradiction.

'I hope you are not trying to teach me my job,' he said brusquely. 'Do you want me to coop my passengers under hatches? Why should I start them panicking? I have told you that I will wait and see. I have all the information from Mr Carr, our agent. And he agrees with my decision.'

'Information sometimes travels slowly. Epidemics travel fast.'

'There is no epidemic,' declared Renton crossly. 'I'm sorry I spoke of this to you. You are making a mountain of a molehill. They never have epidemics here.'

He stood like a bantam cock, defying further opposition. But Harvey simply answered in an even tone:

'That's good.'

Renton looked at him testily, but it was impossible to penetrate the mask of that impassive face. Quite ruffled he stood silent for a while, then, with his expression still annoyed, he nodded abruptly and went into the chart-room.

Harvey remained standing at the rail.

Yellow fever! Was there something sinister now in the brightness of the bay, something hard about its colour? It was nothing, absolutely nothing. A sick man sixty miles away, perhaps. An exaggerated intuition for calamity! At any rate, he did not care. Nothing mattered to him now.

He turned, making for his cabin, then all at once he paused. On the lower deck, aft of the gangway, he saw Mary and Mrs Baynham talking to a man who had apparently that moment come on board. The man was youngish, handsome in a florid style, with a red and rather beefy face, a small dry, up-twisted moustache, a thick neck and a muscular figure carefully controlled; he wore a tussore suit, immaculate, well cut, matching the light suede shoes upon his feet and the spotless Panama held in his well-shaped hand. He was laughing, his feet apart, his head thrown back so that a fold of skin bulged slightly over his collar in a fashion which to Harvey seemed odious and gross.

Instinctively he detested the man, noting, with a curling lip, the sheen on his sleek hair, the vaguely pompous inclination of his head, the killing glances of his eye, the arrogant complacency which intermingled with the deference of his address.

A grim speculation flashed into Harvey's mind. Is he her lover, he thought viciously; and this meeting the beatific purpose of the voyage?

But whose lover? He was staring now with furrowed brow at Mary. Was there an acquiescence in her face, in that quick impulsive movement of her hands? Her white silk dress clung to her, infused with the warmth of her flesh.

Then, as he remained gazing fixedly at the group below, again a voice addressed him. He started and looked round. Behind him stood Susan Tranter and her brother both dressed to go ashore. She repeated her question, calmly, her eyes quite un-smiling upon his.

'We wondered if you were fixed up for today?'

'Fixed up?' Detached violently from his mood, he echoed the words almost stupidly, aware of her neat and compact figure, the serious directness of her gaze. Her hands were gloved; her small, straw hat cast a softening shadow upon her square brow.

'Have you made any plans - that's what I meant - plans to spend the day?'

'No!'

Her eyes fell - then immediately lifted.

'Robert and myself have an invitation,' she said steadily. 'We have American friends at Arucas. They are kindly folks. They have a pleasant villa, well, you'd say it was real pleasant by its name. It is called Bella Vista. Will you come?'

He shook his head slowly.

'No! I won't come.'

Her eyes could not leave his face.

'It would be a good thing if you came,' she persisted in a low voice. 'The scenery is lovely there. They are Christian people and very kind. You would be made real welcome. You'd be at home there. Isn't that a fact, Robert?'

Tranter, standing with averted head and gaze fixed upon the lower deck, made an unusually gawky gesture of agreement.

'Why should I come?' said Harvey stiffly. 'I'm not a Christian I'm not kind. I should hate your dear American friends and they naturally would hate me. The very name Bella Vista fills me with loathing. And lastly, as I told you before, I'm probably going ashore to get drunk.'

Her eyes fell away from him.

'I beg of you,' she said in an almost inaudible voice, 'I beg of you. I've prayed -' She broke off and for a moment stood staring at the deck. At last she raised her head.

'We'll go then, Robbie,' she declared in an even voice. 'It's a long drive. We can find a carriage on the quay.'

They descended to the lower deck. Deliberately she took the opposite side from that on which Elissa stood.

'Say, Susan,' ventured Tranter as they went along, 'don't you think we might postpone our visit till the afternoon?'

'No, I don't think so at all,' she answered, staring straight ahead. 'We've been asked for lunch.'

'I know. Sure, I know,' he said awkwardly. 'But we don't have to spend the whole day there. I guess the afternoon would have done pretty well enough.'

She stopped and faced him, her recent agitation welling to the surface in another cause.

'This is the third time this morning you've suggested we stop back from Bella Vista. You know it's important we go there, Robbie.' She asked with trembling lips: 'What's wrong with you, and what else is there to do?'

'Now, now, Sue,' he protested quickly, 'You're not to get upset. But, well - what's the harm if I did think we might have taken the morning to go over to Las Canteras with Mrs Baynham? She asked me to accompany her party to the beach. She said we might all take a swim. It's darned hot. And you know how fond you are of the water. Why, back home you were the bestest swimmer ever.'

She gave a little involuntary gasp.

'So that's it,' she cried. 'I might have guessed. And the way you put it over - trying to get me to the beach. You know you always hated to go swimming. You know you never could swim. She asked *us* indeed! Don't you see she's only mocking at you? Oh, Robbie, Robbie dear. What's come of you these last few days? You won't let that woman out of your sight. I tell you she's guying you all the time. Yet you keep running after her like you were crazy.'

Instantly he turned red.

'You've got it all wrong,' he blurted out. 'There's nothing - absolutely nothing I'm ashamed of.'

61

'She's a bad lot.' These words came quivering from her lips.
'Susan!'

There was a silence during which she fought for self-control; then, speaking with determination, she said rapidly:

'I won't stand by and see you made a mock of. I love you too much for that. We'll go to Arucas. We'll go now. And we'll stay there all day.'

He met her resolution with an elevation of his dignity. Knowing himself to be in the right, bitterly disappointed at her refusal to go to Las Canteras, he answered nevertheless, in a calm and lofty tone:

'Very well, then. Let's go. But I tell you plain I'm goin' to speak with Mrs Baynham when we return.' Turning, he walked off the gangplank with his head in the air.

Suppressing a sigh, her face troubled and unhappy, Susan slowly followed him.

Harvey did not see them go. He was in his cabin, eating moodily the fruit which Trout had brought up for breakfast. Telde oranges, thin-skinned and delicious, and custard apples fresh that morning from the market - a luscious meal. But he thought with introspective bitterness of his recent scene with Susan. He had not meant to take that tone; her intention at least was good; her quality - a downright honesty. Angry with himself, he stood up and began to dress. He had been hurt by life; and so, like a snarling dog, he wished to hurt back in retaliation, to strike at life with indeterminate, unreasonable savagery. Moreover, he must wound first lest he himself be wounded once again. It was the reflex of a stricken soul, but he saw it only as a symptom of his own malignity.

He sighed and turned from the mirror. His face, no longer pallid, was hardened by a stain of brown; his hand, with which he had just shaved, no longer trembled; his eye was clear again. His body was recovering quickly, but in his heart there ranged a scathing self-contempt. He despised himself.

A knock sounded on the cabin door, and, lifting his head, Harvey paused. He had imagined himself alone, of all the passengers, upon the ship - left to that solitude he had so insistently demanded.

'Come in,' he cried.

The door flew boisterously open. Jimmy Corcoran entered, his chest inflated, filled by the glory of the morning. A new check cap lay backwards on his head, and round his neck a tie of blazing emerald. Harvey stared at him, then slowly demanded:

'Since when have you taken to knocking?'

'I thought you might be in your dishabille,' said Jimmy, grinning largely.

'And would that have upset you?'

'Troth and 'twouldn't. Not by the weight of one shavin'. But it might have upset you. Yer such a cranky divil.'

Harvey turned and began to brush his hair with firm strokes.

'Why don't you hate the sight of me?' he asked in an odd voice. 'I seem hardly to have been, well, polite to you since we came on this charming trip.'

'Polite be damned,' answered Jimmy with gusto. 'Sure, I don't fancy things too polite. Kid gloves wasn't never in my line. I like a fella to call me a fool to me face and clout me matey on the back like that.' And hitting Harvey a terrific slap upon the shoulders by way of illustration he elbowed himself forward to the mirror where he ogled himself, straightened his atrocious tie, smoothed his plastered lock and blew a kiss to his image in the glass. Then he began to sing:

> *'Archie, Archie, he's in town again,*
> *The idol of the ladies and the invy of the men.'*

'You seem fond of yourself this morning.'

'Sure I'm fond of meself. And why not in a manner of speakin'. I'm the only man that ever hit Smiler Burge right over the ropes. And I'd do it again next St Patrick's Day for love. Don't ye know I'm the finest man that ever came out of Clontarf? Me ould mother told me so. The heart of a lion and the beauty of a faun as Playto says. And this mornin' I'm feeling that good I wouldn't call the Pope me brother.' He went off again:

> *'He's a lady killer*
> *Sweeter than vaniller;*
> *When they meet him*
> *Sure, they want to eat him.'*

Then, heaving round, he said:

'We're all set for the beach. You and me's goin' ashore this mornin'.' Harvey contemplated him.

'So we're going, Jimmy, are we?'

'Sure an' we're goin'.' He emphasised the certainty by smacking his fist into his palm. 'We're goin' to the Canteras Bay. I've just been talkin' to the captain. It's the gilt on the gingerbread

63

all right. There's bathin' there and a little resstrong where ye can grub. I'm telling ye there's a strand of yellow sand would drive ye crazy with delight.'

The spectacle of himself being driven crazy with delight by a beach of yellow sand drew a shadowy smile to Harvey's face. But strangely he said:

'All right! We'll go then, Jimmy.'

Corcoran grinned all over his battered face.

'Be the holy - if ye'd said no, I'd have slaughtered ye. I've got important business to tend to in the afternoon. Private and personal ye'll understand. But all this mornin' ye belong to me.'

They went out of the cabin into the liquid sunlight, crossed the gangplank, and walked down the dusty mole. Strutting along with thumbs in both arm-holes and a toothpick between his lips, Corcoran assumed proprietary rights over the harbour, deplored the indolence of the natives, philosophised upon the women, purchased a bunch of violets for his buttonhole from a crumpled old woman, donated a pinch of snuff to a fly-infested beggar, and finally drew up before a disreputable one-horse tartana.

'Aha!' he exclaimed. 'Here's the ticket for soup, fella. The horse can stand up and the carriage has wheels.' He turned to the driver. 'How much drive Las Canteras, bucko?'

The driver made with his shoulders a gesture indicative of extreme unworthiness and extended four yellow finger-nails.

'Four English shilling, señor.'

'Four English tomatoes! It's too much. I'll give ye two peseta and a pinch of snuff.'

'No, no, señor. Much beautiful tartana. Plenty quick.'

'Ah! Plenty quick me foot.'

The driver burst into a flow of Spanish, making little piteous grimaces of entreaty.

'What does he say?' asked Corcoran, scratching his head. 'I'm slow at the lingo.'

Harvey answered calmly:

'He says that he knows you well. That you are the most arrant humbug that ever breathed. That you have never knocked Smiler Burge over the ropes. That Smiler Burge nearly killed you with one swift blow. He says that you are ugly, old, and that you do not speak the truth. He says further that his wife is dying, that his ten children are dying, that he himself will die of

64

a broken heart if you do not pay him four shillings for the hire of his lovely tartana.'

Jimmy thrust back his cap until it lay upon his collar.

'We'll give him a couple of shillin', then,' he said doubtfully. 'Two English shillin', kiddo.'

The driver's face split in a dazzling smile. With the air of a grandee he flung open the rickety door, leaped upon the box, and flourished his conquest to the world. Two English shillings! It was exactly five times his legitimate fare.

'That's the way to handle them boys,' said Jimmy out of the corner of his mouth. ' 'Tis the business instinct. If ye don't watch out they'll swindle ye hollow.' And he lay back expansively in his seat as they bumped down the rutted street.

## CHAPTER X

MARY FIELDING had come to the Playa de las Canteras. She, too, had heard from Renton of the beauty of this little-known shore, and now, in her wet green bathing-suit, she lay flat upon the sun-bleached sand, letting its soft warmth creep into her. Little drops of sea-water still glistened upon her white legs. Her body, moulded firmly by the waves, held a vibrating life. The curve of her small breast was lovely as a flower, graceful as a swallow's flight. Her eyes were closed, as though to shutter the exquisite abandon of her mood; yet she could see it all, the lovely, lovely scene. The gracious sweep of yellow sand; the water bluer than the sky; the foaming whiteness of the breakers cresting in thunder across the reef; the distant peak - shining, translucent, omnipotent as a god. Oh, she was glad that she had come.

Here she could breathe and, pressed naked to the earth, be herself at last. Within her something rose, whiter than the crested foam, more shining than the mountain peak - a memory, an aspiration, or a mingling of them both. Never before had the conviction swelled so intensely within her that all the life that she must lead was but a subterfuge, the paltry shadow of reality. And never before had she so intensely hated and despised it: the plumaged performance of society, the ritual of Buckden -

yes, even Buckden, rising in mellowed bricks, seemed now oppressive with the crushing dignity of years.

Now, close to the earth's simplicity, it all seemed remote and vague: formless as the loose sand that streamed through her fingers.

Raising herself, she looked over at Elissa and Dibdin, who sat back to back under the shadow of a big umbrella. Elissa had not undressed: her skin did not like the sea. But Dibs, with a sort of senile friskiness, had bared his scaly hide and, like a mummy masquerading in blue serge shorts, exposed his desiccated carcass to the breeze.

Supported by her elbow, Mary listened to their talk. She listened deliberately, filled by a sense of its futility.

'Elissa,' Dibs was saying, 'you're not really bored at coming here?'

For two full minutes Elissa Baynham went on interestedly powdering her nose: the fourth time within the hour she had consummated her passion for perfection.

'You know I'm always bored,' she answered, when all hope of any answer had been lost. 'There are no men here.'

'No men,' giggled Dibs. 'What about me?'

'You,' said Elissa; and that was all.

There was a short silence, then she demanded:

'Light me a cigarette. And don't wet it or I shall have hysterics.' She paused. 'I've suddenly thought of a new name for you - now that I've seen you in the altogether. In future I shall call you Sex-Appeal.'

He found an onyx case in her gold mesh bag, extracted a cigarette with his veinous fingers, and lit it.

Trailing a hand over her shoulder, she said:

'Give it me so I don't have to turn round. The sight of your skin is agony.'

'My skin,' he exclaimed, touched on the raw at last. 'It's a perfectly good skin. Hundreds of women have loved that skin.'

'That was before you took to wearing corsets, darling.'

Dibs quivered with rage, and retaliated on a different flank.

'You're damned silly, Elissa. I don't know what's come of you. Letting that Tranter fellow run after you.'

'Yes, isn't it harassing? He's trying to bring me to salvation.'

'But - but the damned fellow's head over ears in love with you.'

'He doesn't know it.' She took a long puff at her cigarette. 'He's such a bore or I might like him perhaps once. Just once -

for fun you know, Dibs - sorry, I mean Sex-Appeal.'

He stiffened his bony back.

'That's too much, Elissa. I'm hanged if it isn't goin' a shade too far. I don't know what the younger generation is comin' to. In my time we had our affairs, but we had the decency to be discreet about them. We were never obvious. And we were at least polite.'

She answered in a taunting voice:

'You always said, "May I?" - didn't you, Dibs darling?'

'Upon my soul!' he gasped. 'Really, you're a most immoral woman, Elissa.'

'No. Not immoral, Dibs,' she considered. 'Merely improper. I shall never consider myself immoral until I allow myself to have a lover on the sofa.'

Mary, listening with a set face, made a faint movement of distress.

'I wish you wouldn't talk like that, 'Lissa,' she said suddenly in a low voice, her eyes fixed upon the moving sea. 'It's too horrible. You spoil everything.'

'Spoil,' answered Elissa. 'I like that, Mary pretty. Who dragged us to this devastating spot? Who refused Carr's invitation to Quinney's? Who insisted on his coming to lunch with us here? He hated it pretty thoroughly, I don't mind telling you. There was a wounded look about his dignity.' And, making a hole in the sand with her forefinger, she entombed her glowing cigarette-end delicately.

'I hate smart restaurants,' murmured Mary, as in apology. 'Everything stiff and horrid. That's why I wanted to come here. It's so odd and lovely. And Mr Carr doesn't mind. He needn't come if he doesn't want to.'

'He'll come,' said Elissa carelessly. 'His tongue lolls out when he looks at you.'

Something disagreeable flowed over Mary - a sense of sordidness. She shook her head to free herself, checking a thought as yet unformed.

'I'm going to swim again,' she said without warning, and, rising to her feet, she ran swiftly into the foaming water. Beyond the foam, which creamed around her waist in eddying rings, the sea was opalescent, blue and strangely ethereal, like light screened through deep crystal caverns. Her feet left the warm sand, and suddenly she was deliciously beyond her depth, surging buoyantly towards the raft which curtseyed at anchor half-way to the reef. Now she felt clean, her limbs whipped by the tanging brine, her blood enriched by the electric air.

She swam and swam, then with a little cry of sheer delight she clasped the edge of the bobbing raft and swung herself, exultant, upon its matting-covered surface. There she rested with arms outstretched, her cheek pressed closely to the warm, wet fibre. Now she felt herself a thousand miles away from Elissa's flippant tongue. A moment passed, then all at once she became aware that she was not alone. Slowly she turned her head. Harvey Leith lay on the far side of the raft.

They looked at each other for what seemed to her a long, long time. Stripped of his nondescript clothes, his figure had an unsuspected grace; his shoulders wide and narrowing downwards, his legs both muscular and fine. At last, filled with a curious perplexity, she let her lashes fall.

'I didn't think. I didn't know,' she said queerly, 'that you were here.'

'I didn't think I should be here myself,' he answered slowly. 'But here I am.'

'And here am I too,' she said with a little laugh. 'We're afloat again on another ship. Isn't it fun?'

Nothing more banal than the words which she had spoken, yet under the flat surface of these words she felt returning, quivering more urgently within her, that queer unrest which previously had taken her. A sense of something upthrown from the past, of something vital, predestined, stretching towards her from the future. It transformed life, tinting this moment with the colours of her dream, flooding her body with a strange expectant helplessness. Never before had she known this deep and throbbing harmony of emotion, never before had this strange constraint possessed her like a pain. She did not understand, she could not defend herself. Her fingers played nervously with a loose fibre of the matting; she had not the power to look at him.

'It's so lovely here,' she said at last, almost nervously. 'The sea - the sun - the snow upon that peak. So lovely. It makes me feel I've known it always.' Her voice was low, and sounded dull upon her ears, the fine inflections flattened by the constriction of her throat.

Quite motionless, yet swung by the swaying raft as though he floated between sea and sky in some enchanted medium, he did not answer. With eyes fixed, absorbed by the living beauty of her form, he seemed to contemplate the words within himself. So lovely, she had said. He felt his heart pounding the blood hard

68

into his temples. So lovely! He had never thought of loveliness, nor sought the soft mystery of beauty. His life had been hard, like granite, governed by known laws, inflexible. He had been seeking. Yes, truth alone had been the object of his search. And the motive of his search? It was no ardour to aid humanity. Simply a cold stretching after reason - indifferent and austere. But now, under a blinding light which seemed to burn upon him from afar, something fused within his soul, different, immutable.

'They call this island Gran Canaria,' she murmured. 'Grand Canary! There's colour and movement in that name. When I think of this voyage I shall say away down into myself, Grand Canary! It has a thrilling sound.'

Her words, acquiring another meaning, reached him dimly through the blinding whiteness of that secret light. And he asked:

'You leave the ship tomorrow?'

'Yes, we shall stay at Orotava.'

It had a strange inevitability. She was going. To-night the *Aureola* would sail, cleave through the warm darkness to a farther island, and in the morning she would be gone.

'It is quiet at Orotava,' she went on. 'A small place and all unspoiled. That above everything is what I like. Mr Carr has arranged everything for us at the hotel - San Jorge. He is my husband's agent here in the islands.'

'I see,' he said; and all the light within him suddenly was quenched. There had been something; and now it was taken back. His lips drew in; calmly he forced himself to look at her.

'You will have a happy time, I know.'

'You go on, of course, with the ship?' she asked, her eyes bright upon him.

'I go on. And back again.'

A silence fell, forged by their inscrutable thoughts. Suddenly she made that impulsive little movement of her hand, as though capturing an elusive joy.

'Will you have lunch with us today? Oh, yes, please - please do. At the little *cabine* place. It is so delicious there. Mr Carr is coming. And I want you to come too.'

There was a painful pleasure in knowing that he must refuse.

'I'm not alone,' he answered. 'Corcoran brought me down here.' He made a movement towards the outer sea, where, like an old seal sporting amongst the surf, Jimmy's figure was dimly seen.

'He must come too,' she said quickly. 'You must both come.'

'He has to go into the town on business.'

69

'But you - you haven't any business?'

Already he had been sufficiently boorish upon the ship; stung by the very memory, his refusal died upon his lips.

'That's good,' she cried happily across his silence. 'You're coming. You're coming to lunch with me.'

Her words forced a faint smile to his lips, and at that smile she sprang to her feet, arched her thin arms with a sort of innocent delight, and plunged deeply into the sea. The impetus of her dive made the raft so suddenly recoil he rolled after her, falling upon the back of an advancing wave. Beneath the surface he opened his eyes. Shining through the subaqueous light, her body slipped away from him, glistening as a moonbeam and as white. He rose, filled his lungs with air. He wanted suddenly to pursue that flashing whiteness. But he did not. He swung away and swam with over-arm strokes to the *cabine*.

In his dressing-box that smelt of resinous pine-wood he put on his clothes slowly. His skin, alive with pricking currents of life, had a pinkish glow. His eyes looked straight ahead, studying remotely the unreality of what they saw.

When Jimmy came in, dripping water from his matted torso, he explained in the same fashion of detachment the invitation he had accepted.

Corcoran, moving a towel with professional skill, shot him one astounded glance; but he said nothing. Crass impulses of thought seemed struggling within his bony skull. At last he said:

'Faith, yer the proud boy with an invite like that. If I hadn't heavy business on me hands I'd join ye wid pleasure. But at anny rate I'll see ye meet the company before I slip me hook.'

Ten minutes later they went into the little restaurant together.

She had used the word delicious to describe it; and somehow the adjective was just. It was small and very clean, the floor of white scrubbed wood, the tables covered by blue checked cloths, the front entirely open to the sea, the sky, and to that distant haunting peak. At the back a long bar curved, capped by a row of bottles - but, strangely, Harvey had no thought for that oblivion he had craved. And, behind the bar a waiter in his shirt-sleeves sat abstractedly upon a high stool curling a little moustache which was like an eyebrow out of place. In the corner stood - quite incongruously - a yellow automatic piano.

At the sight of the instrument Jimmy's eye kindled knowingly; he immediately went over and with a coin set it gaily spinning into life. A piercing tune rent the air, and, following some intelligent shrugging of his shoulders, Corcoran flung himself into a lively jig. At once the waiter smiled; a languid youth sipping absinthe at the bar smiled; a Spanish family in the corner smiled. They understood; they were appreciative: they, too, knew the meaning of happiness. The music cascaded on. Jimmy's feet moved with a baffling intricacy and a dazzling speed. The waiter began to beat time with his hands; the fat Spanish mother nodded her head with spirit above her tucked-in napkin; the youth, opening his mouth like an excited hound, broke suddenly into a high tenor accompaniment of the song. Throughout the melody vague wafts of good cooking strayed in from the kitchen beyond, mingling with the smell of garlic and the salty odour of the sea.

At that moment Mary came into the room, followed by Elissa, Dibs, and Carr. There was a curious pause: Jimmy, quite out of breath, for once looked sheepish; the youth turned mute; the waiter slipped off his stool and the music shut up with a sudden sepulchral bang. But Mary laughed.

'Lovely,' she cried, clapping her hands. 'A lovely tune. Put it on again.'

Wilfred Carr did not laugh. Framed in the doorway, he envisaged with supercilious eye the whole inadequate environment and shattered it with his stare. Never before had he visited this atrocious place, and never, clearly, would he return. No gentleman could lunch with dignity in such a den save to gratify the ridiculous whim of a most charming lady. His silk-clad figure stiffened as he took in Harvey, standing with hands thrust in the pockets of his ill-made suit, and his companion, the vulgar, battered Irishman. His civility was freezing over the matter of the introductions. He stood aside stiffly as Corcoran made to take his departure.

'Ye'll excuse me,' Jimmy declared, 'I wouldn't be after leavin' you if I didn't have to go. But, truth to tell, I've got a wire and other things besides to settle. Mosth important.' He inferred tacitly that transactions of the first magnitude were on his hands, and he bowed himself gallantly away.

'Who is that fellow?' demanded Carr disdainfully.

'He is a particular friend of mine,' Harvey answered directly. The two looked at each other.

'Oh, yes,' Carr drawled, at last removing his eyes. 'Naturally.' They sat down to lunch in an atmosphere suddenly electric. The romantic little waiter had surpassed himself - not every

71

day, you see, did English milords visit the *cabine*; and the little *contessa* who had ordered the luncheon was so beautiful - *bella, molte bella*. So the stiff coarse napkins had taken stupendous shapes; a tiny bunch of dew-drenched violets lay upon each plate; the small black olives were delicious; the omelette, made with pimentos, as had been demanded, was risen high as El Telde himself. And now they were at the *ensalada*.

'I must,' declared Mary. 'I simply must have some garlic to my salad.'

Carr made a movement of horror which he turned hastily into a cough.

'Of course, of course.' Twisting round, he spoke loudly to the waiter in bad but arrogant Spanish.

'You know,' he said, bending towards her confidentially, 'you should really have let me arrange your day, Mary.' The name came easily from his tongue. 'Lunch at the club. Better - well, rather better than here. Then on to golf. We're rather pleased with our course.'

'But I didn't come here to play golf.'

'Ah, well, you must let me manage things for you at Orotava,' he declared intimately. 'Business takes me to Santa Cruz in a couple of days - just across the island. I'll certainly look over.' His manner, concentrated killingly upon her, inferred subtly that she must necessarily be impressed by his interest and devastated by his charm. That exactly was Wilfred Carr. So many women had told him that he had charm, he knew infallibly that no woman could resist him.

Perhaps he was charming; he had all the qualities. He danced splendidly, played golf well and tennis brilliantly; he rode, had boxed for his college, was sound at bridge and perfectly at home in any boudoir. He was only a country parson's son. But he had been educated expensively so that everything was in his manner and nothing in his head. Yet he had the instinct of self-advancement. At home he had cultivated people, the right people; he had cultivated Michael Fielding; and now, with a soft billet, an easy life, and adequate popularity in the limited society of the islands, he often told himself he had nothing to complain of.

He had met Mary Fielding quite often in England; quite often from a distance he had gracefully admired her. And now she was here, a young and very lovely figure - not quite comprehensible to be sure, inviting a man to lunch at such a ghastly little pub. She had always had that reputation - simplicity and all that, don't you know; rather odd perhaps; some ass had once named her Alice in Wonderland, but - well - in spite of that, or because of it, a most entrancing little creature. Again he bent forward, with a blandishing gesture of his beautiful hands.

'Yes,' he said. 'If you put yourself in my hands I can promise you an amusing time. You must have found it dull on the little banana boat.'

She looked at him curiously, as a child might contemplate a crab.

'Not so very dull, thank you.'

He laughed easily.

'Well, you must cheer up now. I'll be quite miserable unless you promise. You know, most folks think we've a primitive society here. Nothing of the sort. We have every amenity. It's the most charmingly delightful spot you could imagine.' He had all the fulsome adjectives of the colonist who, adopting a country and therein succeeding, now sees that country as the reflex of himself; and he added glowingly, with an eye towards effect upon his hostess, 'Perfect Utopia. Everybody has a good time here - and why not?' He became quite lyrical. 'Man and beast - they all enjoy themselves frightfully.'

Harvey, sitting with a set face, felt a cold wave of antagonism sweep over him; for some reason he felt desperately and unreasonably infuriated. Deliberately he turned towards Carr.

'I saw some mules this morning on the quay. Not exactly healthy. They didn't seem to be enjoying themselves frightfully.'

Carr sat upright in his chair. He frowned.

'The mules are all right,' he said shortly. 'No one takes any notice of them.'

'And the mosquitoes,' said Harvey, whisking at an insect that buzzed about his plate, 'no one takes any notice of them either, I suppose.'

Carr's frown deepened.

'No,' he sneered, 'no one but old ladies and milk-and-water tourists.'

'Good,' said Harvey evenly. 'Even the mosquitoes enjoy themselves. And no one is a whit the worse for it. No fever. Nothing. It's delightful.'

A slow look of understanding crept into Carr's face; he gave a short derisive laugh.

'So that's it. You've been listening to the scare. I might have guessed as much.'

Dibdin laid down his fork with an air of perplexity.

'Look here, you fellows! I don't understand. What's all this you're talkin' about?'

Carr made a vigorous gesture of contempt.

'It's nothing, absolutely nothing,' he declared. 'There's an odd spot of fever wandering about the islands just now. No one with any gumption pays the least attention. You always find somebody ready to cry wolf amongst the natives. But we don't go about in a whining funk. Good Lord, no. We wouldn't be British if we did.' His tone held a magnificent and patriotic intrepidity.

'The clean-limbed Englishman speaking,' said Elissa with a grimace. 'But someone really should have told us. From now on I shall regard every mosquito with a sort of palsied horror. I feel myself itching from head to toe already.'

'We got rather eaten this morning,' Mary reflected lightly, 'coming down the mole.'

'Don't you worry, Mary,' Carr answered soothingly; he patted her arm. 'The whole thing's perfectly absurd. A spot of fever. Good Lord, it's nothing. I'll see you don't take any risks.'

She moved her arm slightly, her eyes curiously aloof.

'There's no such thing as taking risks,' she said calmly. 'Things just happen or they don't. That's what I believe.'

'Of course,' agreed Carr, rather peevishly. 'But for all that I'll see you're all right.'

Harvey was silent; but inwardly he burned. He knew his vague prescience to be absurd - merely the instinct of a scientific mind. But he had once seen yellow fever in a lascar seaman at the Port of London and he never would forget the ghastly ravages of that disease: acute as cholera, deadly as plague. And now to hear this blustering lout proclaim that it was nothing, to see him exploit a flashy, ignorant bravado - it was maddening. Turning his head, he gave Carr a cold, level stare. But before he could speak Mary rose.

'Let's have our coffee outside,' she said. 'Here on the verandah.'

They got up and went out to the small wooden platform which, facing the south, kept its zinc-topped tables in a shady angle of the *cabine*. Coffee was brought and handed in silence. The little waiter had a plaintive air, as if he knew the harmony of the day had been disrupted.

'I'm sleepy,' Elissa said with half-shut eyes.

No one answered. No one had very much to say. Harvey sat

74

glumly with legs extended and hands stuck deeply in his pockets. Dibs' mouth hung open as it did when he was bored - privately he thought Carr a poorish fellow, and the luncheon, too, perhaps it had been heavyish for his liver!

On Mary's face was a sad and wondering abstraction: she seemed busy with a secret both baffling and precious. Once she turned to Harvey.

'On the raft,' she said rather dreamily, 'do you remember? I almost feel myself floating there yet.' And from her eyes, no longer curious and aloof, a strange unknown sweetness came to him.

With coffee-cup in hand, Carr stalked about the verandah, sulking gracefully, pausing only to kick at a lizard which scuttled across the boards. From time to time he stole quick glances at the back of Mary's neck, which was white and very smooth, touched, too, by a wisp of curling hair. She had treated him uncommonly casually, hanged if she hadn't! At last he repented. A smile came to his full lips.

He came and drew his chair up to hers. He was prepared for confidences; but, forestalling these confidences, she said remotely:

'I'd like to get back to the ship.'

He at once bent forward with a rush of effusive protests. It was too early; the *Aureola* wouldn't sail before eight; they might cruise round the Puerto - his launch was at the steps - and she must above everything take tea at the club. He had recovered all his charm and was again ready to be on playful terms with life and her.

But Mary rose, her eyes holding that distant look that sometimes came to them. The others might stay, but she really must go.

The others did not wish to stay. The bill was paid; they started out, walking across the narrow isthmus to the Puerto, where, as he had so emphatically stated, his launch lay waiting. But not, this time, for a cruise. With a wounded air he handed her down the steps; the others followed; then the engine started. As the launch chugged across the bay he had a shred of satisfaction. He was sitting next to her, and under the sheer fabric of her dress he felt her side, all warm and soft. He made a gentle movement with his knee. But she looked straight ahead into the distance. Still, he was not displeased. You never could tell. Women. They were queer creatures.

Five minutes later they were alongside the *Aureola*. He got up

75

gallantly to hand her up the ladder - no one could infuse more subtle pressure to an arm than he - but as he extended his hand someone from behind collided with him violently.

'I'll do that,' Harvey said in a fierce undertone. 'Do you hear?'

'What,' stammered Carr, checked by his surprise. 'What are you doing?'

'Make way,' hissed the other, 'or I'll knock you into the ditch.'

Carr stood for a moment inarticulate, stupefied by surprise - but for all that something in those blazing eyes made him give way. They were all out of the launch before he could recover himself. Damn that fellow, he thought. Damn it - why didn't I hit him? The smile had stiffened on his lips, but with an effort he kept it there.

He took off his hat and waved it gracefully, calling out:

'Don't forget. We shall meet next week.'

And, as he plumped down on the cushions of the launch, with an oath he swore he would make sure they did meet.

## CHAPTER XI

AT six o'clock that evening, as the sun slipped rosy fingers over the pinnacles of Santa Ana, Susan and Robert Tranter returned to the ship - the last to do so, for Corcoran had long been back. Dust lay upon their boots - in the interests of economy they had dismissed their carriage at the Plaza - Susan's shoulders sagged slightly, Robert's air was curt, as though that day a duty rather than a pleasure had been achieved.

They came up the gangway slowly and in silence, immersed apparently in their secret thoughts. Then, as Susan's foot met the deck, she suddenly observed the figure of Harvey Leith pacing up and down beside the after-hatch. Immediately her eyes lit up, her shoulders lifted as though fatigue and fear had momentarily been dispelled. Something sang in her heart: 'He's all right. He's all right.' Her stolid form took on a strange lightness, a bar of light touched her dull hair to gold. So poised, she stood for a moment at the end of the gang-plank, then she followed her brother along the alley-way.

'It's kind of good to be back, Robbie,' she remarked valiantly. 'I guess it's been tiring today when all's said and done.'

To this he made no reply.

Her eyes turned overcast again but with no alteration of manner she said:

'I'll lie down a little now, I guess. My head aches some. You'll be all right till supper, dear.'

His back was rigid but his voice held the sulky note of rectitude unjustly used as, half over his shoulder, he replied:

'I reckon I've always *been* all right.' And with his head in the air he stepped into his cabin and sharply closed the door.

But was he all right? Standing for a moment before the mirror he stared absently at his face, which seemed pale, unfamiliar; then confusedly he sat down upon the edge of the settee and let his brow fall forward on his palm. The visit to Arucas on which depended something of the success of his mission had been actually a weariness and a tribulation: he had been detached, inattentive to the important discussion on the printing of the Spanish tracts, almost neglecting to take away the letter of introduction to Mr Rodgers at Laguna. All day long he had been engaged by another thought. Elissa! The name, even though it were unspoken, had now the power to make him flush. But why? He had no cause to flush. That exactly was the point. Of course! No one could understand but he; Susan, all upon this ship, the whole calumniating universe might harshly misjudge him and with pointing finger condemn his sentiment. He knew that they were all wrong, that his emotion was noble and beautiful and good. Beautiful - he knew it to be so, a generous emotion which glowed within him and made him feel that he was near to God.

Elissa! - she was beautiful! But where was the shame in that? Beauty was God's gift, bestowed with that same breath which infused the quickening clay with its immortal soul. And if she had been a sinner, was that a reason why he should, like the Pharisee of old, condemn, and pass her by? No, no! Before God, a million times no! He had said from the first that he would help her, a lovely woman stooped to folly. Today even to have been away from her, to have lost the opportunity of three long hours, had pained him grievously. Ah, yes, grievously was indeed the fitting word. Again the hot desire took him to be with her - to save her. A vision of Elissa, saved, sanctified and beside him, rushed before him, a lovely vision intermingled by a quivering confusion of sound and colour: of angels' wings beating lightly, of blaring trumpets soaring in harmonious notes, of white garments undefiled and soft pure pinkish lips, of golden gates opening wide and bosoms on which a head might rest. Oh, it was too much, too much for human heart to bear.

Alone there in the solitude of the cabin his nostrils quivered, the colour deepened upon his cheeks, he looked up suddenly and in a vibrant voice exclaimed aloud: 'I kin doo all things in Christ who strengtheneth me.'

With eyes uplifted he sat for some moments as if in prayer, then he rose, washed his hands and face, put on a clean collar and went out of the cabin. He ascended at once to the upper deck.

So much had he hoped and so little expected to find Elissa there that the sight of her sitting idly in a sheltered corner drove the blood violently back to his heart. A few yards off, abaft the deck house, stowed in her chair like a coil of rope or something of the ship's fixed gear, was Mother Hemmingway, alert, malicious and observant. She had not stirred from the ship all day. Tranter did not see her, as he advanced directly to Elissa with glowing eyes.

She looked up.

'You are quite a stranger,' she said languidly. Flattery gratified her, and the servile devotion in his face made her almost civil.

'I had to make a call - honest - just simply *had* to make it,' he explained with eagerness. 'But - well - my thoughts have gone out to you all day.'

She yawned, exhibiting unabashed the firm white teeth set in her big red mouth.

'You're tired,' he said quickly. 'You've done too much.' His solicitude was fraternal; yet he might surely have bestowed a moiety of his compassion on Susan and her weary, racking head.

'I've had an utterly boring day. Too completely unattractive.'

'I suppose you would call my day boring, too,' he answered, leaning his elbow on the rail close to her and smiling into her eyes. 'Though it's hardly a word I'd be liable to use. Still, one has the satisfaction of a duty done. Our visit to Arucas may bear fruit. I mean as regards the success of our mission. The folks there have promised to be financially behind us in our venture. We have an introduction to a most influential planter in Laguna. Now we can go full steam ahead.' He paused reflectively. 'Gosh, it's downright queer. The whole day I've felt quite cold about the prospects of my work and now that I'm here talking to you

I just can't hold myself back. Full of pep! And it means so much to me.'

'Why?'

'All my life I've been bound up in the work. I found grace early. Yes, I was saved when I was quite a boy. And I was a poor boy. I had to battle upwards, put myself through theological school, fight hard to fit myself for my work in the Lord's vineyard.'

She looked at him with unbelieving eyes: he's not real, she thought, not real. Aloud she said:

'Are you telling me the story of your life?'

'No, no,' he exclaimed, and made a little manly gesture. 'It's just that I feel I want to tell you everything - everything about myself, everything that is me. Can't just hold it in.'

A pause came, filled by her curiosity; then she asked with a quaint uplifting of her brows:

'You have never had anything to do with women?'

'Nothing!'

'Not ever?'

He shook his head, looking at her with his luminous, big eyes as a dog might gaze upon his mistress.

'Well, well,' she murmured to herself. 'So it's true. And all the way from Connecticut.'

'Beg pardon, ma'am.'

'I was saying,' she replied, 'that I must call you Joseph.'

He flushed vividly; he did not understand.

'Joseph?' he stammered. 'But my name is Robert.'

'I shall always think of you as Joseph. For me you are born again under that name. And yet I don't know. I haven't decided.'

Her manner was grave but he had the dreadful suspicion that she was making fun of him, and with a pathetic earnestness in his voice he exclaimed:

'It has been a great experience meeting you. So great I cannot think of you going out of my life like' - with a fervid movement of his arm he unloosed the booming platitude - 'like a ship that passes in the night. It seems so purposeless. Something must come of it. Yes, it must. All our talks together cannot lead us nowhere. Oh, I'd give my right hand to be the instrument of your salvation.' His voice faltered and broke off. Quite overwhelmed, he laid his hand entreatingly upon her arm, said with treacly sentiment: 'I'd like to give you something. That's the feeling I have for you. Oh, sure it is. And if you'll have it I'd like you to have something that is very precious to me. I've got a little book that was my mother's. 'Tisn't much - a little book of good words. But I've carried it about with me these last twenty years. Will you - would you take it?'

She looked up, then quickly looked away.

'That odious woman in the corner is staring her eyes out at you,' she remarked casually. 'I don't in the least mind, but probably you do.'

He turned his head, met Mother Hemmingway's unwinking beady stare.

'No, no,' he declared, 'I don't mind.' But, chilled, he withdrew his hand.

'Give me that after dinner,' said Elissa suddenly, 'when we're slipping out of the harbour after dark. Rather mysterious and nice then. It'll round off the day.'

Entranced he looked at her. In the background Mother Hemmingway disencumbered herself from her chair and shuffled towards the companion. She had seen all that she desired; and now a rare malicious delight engaged her. Little ripples of inward merriment agitated her fat stomach as she guided her small tight-laced feet carefully down the steps.

'Crickey me, if it ain't the richest lark,' she kept muttering to herself. 'Sancta Maria, scrag me if it ain't. Pray to Gawd 'as got it proper. Bloomin' 'umbug. Oh, my eye - it's too good - too good to keep.' Squirming with mirth she handed herself along the alley-way, like a little black toad, and entered her cabin sideways. As she had expected, Susan was there - resting upon her bunk with a wet handkerchief around her head.

''Ello, 'Ello,' she cried, with the richest geniality. 'Avin' a little shut-eye. And quite right too. You got to watch your 'ealth out 'ere or the goblins'll get yer. Stryte. Tyke it easy, dearie - like your little brother's doin' on the upper deck.'

Susan uncovered one eye. There was a pause.

'My brother?'

'The syme,' cried Mother Hemmingway leaning against the bunk with supreme good-heartedness. 'The syme 'andsome little 'armonium-pl'yin' gen'lman. And Sancta Maria ain't 'e pl'yin' now. Not 'alf 'e ain't. Not that I blyme 'im. "All work and no pl'y mykes Jack a dull boy." Stryte. That's been the 'Emmingway motta for over a 'undred years.'

Susan opened the other eye.

'What do you mean?'

80

Mother Hemmingway burst into a roar of laughter.

'Don't upset yourself, ducky. 'E's all right is little Robbie. And it's only 'uman nyture after all. Or w'y did Gawd myke petticoats?'

There was a silence, then Susan lay back and closed her eyes with a restrained expression of repugnance.

'Perhaps we might be quiet for a little,' she said. 'I have a headache.'

But Mother Hemmingway was undaunted.

'Lord, I've 'ad 'eadaches on me in my time. Specially after I been swipey. I wouldn't 'arm you, ducky. I only thought you might like to know that brother Bob is 'avin' the time of 'is 'andsome life with Mistress B'ynam. 'Oldin' 'ands. Kiss in the Ring, and Jinny's at the Cottage Door.' Cocking her head in the air she sang in an affected tone:

> '*Oh, waltz me around again Willie,*
> *Around, around, around.*
> *The music is dreamy, it's peaches and creamy*
> *Oh! don't let my feet touch the ground!*'

And in her natural voice: ' 'Streuth, Love's young dream ain't in it. Gave me quite a thirst it 'as.' And turning away nonchalantly she took a swig at the water-bottle and began to gargle her throat noisily at the wash-basin. Susan sat up abruptly, her gaze startled - quivering upon that squat and shiny form. Into her face flowed a harassed look; she rose slowly, opened the cabin door, and went out. Mother Hemmingway, who seemed to have been watching every movement with sly eyes set in the back of her head, suddenly called after her:

'Tyke my shawl, dearie. The sun's goin' down and it's a cowld gyme pl'yin 'gooseberry.'

Then, collapsing upon the settee with her hands clasping her pudgy bosom, she went into peal after peal of shrieking laughter.

Susan mounted stiffly to the upper deck, a whirling uncertainty in her head. One swift, anxious glance showed her that Robert was not there: he had gone below. But Mrs Baynham was still on deck, sitting in a queer reflective langour, the blinding western light behind stamping her large voluptuous figure with luminous intensity. Something in that figure, subtly magnified it seemed, swelled out to Susan like a fantastic horror. Her lips constricted, her expression grew faintly scared. But an unconquerable force was in her. She advanced to the other woman.

'Why cannot you leave my brother alone?' she said directly in a low concentrated tone.

Elissa looked up, then looked away.

'Tittle-tattle in the cabin?' she murmured. 'Little Christian conversations with the Spanish-Cockney friend?'

'You won't put me off like that,' said Susan rigidly. 'I've known for long enough that my brother is infatuated with you.'

'Then why not speak to him?'

'I have spoken to him. But he doesn't understand. He's never been like this before and he's quite hopelessly bewildered.'

Elissa began to powder her nose.

'You mean that you are quite hopelessly scared that you will lose him. It's staring out of your face. For years you've yearned over him, and the first time he looks at another woman you faint with horror.'

Susan's fingers clenched; her cheeks were very pale.

'You're wrong,' she cried in a trembling voice. 'I only want Robert to be happy. My devotion to him is quite unselfish. No one would have been better pleased than me if he had fallen in love with - with a good woman.'

'Oh, Lord,' sighed Elissa, closing her powder box listlessly. 'I thought all that sort of thing had gone out years ago. I really can't cope with it.'

'I'm sorry,' Susan said through set lips. 'But you'll have to cope with it.'

'Do go away,' begged Elissa languidly. 'Please do. I'm quite exhausted. You're too intense. Portrait of early Christian girl being thrown to the lions. It's absolute agony.'

'It's no good being flippant,' said Susan hoarsely; she was choking - her breathing stifled her. 'You've got to promise me now - now.'

All at once the languid air fell from Elissa like a garment; slowly she raised her head and fixed on Susan a stare of insolent contempt.

'You're such a damned little fool that now you begin to annoy me. Can't you holy women ever let things and people alone? You want everybody to be like you. It's such colossal egoism. And you're possessive! Have you patented him - your little Robert - as a second edition of the Saviour? Oh, I don't mind if you have. I don't mind who you convert. But why the devil should you mind who I sleep with?'

'You can't -' gasped Susan. 'You can't talk like that. It's terrible.'

Elissa gave a short laugh; then suddenly she stood up.

'Most amusing - this talk,' she said with patronising rudeness. 'But I think we've had enough of it. I'm going down.' And with her rug trailing from her arm she brushed past, gracefully, to the companion.

Susan stood motionless, her knees trembling, her whole body torn - burning. Within her, something seemed to shrink and fall weakly into an empty darkness. But at least she had spoken. Yes, she had spoken. The thought comforted her. She lifted her face to the dazzling sky whose glorious radiance poured forth, it seemed in glittering chains from the very throne of God.

God! Yes, there was God. It was all right - everything. She could pray. Strength flowed into her, and, with her head upraised to that majestic sky, her lips moved without sound in a passionate appeal.

Suddenly, as though under some cathedral dome a kyrie had been rung, a quiet bell tinkled thrice. And that gentle impassive thrilling woke within the ship. There came a splash of ropes, a creaking of fenders, a few shrill cries falling backwards, fading into nothingness. A breeze awoke mysteriously in the placid air. The ship quickened. Again the *Aureola* was under way.


## CHAPTER XII

DINNER was over: a silent, uncomfortable meal, crossed by many currents of emotion, overhung by the strange imminence of departure. The captain, adept usually in rolling conversation round, had talked little. Something was on his mind, perhaps the thought that he was losing a passenger for whom he had a sincere regard; perhaps a deeper thought than that. His eye had fallen frequently on Mary and he had asked:

'You spend all your time in Orotava - at the hotel?' At her affirmative he had hesitated - an indecision unusual in such a man, then said: 'It is a trim little place. Clean - right by itself. A perfect health resort. And the wind is always off the sea.'

And that was all.

Now Harvey stood on the upper deck, glad after the heat of the saloon of the night's tranquillity. The effervescence of the sunset had dissolved and sunk, blazing, into the waters of the sea. And, as with a sigh of consummation, it was again serene and clear: a calm, white night, lucent with the fluid beauty of pale moonshine. Swung low behind the latticed rigging, the moon, not yet full-formed, held that faintly flawed loveliness - like a maiden trembling upon maturity. The stars, too, were timid in the high translucent heaven. On the ship's port quarter, fading, yet brighter than the stars, the lights of Las Palmas pricked the sky's clear rim with tiny glittering points.

Without haste the *Aureola* slid onward at a bare five knots, lolling a little in her gait, as if conscious that her passage was brief and the need to anchor before dawn remote. The clucking water played about her sides and stern; the sound rose up like bubbles, breaking with quiet echoes and a gleam of silver.

Leaning over the forward rail, Harvey let his gaze sink into the warm oblivion beyond: sea, earth, and sky united and at peace. But in his heart there was no peace.

Suddenly a step came behind him, a hand was laid upon his shoulder. He did not move; without turning his head, he said, in a tone constrained strangely by his melancholy:

'Well, Jimmy, did you get your business done?'

'Sure an' I got it done,' cried Corcoran; in the universal still-ness his voice resounded with a cheerful magnitude. 'And sent me wire to Santa Cruz an' all. When old Bob gets it he'll be dancin' wid delight. I tell ye I'm all set for the big-time business.'

'You've been very mysterious, Jimmy,' said Harvey absently, 'about this business of yours.'

'Aha!' cried Jimmy. 'There's time and place for talkin', isn't there? And no man ever made a fortune by openin' his mouth a mile.' He broke off, gazing surreptitiously at Harvey's dark, severe profile; then with a sly show of confidence he declared: 'But yer a friend of me own, aren't ye? I don't mind tellin' ye what I'm afther.'

'Some other time then, Jimmy,' Harvey said quickly. 'I'm not just in the mood for touching intimacies.'

'All right, all right,' said Jimmy agreeably; he withdrew his arm, struck an attitude of offence, made with his fists some exaggerated passes into the unresistant air; then, panting a little, he took snuff. 'See! That's the stuff. All in good time, says you?

Right, says I. But you'll come ashore wid me at Santa Cruz and meet the Professor or me name's not Jimmy C.'

A short silence fell, then Jimmy cocked his battered ear.

'Do you hear him?' he said, his grin slow - invisible yet rich. 'He's like a cow in a china-shop.'

Abaft the chart-room they heard the quick padding step of Robert Tranter. He was humming - sure sign of his disquiet. When indecision seized the evangelical mind, Tranter would hum; and now, emerging from his thick pursed lips, came the sibilant strains of 'Swing low, sweet chariot.'

'Jumpin' Janus Macafferty,' Corcoran went on, 'but he's a slob of putty, that one. Playto was right when he said that sinse was a thing that could niver be taught. And the lump of him too an' all, yamblin' about like he was moonstruck. Faith, his sister's worth six of him.' He yawned, clenching his fists and stretching them luxuriously upwards. Then, with an extremely casual air, he declared: 'Well, I'm for down below. A little quiet chat, with Mother H. and Hamble. Just a little social talk, ye understand. Nothin' more. S'long. In the meantime, that's to say.'

A phantom smile hovered over Harvey's face - Corcoran's evasions were too absurd! - then quickly faded. He turned to the rail, seeking the solitude of the sea, the massive silence of the night. But a moment later he was again disturbed: Tranter stood at his elbow.

'Musing, Dr Leith, I see. And a wondrous night it is for communing with the stars. Yes, sir! A little close, perhaps. Kind of humid, don't you think? I must own I'm perspiring.' The sound of breathing came through the effusive heartiness of the voice. 'The folks ought to be on deck getting the air.'

'The folks ought to do as they want to do,' said Harvey with gloomy impatience.

Tranter laughed: his ready, emotional laugh which to-night seemed more ready, more emotional - drawing up with a gulp almost upon the edge of hysteria.

'Ha! Ha! Sure, they ought.' He talked as if to reassure himself with his own rich overtones. 'Why, yes. Up to a point, that is to say. I only meant the ladies might find it pleasanter on deck. Now, I wonder where they can have got to.'

Harvey swung away, nauseated by something flabby in the words, something frightened yet persistent.

'Mrs Baynham went to her cabin immediately after dinner,' he threw back curtly over his shoulder. 'I heard her say that she was tired and that she was going to turn in at once.' Turning abruptly towards the companion he walked away, dimly conscious of the sudden wave of desolation that flooded the other's face.

Gone, vanished for the night into the inviolable sanctuary of her cabin! - and after she had *promised* - it was a cruel blow for Tranter. The small, limp leather book bulging his breast pocket seemed to press suddenly upon his heart like a weight of lead. Crushed, he stood for a moment with a curiously abject air, then, lowering his head, he began slowly to walk up and down. Now he was not humming.

Below, Harvey paused outside the entrance to the alley-way. Should he too turn in? He was tired, exhausted by he knew not what. An ugly memory of Tranter's face obsessed him, drawn like a smear across his mind, evoking in him unreasonable anger. This emblem of sickly tenderness exhibited so nakedly - it crystallised his whole belief in the fatuity of love. A biological necessity, an animal reaction thrust on the victim of gross instinct. No more. Thus he had always coldly thought. And yet the repetition of that thought distressed him as with a heavy grief. What had happened? His clear, fine pride recoiled from a mocking inward voice. And there came other voices. Around him the beauty of the night rose up and with a thousand taunting tongues confused his senses. Beauty - which he had never recognised, which lay at the opposite pole from truth, irreconcilable with his belief.

Sadly he walked forward, past the fore-hatch towards the bow. The ship, with unconquerable serenity, moved calmly through the great stillness. He reached the bow. There, though his face showed nothing, his heart opened and turned with a wild throb. Her figure, straight and fragile as a wand, leaped to his sight in a haze of secret joy. Then he was at her side, leaning upon the taffrail, staring into limitless space, silent.

'I felt that you would come,' she said at last; she did not look at him. 'Now I don't feel sad any more.' Her voice was low, almost colourless and utterly devoid of coquetry. 'It had been so strange today,' she went on, 'I feel bewildered. And tomorrow I am leaving the ship.'

'You don't want to go?' he said - and his words held a painful coldness.

'No. I don't want to leave this little ship. I love it. It is so safe. But I shall go.'

He did not speak.

'Have you ever felt,' she continued in her odd, remote tone, 'that you were caught up in something and had simply to go on - like little strings pulling, pulling you forward all the time?'

He fought for a sneer to lay bare the folly of her remark; but no sneer would come.

'All my life seems to have been like that. This little ship is pulling me forward now; to something - I don't know what. And yet I do know. Vaguely I know without being able to understand.'

'That is quite unreasonable,' he said, in a low voice.

'Oh, I know it isn't reasonable. But it's there. You laughed at me before when I told you about my dream. You think I'm silly, perhaps - crazy! But, oh, I can't help myself. Something is haunting me. It keeps hovering about me like a great bird. It won't leave me alone. I've never been to these islands before. And yet I feel dimly that I'm going back. I've never seen your face before and yet - oh, I've told you this before! Think what you like, it is true - true as death. On the raft, today, I felt most wonderfully I knew you better than I know myself.' She ended in a little gasp which floated outwards like a white bird lost and fearful, far away from land.

He forced himself to say:

'Queer fancies come upon the sea. They have no relation to life. In six weeks you will be back in England. You'll have forgotten everything. And your little strings will be pulling you gaily to smart restaurants, to the opera, to those tea-parties that you spoke about the other day. A most attractive life!'

For the first time she turned her head towards him. Her face, blurred and haunting, had a strange whiteness in which her eyes were darkly mournful.

'That's just the surface,' she said sadly. 'I don't like it, I've never liked it. Never. I'm out of place. Somehow I don't fit in.' A queer note of pain crept into her voice which quickened insensibly. 'You think I'm not grown up, that I understand nothing of life. But I do, and that's why sometimes I can't bear it, oh, that's why I must get away - away. It's all so futile, full of noise, and rushing about. No one keeps still - parties, and more parties, cocktails, dances, the kinema, dashing here and there - a non-stop life - every blank moment filled with jazz. Elissa's gramophone - she'd die without it. The one idea - how can I enjoy myself? You wouldn't believe it - there isn't even time to think. You feel that I'm a fool, that I've got no sense of proportion, no sense of humour. But I believe that you only get out of life what you put into it. And with the people I know, it's take - take all the time. It's all bright and glittering on top, but inside there's nothing real. And there's no one - no one to understand.' Inarticulately she broke off and turned her wounded face again to the sea.

For a long time he did not speak, then from his rigid body something answered.

'You are married,' he said in a low tone. 'You have your husband.'

That melancholy, surrounding her form like a delicate shadow, again enwrapped her voice as, like one repeating a lesson, she said:

'Michael is very good to me. He is fond of me. And I am very fond of him.'

The conflict within him was insupportable; words broke violently beyond the barrier of his restraint.

'Then you have no cause to complain. Your husband loves you and you love him.'

Everything retreated; the ship, the sea, the night, all suddenly were still. Her hands pressed together helplessly. She whispered:

'I hate myself for speaking like this. But you've asked me. I can't - I've never been in love. Never. I've tried - but I can't. It's as though all that was torn from me years and years ago.'

Minutes passed. Neither of them spoke. The ship resumed its steady passage, the sea its gentle swell. The sounding and sighing of the water rose passionately again across the drifting air. Stars fluttered into the limpid sky like eyes uncovered and washed clear. They were standing there together in the darkness. Nothing else mattered. Time and space dissolved. A mysterious intimacy united them. The ship no longer was a ship but some strange celestial element wherein a force, regardless of their separate bodies, bore them onwards swiftly and together. Yes, they were together; bound by some force which reason could not compass. Yet it was there, unintelligible, but real. Out of the past, out of the future, mystical, actual. His heart beat madly. A divine sweetness hovered in the air waiting to infuse his blood. Trembling, he desired to know only that she loved him. No more than that. But he was silent - it seemed a violation of that moment to speak one word. At last a bell struck faintly, far behind them. She sighed.

'I must go now. Yes, I must go.'

Silently he turned and accompanied her. Every movement that she made was precious, laden with meaning. In the alleyway they paused, then without a single glance they went to their separate cabins. He dared not look at her. They did not even say 'Good-night.'

A long hush seemed to descend upon the ship. As in that succeeding hush, when the sun had fused in clear and undefiled beauty with the sea, so now there was something lingering yet chaste within this silence. The card players had at last turned in. The vessel seemed asleep.

And then, from the upper deck, breaking the omnipresent stillness, came the rapid padding of Robert Tranter's feet. He ought to have been in his cabin. He had gone down; and gratefully Susan had seen him go. But he had come out again. It was so hot, he simply couldn't breathe. Gosh, a fellow must have some air, come what may.

And so he was on the upper deck, surrounded by the serene loveliness of - well - his Creator's works, moving, moving restlessly up and down; up and down. Gosh, it was hot! He pulled nervously at his collar. A fellow couldn't be expected to stop down a night like this. And yet he supposed he must go down; yes, sir; couldn't stop out *all* night. A wan smile slipped across his face at the reflection. He - Robert Tranter - to do that Don Juan act! Then the smile faded, leaving his expression somehow frightened.

How he wished he had seen Mrs Baynham after dinner! She had promised; yes, doggone it, she *had* promised. Not like Elissa - yes, why shouldn't he call her Elissa, it was her name wasn't it - not like Elissa to break her word. He knew she was a woman who would stick to what she said.

Gosh, how hot it was! He felt all warm and uneasy. Mopping his brow with his handkerchief he tried desperately to compose himself. But it was no use. She had said, hadn't she, that she would accept the book. After dinner. And she had gone immediately to her cabin. The inference which he had faced before rose up and struck him with redoubled violence.

She must have meant him to call at her cabin and hand in the book. Yes, indeed, she must. And why not? He swallowed quickly and mopped his brow once more. Yes, why not? It wasn't that much after ten. And she was leaving the ship tomorrow.

'Leaving the ship tomorrow.' A small whispering voice, that

might now have been his own, kept repeating the words close to his ear.

Oh, he couldn't let Elissa leave like that. No, no. She would think he'd forgotten - a mean trick. No, sir. He couldn't play a mean, shabby trick like that.

All at once he paused in his pacing. With a hypnotised, frightened look in his eyes, he turned and went slowly down the companion. Cautiously he advanced to her cabin door. Quaking, he tapped lightly, fumbled, opened the door.

She was not in her bunk but, half undressed, reclining upon the settee. The rich profusion of her scattered clothing caught his eye; but it was the sight of her - there! - that dazzled him.

'Well,' she said with perfect calmness. 'You've been a long time thinking.'

He did not speak. A loutish look crept into his frightened face. He stared at her again, her hair, her skin, the rich curve of her thigh. His throat went dry. He forgot everything. He stumbled inside the cabin. Then he closed the door.

## CHAPTER XIII

BUT night succumbed in turn to morning and all the warm beauty of the darkness drooped into the ocean like a languid hand. Daybreak came cold and harsh, trailing slow streaks across the sky inexorably. The *Aureola* - anchored off Orotava since seven bells - rode the grey swell loosely, a coil of mist about her mastheads, a thin dank vapour upon her brasswork. To leeward this same fine mist lay banked upon the beach, rising whitely across the town and falling in sullen clouds against the Peak, baffling the vision, in all but tiny shifting rifts through which a snatch of colour - a yellow roof-top, a feather of green palms, a burst of purple blossom - gleamed and vanished fitfully with evanescent, tantalising loveliness. Upon the black volcanic sand the surf obscurely pounded. And sea-birds, screaming and crying about the ship, threaded that distant booming with a note both desolate and ominous.

'By the lumpin' Jonah,' said Corcoran as he stood upon the

upper deck surveying the prospect with Mother Hemmingway. 'I'm not that sthruck on the looks of this lot. Ye can't see much, and what ye can see looks proper creepy.'

Without moving her beady eyes from the distant shore she shifted her cigar to the far corner of her mouth.

''Ark at the byby,' she ruminated contemptuously. 'Just 'ark at 'im. W'y, you juggins, wot do you know about it? W'en this mist lifts the plyce is a blyze of every 'ue. You can't move for the lovelee flowers. Remember George Lashwood's number. "Every morn I buys yeu vi'lets." Great boy was Georgie. Well, 'e wouldn't 'ave 'ad to buy 'em 'ere. Nor you neithers. They jumps up everywheres an 'its you stryte in the bleedin' eye. Not that I give a Sancta Maria w'ether they does or w'ether they don't. That's me. See.'

'I see all right,' said Jimmy gloomily. 'Ye don't give a Sancta for nobody, that's why ye've the divil's own luck at the cyards. When do we sail?'

'We'll up anchor soon enough. W'enever the hoity-toity, Gawd-Almighty passengers is took off. If you don't like the plyce the captain don't like this 'arbour. Not any too good. There's rocks you see, cocky, to leeward. Toss a biscuit on them from the stern. If you'd 'ad my early training in shipwrecks you'd sabe wot that spells. We'll be off in 'alf an 'our, I'll bet. Five o'clock we ought to myke Santa Cruz. Good old Santa! Then you won't see old 'Emmingway for dust. She'll be into 'er little Casa presto pronto. With 'er feet on the mat and 'er elbows on the tyble doin' a bit of comida. And in case you don't rumble it, that means 'avin' a proper feed. Some'ow I 'aven't enjoyed my chow lytely. Not prop'ly. Wot with that bleedin' old toff stuck opposite, you can't let yourself go at it like you'd want to. Like eatin' a fish supper outside Buckin'am Palis. Vulgu-ar, awf'lly vulgu-ar, but the stricken truth.' Suddenly she half turned and gave him a sly side-glance. 'And w'ile we're on the subject of the stricken truth. Wot d'ye think you're goin' to do when you 'it Santa?'

'Business,' he said, largely stroking his chin. 'A foine business app'intment.'

She tittered unbelievingly.

'Let's 'ave it stryte. You cawn't cod me. You and your business! You ain't no Rockefeller. I know what you done that afternoon in Las Palmas. You 'ocked your tie-pin. Yes, cocky, slipped it up the spout so's you could 'ave a little ready for to 'ave a little gyme of rummy. And now you've lost it all to 'Emmingway.'

Complacently she slapped the bag upon her bosom. 'It's 'ere. In the private syfe. And you're back agyne upon your uppers.'

His jaw dropped at her diabolic intuition; had he not been so disconcerted he might have blushed.

'What are ye talkin' about, wid yer athrocious nonsense? Haven't I got a job waitin' for me the moment I stip off the boat? Isn't it all arranged? Isn't me friend Professor Sinnott waitin' to receive me wid open arms - and take me into partnership?'

She stared at him for a full minute in acute surprise. Then she began to laugh. She laughed at first silently, containing the full savour of the joke. Then she let herself go, screaming with mirth, holding on to the rail with both hands to sustain herself.

'Sinnott,' she shrieked, 'old Bob Sinnott what keeps the little amusement plyce by the bull-ring. Oh, my Gawd! a little 'arf-baked shootin'-gallery for the bloods and a one-'orse roundabout for the bambinos. Oh, 'elp me criminy, it's rich. I knows old Sinnott. 'E's no professor. 'E's a ruin. A bleedin' ruin is Bob, I tell you. 'E's on 'is last legs. 'Is plyce is fallin' in pieces and, 'streuth, 'e's fallin' after it. And 'e's goin' - 'e's goin' to take you into partnership -' She exploded into another paroxysm.

He stared at her in incredulous dismay.

'A pack of nonsense,' he stammered, 'a pack of athrocious nonsense. Bob and me was pals in Colorado, sure, he wrote and asked me out.'

She wiped her eyes, took a voluptuous pull at her cigar.

'You wyte and see,' she declared richly. 'You just wyte and see. Old Bob Sinnott owes money all over the plyce. 'E'd clutch at any straw would Sinnott. 'Asn't got a bloomin' brass to call his own. 'E's blotto.'

Dead silence.

'Ah,' he muttered weakly, 'yer all wrong.'

She nodded her head vivaciously.

'I'm tellin' you, cocky. You're on the wrong 'orse. You'll be comin' in to see me soon. Spare a crust, ma'am - so 'elp me Gawd - and break the news to mother. But don't fret! I shan't let you starve. 'Emmingway's 'eart's in the right plyce. An ugly old bit but an 'eart of gold.' She darted a sly glance at him. ' 'Undred and Sixteen Calle de la Tuna - that's the spot. Everybody knows my plyce. Fair word and no fyvour. Say "Mother 'Emmingway's plyce," and look simple. You can ask a peliceman if you please.' She inhaled another luscious puff from her cigar. 'Don't tyke it so serious, cocky. Cheer up. You ought to be like

Mrs B'ynam. Nothin' don't knock 'er about.' She seemed actually to try to rally him. ' 'Aven't you see her? She's walking about like a cat that's had cream. And wouldn't you like to know the reason w'y?' She raised her eyebrows knowingly, then tittered with delicious relish. ' 'Aven't you noticed? Tranty don't seem to 'ave appeared this mornin'. 'Avin' a prayer-meetin' after hours was Tranty. Sleep lyte, sweet chariot. Lie low, sweet 'armonium player, if you don't want to fyce the music.'

Corcoran stared at her with corrugated, distrustful brows.

'Can't you let be?' he said at last - still disconsolate. 'You're always thinkin' the worst of somebody.'

'The worst,' she burst out indignantly. 'Didn't I see 'im standin' like a lost sheep at 'er cabin door, bleatin' 'is 'oly 'ead off to be took in? Didn't I watch 'im -' She stopped short, her eyes drawn suddenly to the figure of Susan Tranter approaching from beyond the chart-room.

'Have you seen Dr Leith?' asked Susan.

'No,' replied Mother Hemmingway with unctuous effusion. 'We 'aven't see 'im, dearie. We just been standin' 'ere discussin' the weather and the flowers and wot not. The be-utiful roses wot bloom in the spring, tra la la. That's gospel, ask Rockefeller 'ere if it ain't. But we 'aven't seen nothin' of the medico. 'E's in 'is cabin like as not. Wot did you want 'im for, dearie?'

'It's not important,' answered Susan quite cheerfully. 'Not so very important.'

'Your brother's not been took bad I 'ope?' asked Mother Hemmingway tenderly. 'Nothing's upset 'im I do 'ope and pray.'

'He does seem rather off colour,' said Susan. 'But it's nothing really.'

'Ah,' breathed the Hemmingway softly. 'P'raps a touch of hindigestion, dearie. P'raps 'e's 'ad a troubled night.'

A silence fell; then, as though to ease that stillness, a faint creaking of oars rose into the captive air, and out of the mist a longboat dimly took form. Manned by eight men who pulled abreast in pairs, standing barefooted in the stern, it drew slowly towards the *Aureola*.

'Here's the boat,' said Jimmy suddenly. 'They'll be goin' ashore now, the three that's for Orotava.'

'And jolly good luck to the goin',' cried Mother Hemmingway, sending the end of her cigar hissing to the water. 'I didn't feel like weepin' w'en they said good-bye to us at breakfast. The little lydy is the proper article, that I will admit. Stryte. "Mary, Mary, quite contrary, 'ow does your garden grow?" You couldn't 'elp but tyke to 'er. But them two others! - well! 'uman nature's 'uman nature, but swipe me if you don't 'ave to draw the line somewheres.'

Again a silence fell whilst, with varying emotions, the three stared at the oncoming boat. And upon the deck below, through his open cabin door, Harvey Leith stared at that boat too. His eyes, dark and fixed, seemed bound not to the little, dancing boat but to some distant inexorable thought. His face, beneath its recent stain of sun-burn, had a curious pallor. All his faculties felt numb: his mind, with a sort of dumb wonder, seemed to contemplate detachedly this figure of himself, so alien - un-recognisable.

The boat drew closer, impelled by rhythmic movements of the heavy sweeps: nearer - and nearer still; then finally it slipped from sight beneath the counter of the *Aureola*'s stern. Now it would be alongside.

His heart turned heavily within him; the mist was void now, encircling him transparently with a fume of desolation; little beads of moisture dropped from the lintel of the door like tears.

Dully he heard the scrape of baggage being heaved, the stamp of feet, the sound of voices; but it all came to him vaguely, without substance or shape. Suddenly he raised his head. She was there, Mary, standing in the alley-way, dressed for departure, her dark eyes upon him seriously, her face curiously intent and small.

'I'm going then,' she said in a voice which barely seemed to reach him.

He stared at her in a dream. She was going.

'I said good-bye - to you all - at breakfast.'

'There wasn't any need, I know that. But I came. The boat's alongside.'

He rose.

'Yes, I saw it come.' He broke off, looked stiffly, unreasonably at his watch. His hands were trembling.

'It's so fantastic going off in this drizzle,' she said in that same small voice. 'Everything seems queer. But tomorrow - I suppose the sun will come again. It makes a difference, doesn't it?'

'Yes, it makes a difference.'

They looked at each other. Her eyes were shining now with a startled, mournful lustre, her cheeks seemed pinched; her figure held a white fragility.

And across his vision flashed the memory of that swallow which

94

had fluttered in weariness about the deck. She seemed suddenly to him like that tired little bird.

'Once you are on shore you will feel more settled,' he said resolutely. 'I know you are sad at leaving the ship.'

'Of course.' She tried to smile but instead she sighed, as from a catching at her heart. A large tear welled up beneath her lashes and rolled slowly down her cheek. 'Don't mind that,' she said indistinctly. 'It's nothing, really. Quite often I can't help making a fool of myself.'

'Are you all right?'

'Oh, yes,' she gasped. 'I really am. Don't bother about that.'

With head lowered and averted, as a startled bird might nestle for sanctuary upon its own breast, she stood motionless. Suddenly she held out her hand.

'Well -'

He took her hand; it was warm and small; his heart constricted with unbelievable pain. He said thickly:

'I'm not coming to the boat.'

'No - don't come down.'

The anguish in his heart drove him unnecessarily to explain:

'The others - they will be there.'

'Yes.'

'So this - this really is good-bye.'

She echoed the last word as though it terrified her; stood again for a second motionless and forlorn; then all the desolation of that hollow air rose up and ravaged him. No longer was her hand in his; no longer did her glistening eyes swim hauntingly before him. She was gone.

He sat down stiffly upon the settee and let his head sink upon his hand as though he could not face the day. He did not see the longboat as it stole from the ship and slid back towards the misty shore. Never before had he felt so terribly alone. He had passed his life in complete oblivion of his peculiar solitary state; but now, as though unleashed, those years of isolation swept over him in one sustained intolerable pang. He became aware of himself as a harsh, outlandish figure; without the gift of friendship; without the power to make himself beloved. Wrenched from his work, outcast upon this ship by destiny, he had been borne towards strange shores where for an instant he had stood as upon a threshold, his soul aquiver with wonder and delight. But now the wonder was dead, the quick delight dispelled, and in this ship - the instrument and symbol of his destiny - he was returning, moving backwards drearily the way that he had come. A frightful surging bitterness tore at his throat. Overhead the stamp of feet bore down upon him through the deck, and rasping across his ears came the shout of orders, the heavy straining of the winch as it coiled the anchor cable relentlessly upon its drum. But he heard nothing as he sat there, his wounded eyes filled with a fatal sadness, staring straight in front of him.

The rain increased, pouring dankly through the grey and humid air, dripping mournfully from the sodden shrouds. And the wind swept up inscrutably from the ocean, prying inshore with sudden clamouring gusts, capping the swell with tiny, snapping crests.

The sea-birds screamed and cried: circling and dipping; circling and dipping; again, again, all lost and desolate. Desolation hung from the curtained sky; and something lonely and forsaken. Tomorrow the sun might blaze again, and airs dance lightly over the vivid earth; but now, as the *Aureola* pounded her bows into the heavy outer seas, there was only sadness - and a sense of sad frustration. Pounding her bows into those heavy seas - away, away.


## CHAPTER XIV

YET soon the rain was left behind.

The short passage to Santa Cruz was over, the *Aureola* made fast in sunshine against the curving mole.

One last glance at the town which lay like a brilliant flower upon the breast of the mountains and Susan ran into her brother's cabin.

'We're there, Robbie! There at last!' She felt uplifted; caught by the excitement of arrival; still filled by relief at Elissa's departure. Then, turning from the door, suddenly she paused.

With his back towards her, he was bent over a trunk fumbling with the straps, his air so inconclusive he might that moment have risen hastily in pretext of occupation.

Her eyes widened in surprise; his packing was inevitably her affair.

'Why,' she exclaimed, 'have I forgotten something after all?'

'This buckle,' he mumbled, without lifting his head. 'I was tightening it. Don't seem to grip like it ought.'

She did not reply, but stood watching him with queer intentness as he tugged unconvincingly at the strap. At last he rose and, flushed from his exertion, he faced her.

'Do you feel better now?' she asked slowly.

'Yes.'

'I was kind of worried about you this morning,' she persisted doubtfully. 'I had a mind to ask Dr Leith to see you.'

The colour on his brow deepened.

'No, no,' he declared hurriedly. 'I can't - I don't want to see him.'

'What's the matter then, Robbie?' Questioningly she entreated him to meet her gaze.

But he would not; instead, he turned away and looked out of the port.

'There's nothing the matter. Nothing.'

There was silence.

'Well,' she said at length, with a sudden briskness, 'I thought you might have been on deck with me to see us come in. It's a big place. I guess you'll like it. I had a glimpse of Laguna far up on the hill, like it was set half-way to the sky. And a terrible pretty place it is. Green valleys and woods, plantations too, and lots of palms. I never knew palms could grow so big. A real foreign place. I've got the feeling it's going to mean something for us, Robbie. Just gripped me the minute I set eyes on it. Something - oh, something important. That's how it felt to me. Some have gone ashore already,' she ran on. 'That Hemmingway woman, she was off like smoke. Two girls - believe me they had some queer style! - met her on the jetty, hung themselves around her neck. Gosh, it was a scene. Hardly the thing, I do declare.' She paused. 'And Mr Corcoran's gone off too, all dressed up in a new bow tie. He looked swell, but hardly took good-bye. Kind of in a hurry.' Again she paused. 'And now I guess it's time for us to get a hurry on as well.'

Unresponsive, he kept his gaze fixed through the port.

'When does Mr Rodgers come?'

'The minute the boat docked he'd arranged to meet us. So they said at Arucas. Don't you remember, Rob? We ought to go and take good-bye of Captain Renton right now. He's been downright kind.' She paused. 'I guess he had his doubts about us at the start. I heard him say missionaries weren't in his line. Kind of mistrusted us for sure. But I reckon we've showed him a bit different.'

He made a restive movement with his hands and involuntarily swung round, his lips working, his nostrils dilated like the nostrils of a nervous horse.

'Susan,' he exclaimed; and broke off.

'Well?'

'Can't you see,' he cried almost hysterically. 'Can't you see how I - how I - oh, can't you see how I am?'

Her steady eyes would not leave his face; she took his hand and pressed it between her palms.

'I do understand, Robbie. And oh, my dear, I do respect you for it.'

Dumbfounded, he echoed:

'Respect me?'

'And why not?' she answered vehemently. 'You couldn't deceive me. I do see that you're unhappy. God knows I've seen the whole thing from the beginning. You've had to fight, Robbie, and if the fight has been dearly won, then the merit of the victory is greater.'

'But, Susan -' he whimpered.

'I know how you feel,' she broke in quickly, 'your sensitiveness. Yes, yes. It was something you've never had to face before. I know she was beautiful. But she was bad, Robbie - oh, downright bad. If you'd been weak she would have spoiled everything - oh, your whole life. Couldn't you feel how uneasy I was? I prayed and prayed that you'd be all right. Well! She's gone now - and don't I just thank God we've seen the last of her.'

He stared at her, stupefied, his mouth open, his large eyes glistening and full.

'Remember,' she said in a low, reassuring voice, 'He Himself was tempted, Robert. That thought should take the bitterness from your heart.'

A sort of wail broke from between his lips; incoherent words trembled upon his tongue. Hysterically, as with an exaltation of remorse, he gathered himself to speak when suddenly there came a knock upon the door. The sound, peremptory and sharp, split like a pistol-shot across the air. Both turned as the door swung open and a man stepped in.

He was tall, fair-haired, and spectacled, with a bony, dried-up frame which made his shoulders seem too high and his white drill suit too large. His air was casual - the composure of complete pre-knowledge - but a bleakness about his mouth and a sombre glint within his eye betrayed some secret force which dwelt within him like smouldering fire. For a moment the weight of his scrutiny rested upon them; then he advanced a hand which was dry and hard, with a furze of red hairs upon its back.

'You're on time,' he declared calmly, in a harsh, twanging voice, as though they had arrived for lunch in some cross-river ferry-boat. 'And I'll say you're welcome. Got your traps fixed? My buggy's standin' waitin' ready on the pier.'

'Well,' said Susan with a little gasp. 'It must be - it's Mr Rodgers, isn't it?'

He nodded his head in acrid acquiescence.

'Aaron Rodgers is my name. Planter from James River way. Threw it down when the blight come on. Three years now I've been on this godless island. Raisin' bananas, lucerne, and citron. Glad to give you hospitality till you get your home set.' His eye, rising swiftly, lit sombrely upon Tranter.

'Pleases me well - your comin' here, brother. This place is a sink. Choked and festerin' with black godless ignorance.'

Under that darting glance Tranter flinched and wilted; the ready colour flooded his cheeks once more.

'Not more pleased than we are, sir,' he mumbled, as though shielding himself. 'Powerful glad to meet you.'

'The time is ripe,' returned the other inscrutably. 'If you can't lead souls to salvation now, then you can leave them to rot in hell.' He paused, and with a grim, dramatic relish bit out the words: 'You've walked in on the worst sickness that's struck this place for years. Yellow fever. Bad. Rank, tearin' bad. From Africa they say it come over, carried on a Liberian tramp-steamer. But to my mind it is a visitation. No more, no less.'

'We did hear a word of it,' said Susan, 'but we understood it was very slight.'

'Slight,' he echoed, with scathing contempt. 'It's bad - poisonous bad. They're tryin' to hush it up. But, as God's my Maker and my Judge, they've gotten a mighty big song to hush.'

Susan compressed her lips.

'Is it in Laguna, the outbreak?' she asked seriously.

'It's all over the upper side,' he answered acidly. 'They got their hands full to keep it out of Santa Cruz. So full they ain't got a proper thought for us. And more - the pest is travellin' west. They got it on the other islands too. Started way down in

Las Palmas last week, they tell me. But Laguna is the centre. There's an estate on the town outskirts stuck right by my place. Casa de los Cisnes. Belongs by an old half-wit Spanish dame.' A cold note of bitterness crept into his voice. 'She's what they call a marquesa. Can you beat it! But blue blood don't keep her place together. It's all to bits. Fanegads of prime land scorched up and showing nothing but weed. Short of water she is. And she won't get none while I'm about. Well, that's where the hotbed is. She's lost half her peons - the few poor trash she did have. The graveyard's full.'

A short silence followed these chilling words; then Robert drew a deep breath, charging himself, it seemed, with lush enthusiasm.

'Well,' he declared, 'there's plenty work for us to do. Let's go to it.' His voice was deep, but there was pathos in its depth, and in its breaking resonance an emotion which rang strangely false.

'C'mon then,' said Rodgers shortly. 'Get your traps ashore.' And with an air of stern gravity he led the way out of the cabin into the sunshine, whose hard brilliance now held something lifeless yet formidable. But now Robert was by no means lifeless. His indecision of a moment ago was gone; his manner, under Rodgers's flinty eye, infused with nervous zeal. He who usually surveyed her activities with an indulgent aloofness immediately thrust Susan aside and began to fuss about the baggage.

She stood watching, pulling on her gloves - despite the heat she would have felt undressed to set foot on land without those gloves - then, at a thought, she turned away slowly and mounted to the upper deck.

Outside the chart-room she encountered Renton. It was on her tongue to say: 'I've come to say good-bye,' when he exclaimed curtly:

'I've been looking for you.' His face had a heated, worried look; in his hand he rustled a sheaf of papers. He paused, then, thrusting out his chin, went on: 'It's about this fever business. I'm afraid there's more in it than we knew of. I hear they've got it pretty bad up Laguna way. Now you don't want to get mixed up in that show. Stay down in Santa Cruz till the mischief's over. Stay on the ship another day if you wish - till you get fixed somewhere. We don't sail till tomorrow.'

A faint smile hovered upon her lips.

'I'm not scared, captain. And haven't they got it in Santa Cruz as well? In Las Palmas, too, for that matter. Mr Rodgers just told us. Didn't we ought to have stopped on the ship there if it's as bad as all that?'

He said something under his breath and his face turned a dull red. The tincture of the martinet which infused his nature made him detest to shift his ground.

'My advices were at fault,' he answered shortly. 'And the agent is going to hear about it. The thing is more serious than I was told. Now I have positive information. You'd better take my suggestion. Stay down in Santa Cruz. There it's quite moderately clear. It'll suit you well enough for the time being. No point in shoving yourself into danger. Only common sense.'

She shook her head, said slowly:

'Sometimes things don't work out best by common sense.'

He made a chafing movement with his papers.

'You will go then?'

'Yes.'

Studying her more carefully, his testy expression altered. He held out his hand, fixed her with a less frosty eye.

'Good luck, then,' he said. 'Keep out of the night air. And don't get nervous.'

A feeling of his regard warmed her. The shadowy smile returned.

'I reckon I'm not the nervous kind,' she said. And, turning, she moved away. She stepped down the companion. Then, as she passed into the starboard alley-way, the light suddenly quivered in her eyes. Advancing towards her was Harvey Leith. They met face to face in the middle of the passage and, with a sort of stupid numbness, she did not make way. He was obliged to stop. For a full ten seconds silence dangled disjointedly between them; then, driven by confusion, she blurted out:

'We're going now. I've just been taking good-bye of the captain.'

He stared at her so fixedly his features were like a mask; it seemed to her that all the bitterness of the early days of their acquaintance was back, so lifeless was his face, his eyes so cold.

'Well,' he said at last. 'Good-bye.'

Instantly she crimsoned, feeling with fresh intensity his deadly power to wound her. And immediately, too, she was confronted by the fact that she was leaving him, that she would never again see him, a fact hitherto so little realised it struck her now like sudden fear.

'And now perhaps you'll let me pass,' he said wearily, 'or shall we sing one last hymn together?'

'Wait,' she cried out. 'Don't go yet. Don't go.' And, driven by the uncontrollable desire to detain him, she thrust her hand forward and held his sleeve.

The feel of his forearm beneath the thin cloth sent a shiver along her skin, which ran shamefully into her blood.

'Will you promise - promise me something before I go?' She stammered out the words, hardly conscious of what she did.

'Why should I promise? I have no obligation to you.'

'Not to me,' she gasped, 'but to yourself. Oh, I'm not thinking about anyone but you.'

He stared fixedly at her plain, upturned face now twitching with her emotion.

'It hurts me,' she went on quite wildly, 'to see how you neglect yourself. Today you haven't been down for a single meal. You eat nothing. Oh, you don't take care of yourself.' Incoherently she broke off, her eyes glistening towards him; then, with a rush of fresh courage, she went on, her tone abandoned, beseeching: 'I know I'm making a fool of myself. But I don't care. I know you hate me. But that won't stop me. There's something about you that makes me burn to help you. I'd put all my trust in you. I know you can do great things. And oh, you've suffered so much. I don't want you to suffer any more. I don't, I tell you. I can't bear that you should suffer. Can't bear it. Oh, please, please let me think that you'll be careful of yourself. Let me know that and I'll - I'll go away happy.' Her hand slipped down his sleeve; convulsively she pressed her fingers into his palm.

'Don't do that,' he cried instantly, recoiling from that tremulous touch as though he had been stung.

'I know, I know,' she cried with a jealous pang. 'I know you're in love with her. Don't think I haven't seen it. Yet even that can't stop me. She can't feel for you the way I do. And she's gone, you see, just as I'll be gone. But my thoughts will go on. On and on. You can't escape them. You can't, I tell you. I'll pray for you. Yes, I'll serve you through my prayers.'

There was a frightful pause filled by her loud and quickened breathing.

'Please don't,' he said in a low painful voice. 'You are upsetting yourself. And all - all for nothing.'

The ring of futility echoing through his tone seemed to goad her; but as she made to speak a voice behind arrested her abruptly.

'We're ready now. All waiting for you.'

It was Rodgers, armed with his level, penetrating stare; and beside him was her brother.

She stood stock-still; then her hand fell back with a gesture of hopelessness. For an instant her eyes strained towards him; then, without another word, she turned; with lowered head she began to walk down the deck.

'Well -' said Tranter indecisively. He stammered his good-bye, offered his hand to Harvey. Gone now was the old effusive, manly grip; the hand was flabby, cold as a fish's tail. Rodgers said nothing. His look encompassed Harvey with a cold disfavour, then he turned his angular back and stalked off.

Harvey stood motionless, his face set and quite expressionless. Thus he watched them cross the gang-plank and enter the waiting conveyance. There was a jingle of harness; a stamp of hoofs; a spurt of white dust. Still motionless, he saw them drive off slowly to Laguna. To Laguna, where there was yellow fever.

## CHAPTER XV

HE alone of all the passengers remained upon the ship, which lay quiescent in a queer silence - like the rifled silence of a hurriedly deserted house. Alone! It was a dreadful word; a word which fastened on to him. He who had craved solitude, who had always been sufficient to himself, was now riven by the pangs of loneliness.

Seated in his cabin with a book upon his knee, he made pretence of reading. But the print was blurred, the words meaningless. A strange, chaotic retrospect of all his life tormented him. Useless - quite useless! The sense of his own inadequacy grew upon him. The incident which had terminated his career at the hospital presented itself suddenly in altered form. He began dimly to be sorry, not for himself, but for those three who had died. Poor devils, he thought, they didn't have a chance.

Impatiently he flung the book upon the bunk, sat staring for a long time at nothing. Then there was a knock, the door opened, and Trout came in, bearing the familiar hot-water can.

Harvey followed the movements of the steward as he set

down the can and silently touched the cabin to order. Then a singular impulse caught him. He took out his pocket-book, extracted a note, offered it to the steward.

'Take this,' he said, 'for looking after a damned ungrateful swine.'

Trout made a delicate gesture of distress.

'No, sir. No, indeed. It's been a pleasure. Time enough when we get back.'

'Take it,' said Harvey roughly.

The steward took it; stood for a second disconcerted; then scraped himself out with a murmur of thanks.

Why, thought Harvey, did I do that? He had begun by cursing Trout; now with a rush of sickly sentiment he had given him, quite inopportunely, a pound. It was too enigmatical for him to fathom. He gave it up. Then his eye was caught by the brass can standing by his washstand; and the prospect of a solitary dinner so suggested filled him with dismay. When the ship was docked, Renton dined unfailingly in his cabin; Corcoran - yes, even Corcoran - had left him; without thought, apparently, of return. He would be alone, alone. Again the melancholy word sank into him.

He had been so desperately self-confident in the past, clenching his fists in the face of friendship, scorning all sentiment with a scathing final wisdom. And now he had learned that his wisdom was not final.

Why had he learned? Love! Six months ago that word would have roused him to derisive laughter; a contemptuous jibe at its inanity. But now he neither laughed nor jibed. He thought of Mary.

Was he never to see her again?

He longed to see her. She had said once, in her inarticulate way, that life was governed by strange and subtle undercurrents beyond the power of reason. At the thought, that strange fatalism which had been born within him quivered with a breath of trembling hope. Through all his life he had expressed himself in terms of hard, incisive fact. But now dimly he was conscious of another force, higher, more intimate than reason. . . .

He sighed heavily, stood up and looked out of the window. Work had ceased along the harbour, but it was still clear. Beyond the breastwork of the mole the roof-tops of the town rose up, one upon the shoulders of another. They were silent yet clamorous. They seemed to beckon. Then, through his brooding, suddenly an overpowering restlessness rose up in him. I can't stay on board, he thought. I simply cannot stay.

It all happened in a moment: the thought merging to decision. Seizing his hat, he swung out of the cabin and made for the quay.

The air was cool; his hurrying steps slackened to a quieter pace; he gained the end of the mole, crossed the road beyond the customs, and entered the Plaza. And there he paused.

The shops were closed; the glittering front of the hotel repelled him; he was surrounded by strangers. What was there for him to do? Around him in the square, beneath the tufted palms, people were strolling up and down. The men walked separately from the women: two orderly promenading streams. There was neither excitement nor commotion; simply an indolent enjoyment of the evening air. The presence of disease within the town made no ruffle upon the surface of its placid life. That life went on, languid and untroubled; today was here, tomorrow could remain; it was sublime philosophy. For a moment Harvey stood watching, then abruptly moved away. Still that restlessness was in his blood. He wandered to the left, out of the main thoroughfare, away from the lights, into a network of narrow streets, where at the turn of an alley an ancient building loomed before him. It was the cathedral, and on a sudden impulse he entered. A service apparently had finished; the scent of wax and incense hung in the air; some women knelt before the central altar, their figures bowed and motionless, steeped in the blue dimness of the place. He stood very still, taken by a strange wonder. He seemed to see the church as it had been years and years ago; heard almost with awe an echoing of all those vanished footsteps; as from a flaming torch the tang of burning cedar came to him. He moved slowly beneath the invisible nave like one who vainly seeks for something - perhaps for peace. Stopping now here, now there, he stared at the broidered vestments, the relics, the thigh-bone of Pope Clement, the cross planted by the Conquistadores. And then he came upon the flags. Before him, in their glazed case, they limply hung, two ensigns taken from Nelson in the assault upon the town. He looked at the flags, thinking of the hands which long ago had touched them. And he had suddenly a curious desire to feel the texture of the tattered stuff. All at once his fingers tingled; across his mind there came a singular sense of pain. And yet it was not pain. A queer emotion, indefinable, evoked by the vision of these flags: a flash of retrospect and melancholy mingling in one swift pang. There was something: then it was gone. He could not place that odd sensation; its source was inexplicable; but it disturbed him none the less, and left him with a hollow sadness.

Still distressed that such emotion could be wrung from him, he turned away, came out of the cathedral, stood indecisively upon the worn steps. Now it was quite dark. From the sea a flashing beam swung round, illuminating his figure for an instant with brilliant light. It was like his thought, that unexpected flash: an instant's light, then plunging back to obscurity.

Behind him lay the shadows of the church. And before him - what? He came down the steps, struck off at random along the water-front. His loneliness was pressing upon him like a curse. And again he was assailed by the desire to escape. He thought: What has come over me? If I don't get away from myself I shall go mad. And, on the impulse, he crossed the cobbled street and turned into a lighted café which stood beside an old lumber-strewn ship-chandler's yard.

It was a poor place, a common wine-shop, low browed, half sunk beneath the level of the street. The floor was of stone, the tables of unvarnished wood. Above, an oil lamp swung from a central chain. Behind the bar a young Spaniard stood in his shirt-sleeves, eating his supper of black bread and olives. From time to time he turned his head to spit the stones across his shoulder: the turning of the head was a delicate concession to politeness. Upon the wooden benches a scattering of customers were seated, all men, all of the class that hangs about a water-front. They looked curiously at Harvey as he seated himself at a table. And he looked back at them. An odd sensation of surprise took him that he should be here; he was confused almost by the transit of his own being from the ship to the cathedral; from the cathedral to the tavern. But had any man the right to question his pre-appointed presence in time and space? It was no mere matter of volition; nor yet of chance. No mingling of circumstances, no splitting of the seconds through infinity, could have brought him to this tavern at this hour. It was his destiny. He felt this with absurdly positive conviction.

The waiter brought him a glass of wine, scuffling his flat feet, which were cased in enormous canvas shoes. Flapping the table clean of slops with a dirty cotton cloth, he laid down the glass, received the money as though it were an insult, and returned to his olives.

Harvey sat with his head bowed forward, looking at the rich brown wine. Then he picked up his glass and emptied it. There was no fear - that stupid craving of the past was gone. That, too, came over him with absolute conviction. How had he ever thought there was escape that way? Not now! His condition now was different; he, himself, had altered beyond all recognition.

He sighed inaudibly and lifted his eyes, which were arrested by an unexpected sight. A man was standing in the doorway. He stood there for a moment looking behind him. Then, ducking his head beneath the lintel, he stepped in. It was Corcoran.

At once he saw Harvey. The two stared at each other, then Corcoran came over, flung himself down at the table, and wiped his brow. His usual air of plausible equanimity was gone; he looked sadly out of humour; his face was dusty, seamed by rivulets of sweat - as though lately he had been in a hurry. Without a word to Harvey, he bluntly ordered a drink, thrust his handkerchief into his pocket, edged his chair to where he could view the door. The moment it arrived he took a long pull at his glass, wiped his lips with the back of his hand; then, as at an afterthought, he drank again, drew a long breath, and groaned. At last he smiled; but it was a doubtful smile, charged with the remnants of acute vexation.

'It's well met,' he declared with a shake of his head. 'But, faith, if I hadn't the lucky pair of heels on me, divil the meetin' this side of creation.'

'What is it?' Harvey asked.

'What is it?' Corcoran groaned. 'It's a painful business altogether. And 'tis all Bob Sinnott's fault to blame, though maybe I shouldn't be sayin' it, God rest his soul, now that he's dead and gone.'

Harvey stared at him in silence. A moment ago his thoughts had echoed in the major key of life; and in his ears had rung a prophecy of destiny. He had seen dimly a vision, felt bearing down upon him a message from the past. And here he was confronted by the ubiquitous Irishman with his fantastic plaint of a Sinnott 'dead and gone'. Oh, was there no sense of values in life? Except this sense of ludicrous anticlimax!

He moved restlessly; conquered a sigh; then said at length:

'Is that the man you call the Professor?'

' 'Tis the same,' cried Jimmy, much upset. 'Him that brung me out here, writin' and askin' me to join him; bustin' wid promises an' hivin knows what - Holy Mother pardon him in purgatory.

An amusement-ground outside the bull-ring, a kind of a fair ye'd call it - that's what he had - they're strong on sich places out in them parts. Or so he told, God forgive him. And Bob had followed the big top all his life, ye see. But I wished ye'd see this place! By the powers, it's a crooked deal that he was afther handin' me, or I'm far cheated. I can't get over it - to think that Bob would do me down.'

'What do you mean?'

Jimmy made an anguished gesture with his arm.

'Sure, Bob must have been on the slide when he wrote the letter. Up to eyes in throuble and over the ears in debt. And he'd borrowed money on the tale of me comin' out to join him. Jumpin' Janus! Can ye think of a better one than that? There was never a man like the Professor for puttin' across the tale.'

'You'd never promised to put money in his business?'

Corcoran was taken with a prolonged fit of coughing - a dreadful wheezy bout which turned his face quite red.

At last, looking up sheepishly, he said:

'Ah! what are ye talkin' about?'

Dead silence.

'I see,' said Harvey ironically. 'Well, if the man's dead, that's the end of it.'

'Sure and he's dead all right,' cried Jimmy. 'He went down wid this blessed fever that's in the town. If he'd only died decent like a month or two ago 'twouldn't have been so bad. But to snuff out on me the very day before I come. Faith, it's the height of bad manners.' His indignation was so tremendous that, remembering those early protestations of 'the grand business partnership' and the 'Professor's' unimpeachable attainments, Harvey had to smile. He said:

'You'll have to come back on the ship with me. Is that what's worrying you?'

'Ah, I'm not worried at all. Faith, I'm not the worryin' kind. I'm just sort of annoyed at the way things has wint wid me.'

'You mean the way things have gone with Sinnott.'

'Wid me, I said,' Corcoran declared resentfully. 'I told ye Bob owed a pocket of money. And I wished you'd seen the dago he owed it on. He was there, if ye please, with a gang of them yellow boys when I got to Bob's place, waitin' for me, primed wid the wire I'd sent from Las Palmas - and, well, a letter or two of me own besides. They come at me like I was Croysus, tryin' to make out I was responsible for what Bob had borrowed. Me, if ye please, that's got me own financial difficulties. Faith, they come at me like a pack of boar-hounds. And, by the powers, they'd have scragged me if I hadn't took a wise discretion for me motto.' He drew a long breath, reached for his glass, raised it to his lips, and added: 'But here I am, ye see, sound as a drum. It's a cliver man that gets the better of the argument with Jimmy C.'

Complacency began to flow into him again when suddenly he broke off; his jaw dropped; he set down the glass untasted.

Three men stood on the threshold of the tavern. They looked round without apparent interest; they looked everywhere but at Corcoran; then with a careful air they came in and arranged themselves at the table by the door.

'Death and the divil,' Jimmy muttered under his breath.

Harvey slewed round and gazed at the three men. They were an ill-looking group. One of them, who was short and powerfully built, with a tight drawn face, lit a cigarette and flicked the match insolently across the room. The other two loafed back on the bench with an air both insolent and languid, as if for the present they were content to watch. The taller had on a *manto* against the evening's chill, and now he threw it off his shoulders with a swaggering conceit. The third man wore a dirty white sweater, burst canvas shoes, and a mangy peaked cap which drooped across his face like a broken wing.

Meanwhile the waiter had hurried over with extreme despatch. And with a deference equally significant he executed the order, brought to the table a bottle of wine. He uncorked the bottle, cleaned the glasses obsequiously upon his apron, poured out the wine; then he stood with lowered head whilst the thick-set man harangued him. He had a violent voice, the short man, and he spoke rapidly, with much thumb-pointing and derisive exclamation. Finally the waiter nodded his head, came over to Corcoran.

'El Brazo,' he said, keeping his eyes averted, 'El Brazo say you will pay.'

'Pay?'

The waiter turned to the group by the door for support; sustained by much nodding of the head from the three he said:

'El Brazo says you will pay for the wine.'

Corcoran sat upright, threw out his chest; the heated, angry look flew back to his face; he elbowed the air like he was pressing forward in a crowd.

'So they think I'm buyin' the company,' he muttered; and to the waiter, but so loudly that all could hear: 'Tell them I'll pay none. Tell them I'll see them in fire and brimstone first.'

Harvey interposed.

Everyone in the place was sitting up and taking notice. He felt disturbance brewing in the air.

'Don't be a fool,' he said sharply, 'you don't want a row in here.'

'Row be damned!' cried Jimmy. 'I've had enough of them dagos!' His blood was up. He buttoned his coat, corrugated his brow at the waiter. 'Tell Brazo from me that he's a dirty yellow hound. Sabe? Tell him dirty, yellow, and a hound. Tell him further that I don't like his face. And tell him finally that he won't get one red peseta out of me.'

The waiter shrugged his shoulders and looked away.

'Perhaps you like to tell. El Brazo says you owe money. El Brazo is matador. He has killed many bulls.'

'He has that,' said Jimmy, 'and then some more.'

'Yes,' said the waiter in mimicry. 'Some more.'

Meanwhile the short man had arisen. Followed by his friends, he came over, lounging, one hand thrust behind his coat. On his face was a wicked look.

'So,' he said, sneering. 'You are going to pay me for what your partner has appropriated. From me, El Brazo, noted for retirement and courage, he has appropriated one hundred pesetas. Yes, you are going to pay me?'

A tension fell on the room; a sigh of bated expectation went up. Harvey rose; so, too, with a bellicose clatter of his chair, did Corcoran.

'Get away,' he cried, thrusting forward his chin, 'or I'll hit ye where ye belong.'

Instantly the other made a movement with his arm. But Corcoran was first. His enormous fist caught El Brazo full on the chin. The crack of the blow echoed in the room, and El Brazo retired with courage upon the floor. As he toppled, a look of vague surprise was in his eyes! then he hit the hard stone surface and was forgotten. Instantly there was uproar; everybody shouted and surged forward. The waiter leaped over the bar; someone flung a bottle. And Harvey made with Corcoran for the door.

They were half-way out when suddenly, through an opening in the scuffle, the long man who was El Brazo's companion flung a knife. It all happened in a flash. Harvey saw the gleam, then the knife was quivering in Jimmy's arm. He pushed forward, slipped, then someone swung a chair and hit him hard over the head. Everything went dark. He had a stupid sense of stamping, shouting people pressing round, of Corcoran dragging him savagely through the crowd. He felt the cool night air. And, inexplicably, through his whirling mind, he had an instant's comprehension. He had been right. Not chance! But in the pattern of it all - the antic pattern of his fate. Dimly he felt Corcoran supporting him down the street. Then everything went black again.

## CHAPTER XVI

HARVEY opened his eyes. He was on a red plush sofa in a small room that smelt warmly of hot coffee, onions, and tobacco smoke. His neck was painfully stiff and his head ached dizzily. Lying quite still he let the room swim out of the haze into some definite perspective. Objects grew clearer. Upon the mantelpiece stood a green marble clock, a box of cigars, two china spaniels with fawn ears and fixed ingratiating smiles, and, above, a needlework text: 'God bless our happy home.' The walls, papered in painful maroon, were hung with violet gilt-framed art: Ormonde winning the Derby; a polychrome Madonna with two attendant seraphs; a nautical gentleman with a beard, in oils; an alluring photogravure of a lady all naked, smiling and unashamed.

He stopped looking. Surely he was dreaming: it was too awful to be real.

But he was not dreaming. Clear sunlight flooded the room through the tightly shut window. It was morning. Cautiously he moved his head. There, at the littered breakfast-table, her short legs crossed, her lips daintily enclosing a cigar, her beady eyes busy with a newspaper, sat Mother Hemmingway.

Harvey stared at her, moistened his lips, then at last he exclaimed:

'How did I get here?'

She did not look up; went on luxuriously with her paper and cigar. But in a moment, with inimitable malice, she reflected:

'So you've woke up, byby dear. 'Ad a nice shut-eye?' And she crackled the paper to another column as though her interest lay entirely upon the printed page. 'I do 'ope and pray you've slept proper and comodo. If you 'aven't, we'll complyne. Stryte, we'll complyne to the management. W'ich is me.'

He raised his hand to his head, felt it carefully. Immediately, as though she had awaited the action, she swung round and grinned at him.

'Well, well,' she declared with relish. 'Does it 'urt? Did a cruel man 'it 'im? Shyme, oh, shyme indeed. W'y can't people be polite and well-be'aved w'en they meet a hexquisitely mannered gen'leman like yourself?'

His look still dwelled upon her.

'How did I get here?'

' 'Andsome Jimmy brought you. Any port in a storm. See the idea. And a fine 'igh-tiddley-'ighty 'e made of it. Spoiled the evening's tryde and bled shockin' all over my drawin-'room carpet. Lucky it's plum shyde. 'Ere! 'ave some breakfast.' She made a sudden movement towards the table. 'Sit in and 'ave your pick. W'y I does it I don't know. I'll wyke up with a pair of wings some d'y - so 'elp my bleedin' 'eart.'

'Where is Corcoran?' he asked.

' 'E's all right. Right as ryne, 'e is. Downstairs in bed. Nothing but a sham. 'Is arm's scratched, that's all. 'Ad his breakfast a 'our ago. Ate about a pound of 'am, too, the greedy 'og.'

Harvey sighed and stood up. Then, gingerly, he advanced to the window and looked out. The room was high, and before him, across the quiet street, lay the water-front, the bay, the jutting mole on which his gaze, moving uneasily, was suddenly arrested.

For a long time he stared at the gap where yesterday the ship had berthed, then a sharp exclamation rose to his lips. Lifting his head instinctively towards the horizon, he made out a tiny blur of smoke that might have been a ship. That, perhaps, was the *Aureola*. He did not know; he only knew the ship was gone.

He turned slowly, met her eyes, which had all the time been fastened on him with sly avidity.

'Why didn't you let them know?' he said heavily. 'Renton - anyone. You might at least have done that.'

She tittered; broke suddenly into her boisterous laughter; slapped the table with her hand.

' 'Ark at 'im,' she declared vociferously. 'Just 'ark at 'im. W'y don't you see that's old 'Emmingway's joke? It's the funniest thing since Noah got stuck on Harrarat. Carajo! It'll kill me.' She held her sides. 'I knew - I knew Renton wouldn't wait for Gawd Almighty. I saw the ship syle from that very window. But I saw you was tired, ducky. So I lets you sleep.' She squirmed with laughter, then, altering her tone abruptly, she rattled the plates invitingly. 'Come on, do. Don't be down'earted. 'Ave some chow. I've 'ad mine, so I don't mind. There's sausidge and tomato. A little of wot you fancy does you good.'

He contemplated her with a wrinkled brow, then, still looking at her, drew forward a chair and sat down at table.

'That's the ticket,' she cried, pressing food upon him. 'Gawd bless my soul but I didn't think w'en you was so polite to me on the boat I'd get the chance to return the syme with interest. Carajo, no. 'Ere! This coffee's gone wishy. I'll get some 'ot.'

'Thanks! It may surprise you, but I'm hungry.'

Whilst Harvey buttered a roll, she made a long arm and pulled upon a hanging bell-rope. There was a pause, then a Spanish girl entered. She wore a bright pink petticoat, no stockings, and high-heeled shoes; her hair hung over her generous young bosom in two glossy, untidy plaits; she smiled first at Mother Hemmingway, then lingeringly at Harvey.

'Hey, Cuca. Bring some coffee. Hot coffee. Presto, pronto.'

'Si, señora.'

'And tyke off the smile, Cuca. It don't myke no beans with this señor.'

'Si, señora.' But Cuca was smiling as she went out of the door, and still smiling when she returned with the steaming coffee-pot. It was not an amused smile, but simply a look of unconquerable amiability which seemed fixed as though she could not put it off.

'Nice little bit is Cuca,' said Mother Hemmingway when the girl had gone. She poured the frothing coffee and passed the cup. Then she sucked her teeth reflectively. 'Been with me five year come Ash We'nsday. 'Appy as a lark. Refined, too, in 'er own quiet w'y. Put on weight, she 'as, since she been with me. Sancta Maria, but 'er figure's come up a treat. You should 'ave seen 'er when I took 'er. My 'at, she was thinner'n a rat's tyle. You wouldn't believe it, the upbringing she'd 'ad. Yes. 'Adn't it been neglected shockin'? W'y, she 'adn't even been confirmed w'en I took 'er. Yes, mister, call me a liar to my fyce if I didn't 'ave Cuca confirmed the first week she was in this 'ouse.'

Harvey, slicing cold sausage upon his roll, said nothing.

'You wouldn't believe it, I sye,' repeated Mother Hemming-

way with unctuous vehemence. 'I treat all my gals 'andsome, so
'elp me, criminy. I don't run no Sunday-school class 'ere, I'll
admit it. But I runs it stryte. See? Fair wind and no fyvour.
And them that don't like it can vamos.'

Vaguely Harvey had suspected the latitude of Mother Hemmingway's establishment. And now that suspicion was amply confirmed. But the knowledge awoke in him neither scorn nor disgust.
Within him something had changed. There came over him,
instead, from deep down in the roots of his soul, a curious
acquiescence. Life must be accepted, not scorned. The run of
his misfortunes had wakened in him a tolerance he long had
needed, a saving humility he had sadly lacked before.

'This coffee is good,' he said, looking across at her. 'And so are
these rolls. Almost better to have missed the ship than this
breakfast.'

Caught by the unexpectedness of the remark, she drew herself
up, instantly on guard.

' 'Ere! wot's wrong with you, cocky? No funny-bones 'ere.
None of your 'umbuggin' sarcasm for me.'

'I'm not sarcastic. I appreciate your hospitality more than you
seem to think.'

She tossed her earrings with a wounded air.

'You ain't generous. That's the trouble with you, mister. You
thinks you know the whole issue. 'Igh up on the throne, superior
like. But you've a lot to learn. Believe me, you 'ave. 'Ere I ups
and tips you a free feed, friendly. And you turns round and spits
in my eye. Be broad, cawn't you? Try and learn something that
'asn't come out of a book.' And she picked up her paper in a
huff, began indignantly to read it.

He studied her with a wry smile.

'Perhaps I've learned more than you imagine. Perhaps I've
been doing a little thinking these last few days.'

She threw him a suspicious look, went back to her paper.

'P'raps you've thought out wot you're going to do in Santa,
cocky. P'raps you're clever enough to think that one out.'

'Have you any suggestions?'

Still distrustful, she answered with a sniff:

'Stay 'ere if you like. Then you'll find I'm not so black as you
paint me. You think the worst of everybody, you do. If you want
the truth, I didn't know the bloomin' boat 'ad gone. Thought
it wasn't leavin' till the afternoon. Dropped me all of an 'eap
w'en I saw it in the bay, 'al an 'our ago. I don't wish you no 'arm.

Stay 'ere if you like. Tyke it or leave it, as the lydy said w'en she threw a banana to the sea-lion.'

He sat with a phantom smile upon his lips, his manner quite devoid of animosity. There was a long pause. Then she looked up and, gazing at him closely, she suddenly tapped the paper in front of her.

'If you're 'ard up for a job, w'y don't you 'it out for Laguna? You're a doctor, ain't you? Leastways, if we believe all we 'ear. And there's a rare rampagin' fever up there. Passing out like twelve o'clock they are. The Spañola medico 'as just took wings - it's in this mornin's *Gaceta*. 'E's the second to go flyin' after 'is 'arp. And the rest don't seem to like the destajo mucho mucho. W'y not try that, mister?'

He stopped crumbling a fragment of his roll; there was a silence.

'Yes, why not?' he echoed.

The malicious look lurked once more in her button eyes as she scrutinised his face.

'You don't mind w'ether they tyke you away in a nice black box,' she suggested insidiously. 'Not you! You don't mind nothing like that.'

He hardly heard her words. Filled by that new fatalism, he sat considering his position.

He would go - yes, he would go. Why hadn't he thought of it before? Something deeper than circumstance had arranged it. He had the strange sensation that this was a moment he had long awaited.

'You'd 'ave to go to Hermosa village,' she went on. 'Up by Casa de los Cisnes. That's the 'ouse where the bother started. And a rummy plyce, too. No one goes near it mucho, best of times. Tumbling to bits. She's 'alf-cracked too - the old bird what 'angs out there.'

'I will go,' he thought again. 'Yes, I must go.' The sudden impulse quickened within him and he repeated half to himself: 'Casa de los Cisnes.'

A silence fell, during which a blinking curiosity showed in her shiny red face.

'You 'ave got guts,' she said suddenly. 'I'll say that for you.' Hastily she corrected herself. 'But, 'streuth! you'll come a mucker if you do go up.'

He thrust back his chair. As though drawn by an invisible hand, he rose from the table and advanced to the door.

'Sancta Maria,' she cried, astonished. 'You ain't going pronto. You got to 'ave a rest. And, blimey, you'd look the better for a shyve and a shine.'

'I'm not going yet,' he answered. 'I want to see Corcoran. It's time I looked at his arm.'

' 'Arf a chance, then. Don't rush at me or I'm liable to 'ave a weakness. And don't go without me or you're liable to lose your way.' She winked archly, crushed the end of her cigar upon a plate, and got upon her diminutive feet. Leading the way across the landing, she descended a short flight of uncarpeted wooden stairs and swept along a narrow corridor. A frowsy comfort filled the place. From below came a clatter of pans, a burst of high laughter, the sound of female voices raised in argument.

Then with an air the Hemmingway drew up and flung open the door of a large and dingy bedroom. In the middle of the bedroom stood a large gilt bed draped by a stained flamboyant quilt. And in the middle of the bed was Corcoran. Clad only in his blue and red striped day-shirt, he sat propped up against the musty pillow with a sort of placid unconcern. His arm was bandaged; upon his nose his steel-rimmed spectacles lay; and on his knees the tattered, dog-eared Plato. His lips moved silently; he did not hear them come in.

'Wyke up, grandma,' cried Mother Hemmingway loudly. ' 'Ere's little Red Riding 'Ood come to see you. Cawn't you smile and look 'appy? You that bled shockin' hover the best carpet in the 'ouse.'

Jimmy raised his head and looked owlishly across his glasses at Harvey. Then he gave an exaggerated start of amazement and delight.

'Well, well,' he cried, 'if it isn't the greatest pleasure of the mornin'. Respect me emotion if ye please, for, faith, I thought ye'd gone and left me widout one word of a good-bye. But tell me quick, now. Why aren't ye on the boat?'

'The ship's gone. Sailed without me.'

'Well, well,' said Corcoran again, 'if that isn't the worst of black misthfortune.'

'Be quiet,' Harvey said. 'You knew all the time it had gone.'

'Did ye ever!' Corcoran persisted with a blarneying grin towards Hemmingway. 'And afther the throuble I got 'im out of, an' all. For him to turn on me like that! But niver mind' - he turned to Harvey - 'it's a treat to know ye're still beside me. And a sight for sore eyes to see ye walkin' on yer feet again.'

Harvey went up to the bed, began to unfasten the bandage.

'How does it feel?' he asked briefly; and, bending, he inspected the wound, which had pierced the triceps muscle superficially.

'Sure, it feels nothing at all. To a man like meself that's took hard knocks and gave them - why, this isn't nothin' but a pin-prick. I only hope that one of thim days I'll meet the yellow boy that done it.'

'A few days' rest and you'll be all right,' said Harvey. He replaced the dressing, rebound the bandage neatly, and stood up. Then his voice turned stiff, his manner constrained. 'In the meantime I'm going to Laguna. Going to have a look at the epidemic up there.'

Caressing his bristling chin, Jimmy absorbed this information.

'Well,' he said at length, 'that's fine. But what about me? At the moment me business plans have fallen thru'. I'm uncertain in me outlook. Faith, I'd better come along wid ye.'

'That's quite absurd. You can't possibly get up for a couple of days.'

'Then I'll come after ye when I do get up. Faith, ye'll not lose me easy as that. I'll be afther ye the minute I put foot upon the ground.'

'It's no use,' Harvey insisted. 'I don't want you.'

'So much the bether,' answered Jimmy, with his grin. 'I'll come just to annoy ye.'

And, using his free hand, he fumbled beneath the pillow and solemnly took snuff.

# CHAPTER XVII

IN the late afternoon, as the sun drew down to the western shoulder of the Peak, Harvey set out to walk to Hermosa - the village below Laguna. The distance was considerable and the ascent steep - free of the town the road rose sharply in short vertiginous slants - but he had a grim, unreasonable determina-tion to make the journey on foot. Somehow it eased the tumult of his mind to inflict this rigour upon his body; and as he climbed higher into the vibrating air, coating his shoes with dust and his brow with sweat, a sense of calmness came to him. He was walking directly towards the sunset, a dark mote in that glittering river of light which poured over the jagged lava cliffs of Telde. Above the volcanic lip a tiny shining cloud lay like a puff of steam. The sky sang with colour which the earth re-echoed. On either side the dark green leaves of the banana-trees hung low, their wind-torn fleshy fronds adroop in the pellucid calm. Round reservoirs of brackish water, yellow and precious as gold, lay listless, glinting obscurely through the plantation foliage. At one pool three mountain goats were drinking. He climbed higher, traversing a grove of eucalyptus-trees, tall as cedars and gracious with their aromatic attar. Then the road opened out, the trees fell back, and beneath him the bay was spread tranquil and remote, dotted with toys of ships and tiny pointed sails. Around the bay the town lay flattened, its miradors foreshortened, its balconies set out like little mouths to catch the air, its mass of huddled roofs gashed by the silver brightness of the Barranca Almeida. But another turn of the road dissolved this vision of the town and instead a range of bare basaltic hills reared themselves coldly. Great lava slags with huge embedded boulders absorbed his gaze.

Now he had been walking for about an hour. A moment later he passed through the hamlet of La Cuesta: a handful of houses, a glass-cased shrine with its flickering light, a white-walled church. It seemed deserted or asleep. He left the village and mounted higher on the narrowing road. Presently, about a mile further on at a steep-angled bend, he saw before him the small, slowly moving figure of a girl carrying a water-jar. He quickened his pace, made up to her.

'Señorita,' he asked in his slow Spanish. 'Is this the way to Hermosa? The village beneath Laguna.'

Still walking, she studied him obliquely without moving her head burdened by the heavy jar. Her eyes were darkly lustrous above the weathered scarlet of her torn blouse. Her body was erect, her hips swayed forward with unstudied easy grace. From the thin dirty fingers of her left hand a yellow blossom trailed. She was not more than fifteen.

'San Cristóbal de la Laguna,' she said at length; and then, 'La Laguna.'

'Yes. Am I on the proper road?'

'The road? It is the King's road.'

'The King's road?'

'Carretera reāl. The old road. Assuredly it is a proper road.'

'But is it a proper road for Laguna?'

This seemed to amuse her; her smile was dazzlingly white; but for fear of upsetting her jar she might have laughed.

'Ay de mi,' she cried. 'How tired am I of ever fetching water.' Then she seemed to forget all about him. They walked together in silence around another loop of the interminable road. She waited till they swung past a clump of cork-trees, then indolently she raised the yellow flower and pointed.

He lifted his head. There, quite close, above its range of grass-topped walls, rose the sombre towers of an old citadel.

'De la Laguna,' she repeated. 'San Cristóbal de la Laguna.'

The words had a queer melodious sound.

'There is sickness in the town?' he asked.

'Si, señor.'

'Much sickness?'

'Si, señor.' She put the flower in her mouth and began in-differently to chew the stem.

'I wish to find Hermosa. The Casa de los Cisnes. Can you tell me where that lies?'

Again her oblique lustrous eyes considered him. She removed the flower between two stiff fingers as though it were a cigarette.

'That is where there is much sickness. At Laguna it is finished. At Hermosa not so much finished.'

'I want to go there.'

'Not so much finished,' she said again; and with a precocious air, 'Jesu-Maria. There is a curse.'

On they went again in silence, then, about a quarter of a mile from the town, abruptly she drew up, pointed to a side path with the languid yellow flower.

'Behold!' she said flatly. 'It is that way, señor, if you must go.'

The side path which she indicated drew back from the high-way through a grove of pines, and, when briefly he had thanked her, he swung towards it. As he stepped into the shadow of the trees he felt that she was watching him, and instinctively he spun round. It was so. There she stood, watching; and, under his eyes, she shifted her jar, crossed herself, moved hurriedly away. And then, quite suddenly the sun went down beyond the far serrated sky-line. All at once the air was colder, as though touched by clammy fingers.

The wood was gloomy, the path narrow, scored by deep ruts and dry as bone. The massed trees hung low - dark with whisper-ing conspiracy. A loose stone, on which he stumbled, went clattering down into a dry ravine. At that the trees drew closer, affrighted; and then a queer light air went through them, murmuring: 'Hush - oh, hush - oh, hush.'

The sinister stillness of the copse sank into Harvey and keyed him to an answering melancholy. Like some symbolic figure he might have waded through the shadows, further - and further still, into the core of a last obliterating obscurity. But suddenly, a hundred paces further on, the trees thinned out; he crossed a wooden bridge and came again to open land, on which a house stood girt by its estate. It was a small estate but he judged it to be the place he sought - a valley of red prolific earth fed by a precious trickle, burdened beneath the tangled richness of its vegetation. So fertile the soil, so luxuriant the growth, the whole plantation throbbed with a note of wildness: a garden rank, untended, but massed with savage beauty - all fecund with a glorious primeval loveliness.

Staring through the huge wrought-iron gates Harvey caught an awed breath: flowers - such flowers! A surge of untended blossom shimmered madly across the dwindling light. Masses of wild azalea stabbed his eyes with crimson that was like pain; pale irises floated in an opal sea; a purple convolvulus twined its trumpets amongst the banks of granadilla; the crane-flowers darted, blue- and yellow-winged, poised in a still perpetual flight; and, over all, the freesia flowed in waves, white and perfumed, delicate as foam.

With a start he collected himself. He lifted the brass-ringed handle of the gate, twisted and rattled it, pushed with his shoulder upon the rusty bars. But without avail: the gate was locked. No matter - the retama hedge which encircled the domain was raddled with a dozen gaps. That was in keeping with the place. He made to move, when, suddenly, his eye, uplifted towards those massy gates, was taken by an emblem wrought upon the arch above. It was a swan, in beating flight. A swan - in beating flight!

Fascinated, he stared at the emblem of the swan, which seemed imbued with meaning and with life. Casa de los Cisnes. Of course. He caught his breath, his whole body rigid. Why hadn't it dawned on him before? Casa de los Cisnes - the House of the Swans.

He stood a long time there, his head thrown back, his being flooded by wonder and a strange excitement. The House of the Swans. Then he sighed and turned away. It was nothing; it could be nothing but mere coincidence.

Shaking the thought aside, he took three paces to the right, stepped through the hedge gap, and gained the weed-infested drive. Two little adobe houses stood on either side, and at the first of these he paused, knocked loudly upon the narrow door, then knocked again. There was no answer. Nothing but the empty echoes of his hammering. The door was fastened, the windows shuttered, the house deserted and strangely desolate.

Quickly he turned to the other hut. Here the door lay wide, the dim interior of the single room flung open to his sight. It was empty of life. But on the earthen floor a blanket formed an ochre square and on the blanket a dead man lay, his dull eyes blankly staring, his mouth dropped open as though surprised. Two candles guttered at the pallet's foot, washing the dead face with a fitful light. And the scent of the freesias filled the air like some sweet unguent.

There was nothing to be done. Harvey turned away, closing the door behind him. He began to walk up the drive which swung southwards in a gentle curve leading him towards the casa, looming whitely against the slope of hill and the sombre background of the trees. It was a noble dwelling fashioned of creamy stone, low yet stately, but fallen to sad disorder: the portico sunk down, the balcony adrift, the shutters rotted and awry, the walls all stained with damp and lichen. Two great urns that flanked the door were tumbled on their sides.

He climbed the worn steps, between the crevices of which a vivid scarlet fungus lay like blood, and rang the bell. Minutes passed with dragging slowness. Again he rang the silly, echoing bell. Then a middle-aged servant woman in a dress of spotted calico opened the door. She stared at him through the grudging aperture as though he were an apparition until he said:

'I want to see your mistress.'

Then her face, enclosed by the tight-drawn inky hair and a red and yellow scarf, grew suddenly evasive and afraid.

'It is late, señor,' she answered. 'The day is ending.'

'It is not yet ended.'

'Before God, señor, the sun is past the Peak. Tomorrow would be a better day.'

He shook his head.

'I must see her.'

'But, señor, the marquesa is old. And she has trouble. She does not receive.'

He took two steps forward, causing her to retreat before him into the hall.

'Tell her I am here.'

She stood, her eyes searching his face, her hands moving indecisively about her apron, then, muttering, she turned and went slowly up the stairs.

He looked round. The hall was lofty, reaching darkly to the arabesque-encrusted roof, echoing to the voice like an old church nave. The faint light had a sombre quality issuing from a single, deep-set window stained with a faded emblem of the Swan. Upon the plaster walls curved swords were swung in patterns. As they had swung for years. Striking the silent emptiness, formidable and grotesque. Beneath the scimitars a shell of armour stood like a shrunken figure of a warrior knight, palsied of arm and bent of knee, but still intimidating - the spear advanced, the visor parted with a grim pugnacity. The figure bore down on Harvey. The whole place affected him strangely, made him almost afraid to stir a foot. And he felt empty - weak. I'm tired, he thought defensively. I've walked too far.

Suddenly arose the sound of footsteps upon the wooden staircase. Abruptly he lifted his head. A little old woman was descending from the gallery above. She came slowly, one aged claw clutching the heavy polished banister, one slurred foot dragging upon the other. Yet for all her slowness she bore her small thin figure upright with the dignity of race. She was dressed entirely in black even to the band around her pompadour frizzed hair, and the fashion of her dress was of a bygone age: the skirt trailing, the sleeves puffed, the neck-band ruffled and high. As she drew nearer, Harvey saw plainly the marks of her senility. Her skin was parchment yellow, scored with a maze of wrinkles, the tendons of her neck taut as the leg-strings of a fowl. She had a little tight-drawn aquiline beak and a tiny pouting mouth. Her dark eyes were pouched and glazed. She wore a score of bangles on her wrists, and on her fingers a galaxy of ancient rings.

Immediately Harvey saluted her; announced himself directly.

'I am an English doctor,' he said. 'My name is Leith. I know you've got fever on your estate and in the village near. Very bad fever. I've come to give you my assistance, if you'll have it.'

Like a little black-clothed statuette she stood, with all the stillness of great age, seeming to look right through him with her opaque yet living eyes.

'No one comes here,' she said at last, and her voice held a

curious sing-song cadence. 'No one comes now to the Marquesa de Luego. She is very old. All day she sits in her room, descending only when she is summoned. What else is there to do, I pray you, señor? Prayers have great virtue, have they not? So Don Balthasar said. He, too, is dead. Not so is Isabel de Luego. So she sits in her room and waits till she is summoned. Assuredly it is a kindness for you to visit her.'

Yes, she is queer, he thought, she is talking about herself. But there was about that oddity a pathos which struck straight into his heart.

'It was scarcely kindness,' he said. 'I was in Santa Cruz. I heard of the sickness you have here - and in Hermosa. The plain fact is that I had nothing else to do. So I came.'

'It was an act of grace, señor - which grows by the denial. Have they taken your horse? What was it you required? It is forgotten. Pobre de mi. So much is forgotten. And so many have gone away. But you must dine. Good advice comes from the aged. Assuredly you must dine.'

'There is no need,' he said quickly. 'Let me see first where the sickness is.'

'In the village. There, so many sick. And now so many are dead. Here on the fiunca they are all dead or run away. All but Manuela and me. Pablo - he was the last. Pablo, the gate-keeper. He died at noon. After, you shall see.' She gave a little ghostly laugh, and, turning to the woman who stood in the background listening with a sullen face, she exclaimed:

'Manuela, the señor will dine tonight with the Marquesa de Luego.'

Manuela's look grew more sullen: she made a gesture of distrust.

'But, marquesa, it is already upon the table, your supper.'

There was protest in the voice: but it fell upon the air. The marquesa was repeating to Harvey with a childish lift of gaiety to her voice:

'You see, it is already upon the table. Assuredly you are expected. And the marquesa? Already she has made a toilet most elegant. Is it not good chance? Come, señor.'

She led the way through the hall into a long room panelled in dark encina wood and hung with faded portraits framed in tarnished gilt. For the rest the floor was bare, the ceiling painted with the figure of an enormous swan, one wall hidden by an enormous ebony *aparador*. And in the middle of the room upon the walnut refectory table was laid out a simple meal of fruit, cold fowl, cheese, and milk.

Sulkily Manuela set a second place, pushed forward another heavy hide-backed chair; darting a final covert glance at Harvey, she withdrew.

The marquesa seated herself with a little mincing air, poured out a glass of milk abstractedly, let it stand before her. Then she took a fig from the dish and began to slice it into green and scarlet pieces.

'You must eat,' she said, raising her head delicately like a bird. 'He fasts enough who eats with reason. That cheese is good. It is made with cardo - from the wild artichoke. Little blue flowers. Yes, little blue flowers. I have picked them when I was a child. And that was not yesterday.'

Harvey took some cheese and rough, yellow bread, shook off his own strange sense of unreality. He wanted to hear more about the epidemic.

'How did this trouble begin?' he asked.

'Trouble, señor? What is life but trouble. Out of the mire and into the swamp. It is a saying. There was a man José returning to his family. A sailor who came upon a ship. Then he died and others after him. It is like the old Modorra plague that came to Laguna when Ferdinand was King. You will find now sometimes little heaps of bones in the hill caves. That is where the Guanches wandered out to hide themselves and die. A long, long time ago.'

Touched almost by awe he said:

'Your family has been here a long time.'

Her eyes looked beyond him contemplating the past.

'But, señor, you do not understand. What is a long time? Not months, not years. Puneta, no señor. It is longer perhaps than that.' She paused dreamily, and lifting her hand, directed his gaze through the narrow window to where in the darkening patio a most fantastic tree rose up, its smooth, tube branches uncouthly twisted, like some beast in mortal agony. 'You see that tree, señor. It is the dragon-tree. Still young, that tree, and yet four hundred years old. No, no! I do not jest. It is four hundred years since Don Cortez Alonso de Luego, el Conquistador and Adelantado, came to this house. From here he made war with his levies from Castille. On the Guanches. At La Mantaza. At the Tower of Refuge. And was wounded at the Place of the Massacre. Since that time, señor, always the de Luegos have lived here. Always, always.' She sighed and let her small hand fall upon her lap. 'But now all is changed. My brother, rest to his soul, lost - lost all - years past - in the fall of cochinilla. Everything was then planted in cactus for the cochineal. But another tintura was found, you understand - all made from quimico. It is no good then for cochineal. My brother, alas, is ruined. And dead now ten years. Since then nothing but misfortune which comes by the yard and goes by the inch. Weeds are not hindered by the lack of water. No one to control but Don Balthasar. And he is dead. Dios mio, it is sad, señor, for Isabel de Luego. She is old in truth. But she still has love of life. The more of life the more of love of life. That is a proverb of Galicia. And here, too, the sun is warm on old bones. Take more milk, señor, if you please. It is sweet, like honey.'

Obediently he poured himself a measure of the warm goat's milk which frothed into the tall, fluted glass. He saw it all: surviving an age when the authority of lineage was paramount, her brother ruined by the discovery of aniline dyes, she was here - old now, enfeebled and alone, victimised, perhaps, by an indolent peasantry, a dishonest overman, stricken even by a disastrous epidemic, the pitiful survival of a noble race.

'Ah, señor,' she exclaimed suddenly, 'better had you known the true Casa de los Cisnes. Not fallen down like this; but the fountain playing in the patio and many happy, ordered peons all singing, singing in the groves.' Moved by her own words to a strange excitement she rose quietly and stood upright, staring fixedly through the long window into the shadowed patio beyond. The room was almost dark now and her tiny shrunken figure bore a ghostly quality.

'Never did you hear such singing,' she declared in a high-pitched tone; her lip twitched slightly; a patch of colour mounted her withered cheek. 'Never, never. Singing in the carob grove. Often I can hear it when the darkness falls.' Her face quivered, lit by the glory of the past, and, to Harvey's acute distress, in a voice which leaped and wavered she began to sing:

> *Al acabarse el trabajo,*
> *Y a la puesta del sol,*
> *Nos juntamos en la alameda:*
> *Brillan las luciernagas como estrellas,*
> *La luna en el cielo está.*

A singular silence followed. The marquesa made no movement to resume her seat. but, still standing, with eyes sunk in that dimensionless stare, she began remotely to eat her fruit, to drink some milk. Moments passed, then suddenly her head slipped down and she caught Harvey's troubled gaze upon her. Slowly the trance dissolved, and, back in reality, she gave a fragile laugh. And lighting two candles that stood upon the table she sat down as quietly as she had risen, clasping her mottled hands upon her lap, breathing a sigh that made her shrunken bosom fill.

He looked down at his plate and began awkwardly to crumble his bread.

'I am sorry,' he said in a low voice. 'Sorry that such a great misfortune has taken you.' He paused. 'And now, if you will forgive me, I must go.'

'Yes,' she said at last, 'you must go.' Then seeming to scrutinise him afresh, 'You are English, and you come at sunset. Dios mio, it is strange. Not for years has an Englishman placed foot in Los Cisnes. And then assuredly it was not you.' A singular smile trembled upon her face. 'How indeed could it be you? For that too is old history, señor, when your English Nelson made battery on Santa Cruz. He was defeated, as you will know. Ay, ay, ay - but the Spanish garrison was brave. And thereafter, the fighting being done, an Englishman came here at nightfall. No, no, it was not you!' The smile ran to a trickle of laughter, childish yet somehow secret. 'It is all written down in a book. I have read it many times within the libreria. Some day I will show you. It is so sad and strange. He came with his beloved to seek sanctuary. She was sister to an English captain. Here he left her, and here returned. Pobre de mi, but life is cruel. When he returned she was not there. Gone away, gone away.' Watching him, she let her voice tail to a thin whisper that was almost of lamentation. Then again there was silence. The candle flames above the table flickered gently, sending shadows swaying around the panelled walls. And Harvey's thoughts swayed with the shadows. Caught suddenly in his throat by an emotion quite unknown, he felt as though, in this strange place all peopled with the shadows of the past, a spell were binding him.

The House of the Swans. His mind raced for an instant in the mazes of a haunting labyrinth; then tremblingly withdrew. Thoughts darted hither, thither - strange, frightening thoughts - like scared fishes in a pool. He was hostile to these thoughts and yet they shoaled about, unreasonably, tormenting him. His whole identity seemed slipping from him, merging with the thin shades which floated round the panelled walls.

He started, with an effort composed himself. He saw that she had finished. He pushed back his chair, and got up.

'I must go,' he said again. 'If you will allow me, I will go to the village.'

'Yes, yes. You will go if you must go. Who am I to interfere with fate? It is not far. Manuela will show you the path.' She rose, and with her shadowy smile and that queer immobile bearing of her body, preceded him from the room.

'Manuela,' she cried, clapping her hands in the hall. 'Manuela, Manuela.'

They waited without speech until the woman came, gliding noiselessly from the shadows in her felt-soled shoes.

'You will take lantern, and guide the señor to the village, Manuela.'

The serving woman's lowering face drew instantly to a look of fear, and, with her head, she made a violent spasm of negation.

'No, no,' she cried. 'No so. I have borne plenty. There is sickness in the night air.'

'Tell me the way,' said Harvey quickly. 'That is enough.'

'Yes, I will tell. And there is a great moon to light you. No need of lanterns or of me.'

The marquesa gave a little gesture of impotence.

'Pobre de mi,' she sighed. 'Manuela will not go. Will not, will not, will not. How often is that heard. But she is all that now remains to me. Listen, señor, and she will tell you. Then return, I beg you, to this house of meagre hospitality. You, too, have known misfortune. It is in your face, señor. Love and grief - they cannot be concealed. But God draws straight with crooked lines. Who knows but there is fortune in your coming. For you, perhaps; and me. And now - adios.'

She turned, with naïve dignity, and began slowly to ascend the stairs. The tap-tap of her heels upon the wooden steps came sounding back, and then the upper darkness of the gallery engulfed her.

At the door Manuela awaited him, and, when he had taken her surly directions in silence, he set out. The night was clear, the garden lit by a moon now all but full. Across his nostrils the perfume of the freesia came up in lazy drifts. Nothing stirred. Even the fireflies hung motionless upon the granadilla leaves. They shone like small, unwinking eyes.

The path ran eastwards and uphill, luminous as a river in that ethereal light. Wading this visionary rivulet he passed an

127

orange grove in fruit, a patch of old banana-trees all rank with undergrowth, some empty packing sheds, a roofless forge, an empty wagon side-tilted from its broken wheel. Everywhere was life; and everywhere decay.

When he had gone about a quarter of a mile, he crossed a low, stone wall and saw above him a dim cluster of lights. Three minutes later he was in the village street, conscious instantly of the blight which lay upon it like a pall. The place seemed deserted of all but some skulking dogs when suddenly, across the way, the black doors of the church swung open and from the dim interior a slow procession wound: censer-bearers, acolyte, and priest. And then the mourners, linked by thin cords to the bier. Harvey stood still, and, as the small white coffin passed, he bared his head. No one took any notice of him. A child, he thought instinctively; and as the funeral train turned into the graveyard his narrowed eyes observed the mounds of fresh-covered earth. He moved forward. Further up he made out a group of soldiers standing around a wagon beneath a naphtha flare. Packing cases littered the road around them. Two nuns, walking swiftly, came towards the soldiers.

'At last I am here,' he thought. 'At last I can do something.'

He did not wait. The door of the first house stood open and impulsively he plunged into the lighted room. As he entered, a woman straightened up from the corner bed where she had been tending a peasant girl. She turned and confronted him; then a little gasp broke from her lips. The woman was Susan Tranter.

## CHAPTER XVIII

Two days before, when the *Aureola* pounded out of Orotava Bay, Mary Fielding watched her go. Standing upon the balcony of the San Jorge, wind and rain beating across her eyes, she saw the ship fade into the scattered mist. The masts were last to go; but they, too, vanished coldly from her sight; and she was left alone with sadness. With the sound of the throbbing engines still running in her head she stood motionless for a long time; then she turned, passed through the wide French windows to her bedroom. It was a charming room: spacious, immaculate, the furniture in taste, the caoba-wood bed hung by a crisp mosquito-net. She sat down in a wicker chair beside her neatly piled luggage, conscious of a frightful sinking in her heart. She ought to ring for the maid to unpack, to go in and see Elissa, to look at her mail - an enormous pile of letters lay upon the topmost trunk. She ought not to sit like this, weakly, with hands drooping upon her lap. But she could not shake her listlessness away. Something was hurting in her side, a pain - it was hurting intolerably.

She bit her lip. Don't be a fool, she thought, a hopeless idiotic fool. Nervously she jumped up, pressed the bell, and waited.

The maid entered, a short mulatto girl whose cuffs and collar matched the glistening whiteness of her eyes. Then, at a word, she went over to the trunks, began to work her small, coffee-coloured fingers amongst the fastenings. Mary gazed at her in silence, moved restlessly to the window. With hands pressed together she stared at the shifting drizzle.

'When will it stop raining?'

The mulatto girl looked up, exposing cheerfully a row of dazzling teeth.

'Please, madama, nice weather all the time come good. So Rosita say.' Her tone was husky, with a sort of comic rhythm. The old Mary would have loved that funny voice. But now she could not even smile.

'Soon it will be fine?'

'Yes, please, madama, tomorrow. Come fine, mañana.' Rosita repeated the favourite word, rolling it from out her lips as though she savoured it.

Tomorrow! The thought struck Mary with a fresh pang: tomorrow and tomorrow; the next day, and the next - all those empty days stretching blankly, endlessly away from her. Again her eyes were mournful with tears; she pressed her cheek against the cold window-glass; and then she sighed as though her heart must break.

But the day marched forward ruthlessly. Her unpacking was completed; the maid smiled and curtseyed herself out; and now the gong drummed out for luncheon.

She descended slowly to the dining-room, joined Dibs and Elissa at a corner table. They were in excellent humour, Elissa delighted by the sophistication of the place, Dibs by the unexpected promise of the cuisine. But their laughter met her like a blow.

Everything was delightful: the service quiet, the food good, the room lofty and serene with cool, branched shrubs. Yet she had no appetite. She touched but did not taste the mullet cooked in white wine which sent Dibs into ecstasies. Her conversation likewise was a sheer pretence. All the time she was hiding that pain which burned in her side.

After lunch they went into the lounge. The rain still dripped from the smoky sky, and Elissa, inspecting the outlook with a dubious eye, proposed a game of bridge.

Bridge! Mary opened her lips to refuse. Then she checked herself. She hated bridge, but no matter, she must make an effort, really she must - so her thoughts ran on - an effort to be less self-centred, more companionable to the others. She took hold of herself, nodded her agreement.

Chairs were brought, and cards. They settled down to bridge. The fourth was a correct little oldish man with a cropped moustache, long jacket, riding breeches, and an army manner, who from the first had angled for the invitation to join them. In a well-bred fashion he had angled; for he was a well-bred little man. It was not long before this emerged with just the casual inconsequence which made it right. He knew, of course, their names and antecedents - each morning it was his practice diligently to scan the register - and was swift to discover mutual acquaintances of rank. He wintered abroad for his 'little woman's' sake, did sketches, organised excursions, spluttered slightly when he spoke, and thanked God he was an English gentleman. His name, Forbes-Smith, inevitably, was hyphenated.

The game wore on interminably: shuffle, cut, deal, call, the laboured business of playing out the hand. No sooner ended than the tedious cycle recommenced. To Mary it seemed so strange and aimless. Why was she sitting here, holding these shiny coloured cards, forcing herself to speak, to smile? Her head was muddled. Forbes-Smith's flattery immeasurably distressed her. She longed to be alone, to be at peace with her own thoughts.

But it was after five before the final rubber ended. Then came the reckoning, a silly argument between Dibs and Elissa about the score, a determined effort by Forbes-Smith to introduce her to some 'charmin' people' in the lounge.

It was almost the hour of dinner before she could get away. Upstairs she bathed her throbbing temples, changed into the first frock which took her hand, and again descended to go through the semblance of a meal. Then, making a plea of tiredness, she was free at last to seek the sanctuary of her room. She shut the door, leaned her side against it wearily, then, with a gesture of abandon, threw the windows open.

The rain had ceased, and from behind a bank of cloud the hidden moon diffused a tender radiance. The night was hazy but luminous. The light, lace curtains swayed gently in the rain-washed air. Faintly came the croaking of frogs mingling with the muffled rhythm of the surf. Beneath the balcony a bank of lilies gleamed. The scent - so like the scent of freesias - rising in heavy, intoxicating waves, caught her breast with a sudden pang. It was too hard - too hard to bear.

Slowly she undressed, letting her dress slip from her to the floor. The damp air cooled her hot body. Now she was in bed, lying upon her back, staring with wide eyes into darkness. She had no sense of time. The croaking frogs went on; the booming surf went on; around her the night sounds of the hotel rose up in sudden starts, uneasily defeating sleep. The mosquito-net, which draped her bed with all the stark whiteness of a shroud, seemed now to stifle her.

Was she ill, that she should feel like this? The thought never entered her head. But for all that she was fevered. And in her blood there had begun to stir insidiously the toxins of infection. Of this she knew nothing; she only knew that she could not rest. Three hours dragged past before a wavering slumber closed her stinging eyes. Down, down she sank through fathoms of forgetfulness. And then she dreamed.

Never before had her dream so vividly possessed her. It began, as usual, by the courtyard fountain: the old cracked fountain with the metal swan which seemed to swim absurdly in the waterless basin. Little green lizards basked lazily upon its rim, blinking kind eyes when she came near. The paving stones were friendly to her feet; the dragon-tree held up its old stupendous limbs; the lovely scent of freesias was in the air. But of course she could not linger. She fled to the garden, and, as she ran, two great white swans rose from the pomegranate-trees and soared trumpeting towards the mountains. The beating of their wings was glorious. She clapped her hands and darted towards the orange grove. Then all at once a new emotion struck her. She paused, transfigured by a marvellous surprise. He was there, again, within that grove which was her own special playground. As she had seen him there so often. But his face was no longer vague, his figure no longer shadowy. She could see quite plainly. It was he. Oh, it was true - after all - she hadn't been wrong. This time he could make no denial. Her heart turned and leaped, unutterable joy rushed over her. She stretched her arms and ran towards him, laughing and crying in the same breath.

Laughing and crying in one wild breath. Oh, the happiness was rapture - no living breast could hold it. Singing, her heart swelled and swelled. Nothing in life or death could match this moment's ecstasy.

She knew at last, as with the revelation of all time, why she was here. It was for him whom all her life she had been seeking. And now the garden was complete. No longer need she dread her loneliness; no longer need she creep away despairing of her childish folly. He was here, beyond the edge of pain, freed from the fetters of illusion. And all her life, forecasted, had lead her to this meeting.

His face, unconscious of her face, stirred pity through her joy. She must declare herself to him, make answering gladness leap into his unseeing eyes. Longing, she whispered his name. He did not hear. Again she spoke his name, more loudly, and made to run towards him. And then, in one swift instant, the new-born rapture of her soul was slain. Upon her lips the smile died coldly. She could not understand. She could not move. She pressed forward, but her feet were prisoned, her body bound. She struggled. Fear and hope were mixed inextricably. Straining she fought to move, torn now by the anguish of defeat. And then, with a little sobbing cry, she woke.

Her eyes, glazed by terror and despair, met the bright perplexity of the new day. She gasped. She was not in the garden but here - held by the staid reality of her bedroom. Hardly breathing, she lay rigid, still dazed by the nightmare-ending to her dream. And then she shivered. So near, so very near, it might have been within the sound of this same booming surf! Yet now so far away! A long sigh came from her. She was bewildered, crushed by the bitterness of unfulfilment.

Rosita, entering with the morning tray, found her with her cheek pressed against her arm; as she pulled the curtain briskly, she declared:

'See now. It is very much fine today. And, as I have explain, madama have plenty sun.'

Mary stared at the maid in silence, thinking still: So near, so very near, it might have been within the sound of the same booming surf. Suddenly, driven by an unknown hope, she said:

'Rosita!' - her voice was queerly secret and remote - 'Is there a garden near; an old, old place where swans come sometimes, about sunset?'

Rosita paused, round-eyed. Then deferentially she laughed, nodding her head as though admiring a most superior wit.

'Please, no, madama. Maybe Rosita queer 'nough but she never know nothing 'bout that.'

'You are sure - quite sure?'

'Please God, yes, madama.' Her laughter swelled. 'Plenty gardens, oh, please God, plenty. But not like that. Twenty years now I live here and all that time I never see not one swan.'

Mary made no reply. Only half her mind was conscious of Rosita's answer; the other half was far away, detached, ringing with mysterious premonition.

She got up and slipped on a dressing-gown. As Rosita had said, the day was lovely. But already it was very warm; at least she felt it warm; and her head was curiously dizzy. As her eyes drifted towards the blue sea beneath she thought absently how cool and how refreshing it would be to bathe. Yes, she must bathe. Her costume, holding still some grains of sand from the Playa de los Canteros, evoked a poignant recollection. Yet the recollection did not linger. It passed, a fleeting pang, across the strange perplexity of her mind. She took towels and went down the broad, stone steps past the lily bed towards the water's edge.

The beach was quite deserted, the sea touched merely by a creamy flicker of wave. She swam lightly, feeling the water thin and unsubstantial as an azure ether. All her body was fluent now and vaguely severed from reality. Though she scarcely noticed, her left arm was stiff and on her wrist a tiny reddish patch had risen. It was a mosquito bite. Three days ago, crossing the mole at Las Palmas, she had been bitten by an infected insect. 'What is to happen will happen.' She had said that. And, 'Not chance but destiny which turns our lives.' And now, the victim of her own prophecy, a dreadful turn of destiny confronted her.

She had been infected with yellow fever.

This strange lightness of her body, the strange clouding of her mind were but the symptoms of that fever's onset.

She came out of the water, her ears singing. She dried herself, put on her robe, and started back through the grounds of the hotel. For some minutes she wandered about, her air vaguely distraught, that humming still within her ears. Suddenly, at a turn of the path, she came upon an old man upon his knees weeding a bed of purple lupines. He wore a wide straw hat upon his head, and, in his long dried ears, thin rings of gold. She stared at the old man's wrinkled, sun-scorched neck. He went on weeding calmly, patiently, but at last he half turned, gave her a slanting, timid smile, murmured a salutation.

She answered him. She could not smile, but inside she was laughing queerly at herself. Oh, how queer, how foolish she was! Always had been - always would be! It was a joke, of course, a dreadful joke. But she couldn't help herself. She must ask the old peon her question. He would laugh at her to be sure, just as Rosita had done. But what did that matter? She was laughing at herself in any case, laughing deep down in the secret places of her throbbing heart.

But when she spoke he did not laugh. He got upon his feet, searched her face gravely. He was silent so long she repeated her words.

'Assuredly, señora, I understand,' he said hesitatingly. 'Perhaps I would know that place.'

The fact that he did not disown her question brought her a sudden inner trembling .Wide-eyed she stared at him.

'A long time ago,' he went on, 'I have worked across the island for the family of the de Luego. Oh, yes, señora. Then the Estancia was great, oh, very great.' He fingered his hat-rim, stumbling to express himself. 'And the armas of that family - it is a swan, señora - a flying swan.'

A sort of vertigo came over her, she shaded her eyes. Surely it was the sunlight that was blinding her.

'It is upon the gates - the big, iron gates beside the yellow lodge?'

He reflected, then said:

'Yes, indeed, señora. And upon the fountain in the patio.'

But Mary interrupted with a little cry.

'The fountain is dry, and little green lizards run about upon the rim. Outside the porch there is a bed of freesias. Then below the drive there are orange trees, hundreds and hundreds of them.'

He smiled gravely, creasing his tawny eyes.

'But yes, señora. It is exactly so. You have been there, it is clear. A La Casa de los Cisnes.'

La Casa de los Cisnes! She repeated the name as if to let it sink into her, as though fearful of forgetting. Then she whispered:

'Is it far - far from here?'

He rocked his head from side to side.

'No, no, señora. It is not far. And an easy way. First to Santa Cruz señora, then to Laguna where anyone will know the old Estancia. Oh, but it is easy. One day upon the little barca which leaves the bay at noon each day of life. Thereafter one little drive. It is nothing.'

The words ran together through her head, resounding, clashing, shivering with dazzling brilliancy. She had a sort of divine friendliness towards the old man. She heard herself thank him. Her own voice - of course - yet apart from her. She was no longer conscious of her surroundings but away in the splendour of that other garden.

She knew exactly what she must do; and the knowledge filled her with a marvellous delight. She was calm - excited yet assured; only a tiny part of her felt bewildered and afraid.

Dimly she was aware of herself returning to the hotel. She went to her room, washed her flushed face, brushed her hair, and carefully put on the dress she had worn at Las Palmas. Her eyes held a high brightness as she looked at herself in the glass. She took some money, thought for a moment, wrote a few lines to Elissa upon a sheet of paper, then placed this deliberately upon her dressing-table.

She was ready - at last. As in a trance, she slipped out of her room. All eager and on tiptoe. No one must hear her. No one must see her go. About her was that queer secret intensity. As she descended the stairs and gained the porch she paused, taken again by that intolerable nostalgia. Casa de los Cisnes, she thought again. All her body trembled. I'm going she thought, at last I'm going. And lifting up her head, with distant eyes she set out upon her journey.

## CHAPTER XIX

THE evening dew had begun to lie upon the broader cactus leaves as he walked towards the house. His shoulders were hunched forward, his head lowered. All that day he had been working in Hermosa. It had been a bad day, an unprofitable day, an utterly exhausting day for him - breathing the sickly air of pestilence and the fume of burning fomites, dealing with ignorance, incompetence, and dirt. Troops were in the village, he had found the Spanish commandant suspicious of his assistance. Both insolent and suspicious: 'We did not *ask* the señor! -' To crown it all he could feel that the worst of the epidemic was over. Like a fool, he had arrived too late. It was a galling thought. But he hadn't been put off. The whole day he had worked like a nigger. He had done his level best. And now, jaded in mind and body, he came round and up the drive.

Then, as he crossed the patio, he raised his head and saw her. Instantly he stopped, like a man stricken mortally. His face went dead white; he pressed his hand across his eyes.

'It's the heat,' he thought painfully. 'It must pass.' But when he withdrew his hand she was still there. An unbelievable emotion surged over him, so unexpected and so exquisite he could only stammer:

'Mary,' and again, 'Mary'. It was the only word his lips could shape. She was here. The light spanning the shimmering courtyard shone upon her face, irradiating it beyond beauty. Her eyes looked towards his eyes. Her figure swam towards him, slender as a young tree, lovely as a strain of music. And within his soul something went leaping and leaping - oh, joyfully! - like a flame.

Now she was beside him.

'Why did you come here?' And the voice was unrecognisable as his. Her face, too, was pale; but her eyes, still fixed upon his eyes, smiled towards him.

'I'm glad,' she whispered. 'So terribly glad I've found you.'

There was silence. Something suffocating rose into his throat.

'I thought I should never get here,' she whispered again. 'That I should never see you any more.' Her body leaned a little towards him. She seemed weary, like one who has reached a long day's end.

'Mary,' he cried out, 'I can't understand. Why are you here?'

'It is all right,' she answered dreamily. 'Now that I am with you it is all right. And here it is like being home.'

Between them the air vibrated. Yet the heavy brightness of her eyes made him afraid. They were shining, but the light was more upon the edge of darkness than ever he had seen before.

'You are tired,' he said in a choking voice. 'You must have something - something to eat.'

'I'm not hungry. But I am thirsty. Yes, I'm very thirsty.'

He tore his gaze away from her. With averted head he said:

'Come, then, and I'll get you some milk.'

As he entered the house the blood pounding in his temples seemed to reverberate in hollow echoes which confused all thought. He went into the refectory. No one was about: it was already well beyond the hour of dinner; he saw from the table that the marquesa had already made her meal. With an unsteady hand he poured out a glass of milk. When he returned Mary was in the hall.

'Thank you.' She drank, looking at him over the rim of the glass. Then she sighed. 'It is good. I had a headache. But that is gone now I think.'

He took the empty tumbler carefully. Again his hand trembled - lest he might touch her fingers.

'You must rest. Really you must rest. You look dead tired.'

She shook her head - carefully - as if afraid she might bring back that splitting pain.

'No. I'm not tired now. I feel better. I feel all happy and light somehow - like air. And I want to go into the garden again.'

He tried to force a smile but no smile came to his dry lips.

'It's rather late, isn't it, to think of that?' Once more, despite himself, he spoke her name. And she repeated it in that distant tone, saying:

'It is lovely to hear you call me that. It reaches away down deep and far, far back.' Impulsively she pressed her hands together and exclaimed: 'Let's go outside. That is where the freesias are - hundreds of them - cool and beautiful. And there is the orange grove. I want to feel I'm truly there. Oh, don't you see I'm happy and excited. It's so wonderful to know it's real at last, that we are here together, that I don't have to wake up alone and sad.'

Her words, spoken with a dreamy earnestness, alarmed him; he wished at once to protest and to obey. As he gazed into the smiling darkness of her eyes, within his mind a warning sounded. Again he was afraid. But the tenderness of her mouth dissolved alike his fear, his faint resistance. He could no longer think. He wanted only to be near her. He followed her through the silent hall.

Outside the portico, the shallow steps, creviced with their scarlet lichen, held her motionless for a moment. Gazing to the west, standing close to him, she drew a long, deep breath in which seemed mingled sadness and delight. There, upon the lava peaks, the sun, a bubble of fire, had burst and splashed the sky with wild, empurpled flame. Cupped by the vaulted heaven the blazing tongues sank downwards and greenish lights appeared, translucent, quivering upwards into the pale yet darkening canopy. Moments passed and then she sighed.

'When you stand near to me like this I feel the sunset throbbing in my heart.'

He did not answer and again the silence linked them. The words he might have uttered were gross beside the singing sweetness of that silence. Slowly before their eyes the day languished as with love, swooning towards the arms of the dusk.

Then she stirred. With eyes upturned and unveiled she smiled at him, began to walk towards the orange grove. The freesias, outsoaring upon the pathway, brushed gently against her skirt; stooping, she trailed her fingers among their draped whiteness, soft and caressing, caressing as a sea.

'I've been cheated of this before,' she murmured. 'Always when I went to clasp the freesias there was nothing. All vanished and cold.'

Suddenly, overflowing the barriers of reason, a haunting illusion grew. It swelled and swelled. There came to him quite vividly an intuition - mad yet splendid. All his faculties resisted. But in vain. He was lost - and went plunging downwards, downwards through space and time. In a low voice he said:

'This is the place you told me of? You are sure?'

'Yes,' she answered with perfect naturalness, 'I'm sure! That is why I feel that I am truly home. Everything the same. The house, the courtyard, the funny twisted tree, the orange grove. Everything the same. And my freesias, my lovely, lovely freesias.' She broke off, a poignant sweetness in her tone. Then with a little gasp she added: 'And you. I know at last, you see. The dream is nothing, the garden nothing, without you. For we have been here before. Oh, linked by something more than dreams. I know it to be so.'

Her voice was faintly strained as though she willed desperately that he should understand. And again, at her words, dimly, as with recollection through the thick texture of reality, something rose and turned within his soul. It was madness: a mad and shapeless myth. But here on this volcanic isle, erupted from the rim of sea back through primal aeons, the facts of life were myths and every myth a towering actuality. Suddenly, as a star might gleam athwart a shadowed world, the meaning of their meeting grew clear to him and it was as if life had suddenly begun. He could not explain, he could not fully understand. He could only believe.

He drew nearer to her. The beauty of heaven and earth was sublimated in her eyes and flowed towards him in a burning stream. He loved her. It could not be denied. They stood now in the orchard of the orange trees. Darker grew the dusk, and, like a slow-swung thurible, silver and alight, the moon sailed lambent into the sky, touching the trees with radiance. Beneath one tree she paused and raised her hand into the fragile branches.

'Look,' she whispered. 'Is it not lovely and strange?'

The tree, laden with heavy, ripened fruit was burdened, too, with blossom and with bud on which the moon made lovely gleamings. Blossoms and fruit; innocence and knowledge; a twofold dignity which she mysteriously possessed.

He thrust up his hand through the drooping foliage and clasped a shining orange. It lay within his fingers, cool and smooth as a virgin breast. He did not pluck it. Nor had she plucked the fruit but merely a tiny sprig of blossom which now distilled a fragrance from its calyces against her cheek.

Suffused by trembling tenderness he looked at her. The thin line of her bosom outlined by her upraised arm offered itself innocently to him and he longed to clasp it as he had clasped the fruit.

'Mary,' he said; and again her name sounded so exquisite upon his lips that tears came into his eyes. 'I have never known anything like this, nor anything so beautiful as you. I can't understand. But I know that all my life has been nothing up till now.'

Though through ages she had waited for this moment, her eyes, closed by the perfume of the orange flowers, opened timidly towards him. The strange pulse, which through the day had troubled her, began again, beating, beating behind her brow. She thought: perhaps it is happiness which makes me feel like this.

In his blood the surging eagerness increased, and his face, no longer gaunt, wore that wild arisen joy. Winging to him came the thought that he had never touched her. No, he thought, not even have I touched those fingers that might fall so cool and soft upon my lips. His body trembled. He stretched out his hand towards her.

Surely now she was lighter than the moon-drenched air. But

the pulse within her head was beating, beating, beating - confusing her beyond thought. As in a trance she placed the slip of orange-blossom in his hand. With fumbling touch he thrust it amongst the tresses of her hair. She tried to smile. How stiff her lips were suddenly, and how dry! She could not smile the quickening tenderness that enkindled her.

He was close to her, so close the opening sweetness of her body exhaled to him. He held his breath. Together in this deserted house, enwrapped by the scented ardent night, alone. All changeless and predestined. The orange-blossom in her hair gleamed palely. Nothing in heaven or earth could now arrest their love: this love which he had never known before, which now incredibly was his.

'Are you happy?'

'I am happy,' she answered breathlessly. 'That is all I know. I feel light and free. Away from everything.'

Her heart swelled like the throat of a thrush. She felt his body melting towards her; but cruelly her own body had become a cage which stiffly baulked the flowing ardour of her spirit.

With all her soul she longed for him. Not to assuage that longing would mean the bitterness of death. I love him, she thought wildly. At last I have found love which wearily all my life I have awaited. And, fleeing the racing darkness of her mind, she said wanly:

'I came here because I love you. Oh, my love, do you understand? There is nothing in life but you.' Then piteously she pressed her hand to her brow.

Startled, he gazed at her, torn between joy and fear. The pallor of her brow blinded him; and, beneath, her eyes seemed shadowed, suddenly worn by an inward fever. Instinctively he took her hand. It burned him like fire, burning, burning like the hot beating in her head. The colour ebbed slowly from his face so that his lips were white. Where there had been singing, now there was panic in his blood.

'Mary, beloved,' he cried. 'Your hands are burning.'

'It is that queerness,' she answered thickly, 'come back again. But it will pass like it did before. What does it matter when I love you?' She tried again to smile but now her face was like a mask mocking her from afar. Not one, but many masks, leering amongst the shadows of the orange-trees. And, through it all, with anguish she hungered to let herself dissolve into the sweetness of his kiss.

Then all at once she felt herself defeated, shrivelled. Forlornly she made to say again: 'I love you'; but no words came. Instead, those leering masks revolved about her, faster, faster, circling at giddy speed; and then the earth rose up and darkness struck her. Swooning, she fell towards him into his arms.

He gave an incoherent cry, riven by a dreadful thought. Supporting her weightless body, again he took her hand. Her pulse beneath the thin archway of her wrist galloped madly. Against his cheek her cheek lay burning. Her whole body was aflame.

'Oh, God,' he groaned aloud, 'why didn't I think before? It's fever.'

Her white lids lifted, and for a second her eyes looked into his all wide and mournful like a wounded bird.

'At last,' she whispered weakly. 'But how awfully queer I feel.' And then her head drooped forward upon his arm.

For an instant he gazed fixedly at those shuttered eyes, then with passionate haste he gathered her, and, half running, half stumbling, bore her back through the garden to the house. The door gave to the violent impulse of his shoulder. In the hall he did not pause, but, calling loudly: 'Manuela! Manuela!' he mounted the stairs swiftly and entered his own room. There upon the old brocaded coverlet of his bed he laid her, and, panting, knelt down beside her. At the sight of her prone body, so helpless upon that bed, a thought came which lacerated him. Tears ran into his eyes, blinding him. Distracted, he pressed her limp hands within his own.

Suddenly, at a scraping sound, he turned quickly. Manuela was behind him peering from the shadows with her sombre startled eyes. Without rising from his knees, he said hurriedly:

'The English señora is ill, she has fainted. Will you bring some water, please. Quickly.'

She did not move, but, after a pause which seemed to him intolerably long, she said flatly:

'And what business has this English señora to be here?'

'No business,' he cried. 'But she is ill. Bring water quickly in the ewer.'

There was a silence. The serving woman, staring blankly, seemed to turn strange theories within the dull caverns of her mind. Then all at once she bent forward, peering across his shoulder, her eyes starting beneath her sallow brow.

'Sea por Dios!' she exclaimed shrilly. 'She is ill, you say. Dios mio, I know that look upon the face.' Her voice rose.

'Dios mio, but it is writ upon her. She has the sickness!'

'Be quiet,' Harvey cried harshly. 'Get water, I tell you. You must help me. Do you understand?'

Manuela drew back, posied for a violent protest. But she made no protest. She stood with arms crossed, strangely motionless; then her mouth closed like a trap. Without a word she swung round. Darting one last look across her shoulder she passed stealthily from the room.

Immediately Harvey rose from his knees and lit another candle. His hand trembled, so that the liquid wax ran down and splashed in warm gouts upon his fingers, but, shielding the flame, he held it near, gazed deeply into Mary's face. It was flushed now, the eyelids slightly swollen, the lips scarlet as a wound. A low groan broke from his lips. He knew it was as Manuela had said.

Manuela! Would the woman never come? His hands clenched savagely, with sudden determination he shot from the room and raced downstairs, calling aloud her name. 'Manuela! Manuela!' The cry had a lost sound, rising and falling through the dark emptiness of the hall, the refectory, the kitchen. There was no answer. He called and called, then, suddenly, in the deserted kitchen, he stopped, struck by a knowledge of the truth. Manuela had taken fright. She had run away.

His expression changed slowly. So he was alone - save for the old marquesa, who now must be asleep - alone with Mary in this benighted house. For ten seconds he stood quite still. Some broth simmering in a pan upon the charred wood embers made a gentle hubble-bubble of sound. From outside the faint croaking of frogs stole in like voices raised in mockery. Then his eyes hardened with sudden resolution. He threw off his jacket. Turning, he seized a brimming water-jar that stood upon its low, slate ledge. Clasping the dewed earthenware in his arms he went rapidly upstairs.

She lay as he had left her, her scarlet lips parted, her bosom rising to her quickened breaths. With a set face he began to unfasten her dress. His fingers were stiff and cold as ice yet now they did not tremble. But within him his heart trembled, flooded by a mortal anguish. She wore so little, her body was so light, her clothing slipped from her like gossamer. One by one he placed her garments upon the chair, her dress that seemed fashioned for her fragility, her stockings that drooped to nothing in his hand.

Tiny beads of sweat broke coldly upon his brow, the fine edge

142

of his nostrils seemed cut from stone. But he went on. He knew it was imperative: he must combat the rising fever. Her skin was white like silk, her breasts unguarded, small and firm, pink-tipped with innocence. Soft shadows fell aslant her outstretched body, draping its lower nudity. About her unresistant form there floated a marvellous serenity.

At last, with a convulsive gesture, he threw back the coverlet, and, clasping her gently, lowered her upon the coolness of the sheet. As he moved, her arm fell limply and seemed to seek its place around his neck. For that single instant her heavy eyes opened and consciousness returned.

'It is so like me,' she muttered brokenly, 'to be a nuisance to you.'

Before he could answer she was away, falling, falling down darkly into a deep oblivion.

He took water and began rapidly to sponge her naked body. His mind worked desperately. He thought with supreme intensity: I must save her. I will save her. If she dies then I too will die. That does not matter. Nothing matters but that she shall be saved.

Under his moving hands her skin grew cooler, moist with the spring water which lay between her breasts like dew. Deluding himself, he fancied she breathed more peacefully; with fingertips upon the thin column of her throat he tried to feel a slackening of her racing blood. Nothing, he thought blindly, nothing matters if only she will get well. Again those words formed and reformed within him until they suffused his very soul and rose soaring from the tenebrous room - an inarticulate aspiration to the watching sky.

He flung down the towel, covered her lightly with the sheet, stood over her. Then at a thought he went downstairs into the kitchen, poured out a cup of the simmering broth and returned. When the broth had cooled, he supported her tired head gently and gave her to drink. Instinctively, like one half sleeping, she drank deeply with soft and drooping lip. To see her swallow the thin cold soup afforded him an exquisite comfort. Courage came to him. Quietly he put away the empty cup, quietly he sat down beside her. Bending forward he took her hand in his, let her fingers rest upon his palm. Immobile as a rock he let his strength flow out to her.

The minutes passed silently. The vigil brought him strange felicity. Hope ran into the coldness of his heart. He had pledged himself to save her. Outside, the croaking of the frogs went on - a passionless uncomprehended cry. A night bird brushed the window with soft wings. The moon swung round, flooding the room with gracious light, loitered awhile and then was gone. And there through the long still night he watched and tended her.


## CHAPTER XX


THE candles guttered to their sockets, the dawn broke fair and clear, the leaves stirred softly, preening themselves from sleep, and Susan Tranter came down the hill to Los Cisnes with an eager step.

A shy flush was on her cheek. Kind of early, she reckoned, to be calling at the house. To be sure it was! Yet, as she picked a flower and thrust it in her dress, she thought: There isn't any harm. We're working together, aren't we? He'll be at breakfast, with - oh, that quietness in his face. He may even smile to me. We'll go together to the village.

Yes, it was happiness for her to be linked with Harvey in such a cause. The outbreak, it is true, had passed its zenith; signs of its abatement were in the air. The form was fulminating, falling as swiftly as it had risen. And, in spite of Rodgers's reviling, the authorities had now taken action. Not the kind of action, she thought, that a real live organisation might have put over. No, indeed. But it would serve its purpose. The civic guard were in Hermosa, and an army surgeon; the dead had been buried, the houses fumigated, a makeshift hospital constituted, a drastic ring of quarantine drawn round the village.

There was less to do than she had wished. But still, it was a noble work. And to do that work by Harvey's side - ah, there lay the happiness, a thrilling happiness which overcame even her uneasiness upon her brother's account. Something was wrong with Robert. She did not wish him to be involved in the business of the epidemic. It wasn't his work. He wasn't strong enough to expose himself to infection. Yet, to see him moping all day in apathy, goading himself to false activity under Rodgers's caustic eye - it gave her a fathomless disquiet.

But even that could not quench the sparkle of her eye, nor curb the briskness of her step, as she pushed open the door and entered the hall of Los Cisnes. With brightness in her plain face she went into the refectory. No breakfast was set; no one was there. Surprised, she hesitated, then, with a little twitching smile, she reflected: Slept late, of course - he hasn't come down yet. The smile remained upon her lips as at a secret thought. Then she turned, slowly ascended the staircase, paused once more. Diffidently she knocked upon the door of his room.

'Are you up?' she called.

There was a strange silence; then from within his voice answered. But, though she held her ear close to the panel, she could not make out the words.

Another silence followed, and again his voice came - more clearly, bidding her to enter.

She turned the handle and went in. She took three steps forward, then her smile went wrong. Her mouth stiffened and all the brightness of her look dissolved. Her eyes slipped from his haggard face to the figure upon the bed. A short cry rose, and was stifled coldly in her breast.

'She is ill,' he said in a flat voice. 'It is that cursed fever.' And he turned away his head.

The world had suddenly gone dead for Susan. She did not think to ask why Mary should be here. Enough that she was here, a blow undreamed of, shattering hopelessly all the new zest of life. Her eyes, travelling dully about the room, took in everything: the sodden towels upon the floor, Mary's bare arm, her hand resting in his hand, the heap of silken underclothing lying nakedly upon the chair. At this a spasm of pain went through her. But she forced herself to speak.

'Is she very ill?'

'Yes.'

'And she has nothing here - not - not even a nightdress?'

'What does that matter?'

A pause.

'Did you sit up with her all night?'

'Yes.'

'You worked all day yesterday. You sat up all night. You must be very tired.'

He made no answer; and she, too, was silent. Then, aware dimly that some explanation was due to her, he told her briefly of Mary's coming on the previous night.

She listened with averted eyes; then she said:

'You can't keep her here. She'll have to go to Santa Cruz. There's nothing here fit for a sick person. You've no drugs, nothing.'

'I can get everything I want. She can't be moved. I won't have her moved.'

Susan made no reply. She was staring intently, ridiculously, at the floor. A long sigh shook her without escaping from her lips. She moved, came slowly forward, took off her hat, her cotton gloves, and placed them upon the table by the window.

'Well, you'd better rest now,' she said at last; her voice, extinguished, would not rise above a monotone. 'You must be terrible tired. I guess I'm going to look after her.'

He did not appear to hear, but as she began to tidy up the room his eyes, looking sideways, followed her careful movements. And at length he said:

'Do you mean that you will help me to nurse her?'

'I'll nurse her. Nothing else for it, I reckon. It's my plain duty.'

He studied her intently with his sleep-tormented eyes, then he said quietly:

'I shall not forget. You are really good.'

Susan stopped short as though she had been stung. And she flushed instantly - a shameful colour that mounted upon her brow. It seemed as though she would not speak, when suddenly she cried:

'You're wrong,' and now her voice was not a monotone. 'It isn't goodness that makes me do this. It's something quite different. I tell you it isn't goodness. It's the worst kind of jealousy. I know you love her. Don't you see I can't bear even to think of you touching her. That's why I've got to stick around and do for her. So's I can be here. So's I -' Choking, she raised her hand to her throat. Her eyes fell upon the garment she had been folding. With a sob she let it slip back upon the chair.

He got up and looked out of the window. Minutes passed, then in a calm, completely altered tone she spoke.

'You got to go and lie down.'

'I am all right.'

'Please be sensible. If you want to be at your best -' She stopped, but continued doggedly: 'For her sake you got to have sleep. I'll take duty now. I'll send a letter over to Robbie to let him know what's happened. You've got to have sleep.'

He seemed to weigh the reason of her words, then with grudging decision he moved from the window.

'Very well. I shall lie down for just one hour. You know what to do?'

'Yes.'

'You see, we must get the fever down -' He gave her his instructions, striving to infuse his tone with confidence, and then he added: 'It will be acute. Soon - soon there may be more to do!'

She nodded her head in tragic acquiescence, looking up at him with lacerated eyes.

His gaze left hers, then slid across her shoulder towards the flushed face upon the pillow. For a moment his soul lay naked - anguished and afraid; then he turned and went out of the room.

He crossed the corridor and, at random, entered another room. It was not a bedroom, but a stately chamber full of gilt furniture and dusty hanging lustres, shuttered against the light, with curtains frayed and carpets raddled by the ants - the ghastly ruin of a noble room. He did not care. Tearing open his collar, he flung himself upon a brocaded sofa and closed his eyes.

He tried to sleep, but sleep would not come. At least, no sleep that merited the name. The room had a musty smell like shut-up cupboards tenanted by mice. It seemed to him that the dangling lustres were waiting - waiting to play a tinkling tune. He tossed and turned upon the hard settee. Visions marched across his mind, not in orderly array, but massed distressingly, pressing, pressing upon him, inextricably tangled in their forward sweep. And always Mary was there, pleading piteously for his aid. At times it seemed that he heard voices; then came, too, a loud knocking, the sound of some arrival.

For about an hour this troubled rest endured, then abruptly he opened his eyes. Unrefreshed, he stared numbly at the gilded ceiling on which the painted swan with outstretched neck and pinions winged fantastically towards him. Despite himself, he shivered. The repetition of the emblem upon the ceiling of each room conveyed to him a sense of something ominous, inevitable. He felt suddenly chilled - menaced vaguely by the unknown.

At last he rose, shook off his lethargy, and went out of the room. But in the corridor he paused, his ears caught by the sound of a guarded yet heavy step beneath. Surely he knew that step. He listened attentively, then, moving quietly past Mary's room, he descended the stairs and entered the refectory. Yes, he had known who it was.

'Well,' he said, 'you've come.'

From across the chair on which he straddled, Corcoran smiled at him - that familiar, battered smile charged with unconquerable optimism.

'Sure. Didn't I tell ye I was comin'?'

'I'm glad,' said Harvey heavily. 'Yes, I'm glad that you have come.'

There was a silence, during which Corcoran shot furtively one serious glance at Harvey; then, pulling out his snuff-box, he tilted his head, affected to consider it with stupendous interest.

'I know how things are,' he said. 'Had it all from Susan T. She let me in, ye see. I near fell off the step at the soight of her. I'm sorry! Honest to God, I'm sorry - at the throuble - an' all. Faith, I'll do what I can to give ye a hand.'

'What is there for you to do?'

'Ye've got to eat, haven't ye? I'll get me sleeves up and have a turn in the cook-house. Sure, I've cooked for fifty in me time - back on an Oregon loggin'-camp. I'd like to have a slash at this place - kitchen and all. 'Tis a likely spot, but it's needin' someone with a sinse of order in his eye.'

Harvey listened with a set face; then he said:

'I might want some things from town. You'll get them for me?'

'Faith and I will too,' answered Jimmy soothingly. 'Didn't I run over with a note for Susan T. a minnit ago? I'll do anything that's useful. Talk sense. And, by the same token, I'll stand by ye if yer afther runnin' into throuble here.'

'Trouble? What do you mean?'

'Oh, just things I've been pickin' up down the town. Off and on, ye know. Nothin' special. Just odd bits of things.'

'What things?' cried Harvey tersely.

Jimmy breathed upon his snuff-box, rubbed it gently against his trouser-leg, then slipped it back into his pocket.

'Them two others has come over from Orotava,' he answered easily. 'Dibdin and Mistress Baynham. Stayin' at the Plaza, they are. And more. The agent fella, Carr, dropped into town last night and started raisin' hell to find the little lady. Betwixt one thing and another, I'm thinkin' ye might be havin' throuble to keep her here.'

'I intend to keep her here.'

'Of course ye do. Of course, of course.'

A word trembled on Harvey's tongue, but it remained unspoken. Just then the door-bell rang, a vicious pealing which was repeated with the same unnecessary force before the first jangling echoes had died out. The two men looked at each other, and into Corcoran's face there swam a look of righteous vindication.

'Didn't I tell ye?' he muttered. 'They've come afther her.'

'See who it is,' Harvey said curtly.

Jimmy felt for his toothpick, concomitant of his most absolute composure; thrusting it delicately between his teeth, he lounged from the room. A moment later a quick rush of footsteps sounded in the hall and a man burst into the room. It was Carr. At his heels came a little Spaniard with a small neat yellow face and a large neat leather bag.

Behind them, closing the door with studied nonchalance, was Corcoran.

Carr wasted no time: his heavy face was flushed, the veins of his neck congested; he looked a man whom anger had made to hurry. In one second his arrogant gaze flashed round the room then came to rest on Harvey.

'Mary Fielding is in this house,' he said, 'I've come to take her away.'

Harvey looked at him steadily. He did not answer for a long time.

'How do you know she is here?'

'On Tuesday she left her friends in Orotava. She had been queer - obviously unwell. The next afternoon she was seen in Santa Cruz enquiring the road to Laguna. We know she took a calèche to Los Cisnes. Last night, from the woman Manuela, we had positive information of an English señora who is ill with fever in this house. I know she is Mary Fielding. Now are you satisfied? I have a doctor and a closed car. I am going to take her away.'

Harvey's eyes came to rest on the Spaniard.

'You are a doctor?' he enquired civilly.

'Si, señor.' The little yellow man drew his small pointed boots together and made a deprecatory bow.

'Apothecary, graduate with commending of Seville. And with papers of recommending from many good families I have awaited upon.'

'Good!' said Harvey, 'apothecary graduate with commending and recommending. Very good.' Reflectively his gaze wandered back to Carr. 'And you are going to take her away?'

149

Carr's colour deepened.

'I've said that once,' he answered sharply. 'I don't propose to say it again. Where is she? Where is her room? I'm going up there now.'

'No,' said Harvey in the same even tone, 'you're not going up. And you're not going to take her away. She came here of her own free will. And now she is ill - desperately ill. Do you understand? And your surgeon apothecary is not going to look after her. I shall do that — here, in this house.'

'You!' sneered Carr. 'I know all about you. I've been making a few enquiries since I met you. I wouldn't trust a dog to your care. And here! What sort of place is this for a sick person? You've no nurse for her, no treatment, nothing.'

Harvey gave him a pale, cold glance.

'I have a nurse for her. I know what I am doing. And I say that it is madness for you to move her. She must not be moved until she has her crisis. Your Spanish friend will tell that I am right.'

The little apothecary, thus appealed to, put down his bag and made a timid non-committal gesture with his shoulders.

Carr took no notice; he was scowling; his eyes, slightly injected, were fixed on Harvey.

'You!' he said again, more loudly. 'I tell you I don't give a damn for your opinion. I've told you what I mean to do. And I don't intend to waste any more time. I'm in a hurry. I mean to find her.' He took two steps forward; but Harvey was at the door before him.

'No,' he said in a voice like ice, 'I think not.' He was surprised to find himself so calm. His whole body was set to an inordinate calmness. He felt himself poised like a runner keyed to the signal-gun. Within, his purpose burned with a cold intensity. The thought of physical violence, of interference from this hectoring fellow, made his determination glacial.

'Let me pass.'

Harvey shook his head slowly.

They faced each other closely; suddenly a corded artery stood out on Carr's temple.

'And who,' he said thickly, 'who is going to stop me?'

'I am.'

There was a rigid silence. The Spanish doctor, utterly dismayed, slipped back against the wall. Jimmy stood tense, his eyes alight, his nostrils expanded, his big hands clenching and unclenching in sheer delight.

On Carr's face there was a wicked look; with his head half lowered, he had a bull-necked pugnacity. He looked out and out a dangerous customer.

'So,' he sneered heavily, 'we think we can fight, do we? We are athletic as well as intellectual. Isn't that pretty?' All at once his tone altered; he thrust out his jaw. 'Get out of the way, you fool. I'm stronger than you. I know everything about this game. Get out or I'll wipe the floor with you.'

Harvey did not move. His face had a cold pallor; his lips, drawn together, held the vestige of an inner smile.

'Will you get out?' cried Carr again.

Once more Harvey shook his head, his eyes still fixed on the other's face.

'Then, by God, you'll get hurt,' shouted Carr, and with his hands up and his head down he rushed forward. Viciously he shot out his left, missed, then swung with his right. The blow caught Harvey heavily upon the head. As it went home, a sort of sneering grin ran over Carr's face. He was a trained boxer. He saw that Harvey had no style – his hands were low, his guard open – and he thought wickedly: He knows nothing; I'll punish him till he drops.

Crouching, his lower lip protruding mockingly, he sparred lightly, then feinted, to land on the jaw with his left. But the blow never landed. Harvey suddenly shot out his right. Let go unexpectedly, the knuckled fist smashed full into Carr's face with such force it seemed to flatten back his nose. His head jerked over, a spurt of blood gushed down his nostrils, the smile twisted upon his mouth. He swallowed painfully. The saline taste of his own blood ran into his throat. He drew back, shook his head, then bored in again with a fierce rush. The rush carried Harvey back against the door. His shoulder struck heavily against the solid wood, but he side-stepped and hit Carr hard in the wind. He felt his fist go home with a soft thud. Carr winced. He was getting more than he had bargained for. His temper gone, his lip now drawn back in a fixed snarl, he rushed in again and went for Harvey, using both hands to head and body. For a full minute he forced the fighting without landing clean. Harvey kept away from him, always a fraction too soon. His quickness was extraordinary, his eye steady, hard with a deep-set bitterness. He knew nothing of boxing. But he knew he must get the better of this fight. High on his cheek-bone was a livid weal; he breathed through his nostrils; he seemed waiting, waiting all the time.

Carr was trying everything he knew. His arrogant air was gone; he was feeling now the flabbiness of his condition. He seemed desperately anxious to get home a decisive punch. Moisture ran down behind his ears; his quick, indrawn breaths hissed through his teeth. He hit Harvey heavily in the neck, bored in to a clinch. Using his weight, he butted Harvey hard under the chin, fell on him savagely, wrestled and tripped him across his knee.

Harvey went down, twisting his leg. But he was up in a second, fought off Carr's rush, and fell into a clinch. In that panting breath upon his cheek he heard the signal he had awaited. He broke away. For a moment he stood off, poised on his toes, then with shut teeth he dashed fiercely into Carr. He seemed to have saved everything for this. He showed no science, but he fought like a demon. Carr took heavy punishment, tried to cover up, and failed. A blow to the head sent him staggering to his knees. He knelt there for a while, then he rose, panting. Smeared with blood, his face was an ugly sight. His collar had come adrift; his hair fallen across his eyes. And he was wild with rage. He went for Harvey madly. His jaw was uncovered, and, like a flash, with all his strength Harvey shot out his left. The delicious thrill of that impact ran up his arm and into his blood like tingling fire. It was a moment to live for.

Carr fell with a thud. It was all over. Harvey wiped the sweat from his eyes, stood watching. Slowly Carr rolled over on his side, lay for a moment with glassy stare upon the ceiling, then struggled to his feet. One eye was closed; his mouth seemed full of blood. Supporting himself against the table, he coughed once or twice, groped in his pocket, pulled out a handkerchief, and pressed it painfully against his lips.

'I'll remember this,' he said with difficulty, looking at Harvey from the corner of his eyes. 'I don't forget easily.'

'Sure ye won't forget it,' broke in Jimmy; he paused, let out a long, ecstatic sigh. 'Ye've had such a hidin' it'll stick to ye for the rest of yer born days.'

'You haven't finished with me,' went on Carr, still staring slantingly at Harvey. 'I know how to deal with you.'

Harvey said nothing.

'You've landed yourself in a pretty mess,' continued the other. 'And I warn you, if anything happens to Lady Fielding you will be held responsible. I am going to cable to her husband. Immediately I have his authority I shall act.'

Holding his face tenderly, he threw one last vicious glance at

Harvey, then, with his head down, brushed past to the door. The apothecary, impelled at last to action looked helplessly from one to the other, bowed jerkily at nothing, then followed like a puppy-dog.

As he went by, Harvey reached out his hand and said quietly: 'Leave me that bag.'

'But, señor,' stammered the other, pale to the lips, 'my medicaments are contained -'

'Don't be afraid. You shall have it back. Later.'

'Assuredly, señor. Most assuredly. But there is the question of usage. For me there is need of immediate usage. And it is not convenable to deprive quickly. We of the profession - we must conduct ourselves, señor, with moral, with behaviour, with deportment.'

Firmly Harvey took the bag. The apothecary stood limp, then, raising his hands and eyes to heaven, he gasped aloud one word and fled the room to safety. There was a moment's silence split by the heavy slam of the outer door, then Jimmy pressed forward, his battered face ecstatically abeam.

'By God,' he cried, 'that was a fight. Sure, I wouldn't have missed it for the money in Klondyke. You gave him two stone and knocked a tune out of him. Oh, didn't you spoil his mug! It's the prettiest fight I've seen since cracky Joe put out the Smiler. Oh, tricky, tricky, lovely.' His lips worked with his delight; he took snuff twice rapidly; then felt Harvey's bleeding knuckles with gentle, appraising touch.

'Nothin' broke, thank God. These thick-necked customers take a lot of knockin' out. Oh, my sammy, what a hidin' he took. Didn't he ask for it? And didn't he need it? Are ye all right yourself, now? Are ye sure?'

'I'm all right,' said Harvey. He walked over to the table, lifted up the bag, and pulled it open. It contained, as he anticipated, a serviceable equipment of instruments and drugs. He snapped the catch shut, picked up the bag again, and stepped across the room. At the door, standing with one hand pressed against the lintel, he gave Corcoran a final look.

'I'm going up now,' he said. 'Do what you can down here.' Turning, he went upstairs to the sick-room.

## CHAPTER XXI

AFTERNOON of the same day. And Corcoran was in the kitchen, which he had made, instinctively, his own. The beaten blue clay floor, wide-open fireplace, and lofty cone-shaped roof - designed five hundred years before to carry off the fume of roasting meats - were somehow congruous to his nature. But the sad disorder of the place offended even his indulgent eye.

Discarding coat and vest, he had set himself in gentlemanly fashion - hardly to clear the litter, but to 'put a top on things,' to draw just a 'dthrop of wather,' to furnish leisurely a few utensils against their later use.

He was whistling softly. He liked a job like this - sure, he did! - it brought back memories of the old place yonder. There was, indeed, about this spot a native ease that pleased him proudly. He was content. Suddenly, at a quiet sound, he paused, glanced up from his work. The marquesa stood in the doorway, her hands folded, her bird-like eyes bent immovably upon him. At once he stopped his gentle whistle and with a conscious air tucked his shirt more modestly within his waist-belt. Then he rubbed his chin with the back of his hand and eloquently broke the silence.

'Turned warmer of a suddent, don't ye fancy? Faith, for all that it goes against the grain to let you catch me unbeknowns without me collar.'

Still framed by the doorway, she said:

'Where is Manuela?'

'If it's the woman yer meanin', she's gone this long while back. Or so they tells me. And she's left a pretty pickle of a mess behind. Bad scran to her, ye'd think she'd stirred the kitchen wid a stick. I'm doin' me best to get things straight.'

She pursed her tiny mouth perplexedly.

'But I do not understand. You, a guest! Thus you demean yourself and me.'

'Ah, now! Honest work never demaned nobody,' he boasted, with a virtuous hitch to his braces, 'no, indade, not the finest fambly in the land. And as for the other, sure, doesn't Playto say it's proper to bestow fayvours on them what needs them?'

'I do not ask favour,' she answered gravely. 'Here, Isabel de Luego bestows favour. But without doubt you are gentle. And your family? You have said that it is truly fine.'

'None bether,' he assured her blandly. 'Descended from the Kings of Ireland on me father's side. I could giv' ye the pedigree. There's the blood of Brian Boru in me for a sartinty.'

She gave a little exclamation, and came mincing into the room towards him.

'So, it is pleasure. Truly, you have the air of caballero.'

For a moment he gallantly sustained her naïve yet hooded scrutiny; then sheepishly he looked down, wiped his palms on the seat of his trousers, and declared:

'Well, that's the way me father had it, anny way. The more so when he'd got a dthrop of flip in him. Maybe we was and maybe we wasn't such great things. But an Irishman's a gintleman whatever way he's born. And show me the man that denies it. I'll paste him like Harvey done the agent.'

'Yes, you have fought,' she murmured. 'Your face - so bravely ugly - scarred like a matador's. It does not prepossess. But behind there is a heart.'

He shifted his feet and reached ineffectually for his snuff. Then he grinned.

'Sure, there's a heart. Big as a boat. Couldn't have swam along without it.'

'You have had trouble. Ay, ay, ay. It is writ upon your beautiful unloveliness. Trouble enough to break the heart of strength. But be not put down. Always there is an ending. For you perhaps there is an ending now.'

Doubtful still as to whether her intention was derisive, Jimmy threw her an uncomfortable glance from beneath his tufted brows.

'You've had trouble enough yourself by the look on it.'

She smiled, netting her face with sad yet elfish wrinkles.

'Jesus Maria,' she murmured. 'Speak not that word for Isabel de Luego. Be it known she is surrounded by infamy. Or was. Everything gone to loss. Everything to pieces. Make yourself honey and the flies will eat you. Breed up crows and they will peck your eyes out. Don Balthasar was the only one. And now he is dead.'

Jimmy scratched his head, thinking: Don Balthasar. He was the biggest crow of the lot by the look on it. And he had her well blinkered. Aloud he said:

'Ye've got a tidy piece of land here, ma'am. Faith, it's a shame to see it fell to such rack and ruin. A man - a good man, mind ye - could make it ship-shape in a twel'month. Didn't nobody niver want to give ye a hand with it, now?'

'Words of the mouth are like stones of a sling. Many would promise, none would do. They do not work; they rob; above at the finca of the Americano they withdrew the water from the stream, though it is forbidden. Land will not prosper in a woman's hand. Ay, ay, ay, it is hard for Isabel de Luego.'

'The scoundthrels,' muttered Jimmy in powerful sympathy, 'to be humbuggin' ye like that. It's athrocious. Why, with a bit of sound overlookin' by a capable fella this place could make a glorious come-back. It's a lovelee spot.' Enraptured by a growing idea, Corcoran open his mouth to extol the virtue of his sentiment. But she murmured:

'So, señor! But you, too, take heed of words. Speaking witout thinking is shooting without aiming.'

He closed his mouth again. The expression on her face baffled him. There was a curious silence.

'Ah,' he muttered. 'Maybe I'm a bether shot than ye think.'

'No doubt you have done many things,' she went on imperturbably. 'No doubt you have travelled far. And no doubt you must travel farther.'

'Be hanged to the farther,' he declared. 'I'd give me Sunday hat to be settled in a tidy billet.'

Again there was silence. He waited quite breathlessly: would she or wouldn't she be takin' the hint?

'You are a heretic, of course,' she sighed. 'Alas, it cannot be else!'

Then Jimmy had an inspiration. Thrusting his fist into his trousers pocket, he solemnly produced, not Plato, but a string of worn beads. It was a rosary, and he dangled it reverently before her eyes.

'Look at that, will ye?' he murmured piously. 'Divil the heretic would be carryin' that about wid him. Over the seven seas it's been wid me.' It was true: he carried it like a charm wherever he went, but once only in a twelvemonth would he say an *ave*. 'Me ould mother's beads they be's - rest to her goodness. And, by the holy, they've steered me straight, through sorrow and through gladness.'

She looked, not at the dangling beads, but far beyond them; then vaguely she smiled.

'Madre de Dios,' she pronounced, as to herself. 'I would have said before there was more noise than nuts. But perchance after all there is a kernel.'

It was impossible to mistake her meaning. Completely taken aback, for the first time in five years Corcoran blushed. His jaw dropped; a vivid scarlet mantled his corrugated brow.

Then, still without looking at him, she murmured:

'Be at ease, señor. A blush on the cheek is better than a stain on the heart. I have a regard for you. Later we will talk.'

Turning without warning, she trailed slowly from the room. And Jimmy stood gaping after her like an old carp waiting to be fed. At last he moved, let out a long dumbfounded breath.

'Did ye ever!' he declared to the ambient air. 'Did ye ever meet the like!' He was obliged to ferret in his waistcoat, hanging upon a chair, and to recover himself with snuff. Then, as his gaze slid out of the window and fell upon the rich enclosure beyond, the recurrence of his thought made him hug himself.

'Jumpin' Moses,' he muttered warmly, 'but wouldn't it be powerful grand if she's got the same notion as meself in that bit of a headpiece of hers. Sure, it's a little kingdom-come of a spot. And a man could put shape intil it quicker'n eat sausidge. The sun's glorious; the soil would make buckshot sprout. Eighteen months and I'd have a new plantation bearin'. I'd bring smoke out a them lazy yellah boys, thievin' a poor old woman like they been. It's a black burnin' shame just to think on it. And besides, what a life for the gintleman! "Good mornin, Don Corcoran, and what are yer honour's orders for today?" Sure, it's got the pig in the backyard knocked to glory. Oh, faith alive, I'd be settled aisy for life if she'd only rise to the occasion.' Tenderly he restored the rosary to his pocket and patted it lightly. 'Me mother always said good would come of ye. And, be the saints, for once the ould lady wasn't far wrong.'

In an excess of holy zeal, he seized the dish-cloth and began to assault the greasy pan, while at the same time he broke lightly into:

> 'Oh! I'll knock a hole in McCann
> For knockin' a hole in me can.'

He was still polishing when, five minutes later, the door opened and Susan Tranter came into the room. The look upon her face drove the smile from his lips and he stopped dead in the middle of a bar. Swept by the optimism which could so readily elate him, he had forgotten - of course he had forgotten! - but now a sudden flash presented the melancholy situation that had slipped his mind. His face fell comically; he made with his tongue a distressful sound reproaching his unpardonable neglect; and following a pause he said:

'Is she - is she any bether - herself - upstairs?'

Susan shook her head without speaking. She was pale, and her lips and eyes had a curiously rigid look. Even her body was stiff, as though purposely she held herself erect and taut, containing with all her resoluteness the burning conflict that was in her.

'Ye'r tired,' said Jimmy, pulling forward a chair. 'Ye'r lookin' all wore out. Sit down and rest ye. I've a drop of broth here that'll put pith in ye.'

Again she shook her head.

'I'm going for my things. I must see my brother. Then - then I'll be back.' There was a queer finality in those few slow words which touched his ready sentimental heart.

'Ah, come on now,' he coaxed her. 'Just slip off yer legs for a minute. Sure, what harm will it do? And, if ye don't fancy soup, say the word and I'll give ye coffee in a jiffy.'

She did not sit down; but neither did she go. She stood gazing at him with those rigid, troubled eyes; then, as if drawn by a force which could not be escaped, she said frozenly:

'She is not better. She is worse, much worse.'

He gave her a quick look, then with averted face meditatively stroked his chin.

'Why don't you say something?' she went on in a suppressed tone. 'I say she's worse. The jaundice is beginning. She has been very sick. She is delirious - raving about all sorts of nonsense - gardens and fountains and her' - the words suddenly came flat - 'her freesia flowers.'

'Well, I'm sorry,' he muttered heavily, 'downright sorry to hear it.'

'Sorry! There's every reason to be sorry!' Her voice rose to a vibrant pitch. 'I don't think she'll get better. I feel she's going to die. A terrible conviction that I've got' - her voice was rushing, climbing - 'that terrible conviction of death - death in the air. Can't you feel it, beating over the place like wings? Darkness pressing in, and disaster. She is lying up there. And he is with her. And all the time I'm thinking -' She did not finish. Her plain features were suddenly distorted - she choked upon her words. There was an uneasy silence.

'Well, well,' he said at length, as though to pacify her. 'Ye must be aisy. 'Tisn't like ye to be this way. While there's life there's hope. And you're doin' yer best, aren't ye?'

But his manner increased her agitation.

'Doing my best,' she cried out. 'Of course I'm doing my best. Doing everything - everything. I'm fighting - fighting with him to save her. But don't you see -' She broke off and caught his arm quite wildly. Her voice fell to a whisper. 'Don't you see I love him? And in my heart I don't want her - I don't want her to get well. Oh, God in heaven, it's terrible, terrible - me - to be thinking that. But I can't help it. And it's killing me.'

Her distress was painful. For an instant it looked as though she would burst into scalding tears. But no, she did not weep. She gritted her teeth upon her sobs; her twitching cheek grew stiff; her hand fell from his arm.

'So now you know,' she whispered, labouring with her choking breaths. 'At least I've told somebody - what I am.'

There came again a heavy silence, then in a low voice she said:

'I'm going - going to get my things.' And in spiritless, disjointed fashion she moved through the side door into the patio, followed by his perplexed, commiserating eyes. Restrained only by her will, the anguish in her bosom almost stifled her. Her heart seemed burning, bursting with the commingling of pain and love.

Yet as she walked through the cool air she struggled for self-control. She took the long way by the stream, climbing slowly the path that wound along the cracked and crumbling bank. Eased in part by her feverish self-accusation, gradually she grew calmer. When she arrived at the Rodgerses' house her face was again composed.

There, upright in a rocker upon the bare porch, sat Aaron Rodgers himself. He did not rise as she approached, but threw her a sour, suspicious look and went on rocking himself with rapid sanctimonious jerks, like a holy roller in an ecstasy. She stood before him.

'Where is my brother?'

A definite pause intervened before, with eyes fixed forbiddingly upon infinity, he answered.

'Ain't here.'

A wave of disappointment swept her. She had wanted so much to see him - her own dear Robbie.

'Where is he?'

'Gone to get quinine,' he admitted grudgingly. 'Always dosin himself with that stuff when he might be doin' a mite of good. Yeah, look as wild-cat as you please. I'm talkin' about that brother of yours right now. He's the most doggone disappintment for a missioner that ever come my way. He ain't done a thing since he arrived but hang about and look goofy. Ever since he got your note he's been buzzin' mad. I'll tell him somethin' when he comes back from Santa Cruz. And he's goin' to like it none too good.'

Though now habituated to Rodgers's mean, inhospitable tongue, an outburst of indignation quivered within her. But she thought wearily: What is the use? And she said simply, as she moved into the house:

'My brother is not strong. You forget that he hasn't had time to settle down.' An unusual note of bitterness crept in. 'Give us time to get things straight before you ask for miracles.'

His acidulous 'Huh!' flew after her as she mounted the creaking pinewood stairs. But again she gave no heed. Rodgers's waspish rudeness! - it was as naught to bear beside the burden of her own distress.

She entered her room, drew her suit-case from beneath the bed, tugged open a drawer, gathered some clothing, a towel, sponge, and toothbrush, flung them listlessly into the case. Her preparations took but a moment. She knew her hair to be untidy - all mussed up, she thought bitterly, and mousey! Her eyes, too - sure, they must be a lovely sight! But she made no effort to repair the damage. She did not even look at herself in the glass. For a second she thought of leaving a note for Robert, but reflected that she had already written him her plans. Yes, she was ready. With suit-case in hand she descended the stairs, passed again through the porch.

Rodgers, rocking grimly, affected not to notice her, but she had not gone two paces beyond the step before his voice rang out.

'Here!' he shouted, 'where are ye goin' with that valise?'

She turned, faced him steadily.

'You know where I am going. I am going back to Los Cisnes.'

'What'ye mean?' He half rose from his chair. 'Mixin' up with that rotten bunch. Come back. D'ye hear? Come on back. What'ye think yer doin'? You ought to be ashamed to walk out on a man like this.'

'You know why I am going,' she answered fixedly. 'And when he comes in you'll tell my brother that I have gone. Tell him I don't want him to come down.' She meant to say: 'It isn't safe,' but instead she corrected herself and added: 'There is no necessity.'

Then, quite unmindful of his protesting shout, she turned and moved off down the stone-flagged drive between the green retama bushes. She walked slowly, her head inclined, her valise dragging upon her shoulder, her figure outlined against the light. And somehow there was a strange loneliness upon her.

## CHAPTER XXII

BUT Robert Tranter had not gone for quinine. Though in Santa Cruz he was searching now ostensibly for a shop which bore the sign 'Quimico,' in his heart this earnest-faced apostle of the Seventh Day Unity was not caring a button about quinine. The errand was a blind, constructed by his crumbled self-esteem to evade the acid-tongued suspicion of Aaron Rodgers. There was something - something *right* about this message for quinine. Honest - there was! Yes, he almost deceived himself. And all the time his big feet led him insidiously towards the Plaza.

Yet when the pharmacy was fortuitously discovered, his lips made a little clicking sound of satisfaction. Why, here it was, of course. He entered; ordered the medicine openly; sat upon one of the white chairs ranged in a row within the clean white place, his moist palms clapped upon his knees, waiting.

He began to hum a hymn tune, and, as he hummed, silly little verses went with the tune. He couldn't help it; they just came.

> *'From up aloft Robert was seen*
> *Waiting on his nice quinine.'*

And another one:

> *'I watch the chemist stir his rod,*
> *Nothin' wrong with dat, O Lawd.'*

He blushed. Funny sort of poetry, he guessed! Yet religion was so mixed up with a man's daily life you just couldn't get away from it. Didn't want to either! When the package was prepared he attempted a feeble joke with the white-coated chemist behind the counter.

'Reckon you don't serve chocolate sundae in your drug store?' A trifle hollow, perhaps, like the laugh which accompanied it, but still a joke.

The chemist did not smile. Watching the other's nervous grimace he said brusquely:

'Cuatro pesetas, señor.'

'Sure!' - fumbling in his pocket - 'You didn't think I wasn't gonna *pay* you?'

Then Robert was free - quite free to return to Laguna. And yet upon the pavement outside the shop he dallied. Around him the life of the town flowed heedlessly, yellow-faced men shouldering past him, women gliding, hooded in black shawls, mules tugging reluctantly against the yoke, a huckster crying aloud his raw, sliced water-melon, a woman swaying along - a basket of fresh-washed linen upon her head. At the corner of the street a civic guard in shiny three-cornered hat stood planted with his feet apart, his hands behind his back, his eye observant.

Robert stirred uneasily. Was the fellow watching, actually watching him? Why, it was preposterous! He stared back with a certain hauteur, and then, as at a secret thought, his eyes fell down. Suddenly he moved off down the street. He needed a walk, you see; time enough to go back when he'd had a stroll. A fellow ought to have a stroll after being cooped up on the hill. And it was towards the Plaza that he strolled.

The nervous look was back upon his face - a loutish, chalky look - as he came into the Plaza and crossed the blue and yellow tessellated square. Hardly knowing what he did he halted, sat down on an iron seat beneath some palms. There in front of him was the hotel - Hotel de la Plaza - the letters gilded across the stucco front. When he had received Susan's note from Corcoran he had jumped to a swift conclusion. His reasoning was wrong; but not his intuition. He had asked one agitated question, which Corcoran unguardedly had answered. That was enough. Since he had known that Elissa was in this hotel a burning impulse had tormented him - an impulse in which he saw the solution of his difficulties, and the end of his distress.

A light colour had risen to his cheeks, agitatedly he fingered his watchchain, then actually he moved his lips in prayer.

'O God, help me,' he groaned, 'help me to see her. You understand how I feel. I want to make things right. You know how *much* I want to see her. O Lord, help me now.' And abruptly he rose and walked swiftly into the hotel. His rush carried him into the lounge which opened out of the vestibule; and there, in wicker chairs beside one of the many small tables, were seated two men. Robert hesitated whilst he took them in - Dibdin, whom he recognised without enthusiasm, and Carr, whom he had never seen before - then with less impetuosity he advanced towards them.

His reception was chilling. Dibs offered a toneless word; Carr turned on him one sullen, swollen eye then pointedly turned it away.

'I wanted to say,' stammered Robert, 'how downright grieved I am at Lady Fielding's illness. And how glad that my sister Susan can be of service to her. Yes, sir, I honestly am. I sympathise deeply with you over this calamity.'

He rested his fingers upon the table edge, leaned towards them in an effort to convince.

There was a long unresponsive silence, then Dibs threw out:

'What are you doin' down here?'

'I came down from Laguna on an errand. To fetch some quinine, in fact. And I just looked in to offer my condolences to you - to you all.'

Dibs let his monocle drop to the end of its silken cord; without further ado picked up his conversation with Carr where it had been interrupted.

'If only that other cable would come,' he said, 'then we'd know how we stand.'

Carr exclaimed:

'Why the devil he asked for further information I'm damned if I know.'

'Michael's got his own way of lookin' at things,' Dibs said, and paused. 'Can't we do something on our own?'

'They're such fools at the Juzgado. And so damnably slow. It's the quarantine ring that's upset them. They won't go in or out of the blasted area. They'll take days to move.'

There was a silence.

'The point is,' said Dibs in a laboured tone, as though he had said it a hundred times before, 'that she walked out on me. How can I be to blame for that?'

'Oh, shut up,' cried Carr. 'I'm sick of your infernal whining. You haven't got the guts of a louse.'

They started to quarrel for perhaps the hundredth time; and

Robert stood listening with a hangdog air. He burned to ask them where Elissa was; but he did not dare. His bumptiousness was gone. All his moral stiffening turned to a watery paste.

He shifted his weight from one foot to the other, then blurted out:

'I guess I'll say good-bye, gentlemen. I hadn't ought to stay too long. So I'll be going.'

He waited, hungry for the comfort of a civil answer, but neither of them looked up; and so, his eye disconsolate, he swung round, drifted towards the door.

But in the vestibule he paused, his heart pounding, the flush risen more highly to his cheek. Oh, Lord, he thought agitatedly, I can't go away like this. Back to that lonely barracks at the Rodgerses' place. Simply can't go away. Must see her or I'll go plumb crazy. With a fearful side-glance to see if he were observed he turned to the negro porter at the desk. Moistening his lips he said:

'Is Mrs Baynham in the hotel?'

The nigger porter pocketed the little wooden twig with which he had been polishing his teeth and hastily stood up.

'Yes, sah, Mis' Baynham in her room.'

He repeated:

'In her room?'

'Yes, sah. Suite t'ree, sah. First floah front.'

'You might - you might show me up.' By a powerful effort he managed to keep his voice composed. But, as he ascended the stairs behind the porter and paused before a yellow-painted door upon the first floor, the last vestige of his composure crumpled weakly. His face wore a look of sickly self-consciousness as he entered the room; and he stood in the middle of the polished wood floor fingering his watch-chain with damp, stupid fingers.

'I called,' he said thickly, then his parochial voice broke and he had to start all over again. 'I was passing. Happened to be passing. So I thought - thought I might call.'

She stared at him with hard, unfriendly eyes. Reclining upon a wicker chaise-longue at the window, she had the look of a large, sulky cat. Her silk kimono, worn for the heat, fell with voluptuous lightness around her outstretched, languid figure. Her hair was unbound, her arms bare beneath the wide, blue sleeves, her bosom hardly covered.

But she made no effort towards delicate concealment. She

simply lay and stared him out of countenance. At last she said:

'So you thought you might call.'

He took a step forward.

'Oh, Elissa,' he whined, 'surely it is God's providence that we meet again. There's no way else to explain it. I thought you'd gone for good. It's like a miracle to me. Oh, but I've prayed for it. Yes, before God I have prayed for it.'

'You've prayed for it?' she repeated incredulously. 'Prayed for that?'

'You don't get me,' he cried. 'I don't mean any wrong. I've repented. Upon my knees I've told God I'm sorry. And don't you see, this is how He shows He understands. He brings us together again. Oh, Elissa, dear Elissa, we love each other. And why shouldn't we? It's wonderful. God created man and woman for each other.' His lips twitched; his eye glistened; throwing out his hand, he declaimed brokenly: 'The Lord God, He made woman and brought her unto the man. And Adam said: "This is now bone of my bones, and flesh of my flesh." '

There was a dead silence; then she said cuttingly:

'Is that all he said?'

No irony could restrain him. Surging forward on a wave of hysterical emotion he rushed on, quoting abandonedly:

' "Therefore shall a man leave his father and his mother, and shall cleave unto his wife; and they shall be one flesh. And they were both naked, the man and his wife, and were not ashamed." '

Her eyes widened; and she cried:

'Are you mad?'

'No, not mad. Only mad for love of you.' His breast heaved; tears rolled down his cheeks. 'Oh, Elissa my beloved, we have sinned together. But now we belong to each other. You are mine - you whom my soul loveth. Now I will be glad and rejoice in thee.'

Sharply she cried out:

'Stop that idiocy. I won't have it. Throw any more of that sanctimonious mush at my head and I'll have you chucked out of my room.'

He flung himself on his knees, blubbering, before her.

'Oh, no, Elissa, no, no. You don't understand. It's beautiful, the Song of Solomon, and I never knew it till I met you. All those long, dark nights without you it's been singing in my head. Singing, singing. "Honey and milk are under my tongue." "Thy lips, O my spouse, drop as the honeycomb." Let me kiss you with kisses on my mouth, oh, can't you see - can't you see I'm asking you to marry me?'

She drew back. For a full minute there was no sound but his heavy, panting breath. Then all at once she collapsed. She gave way to ungovernable laughter. She lay back shaken, helpless. 'Oh, God,' she gasped. 'If I survive this trip I shall be lucky. It's too much. One thing after another. And now this. It's too much - just too much.'

His face, working piteously, entreated her compassion.

'Don't laugh,' he begged convulsively. 'Don't laugh at me. I know you're 'way above me. But you gave yourself to me. You love me.'

Her laughter ceased; she gazed at him with hard derision; then, with a biting contempt, she said:

'Stop that idiotic blubbering.'

'I can't,' he choked, and tried to take her hand. 'I can't help it.'

'Get up!'

'Don't you see,' he whimpered, 'I'm just crazy about you. All my life long I've never thought of any woman. And now I can't stop thinking. I can - I can think of nothing else.'

'Get up!' she repeated coldly.

He stumbled to his feet, stood drooping before her.

'Now listen,' she went on. 'And listen carefully. I don't love you. I think you're the most insufferable idiot God ever made. On the boat I hoped for one instant you might amuse me. But you didn't. You bored me horribly. And you were too idiotic, too conceited to see it. You're all surface, my saintly friend, and quite hollow inside. You're not a man. You're a fool, a selfish Bible-banging fool without the backbone of a spider. I'm selfish and know it. But you - you're the most hide-bound egoist that ever hummed a psalm tune. And you think you're a God-sent minister of the Light - Heaven's gift to humanity. You say you're sincere. That's the worst of it. If you were a hypocrite I might respect you. But you believe you're a saviour. You bound about, roaring salvation. And how you like it. Then the moment you're hurt you start to snivel. Here am I stuck in this wretched hotel with fever about and no boat for a week. And you come oozing in with repentance in your soul and matrimony in your eye. God, it's too funny. Really, you sicken me. Quite painful. Now leave me, please. It's hot, and it bores me terribly to talk like this. I shall perspire in a moment, and that would be too frightful.'

His whole face fell; his big frame seemed to cave in. He stared

166

at her with appalled and abject eyes; then he gulped and cried brokenly:

'You can't mean that, Elissa. Oh, my dear, my own dear. You must like me. I'm decent. I'm straight. I'm kind. I'll give up here and come ba k with you. I'll do anything. I'll - I'll make good - get on for your sake.'

'I'd rather you got out,' she answered indifferently.

'Let me pray,' he blubbered, and clawed at her arm. 'Just lemme pray. That might turn you to me. Don't send me away like this. We belong to each other since that night - that wonderful night.'

'Get out,' she said negligently, again picking up the book that lay on the arm of her chair. 'Please do get out.'

He stood stockstill, and for all his bulk he had a beaten dog's look. Fumbling in his breast pocket he withdrew a handkerchief and blew his nose surreptitiously. Two minutes passed. Now he was gazing at the lines of her indolent figure; a spot of colour crept slowly back into his cheeks. He moved away, stopped; looked at her again. Suddenly his flush rose up again, and he stammered:

'You wouldn't - oh, Elissa, even if you don't want to get married -' He waited, his lips dry, his eyes upon that milky skin, hoping she might help him out. But she was silent. 'Say - you wouldn't -' he stammered again. 'You wouldn't be nice to me -'

'No,' she answered without troubling even to lift her eyes from the page. 'It doesn't interest me at the moment.'

Dismally his eyes fell to the floor; an angry misery rushed over him. The corners of his mouth drew down sullenly; defeated, he no longer entreated; a sense of his humiliation was in his mouth like gall.

'So you won't have anything more to do with me,' he threw out. 'Not good enough, I guess! You can afford to run me down. You - sitting here while your friend is ill - too selfish to go to her!'

'Precisely,' she agreed blandly. 'I told you I was selfish.'

He hardly seemed to hear her.

'Expect me to slink out now, I suppose! Quite finished with me. All right then. I'll show you I don't care two cents for your opinion! I'll show you who hasn't got the backbone of a spider!' He shouldered to the door, twisted the handle, and wrenched it open. Turning, he faced her, flooded by a hot unreasonable resentment. 'Maybe you imagine you can wipe your feet on me,' he cried. 'So superior maybe. Well just wait and see. I'll show you! I say, I'll show you!' His voice rose to a shout, then, slamming the door violently, he was gone.

What he was to show her he did not at that moment know. As, with a burning face, he rattled down the steps and flung out of the hotel he knew only that he felt on fire. Recklessly he struck out across the Plaza - anywhere to get away. But he wasn't going back to Laguna; he couldn't go back to that mean, cursed, suspicious Rodgers. That would kill him. No, no; he'd stay here. He wanted to stay here; and he would stay. He'd show them - show them all!

Then, as with a flash of revelation, he remembered the hotel in the Calle de la Tuna. He knew, of course he knew, the nature of that place; at least he suspected it. He swallowed drily, revolving a curious equation in his brain. He couldn't go there; he knew he couldn't; that was a bad - an evil place. Yet somehow, he hesitated, at once fascinated and afraid. He had to stay somewhere; couldn't go back to that Rodgers; and he wasn't sure - couldn't be sure - as to whether the hotel was bad. It wasn't right to misjudge a place like that, and, if it *was* bad, oughtn't he to go down and try to clean it up! As he equivocated he quickened his pace, began to alter his direction, turning down towards the harbour. And, as he did so, he began, in a fearful, intimate fashion, to pray. 'O God,' he muttered to himself, 'I don't want to do wrong. I don't want to be comin' down here. She's put me to it. Didn't I want to do the right thing? Didn't she sneer at me? O Lord, help me now. Lead me not into temptation.'

He began to walk more swiftly, as though pursued by devils. Always he walked towards the harbour. And always his lips kept moving in that strained, shuffling petition. 'Help me, O Lord. Help me now. Don't lemme do wrong.'

He turned a corner, slipped down a lane where the houses were smaller, dilapidated, somehow more sordid. He heard laughter, sound of a guitar. A woman, standing in a narrow doorway, murmured in his ear as he strode past. What did she say? Five peseta, señor. She was very fat, her breasts like bladders of lard. Her low laugh followed him down the narrow street. He was still praying, and still his eyes were burning as he entered the Calle de la Tuna.

# CHAPTER XXIII

THE sun had drawn to another setting beyond the Peak leaving Los Cisnes confronted by the night. Within the sick-room, shadows pressed insistently. Already the corners were obscure, cloaked by soft darkness that hung like arras. Closer, gently came these insatiable shadows, enclosing the dwindling light as though it were a life that must be crushed and finally extinguished.

Only the shadows moved; all else sustained a fearful immobility. The window stood half open, but no breath stirred to clear the taint of drugs and sickness that was in the air. Outside, beneath the brassy twilight, a thunder heat lay brooding on the land. Within, this same moist heat made breathing stifling.

Beside the bed, Harvey sat with his chin upon one palm, his haggard face quite hidden, his body upright, rigid. Before him, on a small sidetable, were ranged a chart, some basins, a bowl of sterile water, thermometer and hypodermic syringe, a row of medicines - the whole set out with scrupulous exactitude by Susan. At the outset she had stripped and scrubbed the room, and for those last three days had kept it to the stern precision of a hospital ward. Seen dimly in that tenebrous light, she was on his right, resting an arm upon the high caoba-chest as though she were unutterably fatigued. But her eyes, like Harvey's eyes, were fixed upon the bed.

Only the bed was illumined, bathed in the fading yellow glare that slanted down, retreating, it seemed, before the dusk. And on the pillow, caught and circled in that glow as by a halo, was Mary's face, pallid as ivory and thin as bone, the meagre shadow of a face that once had smiled and quickened to the joy of life. Now no smile touched the dry lips. Now in the sunken eyes there was no joy; and but a drain of life.

Suddenly Susan raised herself and spoke.

'Is it time to light the candles?' Her voice was measured; yet strangely hollow and distraught.

Harvey did not answer. Detached by dreadful apprehension he heard her voice; but it conveyed no meaning. Fragments of thought alone pierced through the desperation of his mind. How long he had been seated thus! And yet how short! The measure of a second; the measure of a life. Sands falling - each grain a second, a tear, a life. They ran, these sifted sands, with such incredible rapidity; and then the glass was empty, the tear fallen, the life consumed. It was dreadful to desire so passionately to save a human life. His whole soul was molten with that desire. He had always regarded the emotion centred around the crisis of grave illness with hostility, suspicion, even with disgust. He had seen in the swing of the balance - one way or the other - merely the success or failure of scientific research. But he was changed - completely changed - his purpose burning now where it had been cold.

Mary! - he thought dully only of her name; but it conveyed minutely everything he felt.

She had been ill only three days; incredible the change these days had wrought. But from the first he had known the form of her fever to be acute, racing with malignant intensity towards that inevitable exigency when either she would live or die. He had painfully faced that fact, sustained by his expectation of an early crisis. But that crisis would not come. Remission only had come bringing its blight of transient false hope. And then the temperature had started up again, climbing, climbing towards that burning zenith where life must shrivel and drop back as ashes into the illimitable void. Climbing fever and falling pulse. He knew with perfect certainty what these must bring unless the crisis came. And all his soul was stifled by the anguish of the thought.

Again Susan spoke, spanning a deep abyss:

'I must light the candles.'

She lit a candle and then another, brought them silently to the table. The flames rose straight, unwavering, like spears, causing the shadows to draw back and stand arrested, waiting like mourners banded and weeping by the candles of a catafalque. A big white moth came sailing inwards like a ship; a hum of circling insects rose, importunate as whispered prayers.

Watching that circling flight, she said:

'I ought to shut the window,' and, after a pause: 'The night air -'

He lifted his head and looked at her; the words fell into his consciousness like drops of water from an enormous height. As though returning from a long way off, he said slowly:

'Let me do it for you.'

Rising, he went to the window, closed it. All his movements

were sluggish - he was terribly tired.

He leaned his forehead against the pane. Darkness had swiftly fallen; the very trees so burdened by its weight they drooped quite slackly in the stifling air. Away to the east a rift of brassy light still lingered, like a streak of molten metal, predicative of storm. Somehow the glare was sinister, charging the hot night with fateful imminence. He turned to find her sad, calm eyes upon him.

'There's going to be a storm,' she said. 'You can feel it in the air.'

'Yes - there is thunder - behind those mountains.' But no sooner were the words spoken than they were forgotten. He was staring at her, studying, apparently, her pale and tired face, her untidy hair, her rolled-up sleeves, the bandage on her thumb - which she had burned with acid disinfectant. 'You are completely worn out,' he said at length.

Though his voice was perfectly impassive she flushed instantly and her mouth made a nervous grimace that was meant to be a smile.

'I am not in the least worn out. Not a mite. It's you - you who have done so much. You couldn't have done more. I guess you're - you're killing yourself.'

His attention was not upon her words; looking at his wrist-watch, he said:

'Go down and get some food. Then you must go to bed and rest.'

'But I don't need rest,' she protested in a low, uneven tone. 'It's you. Please, please, listen to me.'

'Go down now,' he said considerately, as though he had not heard.

She made an involuntary gesture of dissent, then checked herself. She looked at him beseechingly.

'Just one night off,' she whispered. 'You simply cannot stand it otherways. You've worked that hard - you're dead beat. You must take tonight - yes - must take tonight off.'

He approached the head of the bed slowly; it was impossible for her to see his face; then he said:

'You know there cannot be another night.'

Leaning forward, she tried to make him look at her; but he did not. His hand fell upon the pillow; he sat down again beside the bed.

She stood watching him, her expression oddly furtive. No

use - no use! Her words had no power to move him. So, with a stifled sigh, she turned, opened the door, limped wearily along the corridor and down the stairs.

In the refectory, supper was set; the candles lit; Corcoran and the marquesa already at table, waiting. The sight of the little prinked-out figure, fantastic as a marionette, caused her a queer unreasonable irritation. She dropped into a chair and began hopelessly to stir the coffee that Jimmy placed before her. For a long time no one spoke. Then Jimmy wiped his brow; solely for the sake of easing the oppressive silence, he remarked:

'Faith, I wisht this storm would break. It's hangin' over us too long for my likin'!'

The marquesa, primly upright in her regalia at the table, declared:

'It will not come yet. Tomorrow, yes. But not tonight.'

'It can't come too quick for me,' said Corcoran. 'Sure, the waitin' is like sittin' on a keg of gunpowther.'

Susan moved restlessly.

Overcome by her fatigue, her nerves were quivering on edge:

'Don't let's moan about the thunder,' she jerked out. 'I guess things are bad enough without that. Reckon we ought to be praying, not complaining about the weather.'

The marquesa lifted her eyes gently towards the ceiling. She did not like Susan - whom she named Americana. Rodgers, the American, had filched the water of her irrigation stream and her enmity in consequence was national. As her own naïve phrase had it: The Americanos had used her ill.

' "A saint's words and a cat's claws," ' she murmured, and smiled remotely. 'It is an old proverb I remember. But for all the proverbs and the prayers, assuredly the thunder will come.'

A hot colour ran into Susan's wan cheeks. She wanted to let herself go, to shout out a really abusive answer at this absurd old woman. But no, she didn't. She looked down at her plate; then she apologised:

'I guess I am sorry for speaking that way. I didn't think. And I'm all to pieces. I guess that's - that's why. I'm sorry.'

'It is not need now to be sorry, Americana,' said the marquesa nodding her head queerly. 'When the thunder comes - the thunder that must not be spoken of - then there will be greater need for sorrow.'

Susan stared at her in apprehension, and she stammered:

'What do you mean?'

The marquesa took a delicate sip of water:

'Some things are not fitted to shape in words. It is best to meditate upon them - to leave them quite unspoken. I might speak much about this gathering beneath my roof. It has, perhaps, a meaning beyond our human understanding. We - who feel so much and know so little.'

'Don't talk that way,' whispered Susan. 'You make me queer. Oh, this whole house makes me scared.'

'Strange things have happened in this house,' the marquesa answered calmly. 'And stranger things may happen. Why should one deceive herself? Without doubt there is calamity so near. Truly I can perceive. Like the thunder, it is in the air. Is it for me? No, no. My time is not yet. And you? You are so strong, so much with spirit. There is one clear solution you will say. For the English señora - this calamity! Ay, ay, ay, you may judge according to your desire.' And she made a movement with her tiny, ringed hand, vague, yet somehow infinitely suggestive.

Susan drew back as though cold fingers had torn aside the veil of her inner consciousness. The room, overhung by the enormous flapping swan, enclosed by its brooding walls, taut with the sultry air, became suddenly terrifying, macabre. She shuddered. It gave to her, all at once, a fearful precognition of disaster which made her want to scream. She felt that Mary was going to die. Yes, she thought quite wildly, I knew it, yes, I knew it from the first.

Even Jimmy stirred uneasily. He threw out his chest.

'It doesn't do to be talkin' like that,' he declared with an entirely factitious cheerfulness. 'You never can tell. I'm not denyin' but what she's powerful ill. But sure, while there's life, there's always hope.' He had proclaimed the platitude with the same resilient fortitude a dozen times before.

Again the marquesa smiled gently.

'Speech is easy. And often it is misunderstood,' she murmured. 'Now I am silent. Only remember that misfortune comes by the yard and goes by the inch.'

A short silence fell; then Jimmy suddenly remarked:

'Misfortune or not, there's one thing I can't for the life of me get hold of. And faith, it makes me none too easy in me mind. Why, will ye tell me, have we heard no more of that Cyarr fella? He went out of this room with lightnin' in his eye, swearin' he'd burn up the cable wires. What he wasn't goin' to do wouldn't

173

bear the tellin'. And here we are with never the sign of a step from anny of them.'

'What step could they take?' answered Susan sharply; she paused, added in a lower voice: 'It is impossible to move her until - until the crisis comes. And only her husband has authority for that.'

He rubbed his chin, sure indication of his speculation, and persisted.

'For all that, something's behind it I'll be bound. And I'm tellin' ye, I'm not easy in me mind about the endin' of it, for Harvey.'

'What do you mean?' she interposed with a nervous quiver of her cheek. 'No one could have managed this case better than - than he.' She could not speak his name; but, leaning forward, she went on hurriedly, defensively: 'He has been marvellous. Don't I know that. Haven't I seen it. And I'll swear to it as well. I'll swear that no one on earth could have done more to save her.'

'And if she doesn't be saved, poor thing,' said Jimmy in a low voice, 'how with one thing and another is that goin' to affect Harvey?'

His question laid bare the very heart of that fear which was worrying her to death. If Mary Fielding died? - and she was going to die! - how would Harvey endure the blame? They would blame him - she knew it - this awful catastrophe following so swiftly upon the other! The responsibility entirely was his - he had made it so deliberately - oh, the thought was dreadful, it terrified her!

She tried to eat the fruit that lay upon her plate. But she couldn't swallow. Torn again by that emotion in her breast, she whispered to herself: 'Oh, help us all, dear God. Please help us now.'

Suddenly, in her unpremeditated manner, the marquesa rose from her chair. Fastidiously, she laved her fingers and her lips with water. Then she crossed herself, murmured a grace of thanksgiving, signed herself again. Finally, she declared:

'She eats quickly who eats little. And it is time now for Isabel de Luego to retire. Si, si - she must go now to her room.' She retreated slowly, with extended elbows and floating mantilla; but at the door she paused, levelled across the ghostly room that elusive, almost sightless stare.

'Al gran arroyo pasar postrero' she said very distinctly; and then: 'Adios.'

It was her valediction.

Susan threw a scared look at Corcoran.

'What did she mean?' she whispered.

He got up, brushing the crumbs from his vest.

'Ah, nothin' at all,' he mumbled. 'I don't rightly understand the lingo.'

She gripped his arm and persisted:

'What did she say?'

'A kind of queer thing ye may be sure,' he answered awkwardly. 'Somethin' about the great stream, and bein' the last to think of crossin' it. But don't be mindin' what she says. She's a powerful decent little cratur when you know her. Faith, she's give me the chance of a lifetime annyway.' He took snuff, and hung about the table for a moment. Then, with a covert glance at her, he moved to the door. 'I'll be goin' into the kitchen now. I've a job of work that wants lookin' afther before mornin'.'

He went out silently, and she was alone. She still felt unaccountably uneasy. Nervously she fingered the peel upon her plate. Tiny beads of oily juice ran into her bruised thumb and set it smarting afresh. But she hardly noticed the stinging ache, thinking dully how uncanny was that old woman, and how very frightening, too.

'A great stream; and be the last to cross it.' What did that mean? In this parched land where all the streams were dry, it was baffling, inexplicable, but vaguely intimidating. At last, with a decided straightening of her body, she put away her thoughts. She brushed her hair from her brow, made to rise. But as she pushed back her chair the door opened, and Harvey came into the room.

She took one quick breath, drawing from his unexpected entry a dreadful meaning. A question trembled on her lips. Yet she could not utter it, but followed him with startled eyes as he advanced silently and sank into the opposite chair. There he looked across at her and shook his head slowly.

'It isn't that.' His tone was quite controlled but behind it lay a mortal weariness.

She faltered:

'She is - she is still all right?'

'She is not all right. Since the fever became haemorrhagic she is infinitely worse. That final bleeding has left her utterly collapsed.'

'Then why have you come down?'

He was a long time answering; then, with a sort of icy sternness, he said:

'She is sinking. Her resistance has completely gone. But her crisis cannot be far off. If she could live till morning she might have a chance. There is only one way to give her that chance. It is dangerous, but it is the only way.'

She whispered:

'What is that?'

Looking at her directly, he answered:

'A transfusion.'

There was a silence; the unexpectedness of his reply left her speechless; her heart beat quickly. Then she gave a little shudder.

'You can't do that,' she stammered. 'It's unheard of. She's got fever. It's not the right thing. Oh, it's not like you to suggest such a thing.'

'I'm not like myself, now.'

'But it would be better,' she gasped, 'better just to wait -'

'And see her die from the effects of that haemorrhage.'

'You can't do it,' she said again. 'It's impossible, here of all places. Now of all times. You haven't got the things.'

'I've got all I want.'

'You can't do it,' she cried for the third time - pressing her hands together. 'The risk, it's too frightful. It might easily prove fatal. And they'll blame you. Don't you see they'll blame you if you fail. They'll say you've -'

He said nothing. His lips were outlined by the shadow of his old ironic smile.

'In the name of God,' she wept, 'I implore you to get some assistance. I've wanted to say this a hundred times before. No one could have done more than you. You've been wonderful. But the responsibility, like this, away from everyone. Don't you see, if she dies, they'll say you've killed her.'

She reached her hand fumblingly towards his arm. At the sight of his tired, sunken eyes her love for him welled over. She couldn't check her feeling. She wanted to kiss those tired eyes - wanted to - wanted to. Tears streamed down her cheeks mussing up - she didn't care! - mussing up her dowdy face. But he did not seem to see her.

'Nothing matters to me,' he answered heavily, 'if she dies.'

Her face altered as though she had been struck; she withdrew her hand, raised it to her forehead to conceal her tears. She snuffled, controlled her trembling lip. At last she said in a different voice:

'If you are going to do it - then - you'll want me - want me to be the donor?'

He shook his head.

'No,' he said, 'I can't have it that way. This is all my affair. I'm going to do it all. Then - if there's any fault it will all be mine.' He paused.

The beating of her heart was stifling her.

'You might let me have hot water, plenty of hot water.' He was speaking calmly, gently. 'And I'll give you the needles - they must be boiled.' Then he got up silently. He didn't even look at her as he walked to the door.

But she rose and followed.


## CHAPTER XXIV


AT the end of the hall there stood an old Castilian clock which Corcoran had found in clogged inertia and promptly mended. It chimed now three lingering strokes. Mounting the darkness of the hall, the whirring echoes floated along the corridor into the sick-room.

Instinctively Harvey looked at his watch, his first movement in an hour: yes, three o'clock. The silence following the striking of the clock was profound. Actually the silence was not complete, for threading the dimness of the room came the thin rasping of Mary's breathing. But this had now gone on so long it had become part of the room, woven to the very substance of its silence. He was alone with her. The others had not wished to go to bed. Susan especially had protested. But he had insisted. No heroic sentiment had moved him - simply the feeling that it must be so. A strange sense of possession had now taken him. It had come, this sense, when he had felt the current of his blood stream languorously into hers. That transfusion - oh, he would never forget it. Never! Sheer madness in one way, nothing else. This vast bare room, the defective apparatus that filled the seconds with feverish anxiety, his own tense forearm bathed in the pool of candlelight, the encircling darkness pressing nearer, Susan's chalk-white face and nervous trembling fingers - it made a contrast against the background of his hospital experience that was simply ludicrous.

A gigantic joke, with Death splitting his sides with laughter in the corner.

It wasn't right, you see - not orthodox, not scientific - this drastic line of treatment. Six weeks ago he would have joined in the laughter of derision and called the whole thing lunacy.

But now - now he wasn't thinking in terms of his test-tubes. He wanted to save one life. The crude equipment at his disposal could not deter him, nor yet the danger - the frightful danger. He saw that she must die unless something were done to sustain her. Not reason, but passionate intuition, was his guide. He had carried out the transfusion. Yes, it was over. Now, inscrutably, they were united; come what might, nothing could dissever that union. He felt it to be so.

The room was unbearably sultry, and his head, already swimming from lack of sleep, was lighter still from loss of blood. Suddenly he rose, extinguished one of the candles which stood upon the chest. The smoky glare which hurt his eyes might also strike painfully on hers. Shading the remaining flame, he bent forward, gazing intently into her face, while upon the opposite wall his shadow took gigantic shape. Then he sighed and dropped into his chair again. Still no change; still that feverish rasping breathing. Her face, held in the mask of unconsciousness, was yet beautiful; her lips, half parted, drooped wanly at their corners; on her thin cheeks a dusky flush stood high; her eyes were not quite closed, but showed a marble slit of white.

Another sigh broke heavily from his chest. Mechanically he took water, laved her dry lips and burning brow. She had rallied following the transfusion, a quicker and a stronger pulse; his heart had bounded up with hope: but now she was back again, lapsing towards the illimitable desolation that was death.

How he had fought, too, during these last days! He had given everything that was his.

He slipped his hand beneath the sheet and clasped her fingers, so thin and unresistant to his touch. The feel of those burning fingers stirred in him unbelievable depths of pain.

He bit his teeth together, devoured by pain. The sight of her, weakened and sinking, the sense of his impotence, racked him maddeningly. Passionately he gathered his flagging strength and willed that it might flow from him towards her. Two tiny human creatures bound only by their linked hands within the vast unreasoning universe. So negligible under the dark canopy of night, they were like atoms lost in a great blackness. And yet they were together. That made the blackness naught, and stripped the vast universe of every fear but one. It was the beginning; it was the end. Nothing could solve the meaning of that simplicity, nothing dissolve its power. With terrible conviction this bore upon him. His whole attitude towards life was swept and shattered; and from the ruins had emerged this shining revelation. No longer could he find a jibe with which to mock the weakness of humanity; no longer was he cold and hard, contemptuous of life. Life now seemed rare: a lovely, precious gift, fraught with strange, unconsidered sweetness.

As he sat bowed beside the bed, there pressed upon his mind the weight of all the suffering and sacrifice the world had known. Dazedly he felt the crushing weight: beauty and love inextricably mingled with the sweat and tears and blood of all humanity.

And with a writhing of his soul - that soul which he had scoffingly denied - he saw his petty arrogance as something pitiful and powerless. His thoughts flew back. With staggering might came the realisation: his work, the very purpose of his work, had failed and been defeated by that same arrogance. If he had cared about the lives of those three patients - how far away it seemed in time and space! - if he had really thought of them as human creatures to be saved? Then he might have been successful. But he had cared only for the vindication of himself and his research. And it had not been enough.

Humility overwhelmed him. Again, as on that last night in the *Aureola*, all his life seemed wasted suddenly and void.

His eyes drew towards her face, then slowly filled with tears. There lay the slender hope of his redemption. A torturing emotion took him. If he could save her! Life would not then be void. Again the burning thought possessed him: If only she could reach the crisis! If only she might live! He knew so well how crucial were these present hours: as though her body, swinging in space, were balanced in a strange, uncertain equipoise from which abruptly it would slip and fall with star-like flight to safety or oblivion.

Involuntarily he leaned over her, until her hot breath fell upon his cheek, and whispered to her.

As by instinct, her thin face smiled weakly. But she neither saw nor heard him. She muttered a few unintelligible words. And then, without warning, her delirium began again.

'Why do they take me away? Why do they take me away? Away, away, away.' The muttered words went on in endless repetition, like a stupid lesson that must be apprehended painfully by rote. On and on, wrestling uneasily within her brain against some power that fought to conquer her. 'Why do they take me away? Away. Away.'

He couldn't endure it. He got up abruptly, began to pace up and down the room.

As he walked, his shoulders sagged forward; his figure had a shrunken look, so that his clothing seemed to hang on him; from time to time he pressed his fingers hard against his temples. And through it all he was listening - listening acutely to that rambling, incessant voice. He had to listen. It was heart-rending. She could not go on like this; he knew it to be impossible.

Suddenly at the window he stopped short. He raised his head and his eyes, searching the amorphous dimness where no leaf stirred upon the sentinel trees, reached upwards without apparent reason towards the sky. There was no moon; the stars were hidden; but vaguely in the east faint streaks of dawn quivered upon the surcharged sky. What lay behind that sky, behind that coming dawn? Soon he would know.

And then, as though in answer to his fear, the muttered voice was silent. He turned swiftly, his heart leaping into his throat. But, though the voice was silent, the rasping breath went on. For a moment he remained motionless, sick with that sudden dread, then slowly he came back and went upon his knees beside the bed. Her pulse was still unchanged: thin, faintly wavering, and slow; he counted it laboriously, confused by the heavy throbbing which filled his own fingers.

What was he to do? What more could he do? He racked his brain feverishly. At last he decided to administer more strychnine. Still kneeling, he charged the hypodermic syringe, prepared her arm, and thrust the needle home. Clasping the fragile blue-veined wrist, he waited. One, two, three, four - how often had he measured those weak and flagging beats! Five, six, seven - how still she lay, how mask-like was her lovely face! Again tears trembled upon his eyes. He loved her: not with the crass desire of his body, but with the melting tenderness of all his soul. He had denied that soaring union of the spirit with a sneer. This was the answer. He had no wish to pray; he could not pray;

but stupidly he thought, and the thought was like a prayer: Nothing matters if only she may live. He asked no more. That alone would be the consummation of their love - for her to live.

She moaned faintly. Again he bathed her brow and lips; there was nothing more for him to do. Leaning against the bed, his eyes scorched by weariness, he waited. He was utterly worn out, but he would not yield to sleep.

The thunder in the air was now unbearably oppressive. It seemed to press forward with the coming dawn. Quiescent, the march of time slipped over him unheeded. Seconds passed, or hours - which, he could not tell. He was waiting, watching her face.

Suddenly an exquisite start ran through his entire body. Kneeling, he remained perfectly rigid for five seconds. He dared not breathe.

Upon her upper lip and brow tiny beads of perspiration had broken. A long, convulsive sigh filled his chest. He was afraid to believe. He was afraid to move. Then slowly, with a pitiful timidity, he stretched out his hand. It was true. Her brow, which had burned with livid fever, was damp. And, as by a miracle stroke, her breathing suddenly had turned easier and soft.

'It can't be,' he thought blindly; 'no, it cannot be.'

Through an eternity of agonised purpose he had longed for this crisis. And now it was here he could not believe. With unsteady touch he reached for the thermometer, placed it with fumbling gentleness beneath her arm. It was a half-minute thermometer, but in his anxiety he let it remain for a full two minutes. His hand trembled so much as he withdrew the thermometer he almost dropped it. His vision was so clouded by fear and hope he could scarcely take the reading. But at last he made out the figures. Her temperature had fallen two full points.

He struggled to control himself. Kneeling by her side, his face impassive, he fought down a wild tumultuous joy. He knew the full significance of the swiftly falling fever. In a violent infection such as this, flaring upwards with feverish intensity, the crisis meant no mere turn for the better. It was a definite indication towards recovery. But he would not yet believe. He was still afraid. He waited breathlessly. When he had endured the passage of another half an hour, he slipped the thermometer beneath her arm once more. This time he took the reading with a firm hand. Her temperature had fallen another point and a fraction. All her body now was dewed by a gentle moisture. Her pulse was stronger, her breathing slower. Even her features had altered in some indefinable fashion for the better.

A great exultant joy burst over him. So exquisite a sob came choking from his throat. And, as though at last she heard him, her eyes opened slowly. She looked at him; with no delirious stare. Recognition was in her gaze and unexpected comprehension of her deliverance.

Then she spoke, her tone so low as to be almost inaudible; but it was her natural voice.

'I've been ill,' she whispered.

The wonder of her speech struck him with unbelievable happiness.

'You are better. You are going to get well.'

She looked at him as though the knowledge caused her no surprise.

'Yes,' she said, 'I know.' Then over her face there came incredibly the vestige of a smile. Something profound and significant was in that shadowy smile. And something steadfast.

The room was quite light now; the shadows were gone beyond return. He gave her to drink, watched her close her eyes.

The ebbing of her life had ceased. Now, instead, fresh life was fast flowing into her. She was sleeping, a sleep of weariness yet of tranquillity. The happiness it gave to him transcended everything.

He had risen to his feet, and for a long time he stood looking down upon her sleeping face. A thrilling exultation that could not be contained was in his heart. He wished suddenly to wake Susan, Corcoran, to spread abroad the glorious news. But he did not.

And then came the consequence of his own fatigue, the quick desire for a breath of air. She was sleeping; she would sleep for hours. And she was safe. He felt quite dizzy now, felt again the need of a freshening breeze. He took one last look, then on his tiptoes slipped gently from the room. Downstairs, he let himself quietly out of the house.

He went into the garden, wandering through the orange-grove where they had stood on that sweet, dreadful night. His heart still sang with that wild and matchless joy. But his steps flagged wearily. For three nights he had not slept. He was dead with tiredness.

There was no breeze. The air was hushed and motionless. No birds appeared to greet the day. The earth lay bare and silent, awaiting the coming of the storm.

What did it matter, the storm, or anything which now might come? She was better, saved, alive! Mazed by happiness, he wandered on, beyond the plantation, into a screen of retama shrubs.

Then all at once he heard a curious buzzing sound. From high up it came, as though a monster dragon-fly were tearing through the brassy sky. Not so much a buzzing as a roaring. A great roaring noise. He tried to look up, but the stark glare of that brazen sky defeated his weary eyes. He was dreadfully tired: at last he admitted it; that perhaps made the awful roaring in his ears. He began to laugh at his own silly fancy. It was too funny for words. But the laugh would not come. His eyes were closing. Drunk with sleep, he staggered and collapsed.

As the seaplane circled and swooped down upon the harbour, Harvey slipped to the ground. He sank into a thick retama bush, which closed over him, and instantly he was asleep.


## CHAPTER XXV


HE did not know how long he had been asleep. When he woke, his watch was stopped. But he judged it must be late. Already the sky was darkening with the early night. Rain had begun to fall in warm, heavy drops. These, splashing upon his face, had awakened him. Free of the first momentary wonder at his position, he lay for a moment in the retama bush staring at the sultry heavens, letting those solitary splashes come upon his brow, his cheek, his eyes. One fell full upon his lips - it tasted quite soft and colourless. And then a crashing peal of thunder broke out of the sky and rolled over him. Marvellous! He saw no lightning, but immediately, as though released by that terrific note, the rain gushed down in torrents.

He jumped up, laughing like a boy, and raced for shelter. How well he felt, how fresh and rested! It was the storm at last - delayed so long that now it had arrived with double vengeance. Another clap of thunder made him laugh again in sheer excitement. There was reason for his mood, of course. The instant he had wakened he had thought: She is better. And, oh, it was a glorious thought, a dazzling, splendid thought. Better - better - Mary was better!

He dashed across the drive, observing with only half an eye that the gravel was churned and cut by new-made ruts. He shot through the door, shook the rain-drops from his coat, and stood gathering his breath in the hall. Still silent the hall—but its silence held no terror for him now. The door of the refectory stood ajar. With a quick step he advanced and looked in. Amidst the silence and the shadows of that strange, familiar room the marquesa sat at dinner, alone. Why, it was funny — It gave him a queer start, reminiscent of their first meeting, to see her thus in her black dress, her trinkets, her solitary, impenetrable stateliness. And she seemed to know that he was there. She raised her head, fixed him with bird-like, unastonished eyes.

'You are come back,' she said calmly. 'Assuredly it is agreeable to me. And you are expected. See, here again is fruit and milk laid out and waiting. Just as it was in the beginning.'

He smiled at her.

'I've had a long sleep,' he said. 'And in rather a queer place. But I'm going upstairs before supper.'

'First you must eat,' she declared composedly. 'The wise man enjoys his little whilst the fool seeks more.'

Her manner amused him as it had never done before.

'No, no,' he said, 'I'm going upstairs.' He paused. 'But I'll drink a glass of milk before I go.' He came into the room, poured out some milk, took a long drink. It tasted delicious. Then, cupping the glass in both hands, he said: 'Where are the others?'

'The Americana — she is upstairs.' That, of course, he had expected; but she went on: 'And El Corcoran — he will return. Meanwhile he has gone to Santa Cruz with the escolta.'

His eyes widened in surprise.

'Escolta — I do not know that word.'

'Words and feathers are carried by the wind.'

He smiled again, this time rather doubtfully.

'I am foolish, perhaps. But even yet I don't quite understand.'

'There is no cure for folly. Did I not say the storm would come?'

Now indeed he stared at her with sudden apprehension. Her impassive face, charged with a sort of fatal knowledge, gave him an unexpected shock.

'Is anything wrong?' he cried. 'Why has Corcoran gone to Santa Cruz? Why don't you tell me?'

She went on cutting a fig into tiny little dice, just as she had done on that first evening. With a gentle inclination of her head she said:

'He who does not look forward remains behind.'

There fell an icy silence. Her evasion suddenly frightened and exasperated him. Without a word he thrust the tumbler upon the table and ran out of the refectory. He dashed upstairs. A fresh peal of thunder broke about his ears as he raced along the corridor. He burst into the bedroom. And there he paused. He couldn't - he couldn't believe his eyes.

No one was in the room but Susan Tranter. The bed was empty, stripped; the window stood wide open to the air; and by that window Susan was on her knees. She wore her hat. She was dressed as for departure. And he saw that she was praying. His heart went cold within him.

'What has happened?' he cried wildly. 'Where is Mary?'

She turned her head; and instantly her pale face was flooded with relief. Hastily, awkwardly, she got upon her feet.

'You're back,' she stammered. 'I'm glad. Oh, I'm terrible glad. We didn't know what had happened - where you'd been. I was afraid. An awful lot afraid.'

'Where is Mary?' he shouted. 'Tell me. For God's sake tell me.'

Outside there came another terrific crash of thunder and a sudden gust of wind rattled the window in its rotted frame.

'She is gone!'

'Gone?'

'They have taken her away.'

'Taken her away?' He echoed her words stupidly, his voice hardly above a whisper; then, in the same tone, a pause between each word: 'Who has taken her away?'

She looked at him with eyes in which jealousy and pity swam, and then she said:

'Her husband!'

He stared at her dazedly. He could not understand. And in a minute she went on fearfully:

'He came early in the morning. You weren't here. He had come by plane, from England - seaplane - you understand. He waited hours here. And still you weren't here. And then he decided she must be moved. He fixed everything. It couldn't have been better done. She's been gone half an hour. But she is gone. Now she's in Santa Cruz.'

He stood staring at her, so horribly still he seemed turned to stone. He couldn't move; he couldn't breathe.

Mary was gone. And it was her husband who had taken her away. Her husband! The thing was staggering and yet so simple. He had thought of everything but that. It stupefied him with is pain, its irony. And then sudden fury took him.

'She wasn't fit to be moved,' he cried. 'It was too soon. Why did you let her go? What in the name of God were you thinking about? You shouldn't have let them take her away.'

Flustered, she dropped her eyes.

'I guess I couldn't help it,' she answered in a low voice. 'I've told you everything was done. Oh, it was managed great. Don't be afraid. She is out of danger. And now-now it's better for her to be in Santa Cruz in the swell house he's taken for her - better than here in this awful dump. She'll get through her convalescence quicker there.'

He pressed his hands against his temples. His face was ashen; a knife, a wicked knife, seemed turning and turning in his side. He couldn't be angry any more. There was nothing to be angry about. A coldness crept over him. There came the memory of her delirium: 'Why do they take me away?' She had cried that out again and again; endlessly repeated. The precognition of this separation.

His mind plunged through unsubstantial vapours. Somehow he seemed to be beholding an event at an enormous distance in time and space. And yet it grew nearer - clearer. All his previous thin and shadowy impressions were corroborated by what he saw. His emotions alone produced the vision and its clarity. But he did see. For a moment. A curtain rolled up and then rolled down again.

Susan raised her head. A stab of lightning lit up the room and revealed the consternation in her eyes.

'Please,' she whispered. 'Oh, please don't be upset. I can't bear to see you upset.' She came up to him breathing quickly, and placed her hand upon his arm. 'Don't you see - don't you see it's better that way? It all figures out for the best. You've done your work. Now there's nothing more for you to do.' Tears of compassion stood in her eyes as she whispered: 'Oh, my dear, can't you see I'm heart-broken to see you hurt so awful bad? Oh, honest - it's true. I swear before God it's true.' Her voice quivered passionately. 'Oh, I'd give my very soul to make you happy.'

He sank into a chair, let his head fall forward into his hands.

Watching him, tears ran down her cheeks. And suddenly all

her love for him overflowed and wouldn't be denied. She'd sworn to herself never - never to give way again. But, oh -

She flung herself down on her knees beside him.

'Listen to me,' she whispered. 'I beg you to listen. You've saved her life, haven't you? That's enough. She's married. And her husband loves her. You can't alter these things. If you love her, then you won't try to alter them. If you do, you'll only make sordidness out of something that's beautiful to you. It wouldn't be you to do that. Oh, no, it wouldn't. For you've been wonderful.' Her breath came pantingly. 'Your skill, your courage, your nobility. Yes, you've got to listen. I don't care. From the moment I saw you on the boat, and saw all you'd suffered written plain on your face, I just went crazy about you. Give me the chance.' Convulsively she pressed his hand in hers. 'Just give me the chance to prove that to you - please, oh, please. You don't love me. But later on you might. Just give me the chance to be with you, to help you, to take care of you. I'll work for you, slave for you. Oh, God in heaven, I'd kill myself for you if only you'd give me just one little chance to show you I love you.'

He lifted his head and looked at her. His face was cold, but in his eyes there shone a strange light of sorrow.

'No,' he said heavily. 'I'm sorry, Susan. But that can't be either.'

The sound of her name upon his lips made her feel weak.

'You're sure?' she gasped.

Silently he looked away.

She, too, was silent, and she was blinded by her tears. Then her head drooped, a shudder went through her body.

'I see,' she said in a choking voice. 'If that's how you feel about it - then - it's just no earthly use.'

She stumbled to her feet. The wind, arisen to greater force, poured through the window and enwrapped her coldly. O, God, she thought, why did You make me like this, so ugly and so hateful? Why didn't You make me so that he could love me? And then within her something finally was crushed and dead. Helplessly she gazed at him sitting with hunched shoulders in the leather-backed chair; a minute passed; then she said lifelessly:

'I was just going when you came in. And now - now I guess I better get along - for good.'

He rose heavily; with eyes still averted he said:

'Shall I take you to your brother?'

She shook her head.

'No. Don't come.'

She stood before him with face uplifted, her arms listless by her side, her whole body wilted, impotent. Then suddenly she reached forward and kissed him. The coldness of his cheek against her burning lips was agony. She sobbed anew.

Still sobbing, she turned and stumbled from the room. She had the agonising conviction that she would never see him again.

## CHAPTER XXVI

At least there was Robert! How she thanked God for that thought as she stumbled up the hill, beating her way against wind and rain to the Rodgerses' plantation.

Now it blew a hurricane; the rain lashed down in sheets, and where the stream had barely trickled a yellow torrent came tearing down. The night's wild desolation was re-echoed in the desolation of her heart. But through it all shone that one precious thought: her brother! Robert, dear Robbie! He would comfort her. Oh, sure he would - and he would understand.

With her hair straggling about her face, her jacket unfastened, her cheap suit-case in her hand, she had a plain and unheroic look. Detached from her surroundings, set back upon the Oke-ville side-walk, she might have been some tired little school-ma'am starting peacefully upon her vacation. But no peace was in her. And the holiday - how strange that holiday was to be for Susan!

She came out of the wood of cedars, drew near to Rodgers's house. Pushing open the gate, she went up the drive. A light burned in a single window upon the ground floor. She mounted the porch, let herself in, laid down her case in the hall. Then she entered the living-room.

In that pallid room, sparsely furnished in yellow oak, that bore somehow a scriptural austerity, and floored with ghastly shining linoleum, Rodgers was seated at the table. By the light of a green-shaded lamp he was reading a small New Testament.

And he was alone.

He looked up, surveyed her from head to toe with a barren

stare, then, tightening his bleak mouth, prepared himself for speech.

'You've come back,' he said; and the coldness of his voice was more than ice.

She felt weak, frightened; she could not cope with his hostility.

'I want Robert,' she said hurriedly. 'I want my brother.'

Rodgers took off his steel spectacles, restored them to their case with the bleak deliberation of a judge. Then he stared at her again.

'Your brother,' he threw out; and his tight lips parted in a sterile laugh. 'You want your brother. Doggone it if that ain't great! Yes, ma'am, I'd call that just great.'

His manner was frightening her more than ever. She hadn't any strength left to stand his bullying. No, no - really she hadn't.

'Don't go on like that,' she cried. 'Is he upstairs? Is he out? Tell me quick. I've got to know.'

'So you gotta know,' he sneered, with a devilish urbanity. 'You really gotta know. Well, well, that's swell! The lady sister of the missioner has sure fire gotta know. It's hard to beat.'

All at once his manner changed, his voice trumpeted with bitterness. 'If you want to know,' he yelled out, 'then I'll tell you. He's gone! Yes, gone - the rat that he is. He's never come back since the day you were here. He skipped out on me to Santa Cruz. That's where he went, and that's where he stopped. He's stopped there, I tell you, stewed up for days in that sink of iniquity.'

She paled; she hardly understood.

'Santa Cruz?' she gasped. 'What is he - what is he doing there?'

Again he flayed her with that savage sneering laugh:

'So you gotta know that as well. I guess there's no end to your demands. But you deserve consideration. Sure, you do, a mighty lot. Comin' all this long way, you and your brother, to bring salvation to this sinful place. Yes, ma'am, a swell example to the natives and your fellow-countrymen - you come bringin' God's word. God's own good word.' And he stroked the book before him with a tense yet fondling touch.

She was absolutely terrified, confronted in this lonely house by his maniac behaviour, encompassed by the screaming wind, the rain, the muttered thunder, and the dreadful mystery of Robert's absence.

She opened her lips to speak, when suddenly he shouted:

'Don't speak. Don't ask no more. I'll tell ye where he's gone.

He's gone to hell, that's where he's gone. I figured he was rotten from the start. And now, by the Lord God of Hosts, I know it. He's in Santa Cruz, sunk in debauchery in the bawdy house of that woman Hemmingway. I've seen it with my own eyes. I went, I tell you, to find out for myself. And he's there, rotten with carnal lusts - lyin' on the foul bosom of a harlot.'

Under those last words, which hurtled like stones upon her, Susan recoiled. But she gathered herself, rose in defence to instinctive denial. She gasped out:

'I don't believe it.'

He rose up and advanced slowly, towering his bony frame above her. His eyes were sombre, menacing.

'You would give me the lie,' he rasped, 'in my own house. Me, Aaron Rodgers, servant of my Maker.' And he raised up his fists as though to invoke upon her the vengeance of the Most High.

She did not move. A fear, more terrible than any he could inspire, rushed over her: the fear that he was right. It gripped her by the throat and stifled her rising cry. In one blinding flash came the thought of Robert caught by something evil and obscene. She shivered.

'Yes, I reckon you ought to hang your head,' he cried, still in that voice of fanatic anger. 'To have named me for a liar. I reckon you ought to kneel and beg forgiveness of God and me.'

She did not hear him; passionately she was thinking: Robbie, he needs me, my own dear Robbie. A gust of courage stiffened her tired body. She raised her head; still facing him, she retreated to the door.

'I'm asking no forgiveness,' she cried abruptly. 'I'm going to find out - to find out for myself. I'm going to Santa Cruz - to my brother - right now.'

Turning, she wrenched open the door, ran into the hall. From a peg she tore down her light coat and began to struggle into it.

He followed her with a heavy step; stood watching her in a silence almost sinister. But, as he stared, the grimness slowly left his face. Suddenly he said, in a voice from which the exultation had departed:

'There's a tornado blowin'. You've figgered that out, I reckon.'

All unheeding, she unhooked a lantern from the wall, and with trembling fingers set herself to light it. The first match spluttered and went out.

'It's none too good a road at any time,' he went on in the same manner. 'And it's a darn sight worser on a night like this. I reckon you don't want to get bogged in the woods or struck by lightnin'. I reckon you want to think twice before leaving my house.'

The lantern was now alight. She snapped it shut, gripped the handle tightly, and made for the door.

He took a quick step forward.

'Say, don't be runnin' out that way. Don't you hear me? It's plumb crazy in such a storm. I ain't got no wrong against you when all's said and done. Stop here till mornin'.'

With her hand upon the outer door, she swung round. Her face was pale, but her eyes were set with a feverish determination.

'I'm not stopping,' she cried. 'I'm going. I'm going now. And I'm not coming back.'

With a sudden jerk she flung the door open; before he could speak, she crossed the porch and ran down the drive. As she vanished into the roaring darkness, she heard his voice hailing her, once, twice. But she gave no heed. With body bent against the hot blast of the wind, she went on, half running, half walking, until she gained the plantation path. Here the lantern's light was merciful: without it she must surely have been lost. Beyond the arc of the swinging beam the blackness rose like a wall. The track, too, was almost washed away by the rush of surface water. It was everywhere, the water; trickling, dripping, soaking, deluging the arid earth. On she went. Her feet churned the rich mud, splashing it upon her dress. The warm, stinging rain plastered her hair upon her brow. She did not care. She floundered on, crossing the bridge above the swollen stream, and gained at last the main highway.

She sighed deeply with relief and made off rapidly down the broad, deserted road. It was the carretera which Harvey had taken on the evening of his coming to Los Cisnes - the same road - but now how different! No placid sunset air now wrapped the listless groves. Instead, the hurricane went whining through the trees, rending the dwarfed stalks, savaging the fleshy leaves - tearing, destroying, whining, whining. Yet it was not so much the wind that hindered Susan as the rain. She had never felt such rain. It teemed upon her in warm, brackish sheets. Her clothing clung to her as to a drowned woman. Little swirls of water formed at her feet. Out of the sodden sky there flared from time to time not lightning as she had known it, but a diffused and spreading glare which rushed across the canopy of night like wildfire.

She went on, sustained by the fierce burning of her will, through the hamlet of La Cuesta, past the brimming reservoirs, under the shoulder of the high basaltic cliffs. But for all her resolution her steps were flagging. Though the gale was following and the way down-hill, her tiredness increased beyond endurance. Her joints relaxed; her body sagged; she was ready to sink with weariness.

And then, to show that God had not forgotten her - oh, sure, she knew that was the way of it! - a wagon came clattering down the hill beside her. She heard the clop-clop of hoofs and, turning with sudden hope, she waved her lantern in high distracted sweeps. With a squelch the team of mules drew up, the boyero peered at her out of the sack which swathed his head and body.

She made a queer figure standing in the deluge, shouting against the wind, her pale face straining upwards in the effort to make herself understood.

'Give me a lift.'

'Pero yo no entiendo.'

'You must give me a lift - oh, for God's sake take me to the town.'

But, whatever his thoughts, her need clearly was urgent. And the night was terrible. He made a gesture of invitation with his whip. In a moment her foot was on the wheel hub. She was beside him and they were off, rocking and bumping down the slanting darkness.

The boyero was from the market at Santa Cruz and he had been caught by the storm beyond Laguna. Now, rather than rest benighted in the hills, he was pushing at dangerous speed towards the town. He did not speak, but from time to time he threw a stealthy side-glance at her profile. Nor did she speak. She sat rigidly upon the narrow perch, chafed by fierce impatience. The breakneck haste was not enough for her. The journey seemed interminable.

But at last they swayed sharply round a narrow bend, and the rain-blurred lights of Santa Cruz loomed mistily beneath. The streets were empty, the Plaza utterly deserted, as they clattered towards the market. Yet through the dead emptiness of streets and square there came a roaring sound: not the rain; not the wind; she could not think it swelled so deafeningly in her ears. And then she knew it for the roaring of a river. It was the Barranca Almeida - engorged beyond its banks, tearing through the town towards the sea.

The wagon drew up at a stable in a side-street behind the market. She jumped stiffly from her seat, fumbled in her dress, and gave the boyero a piece of money. Then she looked around her. She had her bearings; she knew what she was about. In five minutes she was in the Calle de la Tuna, outside the doorway bearing the number that she sought. The door had no fanlight, but there was a Moorish grille whose interstices disclosed the presence of light within. She had no hesitation. At once she tried the handle. It yielded. She drew a long breath and ran into the hall. It was a long hall, tiled in mosaic pattern, edged by a tarnished dado and a row of tattered palms. All along one wall hung little pictures of sailing-ships worked in coloured wools. On the left was a curtained archway through which came light, the sound of voices, and of laughter. The light, reaching into the dimness of the corridor, was hazed by swirling clouds of cigarette smoke. There came, too, as she listened, the thoughtless tinkling of a mandolin.

Susan stood quite still. Nothing particular to cause alarm was in the place. But for all that her whole being rang with a sense of apprehension and disaster. She clenched her hands tightly, went forward down the passage. But as she advanced a woman came out of the alcove.

It was Mother Hemmingway.

A vivid colour rushed into Susan's rain-blanched cheeks and then rushed out again. She hardened herself to face the rancour that must come.

But the other stood silent. She seemed, incredibly, at a loss for words. At length she came up to Susan and stared her up and down. Into her ugly features flowed a curious perplexity. Then she exclaimed:

'Wot you doin' down 'ere on a night like this? Swipe me if I didn't think it was your ghost at first. You're wet - absolutely drenched. Blimey! you 'aven't even fetched a numbrella. Don't you know the weather ain't fit for an 'erring to be bout in?' It was strange, but in her voice there rang a note of odd commiseration.

Susan's state was pitiable. She was soaked to the bone, her hair smeared dankly about her face, her shoes squelching, her sodden clothing oozing water to the floor. But she seemed unconscious of her own condition. She cried out:

'My brother - is he here?'

Mother Hemmingway ignored the question. A gust of energy

seemed all at once to strike her. Taking the other by the arm, she declared vigorously:

'I never 'eard of such a perishin' adventchure - muckin' through ryne like this. Did you think it was an April shower or wot? You'll get your death of cowld. Pneumonia and Gawd knows what. W'y, criminey, I won't stand and see you froze. 'Ere! Come into this little plyce and get your duds dried.' And, before Susan could resist, she pulled her into a small sitting-room which gave off the other side of the corridor. There she thrust her into a chair and, talking with the utmost volubility, began to rummage in a chest of drawers which stood beside the shuttered window.

'You shall 'ave a couple of towels,' she ran on, 'if you'll excuse me 'alf a jiff. I 'ave them 'ere under my 'and. W'ere did I put them? In this drawer they was. Never can get your fist on a thing when you wants it. I'll 'ave them in a tick. Ought to 'ave a mustard bath, you did. Stryte. But I'll get 'old of the towels first. Then you'll tyke your shimmy off and I'll give you such a rub you'll rise all of a glow. Blimey, I cawn't get it out my 'ead. You walkin' in 'ere like you'd swam the bleedin' 'arbour.'

But Susan's mood was not to be propitiated. Tensely she waited. The moment the other turned from the chest she bent over and looked her in the face.

'Where is my brother?' Her tone was low, but it held a thrilling urgency.

Mother Hemmingway made a great ado with her towels: unfolding and flapping them in immense solicitude.

'Brother!' she exclaimed, as if it were the last thought in her mind. 'You're meanin' little Robert, ain't you? Blimey, 'ow should I know where he is? I ain't 'is keeper, ducky. Puñeta, no. And you're the main consideration at the momenta. Wyte till you've 'ad a dry-up and a noggin. Then you can talk about 'im to your little 'eart's content.'

Susan did not move.

'I can't wait. I've got to know. Is he here?'

The other paused. Behind her beady eyes, which beamed inevitably a sparkling malice on the universe there lay for once a singular embarrassment. Suddenly she shrugged her shoulders, offered on impulse a generous lie.

'No,' she answered, ''e aint 'ere. 'Ow should 'e be 'ere? I swear 'e ain't 'ere as Gawd's my Myker.'

'I don't believe you,' said Susan quickly. Her teeth were

chattering now, her lips blue with cold and fear. She reached across the table towards the other. 'Tell me -' Her voice broke. ‹Oh, honest - you've got to tell me if he's in this house.'

'No,' shouted Hemmingway, with a violent out-thrusting of her bosom. ' 'E ain't in this 'ouse. Would you myke me hout a liar to my fyce? I tell you 'e simply ain't 'ere. I swear it on my sacred oath. And that's the end of it.'

Then the door opened and Robert entered the room.

There was a dead silence, broken only by the drumming rain and the rushing of the river. He came in dizzily, like a man who had swung between unknown extremes of exultation and despair; and from his present look, drooping and half fuddled, it was clear he had now touched the pit of his experience. He lurched in aimlessly. He'd been goin' to show somebody, hadn't he? Show somebody somethin'! Well! -

And then he raised his head. He saw Susan. For five seconds he stood transfixed, then a cry that was like a sheep's bleat broke from his lips. He did not speak, but his face spoke more than words, suffused by a ludicrous dismay that shocked the eye. They gazed at each other in silence; at last he looked away - shrinking yet sulky.

She gave a long, long sigh.

'Robert,' she whispered. But the shock of seeing him had frozen her trembling body. She could say no more. He flung himself into a chair.

'What d'you want?' he muttered thickly, resentfully. 'What d'you want coming down here? What you doing here?'

She gave a little choked cry.

'Oh, Robbie, I came to find you - honest I did - to take you away.'

He stared straight at the opposite wall. He had still the dregs of liquor in him.

'Huh! You did - did you? To take me away? And where you think you're goin' to take me?'

At his tone a scream rose almost to her lips.

'Anywhere,' she gasped, 'out of here. Oh, anywhere so long as we're together, Robbie.'

Mother Hemmingway, listening with ill-concealed impatience, felt irritation supplant her ineffectual benevolence.

'That's right,' she cried shrilly to Susan. 'You tyke 'im away. Tyke 'im out of my 'ouse, for as Gawd's my judge I'm sick of the very sight of 'im. Full of 'anky-panky the one minute and

hangles' 'ymn-tunes the next. Laughin' 'is silly 'ead off like
'e was a cuckoo and the next thing - pull the blinds down, Willie's
dead! 'Streuth! I'm used to men, I am, and not to 'arf-baked
'armonium-pl'yers. I only let 'im stay to try to put some guts
in 'im, but 'elp me, jimminy, you can't do that to a crawler.
Tyke 'im away, I say, and good luck to you.'

A shudder ran through Robert; he groaned. He was being
kicked out - *him* - the Rev Tranter - being kicked out of this -
this *hole*.

'You wan' rid of me.' He tried to sneer, but his face was too
slack - he couldn't.

'You've 'it the nail on the bleedin' 'ead, cocky!'

'Huh!'

Susan started forward nervously.

'Oh, come on, Robbie,' she pleaded, with a quivering mouth.
'Come on home now. Come on away with me. Let's be together
again. Come on, dear. Just you and me - oh, honest, it'll - it'll be
great - if you'll only come now.'

He dashed aside her outstretched hand. The last drink he'd
had rose nobly to his support. He wanted to weep for the indignity
he suffered. Get rid of him, would they? Him? Rev R. Tranter.
Oh, God, it was too, too much. Blubbering tears ran down his
cheeks.

'Lemme be,' he bawled suddenly. 'If I ain't fit to be touched I
ain't fit to *be* touched.'

'Oh, w'y don't 'e shut up?' muttered Mother Hemmingway,
and she turned in disgust. ' " 'Too lyte, too lyte,' the captain
cried, and shed a bitter tear." W'y don't 'e dry up and get out -
the blasted fool.'

What! making a fool of him, was she? The little runt. Christ!
He'd show her. He'd show them both - everybody! A man,
wasn't he? His face worked. He jumped up from his chair, which
fell clattering to the floor. He swayed slightly on his feet. His
chest heaved. A luscious emotion suddenly anointed him. He
gulped and cried:

'Mebbe I will get out. Mebbe I don't have to trouble you much
further. I've denied my God, haven't I? I've levelled myself
with the swine? Huh! That's all you know. Don't you know the
meanin' of atonement? Don't you know the meanin' of sacrifice?'
He exploded the last word, swayed on his feet some more. He
was more drunk than he knew. And God! wasn't he showing
them at last? A great - oh, a *noble* idea - swelled inside him. He'd

show them if he had guts - show the whole bloody lot of them. 'I'm lost, aren't I? Lost and damned? That's what you reckon! But I reckon different. You don't know everything. You forget about *sacrifice*.' He clung to the word. His voice, risen to a shout, became suddenly confidential. 'And what have I got to live for?'

Susan started forward. Fear and pity burned in her eyes.

'You've got everything to live for,' she cried. 'We've got each other, haven't we? We'll make a fresh start, Robbie. You and me - like we always been - together.'

He gave a wild, hysterical laugh. His idea was big now - awful big. She needn't think she'd stop it. He'd hardly meant it first go off. But now - oh, now! He flung out his arms and threw back his head.

'I'm gonna make no start,' he shouted. 'I'm gonna make an end. Jesus done it for me. I'm gonna do the same for Him.' A thousand seraphic voices were ringing in his ears, and through that ringing came the roaring of the river. He straightened himself with a jerk, glorying in the splendour of his resolve. 'I've sunk myself in sin,' he bawled in a voice of frenzy. 'But I kin cleanse myself of my iniquity.'

'Don't talk like that,' she gasped. 'You're - you're frightening me.' She rushed towards him, but with his big buttery hand he shoved her away. He had dramatised himself beyond reason. His eye glistened; his nostrils dilated with ecstatic fervour; in his ears the rushing river swelled in a mad celestial strain.

'I've been steeped in evil,' he chanted. 'And now I'm gonna wash that evil out.'

Panic thrilled in Susan's heart. With sudden desperate intuition she, too, was conscious of the sounding of the river. It was like a nightmare. Again she flung herself upon him. But she was too late.

He dashed open the door, rushed out of the room, down the corridor. Shouting, he disappeared into the outer darkness. It all happened in a second.

'Oh, my Gawd,' cried Hemmingway. ''E's gone crazy.' Paralysed, Susan stood with hands clasped upon her breast. Then she stumbled forward. With a frantic cry she rushed after him.

The sudden transition from light to darkness benumbed her sight. She stood on the pavement straining with blind, bewildered eyes. And then she discerned his running figure far down the deserted street; large and dark it loomed, like the figure of one possessed.

He wasn't - oh, he couldn't - her Robbie! With a choking cry she raced after him. The rain beat into her frightened eyes, the wind battered against her panting breast.

She could not gain upon him. And he was making for the river. The knowledge drove her crazy with terror. As she panted on, the thought beat through her brain: He can't swim. It hammered on her in agony through the tumult of the night, and the frenzied beating of her heart.

The noise of the river swelled. Nearer and nearer. All at once the darkish flood burst into view before her.

'Robbie,' she cried, in an agony of love and fear, and again, 'Robbie.'

He could not hear. He was there at the water's edge. His form, outlined against the lowering sky, seemed to poise itself for an instant upon the brink. Then it vanished from her sight.

She shrieked, calling on God for succour. She reached the bank. Dimly she saw him struggling in the current. Faintly she heard a cry that might have been for help. An answering cry leapt from her lips. She could reach him. She could save him. She called again in answer to his call. She clenched her teeth and flung herself into the river. Her plunge made no sound. Darkness and the roaring of the waters enclosed her form. She swam and swam, straining with bursting heart to reach him. Yes, her heart felt bursting. It was weak, always had been weak. But she never thought of that. She was gaining. She was nearly there. She reached out her arm. And then came a sudden surging wave which cast her side against a spur of rock. It was not a heavy blow, but it was upon that beating, bursting heart. Her arm fell back; her body spun giddily around; dully she felt a greater darkness rush upon her. She felt herself fainting. And then, as if that were not enough, brutally the current took her and dashed her head against those hidden rocks. Again and once again. And that was all she knew.

Al gran arroyo pasar postrero.

She didn't know what that meant; and now she would never know.

As Tranter - thrown by an eddy upon a lower sandbank of the estuary - staggered to his feet, sobered now and wholly frightened, and began to wade in frantic haste towards safety, Susan's body floated past him. Scrambling away with his back to the river, he whispered:

'Oh, gee, what was I thinkin' on? Oh, gee - oh, God - oh,

Christ - oh, hell! Guess I was crazy. Guess I near drowned myself. Guess I better get some dry clothes. Oh, Lord, I'm glad - oh, thanks be to God -' And Susan went sailing out into the darkness of the sea.

## CHAPTER XXVII

A FORTNIGHT later, Harvey Leith came down the hill to Santa Cruz. It was afternoon. The wind had fallen, the sun blazed out, the earth was steaming under the shimmering sky. The storm had long passed over and been forgotten.

He entered the town, skirted the market-place, advanced across the Plaza towards the waterfront. He was walking quickly; he looked neither to the right nor to the left. Passing the barrier of the Aduana, he stepped into the shipping office and advanced to the cubicle marked 'Enquiry'. He spoke to the clerk.

The clerk - a young blood with dashing side-whiskers and plastered hair, stared queerly at Harvey, then he shrugged his shoulders with a sort of contemptuous indifference.

'But the señor is unfortunate. Assuredly most unfortunate. The second boat sailed yesterday.'

'And the next one?' - very quickly.

A little curl of the plastered one's lip: 'Not for a full ten days, señor.' A pause. Harvey's face revealed nothing of his thoughts.

'Thank you,' he said quietly. He turned, fully conscious of the odd stare still fixed on him, and went out of the dirty office into the yellow glare of the sunshine. He retraced his steps - very slowly - recrossed the Plaza. Outside a café he stopped, arrested by his image in the mirror. He hardly recognised himself. His unshaven face was like the face of a stranger; one of his boots had burst across the toe; his disreputable suit, torn at the knees and stained by mud, might have been rejected by a tramp. God, he thought - looking into his own gaunt eyes - what a sight!

He moved off towards one of the public benches in the Plaza. The breeze blew a litter of papers about his feet; on the pavement some rotten melon-rind lay festering with shiny blue flies. Thrown away - left over - like himself.

He sat down. Well! - now he could at least sit still. On that night of storm - was it days ago or years? - when Susan left him to go to Rodgers's place, he hadn't been able to do that. No! He'd been forced to get up, his breast charged with a torturing restlessness which drove him to pace the empty room, whilst the thunder rolled, and the ants scurried across the dry boards.

How could he have been still! His thoughts were scattered; his mind writhed and twisted like the cedar-trees before the wind. He could not stay in the house. He couldn't wait for Corcoran's return. He couldn't speak to the marquesa. Mazedly he went out of the hall, through the garden, struck up the path towards the mountains. He didn't know where he was going. Before him the Peak rose dimly outlined in the dying light. It seemed silently to beckon. And he had the strange sensation that to surmount that towering summit would bring peace - oh, fathomless, eternal peace. There, above the littleness of earth and all the puny reaches of the sea, circled by clouds and rare omniscient winds, a man might press his brow against the step of heaven and lap himself for ever in sublime tranquillity. Walking upwards - his eyes affixed to that splendid crest - he had a glimmer of enlightenment. A vision, which words could never formulate.

On and on. Leaving the bridle-path he had been following. Caring nothing for the rain. Climbing further towards the Peak. Conviction growing that he must - must achieve that distant summit. A range of barren slopes covered by calcareous casts of plants and the poisonous shrub verolillo. He crossed them all. The land of a pale sienna colour, the ravines banked with drifted sand. On the ledges of the rock, stunted vines and wild fig-trees - growing, tangled, inextricable as the thoughts within his mind. And then the terraces, bank after bank filled up with rotten pumice-stone. On and on, striving quite madly to reach the Peak. Darkness falling, the rain and wind increasing, the thunder tumbling about the hills. He stumbled on, following the track amongst a desolation of volcanic cinder-heaps. And then he came upon the caves. Cut deeply in the mountain-side - each fronted by its patch of maize sprouting from the lava ash.

The barking of dogs - a row of faces drawn to those tiny burrows in the rock. Faces peering towards him, the faces of the cave-dwellers. Dim forms rushing out, shouting, pressing round him - little stunted people - speaking a language he could not understand. But they would not let him go on. Chattering, gesticulating towards the sky, forcing him back into the safety of the caves.

The caves of El Telde - warm, dry, lit darkly by red embers. There he had lain all night, whilst the storm ranged madly round the Peak.

Next morning he might have gone. But he had remained. Calmer in mind, his body acquiescent to a strange fatigue. They were friendly, the little people, thrusting on him their simple hospitality. They gave him food - gofio - a porridge made from the maize they grew themselves. When the sun broke through, the children came out and frisked amongst the rocks. Quite naked - tiny and timid as squirrels. Seated on the sun-warmed ledge Harvey watched them play. Free of their first suspicion they rolled and tumbled about his feet, clambered upon his knees. A strange experience. Close to the crest of the Peak. Unsmiling, unresistant to their plucking hands, he let the naked children play about him.

Day and night. Each night he had said: Tomorrow I will leave. But he had remained. Why should he go? Where could he go? Better, far better wait amongst the hills. He wasn't needed now - not wanted. Soon they would take Mary from Santa Cruz, just as they had taken her from Los Cisnes. Only when she had gone would he descend to the town. . . .

Today - yes, that was today. He sighed gently - discovering himself, here, upon the bench, back again in Santa Cruz, alone. And now no boat for a full ten days.

The palm fronds swayed above his head. The fountain splashed. Little silver fishes swam in the marble basin at his feet. From time to time he felt people staring at him. An old man tottered past - unwashed, unkempt - begging, selling lottery tickets. His glance dismissed Harvey with disdain. He didn't even bother to offer him a ticket. Strangely, it brought Harvey an odd satisfaction to find himself passed over - unrecognised for what he was.

And then a shadow fell across the beach, wavered and drew up. He heard a sudden shout, felt a slap upon his shoulders. With a start he looked up. It was Corcoran.

Yes - Corcoran - thrust-back hat, straddled legs, swaggering air, invincible grin. But there was a suspicious twitching about the edges of the grin. And the laugh that followed it was queerly near a sob.

'It's yourself,' he stammered. 'Yourself, indeed, that I've looked everywhere for days I - I hardly know ye. I thought ye'd -'

Here his smile gave way. He broke off: he almost broke down. 'Oh, honest, man,' he faltered. 'I'm awful glad to see you.'

There was a silence. Jimmy blew his nose powerfully. Then gradually his grin came back, grew into the old delighted laugh. He was himself again. For a moment he looked as if he might fall on Harvey and publicly embrace him.

'It is you, yerself, it is,' he repeated, rubbing his hands together. 'Yerself and no other. What in the name of hivin have ye been doin'? What do ye mane by scarin' the wits out of a man?'

'You might have known I'd turn up,' Harvey answered stiffly.... What a stupid thing to say! But he couldn't for the life of him have been clever at that moment. He'd never thought - never - that anyone might be so glad to see him. It was something after all - friendship.

'Yes, indeed,' cried Corcoran, plumping down on the bench beside Harvey, the joy of the meeting still irradiating his humid eye. 'Yer the boy for frightenin' us all right. I searched for ye in every corner of the town. High and low, up and down, I sought. Scoured the countryside. Faith, I'd begun to think that you had gone the way of the river as well.'

Harvey looked up. There was a pause. Corcoran's gaze fell. He seemed to wish he had not spoken.

'Ye'll not know,' he said in an altered voice. 'Ye'll not know what has happened to Susan.'

'Susan?' Harvey echoed in wonder.

Jimmy hesitated, then, in a manner both gloomy and subdued, he launched into an account of Susan's death.

'They never got her body,' he ended in a low tone. 'She's out there on the sea-bed, the poor thing. Och, I've been powerful upset about it all. There was always a glint of sad misfortune in the far-off corner of her eye. She ran after things too hard, she did. And that, I'm thinkin' is the way she never got them.'

Harvey stared at him with eyes suddenly wide, horrified. Susan! Oh, it was too horrible - he couldn't believe it. Susan, so eager, so quick to feel -

He must have spoken; for Jimmy murmured:

'She don't feel nothin' now - out there.'

Out there. Out on the sea-bed amongst the cool sea-weeds and the corals, striped fishes darting, quivering above the pallid, unshut eyes. 'Give me a chance - oh, just give me one little chance!' Pleading, her hand outstretched, too eager, too eager after happinness! And now out there. . . .

The thought of it made Harvey shiver.

'I'm terribly - terribly sorry,' he whispered, as though he spoke into himself. And then, after a long time: 'Where is her brother?'

'Him,' cried Jimmy with unutterable scorn. 'Ye wouldn't believe it. He's back again at Salvation. Up to the eyebrows in repentance. Swearin' to God that his sister died to fetch him back to grace. Jumpin' Janus, it would sicken ye. He's brung the harmonium down to Santa Cruz, he's rented a bit of a hall, and he's missionin' fit to burst - slammin' out the hymn-tunes and the prayers wid tears in his eyes. Glory, glory, halleluja! By the powers, 'tis scandalous enough to give a man black ja'ndice.'

Two minutes passed; then Harvey asked:

'And you? What's going to happen to you?'

Corcoran took snuff with a conscious air. But no mere act of snuffing could hide his satisfaction. Thrusting one thumb modestly to its arm-hole he answered:

'Faith, it's happened already ye might say. I'm all fixed up at the Casa. Successor to Don Balthasar, R.I.P. I've got aholt of a dozen yellow boys and I'm workin' the suet off them. I'll knock the place into shape in no time. Druv down here with me own mule team. I'm tellin' ye it's the life of a lord I've landed meself into. And, in a manner of speakin', all by me own endeavour.'

Harvey's lips hardly smiled. But he was glad - tremendously glad.

'That's good, Jimmy,' he said slowly. 'I'm happy about that.'

Corcoran threw out his chest and abruptly stood up.

'Not so happy as yer goin' to be,' he said with a sudden change of tune. 'Come now. It's time we were goin'. I've had me innin's and now it's yours. Come away over to the hotel.'

'The hotel?'

'And where the divil else! D'ye think you're goin' to sit on this holy bench till the boat comes in? Be sensible for the love of hivin and come on.' And taking Harvey's arm he drew him to his feet, led him with some persuasion across the Plaza.

They entered the hotel. Corcoran swaggered into the empty lounge, sank into a chair, and called loudly for the porter.

'Yes, sah.' The nigger hurried over, all gold braid and teeth.

'Ask Sir Michael Fieldin' if he'll favour me with his presence. At his own convenience, ye understand. Tell him it's somethin' important.'

'Yes, sah.'

Harvey jumped up as though he had been shot. His apathy had vanished. He leaned sharply over Corcoran.

'They're here? Here - in Santa Cruz? They haven't gone?'

Corcoran took refuge in a delicate yawn. 'Easy, easy now,' he counselled. 'Don't be flyin' off the handle.' Harvey's lips had turned quite pale.

'But I thought - a whole fortnight -'

'Ah, they're still here,' said Corcoran. 'How would I be sendin' for the man if he wasn't here.'

A pause came.

'I don't want to see him,' Harvey said quite dully. 'And he doesn't want to see me.'

'That's just where yer wrong me boy,' declared Jimmy, lying back in his chair and inspecting his boots - shined to a high perfection by one of the 'yellow boys'. 'Faith, he's dyin' to meet ye. And why not? Ye saved the little lady's life, didn't ye? He's been lookin' for ye all over - as well as meself. Faith, he's one of the kindest. Ye wouldn't meet a more agreeable in a whole week's march. And he's bubblin' wid gratitude.'

'Let him keep his gratitude.'

'Pooh! A pack of nonsense,' returned Jimmy. 'Don't be so impetyus. Ye want to get back home, don't ye? Faith, ye don't want to start beachcomin' at your time of life.' He broke off suddenly, raised his head, then nodded it violently to the man who had entered the lounge.

A coldness came over Harvey as he took in the other. Fielding - Mary's husband - yes, the thought struck coldly, but with a curious unreality. Quite tall, quite broad, quite handsome - in an easy, take-it-for-granted way. His features were all in proportion, the nose straight, the chin beautifully smooth. He had a lot of nice, well-brushed yellow hair. His whole face wore an extraordinary amiability. He was stamped with amiability - as if he couldn't, didn't want to shake it off. His eyes in particular, of an optimistic blue, smiled upon the world and seemed perpetually to say: 'Charming, charming, oh, really charming.'

He drew nearer. He looked very excited and pleased. He threw out his hand, almost rushed upon Harvey.

'Splendid!' he exclaimed. 'Simply splendid. This makes things right - just absolutely right.' There was a hollow pause; then Harvey allowed his hand to be shaken. There was nothing else to do.

'Well, well,' Fielding ran on, 'if it isn't the best thing -' He twitched up the creases of his trousers and sat down. He pulled his chair close, said amiably - but with a very definite gravity: 'Now tell me! Have you had lunch?'

Lunch! Harvey drew back. Was the man really serious? He gave him a suspicious stare.

'Yes,' he lied. 'I've had lunch.'

'Good Lord, what a pity. But you'll dine with us. Heavens! what am I saying! You'll do everything with us. I refuse to let you out of my sight. It's marvellous to see you here at last. Quite marvellous. Mary will be delighted. Absolutely delighted. I know she's been worrying, worrying her head off about you.'

Harvey started nervously, again. He couldn't understand this - this inordinate placidity - so different from what he had expected. Didn't Fielding realise - hadn't anyone told him? Oh, it baffled - enraged him. And suddenly, in a hard voice, he said: 'Hasn't your friend Carr had something to say about me?'

'Carr!' Fielding laughed. 'I never pay any attention to what Wilfred says. Never. He's a good fellow is Wilfred. Terribly good on a horse. But erratic - oh, confounded impulsive sort of chap! His cables - hang it all - his cables almost rattled me.'

'I'm not talking about the cables.' Harvey said thickly. 'I'm talking about something quite different.'

A pause came, whilst Harvey waited, rigid and intent. But Fielding, lost in sudden abstraction, now seemed studying him with a profound, yet indulgent eye.

'Collars?' he remarked at last. 'Yes, it's going to be difficult. Especially the collars! What size do you take? I'll wager it's an inch less than me. I'm 17 - isn't that simply foul! But mind you - everything else I can let you have - a suit that's never been worn - thank goodness old Martin shoved it in - razor, underwear, tooth-brush, sponge, the whole kit. But, hang it all,' he frowned humorously, 'I'm not so sure about the collars!'

No, it was not an affectation. He was really concerned in a mild, half-quizzical sort of way about this little business of the collars. Concerned and quite interested. Harvey could have groaned. He'd expected everything - everything but this bright-eyed banter. He averted his head, stared gloomily at the floor.

'You know,' said Fielding, 'I haven't thanked you yet. Good Lord!' His charming, inconsequential smile flashed out again. 'It's quite marvellous, Mary's recovery. I'm terribly grateful. Sort of thing you can't talk about. She's actually getting up now.

Soon she'll be able to travel - by plane of course. Then we'll let the country air finish the job at Buckden.' He paused, added cheerfully: 'You'll stay with us. Of course you will. That's understood. You might rather care for Buckden. Nice little place. I've a hybrid rose I'd like to show you. Quite new. Not so stuffy, I assure you. I shall bring it out this year. At the Horticultural.'

Harvey sat quite still. The whole thing was so incomprehensible it left him speechless. Fielding must know - yes, he must know absolutely. And yet - this smiling, unruffled equanimity - it did nothing, it simply held the situation in a horrible suspense. He wanted to hate Fielding. But he could not. Friendliness alone he must have loathed. But there was something - something about the man so completely unassertive. He had everything: looks, breeding, charm, and that unconquerable amiability. Yet he seemed placidly to assume that he had nothing. It was impossible to dislike him.

At last Harvey muttered:

'I'm sorry I can't accept your invitation. You return by plane. I'm going back by boat. It's hardly likely we'll meet in England.'

Fielding let out a vigorous protest.

'My dear fellow,' he exclaimed. 'What on earth! You don't know what you're saying. You're not going back by boat. 'Tisn't built yet' - a laugh. 'You're going back by plane - with us.' He took it all blandly for granted. Then, with that same lack of continuity, he gave his knees a definite pat and energetically stood up: 'Come along, now. No time for talking. I've got a room for you. You want a bath and a change. Then we'll nip over and see Mary. It's just a step.'

As he spoke, the swing-doors of the hotel squeaked and clattered. And Elissa came into the lounge followed by Carr and Dibdin. When they saw Harvey, the three stopped short. There was something rather foolish in their sudden combined astonishment. They came over slowly.

'Just the right touch,' remarked Elissa - she had recovered herself and was airily inspecting Harvey's beard - 'to make it spectacular and exciting.'

'And heroic?' Carr added with a sneer; there was still a delicate purple around his left eye. 'We fall on his bosom and weep.'

'Shut up, Wilfred,' Fielding interposed. 'Do you want me to sack you on the spot? Did you go down to Stanford about the plane, or did you not? Answer me, you idiot.'

'Of course I went down,' Carr replied sulkily. 'He's only got one thing more to finish - the oil-feed or something. He said any day next week. Providing the weather's right.'

'Thank God,' Dibdin ejaculated, as if he were spitting out a prune stone, 'we'll soon be quit of this beastly hole.'

Fielding turned round in his reasonable way.

'You're going back by boat, of course. You understand that, Dibs?'

'By boat?' gasped Dibs. His tone was horrified.

'The plane only takes four - besides Stanford.'

'But - surely - four - I mean to say -' Dibs' shocked glance passed from Harvey to Fielding and back again. His watery eyes widened gradually to dismay. His monocle fell out and his mouth fell open. He collapsed, blankly, into a chair.

Elissa shook with laughter. She sat on the arm of the chair, helped herself to a cigarette. But she looked up as Fielding took Harvey's arm.

'Where are you going?' she enquired, eyeing them from behind the smoke. 'Polite afternoon call on the convalescent?'

'No,' Fielding answered cheerfully, 'we're goin' to look for collars.'

# CHAPTER XXVIII

THE roar of the twin engines was hardly noticeable in the insulated cabin of the plane. Now they were all so used to it. Just that steady drone. Nor was there much sense of movement. Tearing along at two miles to the minute they seemed simply to be lolling in the blue above a vast grey feather-bed of cloud. Against the laboured outward passage of the ship this homeward flight was arrow-swift.

Only two days since Santa Cruz.

They had risen from the bay on Thursday, before noon. A calm, clear day; not much sun; the water green and flat as a slab of glass. Risen so unexpectedly that Mother Hemmingway had thrown up her window and thrust out her shiny head - flummoxed, fair flummoxed, she was!

'Gawd blimey, but they've gorn. Carajo coño! And never

looked near us to s'y ta-ta. Such bleedin' unfriendliness - oo'd a thought it. By the pins of the twelve apostles I'll watch my company in future! 'Ere, Cuca, fetch us a drop of nigger's blood. Pronto, pronto, I'm struck all of an 'eap. 'Streuth!'

And Tranter, startled by the humming in the sky, had rushed from his newly-rented mission hall to crane his neck at the retreating speck.

'Oh, gee, they've gone,' clasping his milky hands emotionally. 'Oh, gee, that's rid me of trouble and temptation. Oh, praise God. And I'm gonna make a success of the mission after all. Hallelujah!' And, running back like a big rabbit, he had plumped himself before the harmonium. With all the fervour of the sinner reclaimed, he had drowned all sound in the booming hymn.

> *My sins were as high as a mountain,*
> *They all disappeared in the fountain.*

Only at Los Cisnes had the departure been foreseen. Dibs, of course, had known. But, immured in a sepulchral huff, he had refused to stir a foot from the hotel. At the Casa, however, a huge, white table-cloth flapped from the rotten flagstaff, like a piece of washing gone astray. And beneath it two tiny figures stood - a grey ant and a black ant - waving and waving. There was a mote of light that might have been the glitter of a snuff-box. And then the plane went soaring out across the sea on which the island lay verdant and lovely, like a lily pad upon a pond. The Peak was last to go - melting away into the glittering illusion of the sky.

That night they had spent at Lisbon, swooping upon the Tagus beyond the ridge of Cintra. Then on, the next day, skirting Oporto, Vigo, Lugo, cutting the corner of the Cantabrian Alps, across the Bay to Bordeaux. It was so easy and unhurried. And yet so swift. Going away - going back. The air was colder as they lifted from the broad Garonne and struck north to Nantes; colder, too, was the sea.

The last day of the journey - how quickly it was slipping past. Inexorably. St Malo now, with the sands of Paramé stretched out yellow as corn. But only for a minute. They melted away like the rest, into the sea, the air, the low interminable drone of the exhaust.

Fielding explained the route with real enthusiasm. He had an elegant map, callipers, exuberant delight in doing things to the second. Time-tables, he announced, engrossed him; there had been - in his boyhood - a book by Verne and a gentleman named Fogg. To arrive 'to the tick' - that was real proof of mind over matter. At present he was forward in the cockpit, enquiring of Stanford whether such a thing were so. Or not?

From the rear seat of the cabin Harvey let his gaze slip through the square window at his shoulder. The clouds were thin and fleecy now, as though that great bed had burst and scattered its feathers on the sea below. Snatches of slaty water drifted past. The sun glittered without heat.

Going away - going back. With a stealthy movement he turned his head and looked at Mary. She was staring straight in front of her, her fingers just touching the unopened book that lay upon her knee. She was silent, pale and thin - oh, so very thin. Better, of course, quite fit to travel. But strangely shadowy still, her chin pressed into the fur collar of her coat, her lashes lying darkly on her cheeks.

She was changed in some subtle yet singular way: older, more contained, betraying in her reflection a curious gravity. As though possessing a quality of dignity and purpose, which hitherto she had lacked. Those light and vivid graces, the quick, impulsive movements, all were gone. And instead there was a consciousness of maturity; no longer the eager yet bewildered child; but now a woman.

Was she conscious of his furtive look? He couldn't tell - he simply could not tell. It was grinding, the suspense, he felt it fasten upon him. It bound him so that he could scarcely move. Those last two days it had been the same, and the five days before at Santa Cruz. Afraid to look at one another, rigid, constrained, never for a moment alone, dreading the banal words that must be spoken, each awaiting, yet avoiding a sign - a sign that never came.

He stared at her, his lips half parted, willing her with all his feeling to look at him. Surely she must look at him - one tiny look - it would be enough.

But she did not. She still looked straight ahead, her face shadowy and white, her chin pressed into the soft fur of her coat, her lashes lying darkly upon her cheek. And the next minute Fielding came through the cockpit. He handed himself aft breezily, and sank into the chair next to Harvey.

'Haze is lifting on the floor,' he announced, and slipped his arm companionably over the back of the seat. 'We ought to have a sight of the Channel soon.'

'Yes,' Harvey answered flatly.

'And then for the jolly old Solent. That's where we strike the water again. Engine's running beautifully and she's not bumping a bit. Stanford says not more than an hour now. Absolutely on time. We'll be drinking tea at Buckden' - he considered his watch - 'at five-fifteen to the tick. Dash it all if I'm not sorry in a way! It's been a gorgeous trip. I hated it coming out - must have been anxious, p'raps. Besides - hate being alone. We've made a snug little party, the four of us. Blessed if I wouldn't mind doin' it all over again.'

Over her shoulder Elissa languidly interposed:

'No. My God - no, not for ten thousand! -' She yawned - reflected. 'The thought of Dibs - marooned, you know, that alone keeps me from hysteria. I can see his face still, all worked up - the final look - hardly human. It's really saving my life.'

Fielding laughed - without a shade of rancour. He said:

'You'll buck up when you get back, 'Lissa. Think of it. Spring in England - the hedges smelling of briar, blossom in the orchards -'

'People holding up umbrellas and cursing when the wind blows them inside out. Mud in your eye from all the buses and never a taxi in sight. Oh, don't be so damned encouraging, Michael. I can't bear it. Go away and drive the engine. Send young Stanford in. I want to find out if he's in love with me.' She shot a malicious look at Harvey. 'I don't see why Mary should monopolise the grand passion.'

Michael laughed louder than ever. He flung his other arm around Mary's chair, linking her to Harvey with ridiculous affability.

'You hear that, young funny. She's exposing you - and your glorious flirtation.'

Harvey winced. But Mary, sitting there soft and passive, made no sign; her face remained quite unreadable. Elissa was staring curiously at Michael. At length she shook her head. 'Sweet,' she said briefly, 'and such a gentleman.'

He went on and finished his laugh, then he took out his cigarette-case, offered it to Harvey, who refused.

'You know,' he continued affably, 'jokin' apart, it is really good to get back. Bein' away makes a fellow appreciate his own country all the better. I'm dyin' to show you Buckden. Remember that rose I was telling you about? It's an extra special. And I must let you see my new almshouses. Funny - I've an extraordinary feelin' for almshouses. Quite a hobby, don't you know. My old man started them and I've kept on - you know - buildin'. I'm collectin' centenarians - like another fellow might go in for butterflies. I've got an old codger there only three months short of a hundred and two. Why-'

Harvey shut his ears. He knew Fielding now - knew him with a knowledge both cold and final. He was, as Elissa said, a gentleman - oh, God, what a word! - but he *was*, for all the archaic horror of the term. Kind, charming, good-natured, he wouldn't do an ill turn to a fly; he couldn't - no, he simply couldn't have an enemy in the world. But he never seemed quite serious. Yes, that was it - impossible for him to be serious. Nor would he argue. Contradicted, he dropped a thing, laughed, forgot about it. And he had no jealousy; he was utterly incapable of it. That had baffled Harvey for days. But now he knew it with perfect certainty for the keynote of Fielding's easy indifference. Love had no meaning to him. He had for Mary a fondness: but that was all. How often Harvey had made up his mind to look him between the eyes - firmly, offensively.

'Look here. I'm in love with your wife.' But it wouldn't have been the slightest use. He wouldn't have said: 'Damn you, what do you mean?' He wouldn't even have said: 'What impertinence!' He would have laughed with perfect equanimity: 'My dear fellow, I'm not in the least surprised. She's charming. Try one of these. They're Turkish, but quite mild.' There was something terrifying in this inexorable good nature. The fact struck Harvey with deadening conviction. Oh, the whole thing was maddening. Better, far better, to batter one's head into a brick wall than against this soft and unresisting cushion of down.

'- And *that*,' concluded Fielding, 'really would please me. To break eighty. But only using one hand, mind you. That's the joke. It'd take a bit of doing. Fiendishly difficult course.'

He crushed out his cigarette, leaned smilingly towards Mary.

'All right, young funny? Not too tired? Quite warm enough?'

Her face, pressed into the fur upon her breast, seemed smaller than ever, her tone was dull.

'Yes, thank you, Michael.'

' 'Tisn't long now, you know.' He peered through the window, then started up with an exclamation. 'Why - hanged if we aren't - yes - we're almost there!' He craned his neck, pointing almost exultantly; no one took any interest but himself. 'That's St Catherine's! And Ventnor lying in behind. And the forts outside, and Haslar. Why, this is great! Lord - Stanford's shutting down his engine. I - I must see him.' And, glancing at his watch, he rushed forward to find out all about it.

Five minutes passed. Ventnor grew, then slipped away on the plane's port side. They circled. The Solent - at first a silver streak between the mainland and the island - grew and grew as they lost altitude. They were coming down. Gently the shining surface reached up to them, and then there was a quiet shock. The plane glanced across the water and straightened out her nose towards the breakwater. Two white plumes rose up behind her floats as she undulated along the surface. The propeller flopped round with comical slowness, then finally ceased to move. They drew up a hundred yards from the ramp. Silence: an almost deafening silence. Stanford, pulling off his gloves, came stooping into the cabin, followed by Fielding. He was a lanky fellow with black, unruly hair.

'Well,' he announced, quite calmly, 'that's it.'

Elissa drooped her eyelids towards him.

'Aren't you sorry it's over?'

He smiled, showing a gold tooth at the corner of his mouth.

'No!'

'No,' she mocked. 'That's all I ever get out of you. You've got no soul. And there's oil on your nose.'

Fielding gripped Mary's arm.

'Look!' he cried excitedly. 'There's Old Martin.'

A power launch shot out from the fore-shore, and, passing inside the fort, made directly towards them. As Stanford busied himself with the unfastening of the hatch, it came alongside.

Harvey stood at the back of the cabin. He watched with a cold, impassive face - Fielding, Elissa, and Martin all talking at once, Mary silent, smiling faintly to Martin, but silent, silent. He was the last to shake hands with Stanford, the last to get into the launch. He was conscious of everything acutely, painfully.

'Thought I'd meet you off the Southsea side, Sir Michael,' shouted Old Martin above the thrum of the launch. 'Much handier than Haslar.'

'Splendid, Old Martin.'

'Thought it'd be easier for her ladyship that way - ' His voice strained beyond its compass, piped and broke. He blinked his faded, blue eyes happily, nodding his head. He was a little, dried-up, wispy man with a long nose and a childish, horsy face. Gentleman's gentleman, thought Harvey, with that same dull ache of understanding - throbbing with service and affection - lifelong - quite feudal.

They were at the green steps of the Old Pier, mounting to land, rows of tall houses rising up behind, trams clanging vaguely, a lot of people staring, an obsequious, terribly obsequious, official: 'Careful your ladyship. Oh, please, careful.' Back - back again -

The car was waiting. There it stood, glittering, supercilious, an enormous, blue Rolls. Dark blue, of course, discreet. A man, rigid as something from Tussaud's, stood by the door - shut it with the gentlest of clicks, then sprang. And now they were off, swathed in rich rugs, the figure again unbending, arranged with Old Martin outside, meshing invisible, silent gears.

The town rolled past them, they swung on to the Chichester road, and the country opened out like a pretty picture-book.

'Not so stuffy - England?' gloated Fielding.

'Wait till you see Sussex, though - our little bit.'

Yes, the hedges were in bud, the little square fields had a sheen of green, the cottages stood beneath the trees, everything was neat and tidy - oh, shining as a nice, new pin. But Harvey took no notice of the pretty picture-book. Horrible or exquisite, he didn't care. Why he thought quite wildly, did I come? I shouldn't have let myself be persuaded. Why had he lost all his defences, his rudeness, his sarcasm, his morose indifference?

He was seated next to Mary, so close that he could feel the living movement of her side. Fielding had insisted.

'Sit there, you idiot!' It was agony. His heart beat like a bell. She was staring straight in front of her. But that peculiar flush had risen faintly to her cheek. Never meeting - never fully meeting his gaze - that was so hungry. . . .

'Hot, buttered scones before the fire,' cried Fielding. 'Not so stuffy that either.' He was in front on the folding-seat, shooting out remarks, exhibiting the landmarks with a proprietary air as though he had been absent for a twelve-month. He slewed round again.

'Not far now. Heavens, it's priceless to be back. Not too tired, old funny-bone? We'll have a regular house-warming for you.'

Something stirred in her. She whispered:

'You're not going to have a crowd of people, Michael?'

'Good Lord, no!' he protested. 'You're hopping into bed instanter. But we'll have a glorious party when you're stronger.' He beamed again. 'We'll get up to Town again. By Jove! we'll

213

do a few things - buy a few things - make things hum - what!'

The car slipped on, with its voluptuous, oppressive silence, through Cosham and Havant. More pages of the pretty picture-book.

'Not long now,' Fielding repeated heartily. 'Not long now.'

With a gay little tune upon the horn, they turned off the main road and ran through a red and white hamlet set in a sleepy hollow. A row of ducks solemnly crossing the village green. Some children in pinafores, silent suddenly in their laughter, terribly respectful. And then, with a sweep, into a broad deep avenue of beeches. On they went, for about a mile, through these beeches.

Harvey saw, then, some deer, that stared with mild eyes as they went past. Dully, the knowledge came to him that they were in a park - a huge enclosure. It was the estate, of course, Fielding's estate. It was enormous, rich, rolling away to infinity.

And then, at the top of a rise, they came on Buckden. It didn't look like a house - it was so big. Seen from the hill it had a massive splendour. It was square, solid, grouped round a central court. In front, lawns swept out, velvet and green. Crisp, blue smoke rose from a score of chimneys. Above the chimneys rooks were circling, cawing. A flag hung languidly on its staff. On the terrace a white peacock stood and screamed.

All so rich, so perfect, so vast, it struck at Harvey, it crushed him. Oh, God, he thought, how different it all is from Los Cisnes. That had been but a background for her beauty - this seemed insatiably to absorb her.

The tyres swished and crunched gently on the drive. They circled, drew up before the porch. Some footmen rushed out. And a dozen leaping dogs.

'Home, thank God,' Fielding cried effusively.


## CHAPTER XXIX

THE following evening; and dinner was over. Not the *Aureola*'s austere sea-fare nor Corcoran's slap-dash coffee and tamale. Something quite simple, both simple and good - 'an honest feed' was Michael's homely phrase. 'Let's go and bite something,' he would laughingly declare; and then, more sententiously perhaps, 'Thank God we can always stand ourselves an honest feed.' And so the honest feed began. Little fat oysters from Whitstable; some plain hare soup, nourishing and strong; grilled salmon from the Tweed; a breast of baby chicken which melted on the air; asparagus forced to a tender succulence; a rosy soufflé that foamed upon the plate; a tiny special savoury whose origin lay in Strasbourg.

Not, oh, not fancy, of course. Yet a man might miss a course and not go hungry. Harvey had missed several; and Mary all but one. Three flunkeys alone saved the meal from a wholly bucolic simplicity - each with the epaulettes of an admiral and the bearing of an archduke. For all the turmoil of his soul, Harvey couldn't help wondering dully if they were real. Had each a soul, an individuality, a life of his own? Or, for that matter, was the whole place real? Let there be no pretence - it was steeped in luxury - a sort of creamy, exquisite luxury. You did nothing. That was immediately assured. Everything was done. You were wakened, given tea. Your bath was drawn, the heated towels laid out. Your clothes, linen, boots, appeared miraculously from the blue - pressed, folded, shining. You were shaved, valeted, sent nicely down to breakfast. And that was only the start. Everything, everything - you could have it simply for the asking. A quick revulsion came over Harvey again.

Oh, God, it was stifling! You couldn't lift a cigarette but some menial swam towards you with a deferential match.

Broodingly he stared into the great hissing log, set deep in the marble fireplace. They were in the lounge, he in a corner chair, Mary seated upon the low fender-stool; Michael and Elissa - rapt in the process of digestion - on a deep divan. Silence was on the air. The log hissed and spurted. Upon the old hand-painted Chinese wallpaper silver parakeets flashed in a deep celestial blue. A row of Lelys beamed graciously upon the scene. Masses of orchids stood on the low oak chest mirrored in a surface polished by time and care. Above the mantelpiece a portrait of Mary - he dared not look at it.

'You know!' Elissa, rather exotic upon the divan, had a momentous thought. 'I woke up this morning with the fullest intention of being bored. But I'm not sure. Rather dreamy it's been today. I'm glad you chased me out to church, Michael. Really terribly soothing and nice. Made me think of the missionary man.' A pause. 'I suppose it *was* quite an experience for him. He'll be none the worse of it.'

Mary, crouched upon the hearth, stared far away into the heart of the burning log.

'And his sister?' she whispered.

Elissa made a long arm for a cigarette.

'Don't be awkward, darling. You're destroying my mood.'

Silence fell.

'Yes, now it is gone. Too unkind of you. And not a soul here to be nice to me. What in heaven's name am I to do?'

Mary, listless as before, made no reply. But something rose up in Harvey. He said:

'Why don't you try some work for a change?'

'Work!' Elissa stared - big-eyed, contemptuous.

Michael carefully took the cigar out of his mouth and cocked one nostril to its aroma.

'Oh, I say now,' he interposed. 'We all do our bit, don't you know.'

'Your bit,' Harvey said heavily. 'And what is your bit? You sit here - you eat and you sleep. You have your diversions. Elissa collects lovers. You collect centenarians. You run up to Town. There you eat and you sleep some more. You go to ten silly plays. You exhibit a blue geranium that someone else has grown for you. They give you a medal. You rush back to open a bazaar, a fête, a hogwash festival -'

'But, hang it all,' Fielding smiled, 'there's Buckden, isn't there?'

'You didn't even work for that,' Harvey answered wearily. 'You didn't earn it. It fell into your lap - all the square miles of it, almshouses, peacocks, flunkeys, cotton-wool, and lice.'

Michael chuckled richly.

'You're forgettin' about the taxes. Why, damme, these days it takes all our time to have a good honest feed.'

Harvey made no answer. But Elissa stole a sly side-glance at Mary; then she gave her light, derisive laugh.

'Democracy is in the air. Little whispers of simplicity. Back to the sweets of the unadorned. "Life is sober, life is earnest." Always the motto of the Mainwaring mariners.'

No one replied. There was silence until Michael got up, cut the end of a fresh cigar.

'Don't let's get stuffy. Let's do something. Prove we're not so hanged lazy after all. We'll play billiards. You like a game, 'Lissa?'

'Billiards,' echoed Elissa, as though he had said leap-frog.

'Yes - you like a game?' he said again. 'We'll have a four. I'll

go and see about the table. All of you come through in a second.'
He lit his cigar and strolled to the door.

Elissa sighed, watching him go out.

'Why,' she murmured, with elevated brows, 'why, at terrible and fascinating moments, must Michael always be so boisterous? We were about getting to the point. What we might be going to do! But now -' She threw one glance at the other two and smiled. Then she rose, yawned, and drifted languidly from the room without a word.

They were alone. For the first time since that morning at Los Cisnes - alone. It was so unexpected that she shivered. She sat perfectly still, as though afraid to move. Then, after a long time, she slowly raised her eyes. She looked him fully in the face. All that had passed in those days between slipped away and was dissolved. And with a sudden catching of her breath she cried:

'It's true - what she says! What - oh, what are we going to do?'

Her eyes were big and dark and hurt. But they were steady, holding in their depths a new maturity. The firelight glinted upon her hair, upon her neck and arms - so white against the plain black gown she wore. Her face, still pale, was outwardly composed; but her lips trembled as with pain.

He didn't speak. He didn't move, but his eyes fastened upon her eyes with a sort of hunger. He thought: Yes, at last - at last we shall know - each of us - at last.

'It's no good putting things off any longer,' she whispered. 'We've got to face things out. You know better - better about me now. You see why I've felt I'd have to get away to something simpler, away from this - all pressing in, stifling me. You heard Elissa's jibe. It's true enough. I've never really cared for all this. It isn't me. But I never fully realised it till I met you. And it's true what you say about work. You've wakened something in me. It's time I stopped being treated as the wistful little girl ... time I stopped sighing after gardens. . . . It's not good enough. . . . I'm a woman now. I'd like to do something, to give something, so that I might get something back. And now, more than ever. I'm changed, I'm different. Oh, Harvey, it's only now I've grown up. I married Michael when I was eighteen. I didn't know anything. I liked him - that was all. He didn't ask any more. He never has. But you see' - her voice was very low - 'you see how good he is -' She stopped short. She pressed her fingers together so that they were whiter than her face.

'Oh, it's terrible - terrible - to love you so much and not to know what to do.'

Again his heart was beating like a heavy bell. As in a dream he said:

'You came once to me - at Los Cisnes.'

'I know, oh, I know,' she answered. 'But then I didn't think - oh, I was ill I suppose. I - I couldn't think. It was instinct to go to you -' Her bosom rose and fell. In a torture of feeling he wished to bury his head in that soft breast.

'You know,' he said in a choking voice, 'we both know - there's something binding us together.'

Silence. Then she whispered:

'I've known that - a long, long time. I don't belong to anyone but you. But what is there to do? I'm not free to do as I want. I couldn't - oh, I couldn't hurt Michael.'

'Would he be hurt so very much?'

'I don't know. I can't think. He wouldn't understand. He'd just laugh. Not the least use trying to tell him - you've seen that too. I'd have to go away - just go away without a word. Is it cowardice to give in, or courage? Oh, I've thought and thought until my brain is muddled. I told you on the ship how much I hated everything sordid and beastly.' Her voice broke, but she made herself go on. 'Women who have lovers - affairs that flare up and burn out. Something ugly - that horrifies me. I've tried to have an ideal, some sort of standard. I've tried to live to that. But the standard's all gone wrong now. I can't tell good from bad. And all the time I'm thinking: How am I going to live without you?' Her voice quivered and fell away to nothing in the silence of the room. He took her hand and whispered:

'The standard hasn't gone wrong, Mary. There's nothing in you that isn't good. I love you.'

She raised her head, gazed at him with those wide, dark eyes. 'And I love you.'

Then the door opened and Fielding came back. Cue in hand, he stopped and stared. He coughed; then smiled.

'Come and have a game, you two. 'Lissa's just decided she wants to play pool. It's no fun less there's four.'

There was a dead silence. The colour rushed into Harvey's brow and then receded, leaving it haggard as before. The smile never left Fielding's face. He said:

'Sorry for butting in, and all that. P'raps you'd rather not play. Come in when you've - when you've finished, if you like.'

Then Mary's eyes fell; her whole figure dropped. Steadying herself against the mantelpiece, she said in a light, queer voice:

'I'm tired, Michael. I think I must go to bed.'

Instantly he jumped forward.

'Oh, I say. Oh, really, I'm hanged sorry. Your first night up, too. I'm an ass to forget. Let me ring. Let me do something.'

She left the fireplace and, with eyes upon the floor, went slowly to the door.

'It's all right' - still in that light, strange voice - 'but I think I'll go now - if you don't mind.'

'Certainly. Of course, of course.' Compunctiously he took her arm. He was touched - ah, hanged if he wasn't touched. He must see her to her room. The stairs, you know - oh, sickening of him to forget.

They went out of the room together. And for a long time Harvey stood staring at the closed door. He felt paralysed. If only he could do something, if only he could fight - as he had fought against Carr. He wanted something to knock down, to destroy. But what could he do against the blandness of a man like Fielding? He saw with crushing force that he could do nothing. Then a shiver went through him. He couldn't stand it. No, he couldn't stand it any longer. Let him get away - somewhere - anywhere. He sprang to the French window. He tore aside the curtains, flung open the window, and went out. He cut across the dewed lawn. The cool air did not cool his brow. The recollection of her face rising out of the misty darkness haunted him. Down through the park he went, into the avenue of beeches. The house behind him rose like a great sprawling beast.

He had to get away from it. It was closing round him, stifling him. There! It was like bursting through cotton-wool, his mouth, his eyes, his ears - all full of it - but at last he was free, past the lodge, out on the open road. He walked and walked - striding along with his head down - swinging along like a madman. Suddenly he heard the whistle of a train. And, lifting his head, he saw the red glare of the engine drawing into a station. He took to his heels and ran, brushed past a porter who shouted the London train. It was moving out of the station. He jumped into it, flung himself in the corner of the compartment. There, rigid and silent, he sat as the train tore through the darkness of the night.

# CHAPTER XXX

A DEAD coal dropped in the grate with a final sound. It seemed to emphasise the silence of the room - the shiny, unpleasant sitting-room of Harvey's lodgings. Ismay, sunk in a chair with his feet upon the fender, cleared his throat defensively. He wanted to speak and yet was half afraid to break that silence. Covertly he looked up at Harvey seated opposite under the yellow-tinted globe which shone impartially on the hard, bad furniture, the monumental overmantel, on the dusty workbench in the corner, the drawn venetian blinds, the thick coffee-cups - empty and treacly - on the worn-out arty table-cover - this style two eleven a half, madam, at the sale.

It was evening of the Thursday following Harvey's departure from Buckden. Outside, in Vincent Street, a raw March fog spread up from the river; it dulled the sound of the traffic, which seemed to pound remotely and rather thinly - for it was getting late. Indeed, at that moment the small blue clock on the mantelpiece pinged out rapidly ten tinny strokes. It gave Ismay his chance.

'Well,' he exclaimed, under cover of the echoes. 'You're more garrulous than ever.'

'Yes?'

'You haven't told me the half, man. Not the half.'

'No?'

Ismay moved impatiently.

'I don't deny that you've had a queer experience, mind you - deuced queer.'

'Yes.'

Ismay gave a short laugh.

'Not that I'd have considered you a likely subject for - well - that sort of fantasy.'

'No?'

'Of course not! You always called a spade a spade, didn't you? You always had a nice hard scientific brick ready to heave at what you called the pretty glass illusions of life.'

For a long time Harvey didn't answer. Then he said flatly:

'I haven't got any bricks now.'

There was an odd pause. Then, raising his head slowly, he declared:

'I tell you, Ismay, I've learnt something that's knocked the cold-blooded rationalism out of me. There are more things under heaven than I ever dreamed of - things inexplicable - beyond our reason. Oh, we think we know so much when really we know nothing - nothing, nothing, nothing.'

Ismay sat up.

'Ah, come, man. You're not serious? I don't understand -.'

'No!' burst out Harvey quite fiercely. 'You don't understand it. And neither do I. But, oh, my God, it gives us something to think about.'

There was a dead silence. Ismay made to speak, but did not. He looked sideways at Harvey, looked away again. Then he made a vague gesture with his shoulders. He wasn't going to pursue the subject, d——d if he was. He'd got a practical mind about such elusive twaddle. Show him a perforating appendix now and he'd really do something with it. But this? And, when all was said and done, what did it matter? The main thing was that Harvey was back, sound in wind and limb - ready, obviously ready, to begin again. His plan had worked. He'd said it would. And hadn't he been right? Ignoring the very inferior clock, he took out his thin watch, looked at it, shut it with a neat little snap.

'And what the devil,' he enquired with abrupt cheerfulness, 'are you thinking about now?'

'Something that might have occurred to Corcoran,' answered Harvey slowly. 'Bearing on the subject of keeping up one's chin.' He quoted: ' "Let me depart from it all not lamenting, but singing like the swan." That's Plato, Ismay.' He smiled queerly. 'A great boy was Playto - you should read him, young fella, if yer not too busy.'

'Depart be hanged,' Ismay cried. 'You know you're departing none. You're a different man - thanks to me. And you're going to justify my words.' He got up, took his coat from a chair, and tucked himself warmly into it. Then he carefully pulled out his yellow gloves. Took his umbrella and his hat. Finally, he paused. 'By the by' - his manner quite definitely portentous; he was producing now the plum which he had been saving for the last - 'there's a vacancy at the Central Metropolitan.' He paused again. 'I thought you'd like to know. I thought you might even care to apply.'

Harvey looked up. There was a pause.

'You mean the new place in Tuke Street? They'd never - no, they'd never have me there.'

Ismay inspected his finger-nails with that too casual air he displayed at moments of importance.

'I should apply if I were you.'

Harvey smiled sadly.

'Still arranging the universe, Ismay?'

'A large slice of it, anyway.'

'You mean -'

'I mean that we can get you in. I haven't let the grass grow. Saw Craig twice about it last week. Understand *that*, perhaps? They want you, in fact.' He forgot his finger-nails and became quite boyishly enthusiastic. 'It's a glorious chance to come back, man. A new place - a decent crowd to work with and the most up-to-date laboratory in London. Every opportunity for your work -' He stopped short. 'You'll take it?'

A bar of silence throbbed within the room.

Harvey seemed to draw reflection from a long way off. Work! Of course he wanted to work. A sudden wave of hope assailed him. All his faculties drew from that deep of melancholy and fixed in one bright focus on the future. There had been the past. Now - yes, there was the future.

'Yes,' he said at last. 'I'll take it.'

Ismay rammed on his hat.

'Knew it,' he cried. 'I'll ring up Craig the minute I get back.' His smile spread all over his face. At the door he turned; raised his umbrella to his shoulder. 'You'll show them, Harvey. You'll make them pretty sick at the Victoria. I told you that you'd show them. And you will one day.'

'I don't want to show anybody,' Harvey said slowly. 'That's all changed. I've lost my smug omniscience. I only want to work, to work humbly, Ismay. I only want to try - to try -'

But Ismay wasn't paying any attention. The triumphant slam of the door drowned the words. Ismay was gone.

Harvey stood in the centre of the room. Over the dying embers the last blue flames flickered gently. He was tired. Yet, through it all, an eager, restless energy shone like a light melting through the fog. Work! A quick sigh went through him - oh, an unexpected, a glorious chance, that Ismay had produced. He'd take it - yes, he'd take it. A new faith was in him - a new inspiration.

His body was still lax, despondent. He couldn't help it. Yet, pulled by invisible forces, he moved, went over to his own little work-bench. The same, just the same - microscope, centrifuge, slides, reagents, test-tubes. Dusty, very dusty and unused. From the back the little sketch of Pasteur looked up at him austerely.

Suddenly that rushing aspiration swelled in him. He would try - oh, he would try. Never before had his desire been so intense, never his sense of spiritual awakening so complete. He took up a test-tube in his hand. The feel of it brought him comfort, a divine assuagement. He could work again. He could work!

It was quiet now, the house silent at last, the traffic ceased in the street outside.

He thought of Mary, his gaze fixed and remote, caught by the image of her face. Laboriously he tried to piece it all together. Yet the pieces would not fit - no human hand could ever make them fit. But it had all happened, happened, happened. And then he sighed. That was the past. The future - he didn't know, he couldn't tell. But at least there was the thought of Mary - an ideal mingled inextricably with his work.

As he stood there, with melancholy still upon his face and that bright tiredness brimming in his heart, he heard a sound in the deserted street. It stole into him from the fog. He gave no heed at first. But it was repeated. A queer sound swinging in quietly from the outer door. And the door itself seemed gently to be touched. He turned his head slowly. It's the wind, he thought. But there wasn't any wind. No, it's Ismay, come back for something he's forgotten. But it was not Ismay.

His heart constricted. Again the silent house creaked - a quiet creak as though someone stepped lightly in the hall. He told himself desperately: It's nothing, nothing, nothing. He knew that it was nothing. But his face was white as death. Then his heart stood absolutely still. No sound this time. But a perfume. It floated into the room - distinct, intoxicating. It was the perfume of the freesia flowers. . . .

THE END

# A. J. CRONIN

| | |
|---|---:|
| Adventures Of A Black Bag | £0.75 |
| Adventures In Two Worlds | £1.75 |
| The Citadel | £2.50 |
| Crusader's Tomb | £2.50 |
| Gracie Lindsay | £0.80 |
| Grand Canary | £1.75 |
| The Green Years | £1.00 |
| Hatter's Castle | £2.95 |
| The Keys Of The Kingdom | £2.50 |
| The Minstrel Boy | £2.50 |
| The Northern Light | £0.90 |
| Shannon's Way | £1.75 |
| A Song Of Sixpence | £0.90 |
| The Spanish Gardener | £0.65 |
| The Stars Look Down | £2.95 |

*All these books are available at your local bookshop or newsagent, or can be ordered direct from the publisher. Just tick the titles you want and fill in the form below.*

Prices and availability subject to change without notice.

NEL BOOKS, P.O. BOX 11, Falmouth, Cornwall

Please send cheque or postal order, and allow the following for postage and packing:

U.K. – 55p for one book, plus 22p for the second book, and 14p for each additional book ordered up to £1.75 maximum.

B.F.P.O. and EIRE – 55p for the first book, plus 22p for the second book, and 14p per copy for the next 7 books, 8p per book thereafter.

OTHER OVERSEAS CUSTOMERS – £1.00 for the first book, plus 25p per copy for each additional book.

Name.......................................................

Address ...................................................

...................................................